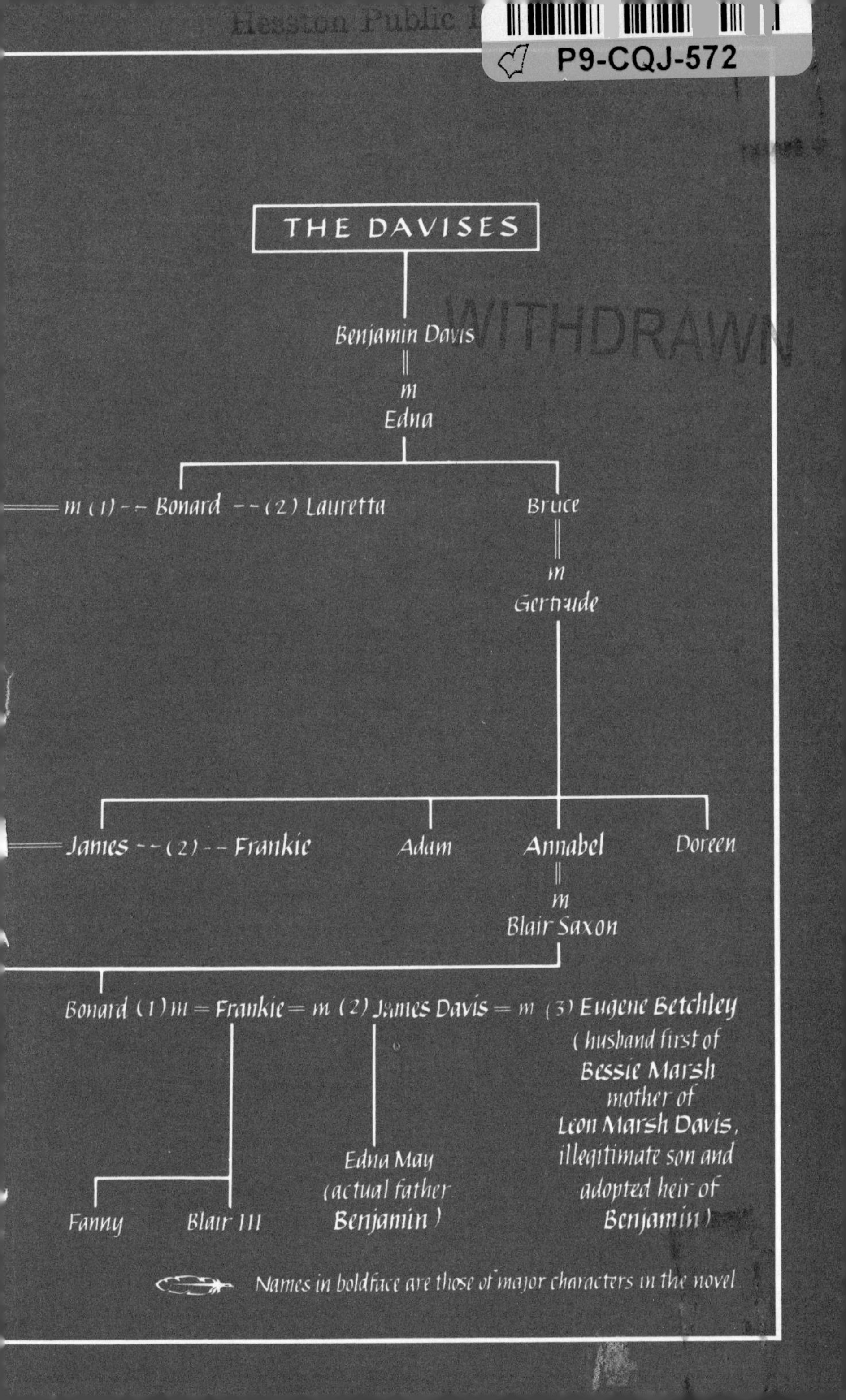
THE DAVISES
Benjamin Davis
m
Edna
m (1) -- Bonard -- (2) Lauretta
Bruce
m
Gertrude
James -- (2) -- Frankie
Adam
Annabel
Doreen
m
Blair Saxon
Bonard (1) m = Frankie = m (2) James Davis = m (3) Eugene Betchley
(husband first of
Bessie Marsh
mother of
Leon Marsh Davis,
illegitimate son and
adopted heir of
Benjamin)
Edna May
(actual father
Benjamin)
Fanny
Blair III
Names in boldface are those of major characters in the novel

Books by Lonnie Coleman

ESCAPE THE THUNDER

TIME MOVING WEST

THE SOUND OF SPANISH VOICES

CLARA

ADAMS' WAY

THE SOUTHERN LADY

SAM

THE GOLDEN VANITY

KING

BEULAH LAND

ORPHAN JIM

LOOK AWAY, BEULAH LAND

THE LEGACY OF BEULAH LAND

SHIP'S COMPANY, short stories

HOT SPELL, play

The Legacy of Beulah Land

The Legacy of Beulah Land

LONNIE COLEMAN

Doubleday & Company, Inc.
Garden City, New York

Library of Congress Cataloging in Publication Data
Coleman, William Laurence, 1920–
The legacy of Beulah Land.
I. Title.
PZ3.C67754Le [PS3505.02826] 813'.5'2
ISBN: 0-385-15459-3
Library of Congress Catalog Card Number 79–7516

PRINTED IN THE UNITED STATES OF AMERICA
FIRST EDITION

To Howard Siegman

Part One

1879

1

Bessie Marsh pulled the reins, halting mule and wagon. To the boy on the plank seat beside her she said, "You can see it clear, now the orchard's bare." He looked where his mother pointed through leafless fruit trees and the oaks and cedars lining the carriageway to Beulah Land. The house at the end did not face the main road as had the old one until it was burned by Sherman's men, but turned rather toward the fields and woods that had nourished Kendricks and their kin for almost a hundred years, since the first of them started the plantation in 1783. It was always thought of as Kendrick property, though all but one now bearing the family name were Negroes who, born there, had chosen to remain after the war, or who had left it and returned. The house was not as fine as the old one, but it was still grand enough with its generous rooms and extravagant porches to appear palatial to the poorer county farmers when they went there to ask a favor.

"That's where we'd be living if they'd reckoned your ma good enough for Ben Davis."

Leon Marsh knew, as everyone did, that Benjamin Davis was his father and that he managed the plantation with his grandmother Sarah Troy. Although he would not be five until April, the boy had heard the story all his life. But the raw January morning made him shiver and imagine the warm indoors of the store they were going to in Highboro to trade the nineteen eggs and four hobbled hens in the back of the wagon for flour and sugar. They had been up before day to milk the cow and feed the stock. Bessie had not bothered to build a fire in the kitchen, since they were going to town; so they breakfasted on buttermilk and cold biscuits, and Bessie advised her mother, who was nearly blind, to remain in bed for warmth until they returned.

"It's cold, Ma," Leon said.

She was gazing through the trees. "It's warm in there, you can bet. They've a fire in every room, and the table set for breakfast. Fried ham and eggs, grits and gravy, hot biscuits and preserves, coffee and cold pie. Leave more than they eat, I expect. No wonder their hogs and niggers are the fattest in the county."

"Ma, let's go."

She waved a hand. "Everything, they have it all."

"Ma—"

She slapped him hard with the end of the reins. He flinched but did not make a sound. Deciding that he looked more than ever like his father, she laughed. The sound splintered the air like falling icicles. "Spit and say: 'I spit on Beulah Land.'"

Thinking of the warmth waiting in Highboro, he pursed his chapped lips, turned his head over the side of the wagon, and spat. Taking that as obedience enough, Bessie flicked the reins on the mule's back, and they continued the journey.

The wagon creaked past the old Campgrounds and over the wooden bridge, and they saw the first cluster of houses. The woman said, "I don't want you to cry like you done last time. If Mr. Sullivan feels like patting me some, it's nothing to you, is it? Maybe I'll coax a can of snuff out of him for your granny. She lives for snuff." The boy looked angry, but said nothing.

The mistress of Beulah Land had also been up before daylight, leaving her husband sleeping and going to the kitchen, where she found the cook Josephine rolling out dough and her helper Mabella boiling first coffee.

"How is she this morning?" Josephine asked.

"I haven't been to see yet; I need my coffee." Sarah Troy drew a chair to the kitchen table as Mabella set down cup and saucer and poured from the pot on the stove.

"Hasn't boiled enough," Mabella warned.

"It will do me," Sarah said, and then to Josephine, "I expect she's no worse or Bianca would have knocked on my door during the night."

"Yes'm." Josephine sighed and sprinkled flour over the rolled dough. "Making sweet potato biscuits." They were one of the many favorite dishes long enjoyed by the fat little woman who lay dying in her room. Finishing her coffee, Sarah touched Josephine on the back to thank her and went for the first visit of the day with her aunt, Nell Kendrick. She often found her asleep, or if awake, with her mind as cloudy as her eyes, but this morning her eyes were open and sensible. It was her maid Bianca who sat nodding in the chair beside the bed. Hearing them exchange greetings, Bianca opened her eyes warily.

"I smell coffee," Nell said.

"Mabella's bringing yours."

"I'll go get it," Bianca announced, and left the room.

"She wants her own," Nell said. They smiled at each other. "How old am I, Sarah?"

"Ninety-seven."

"Am I?" Nell mused. "I was a delicate child; no one thought I'd live to put on my first corset."

"Josephine's making sweet potato biscuits."

"Dear soul."

An hour later everyone had breakfasted according to appetite and begun the day's occupations. Casey Troy, Sarah's second husband (her first having been Leon Kendrick, master of Beulah Land), was a painter and photographer. At sixty-five he was three years younger than his wife, but both led active lives and retained a fair portion of earlier health and looks. Plain at ten, Sarah was allowed to be interesting at twenty, and beautiful from thirty on.

Casey saddled a horse and rode into Highboro with his sketchbook dangling from the saddle horn. He was to begin work on the portrait commissioned by Mrs. Bonard Saxon, still known as "the beautiful Miss Frankie" although she had borne two children and been wife as well as mother for more than five years.

Benjamin Davis always began his day early, coming down the half mile from his house in the Glade and assigning the men their work. Most of them were plowing the highest ground. After looking over the non-working stock, he joined his grandmother for breakfast. He had coffee at home, but his wife Priscilla rose later than he and breakfasted lightly, if at all. Her pregnancy was in the eighth month, and their hope of safe delivery grew each day stronger. In four years of marriage she had miscarried twice.

It was Benjamin's habit to companion Sarah for the hearty

morning meal they both enjoyed as they discussed the day's expectations. Forty-three years different in age, they were alike in their love for Beulah Land and each other. It was true, as his wife and her husband agreed, that each was the other's nearest friend. As Benjamin helped himself liberally to peach preserve, Sarah said, "Was Priscilla awake when you left?"

"I don't know." After a moment's pause he added, "I didn't want to bother her if she was sleeping."

They did not have to look at each other to acknowledge what was unspoken. The courtship and marriage of Benjamin Davis and Priscilla Oglethorpe had surprised town and county, so different had they been. But both went about it with a determination that made it look like destiny, overcoming where they could not ignore the misgivings of friends and the opposition of her mother.

Sarah said briskly, "She'll be content when the child is born."

He looked at her then. "Pray God. Town girls take some getting used to country living."

She nodded as if she believed what they were saying, then offered him the comfort of being teased. "You're mighty sure it's going to be a boy."

"Yes'm, and he's going to be named Bruce Davis for Grandpa."

She watched him fork a bit of preserve onto the last crisp bit of ham. "How can you do that? I like my salt, and I like my sweet, but I want the salt first and the sweet after."

"I like them together. Otis has put the best men on the high west fields. They'll spend the rest of the week plowing their way down." She nodded. "Thought I'd ride into town this morning and look over the gin. Not do anything other than kick a piece here and there to see if it rattles right."

"If it rattled wrong, Isaac would already know it; but you're right to go." When he pushed his plate away, she said, "Stop in Sullivan's and ask if his new nutmeg has come. Josephine won't use any of that old he sold her, and sweet potato biscuits need a touch of it."

Benjamin's sister Jane Todd lived with her husband Daniel and their two sons next door on what had been part of Beulah Land. With the arrival of their second son, their little house in

Sarah's side yard was discovered to be too small. Sarah and Benjamin talked privately about an idea they'd long had and decided to make Jane and Daniel a deed to four hundred of Beulah Land's sixteen hundred acres. Daniel Todd had been a Union soldier who deserted, wounded and half starved, during the last year of the war and found his way to Beulah Land, where its mistress took him in. He paid her with hard work. Without him the place might have been lost, its load of debt the consequence of punitive taxes at the war's end and Reconstruction. Jane knew what Sarah and Benjamin guessed: deep in Daniel's Vermont soul he hungered to own part of the land he'd helped them save and come to love. And so, although he protested when it was offered to him, he looked happy. Accepting the deed, he proceeded to build a house and farm buildings, and to dream lives for his sons, unaware that those who follow must always make their own.

"Grandma!"

"Grandma!"

"Here I am!"

The calls came from Robert E. Lee Todd and Jefferson Davis Todd, aged four and two, named for the general and the president to bring new names into the family as well as to commemorate the past. Sarah's answer coincided with her rounding a corner of the house after gathering eggs with Mabella. It was good luck that Mabella was carrying the eggs, for both boys threw themselves upon their great-grandmother, sure of their welcome, and she swung one under each arm as they made their way up the steps of the back porch toward the kitchen, where Jane waited.

"You spoil them," Jane said.

"Your mother used to say that when I swung you," Sarah answered.

"May the Lord rest her soul," Josephine intoned. Fond of both children, she was partial to Jefferson, called Davy. "Who this baby come to see Josephine?"

He wrapped himself around her long-skirted legs as if he would crush her. "Not a baby—two years old!"

"Look like a baby to me, don't he to you, Mabella? Reckon we better give him a sugar-tit to pacify him?"

"I'm too big for sugar-tits, I want a biscuit!"

"Maybe there's one left, maybe there ain't." Josephine simpered. "Who you love best?"

"You, Josephine!" both boys shouted.

"Well," she said complacently. They followed her as she went to the cookstove and took biscuits from the black pan on top. She made a finger hole in each and filled it with syrup. Holding them high until they stopped dripping, she presented them to the children and watched as they devoured them. "Always hungry as hound dogs. Mabella, clean the chicken mess off'n them eggs like I told you. How many times I got to say don't use water, it weakens the shell? Use your hand like this."

A little later, sitting with Nell while Bianca rested, Jane heard whispering in the hallway and tiptoed to the door.

"Who is it, Jane?" Nell asked.

"Bobby Lee and Davy."

"And who might they be?"

"Mine and Dan's boys."

"Yes," she remembered.

"I'll send them away."

"Let them in," she said to Jane's surprise, for she had never liked having children about her.

They wanted no further invitation. "Come here so I can look at you," Nell said, and the boys obeyed. Awed to silence by the unexpected, they stared at her as curiously as she did at them. "You look like Daniel," she said to Bobby Lee, and to Davy, "You don't look like anybody."

Unabashed, Davy said, "Come play marbles with us."

"I reckon not," she said after appearing to consider it. "I got to lie here and think about going to heaven."

"Are you going today?" Davy said, and Bobby Lee nudged him with an elbow.

"Might," Nell said. "Haven't made up my mind when I'm going."

"Will you grow wings?" Bobby Lee wanted to know.

"I'll tell you a secret: they've already started."

"Can we see them?" Davy asked.

Nell frowned. "A lady doesn't show her wings to gentlemen."

Davy beamed at her admiringly. "Do they have tater biscuits in heaven?"

"If they don't," Nell said, "I won't stay."

2

Casey Troy was uncertain what to do with his horse. He and Sarah visited the Bonard Saxons once or twice a year, but on those occasions they came in a buggy, or in the rockaway if Jane and Daniel accompanied them, and a servant was waiting to dispose of the equipage. Today he came alone and in a professional capacity. After dismounting he stood, reins in hand, as one who pauses to admire the prospect (Miss Frankie was house proud), but hoping that someone inside would spy him. This happened. Annabel Saxon opened the front door of her son's house with the greeting: "Here you are, painter Troy!"

She never knew how to address him. She called Sarah "Auntie" to annoy her, although they were not kin. Sarah's daughter had married Annabel's brother James Davis; Sarah's grandson Benjamin was, therefore, Annabel's nephew. Casey Troy was nobody, as she had said at the time he married Leon Kendrick's widow, and she still referred to him sometimes as "the nobody who married the mistress of Beulah Land."

Casey was on surer ground, for although Yankee-born, he knew Southern manners and understood that a gentleman might address any lady by her first name if he preceded it by "Miss," whether she was maid or madam. "Miss Annabel," he declared, "you look pretty as a picture, if I may say so."

She laughed appreciation. "Who better qualified than you, sir? —painter of countenance and soul! Come and let us see what you make of Miss Frankie. The boy will take care of your horse."

Casey took his sketchbook from the saddle horn and followed her into the house. Sarah would be amused to hear that Annabel had thought to be in attendance as chaperon or, more likely, director of the session. Frankie Saxon came to meet them in the entrance hall. Having allowed her mother-in-law to open the door, she affected surprise, as if she remembered that she was expecting the artist only when he appeared before her. "Mr. Troy! I have just this moment—" She led them beyond her living room into the small sitting room she used for morning visits.

Civilities were exchanged. Frankie asked particularly after Jane and Mrs. Troy. On her first visit to Highboro six years ago, she had almost married Benjamin Davis, deciding to have the banker's boy instead only when she discovered that Bessie Marsh was pregnant with Benjamin's child. The family mammy bustled in behind two skipping children who were entreated to "say howdy to the gentleman" and then consider themselves excused. A quarter hour passed as they remained to be admired. Five-year-old Blair Saxon III recited several verses from the Psalms, secure in the knowledge that no one interrupts the Bible, and three-year-old Fanny demonstrated her curtsy so many times she grew dizzy and fell, bumping her head on the floor and weeping. Thereupon the mammy, young Blair, and Fanny were invited lovingly to leave them. When they dallied, they were told gravely to go; and when at the doorway they still lingered like old actors reluctant to quit a stage, Annabel shouted, "Scat!"

Although she had been told that in the first session Casey would make sketches only of her face, Frankie was carefully dressed, but so she always was. A beauty from a poor Savannah family, relatives of Annabel's other daughter-in-law, Frankie had known her good fortune in marrying even the second son of a banker and had been quick to learn the perquisites of position. A big frog in a little pond she might be, but a pond, no matter its size, is the world to those who live in it or beside it; and Frankie knew it.

Annabel said, "It was my idea, this portrait, Troy." (She decided the last name would do for a business visit.) "Law, yes. I recollected how much admired was the one you made of me all those years ago—"

"You've changed little, ma'am."

"Everyone says my daughter-in-law is a beauty and so she is, but we must catch the bloom before it fades. I told my son: 'Send for Troy, he is the man.' You deal more in the camera these days, I understand; but for lasting there is nothing to my mind like paint on canvas with a stout frame around it. Now, where will you have her pose?"

Casey opened his sketchbook and assumed the preoccupied manner of the artist. He used silence as a shield. Asked again by Annabel where he would have Frankie sit or stand, he merely frowned and ignored her. "On the little settee perhaps? I do think standing beside a pedestal looks common."

Frowning still and wordless, he directed Frankie with a hand gesture to a chair in a bow window where the morning light was clear but not dazzling, and where there were no shadows to mislead him. Annabel chattered a few more suggestions, but when she was ignored by both artist and subject, she subsided into brief outbursts, like a bird in a bush who reminds us of his presence with a trill at intervals without commanding our attention to a full recital.

"Law, so well I remember. Everyone was delighted. Came from all over the county to admire it when it was done. Troy was much sought after, I assure you. Everyone wanted him. But the portrait he achieved of me was the most admired of any of the many. Fancy your not recognizing it as me when you first saw it, Frankie! Everyone vows it is my spit and image to this day."

Casey began to work, and Frankie fixed her eyes on a wax rose in a miniature vase.

"And Aunt Nell—how did you leave the old soul?"

There was no answer but the scratching of pencil on paper.

"Poor thing, I wish she'd die. Better for her, and you all too. She's complained of being an invalid her whole life. Everyone dancing duty and attention on her, never mind the trouble; and look at her, nearly a hundred. Not content with the threescore and ten so sensibly advised by our Creator. Frankie, move your head to the right. The left side of your face— Never mind, the artist eye will make allowance. Nothing terrible, only not as good as the other. Unremarkable with anyone else, but with you we look for perfection."

To ignore her mother-in-law was no longer enough, and Frankie's question to Casey sounded irritable. "How is Mrs. Ben?"

"Frankie!" Annabel said in a correcting tone. "Strictly speaking, Troy is not family. One does not ask a gentleman who is not family the condition of one who—"

"I only hope she is healthy and comfortable."

"I believe she is both," Casey said in a tone as remote as the moon. Closing one eye and holding his pencil vertically, he squinted intently at the subject of the drawing. Both women were daunted to silence. It never failed, Casey reflected.

3

Isaac was a light-colored Negro in his middle fifties who appeared older, perhaps because of his hermit existence. He had one real leg and one carved from wood, a substitute for that crushed under a bale of cotton that tipped and fell on him when he was a young man and first began to work at the cotton gin. He had a solemn passion for machinery, which perfectly suited him for his job as caretaker.

As he and Benjamin paused at the office door after their round of inspection, he picked up a kitten from the floor and held it out by the scruff of its neck. "Take him, Mr. Ben. My old mouser wants to kill him. Never been much of a ma, but never before bad as now. Litter of five, and she kilt every one but him, and would have got him if I hadn't stopped her. I been pondering what to do with him."

Benjamin accepted the creature and looked him over. He was black except for a white strip around his left hind leg and a few white hairs at his chest. "All right, Isaac."

"Maybe Miss Priscilla see some good in him."

"Afraid she doesn't care much for cats." He smiled and scratched the kitten's ears. "I'll take him to Aunt Doreen. She and Miss Kilmer keep up with the cat needs of Highboro." Benjamin stuffed the kitten into a loose outer pocket of his coat, where, after some experimental squirming, he seemed content to remain as Benjamin got on his horse and walked him back through town to Sullivan's store. There were two farm wagons pulled up under the sign lettered *Groceries and Dry Goods.* In one stood a ragged boy he would have taken no notice of had not Bessie Marsh come out of the store just then. He looked again at the boy and recognized his and Bessie's child.

Dismounting, he hitched his horse and greeted her. "Morning, Mrs. Marsh." Everyone accorded Bessie the courtesy title of "Mrs." after Leon's birth. "As though," Bessie put it, "I was married to myself."

"Morning," she said. "Leon, you remember Mr. Benjamin Davis. He was out to see us—" She turned to Benjamin. "Last fall, was it? Say 'howdy,' Leon."

"Howdy, sir."

"Howdy, son," Benjamin replied. Man and boy colored as they exchanged looks, and Bessie glanced from one to the other with pleased malice. Running a hand under her shawl, she pulled from a dress pocket a small can with a printed label. "Bruton snuff," she read. The boy blushed more deeply, and as Benjamin wondered why, Bessie laughed at his puzzlement. "I haven't taken up dipping, though they say it's a comfort for troubled minds. It's for Ma. Mr. Sullivan added it to the flour and sugar he traded me for my hens and eggs, and other considerations."

The boy was staring at Benjamin's coat pocket, which moved. Benjamin drew forth the kitten. "Picked him up at the gin. His ma wouldn't keep him."

"Unnatural," Bessie said. "I call it unnatural to deny your own flesh, don't you?"

"What you going to do with him?" Leon asked.

"Why—give him to you if you want him," Benjamin surprised himself by saying.

"Can I, Ma?"

"Sure, boy! Always take what you're offered and say 'thank you.'"

Benjamin handed the kitten over the side of the wagon. Bessie said, "Hope you won't think my boy's too tattery. He's got better at home Miss Sarah gave him last Christmas, but it's not for every day. That old sweater's warm enough, ain't it, boy?" She pulled the shoulder in a way that further exposed rough darning and worn areas.

Benjamin shifted uncomfortably. "Grandma asked me to stop for nutmeg."

Bessie clapped her hands. "Somebody going to cook something good? You'll find Mr. Sullivan feeling pert this morning."

Benjamin nodded to woman and boy and started into the store, but her voice stopped him. "Hear you and Mrs. Davis are hoping again. Well, you've had bad luck, haven't you?" She used wheel spokes to ladder herself up to the plank seat. Untying the knotted reins, she yanked the mule into a stiff, backward walk before turning him into the street.

The mule knew the way. The boy tended the kitten, and the woman followed her thoughts. When he was nineteen and she twenty-five, Bessie and Benjamin had come together in mutual need, neither innocent, neither seducer. It was a hot and fleshy affair both enjoyed, with nothing begged and nothing promised. She was the plain daughter of poor farmers, he the heir to Beulah Land. There was no question of his marrying her, although he acknowledged responsibility for her pregnancy and promised to help her family in every way short of marriage. And so he and Sarah had done.

Later the same summer he courted the beautiful visitor from Savannah, Miss Frankie-Julia Dollard, but she married Bonard Saxon when she understood Benjamin's determination to stand by Bessie Marsh. And eventually he married Priscilla Oglethorpe. Bessie Marsh was not at the time resentful. She had a mother and a father and other beaux, and she had not expected to marry soon, let alone well, for after the war the ranks of young men were thin. And so he married, and she bore the child. Her father, who was a poor farmer in all ways, contracted consumption and died of it. Her beaux were content to lie with her but not to wake with her;

the bit of land that became hers was insufficient bait for a permanent attachment.

Sarah and Benjamin helped the Marshes, but with bad luck and bad management, Bessie's little became less until now she kept only a few chickens, three or four hogs, a mule and a cow. She tended a vegetable patch, mainly turnips and potatoes, but the land was rocky and sour and its yield was meager. Bessie let her pride go with her youth and was now glad if favors to the storekeeper allowed her some feeling of independence of Sarah Troy and her grandson. It seemed to Bessie that they had all and she nothing. But when Priscilla Davis was cursed with miscarriages, Bessie began to realize an advantage: she had a son.

Still, she could be moved to rage, as she had been this morning when she saw Benjamin Davis, young at twenty-five whereas she felt herself old at thirty-one.

They came to the creek on the edge of town, and after crossing the bridge, Bessie stopped the wagon. "Now," she said to her son, "take him and drown him."

Leon stared at her. "You said I could keep him."

"I said you could take him. The givers don't like their gifts refused. But I won't have nothing that might kill my biddies."

"I'll train him so he won't, Ma."

"We got nothing to feed him."

"He'll catch mice."

"The rats are bigger than him."

"Ma, let me keep him?"

"Do what I told you and let's get home. It's cold."

He had edged away from her on the seat. The kitten, gripped in one hand, complained. Sliding over the side of the wagon, he dropped to the ground, and the woman followed him. He had run only a little way when she caught him. He lost the kitten as she grabbed and slapped him. Stripping a branch from a bush, she began to lash him across the back and around the legs. She administered the whipping quickly and thoroughly, and she was almost warm when she pushed him away from her. The kitten crouched nearby, frightened to immobility.

"You'll mind me now," Bessie said, "or I'll beat you raw."

The boy picked up the animal.

"Take him yonder and hold him under."

The boy carried the kitten to the edge of the creek, where he knelt and did as his mother ordered.

When the creature struggled no more, she said, "Let him go."

Back in the wagon and on their way again, Bessie said, "You'll learn to be hard."

4

The Glade consisted of a few acres of high ground with trees and grass, and a spring that fed a brook. Its rockiness made it useless for farming, so Benjamin, having loved it all his life, built his house there when he became a man and thought of marrying. On the day he and Priscilla climbed the hill as man and wife he dreamed that the next years would fill the house with children and that the Glade would yield its quiet to their rackety games, their ponies, and passing pleasures.

Today, after presenting nutmeg to Josephine and refusing his grandmother's invitation to stay for noon dinner, he rode home to the Glade and, entering it, thought that it seemed quieter to him now than it had when he was a boy. The silence then had been intimate and waiting. Now it was mere stillness. No dog came barking a welcome; no cat, blinking in winter sun, turned his head to see who approached. Priscilla discouraged their having dogs and cats because there was no keeping them out of the house with all Benjamin's comings and goings, and they dropped hairs everywhere. Neither was there sound of domestic fowl or cow; these were quartered in the farmyard below at Zadok's house and barns. Thinking of Zadok's family, Benjamin's eyes warmed. His overseer lived with his wife Rosalie and their five children in tumbling profusion of beast and bird, hay smell, hog smell, and cooking.

Down there Benjamin could feel things growing in the yards and barns and fields about him; up here was pause, cessation.

Priscilla Oglethorpe had fallen in love with Benjamin partly because of his family. Her own—mother, father, sister—she'd thought of as laced and buttoned, prim in dim parlor, hands folded on laps waiting for Kingdom Come. The Kendricks and Davises were forever moving about, getting into and out of trouble, abundantly acquainted with joy as well as grief. Their appetites had never been tame, and their means of satisfaction had sometimes been exceptional and disorderly. It was their energy that had made such a strong initial appeal to Priscilla, for her own family was without it. Her two older brothers had died in the war, and her father Philip, when his left arm was torn off at Shiloh, abandoned himself to mourning the lost sons and the lost cause the rest of his life. Her mother Ann's only anticipation was the Afterlife. Often on her lips was the admonition: "Prepare for Judgment."

That mother whom Priscilla had thought to escape by marriage to Beulah Land exerted a continuing, even, Benjamin feared, an increasing influence upon her elder daughter. And that mother, Benjamin remembered, was expected today with her trunk to spend the remainder of "this painful time" with daughter and son-in-law in the Glade. No death watch could be kept more grimly than the way Mrs. Oglethorpe awaited the birth of a grandchild. On the occasions of her daughter's miscarriages she would express no sorrow or disappointment. "We bow to God's will."

Benjamin unsaddled his horse and entered the house the back way. Rosalie had trained her oldest daughter Freda to Priscilla's kitchen. She had herself been housekeeper to Benjamin before he married. Freda was energetic and clean, a good cook who might become a better one. So far she had received scant encouragement. Priscilla was not accustomed to the robust meals enjoyed at Beulah Land and soon curtailed Freda's free hand in the kitchen. Whether result or cause: Benjamin began to eat away from home, usually with his sister or grandmother or Zadok. He often took no more than one meal a day at his own table.

Crossing the back porch and entering the kitchen, Benjamin

found Freda with her lips stuck out in a pout. "Mrs. Oglethorpe has come," he said.

Freda tossed her head. He patted her shoulder, and she relaxed enough to say, "You be eating more at home now, Mr. Ben?"

"I'll be here for dinner and supper anyway. What are you cooking?"

"My Sunday baked chicken, though it be a Tuesday. Was going to make apple tarts, but Mrs. Oglethorpe say nobody wants them so it's a waste and don't do it."

"Cook them for supper. I'll want them."

"Yes, sir," Freda said, and almost smiled.

Benjamin returned to the back porch, where he dipped water from a bucket into a hand basin and quickly washed his face and hands. He then went to join Priscilla and Mrs. Oglethorpe in the room next the master bedroom, fitted for the child to come during Priscilla's first pregnancy but since turned into a kind of invalid's sitting room. His welcome to Mrs. Oglethorpe was all courtesy and no warmth. He had long ago given up trying to love her and knew she would never love him. She could not forgive him for inspiring her daughter's one rebellion. Losing that battle, she would give no further inch of the field. Bending over his wife's chair to ask how she was, he observed the strained look of her eyes and mouth. Mrs. Oglethorpe had wasted no time.

It was she who answered for Priscilla. "I found her quite dejected. The girl left a window open, and my poor child's hands were cold as a corpse's when I took them in mine. I closed the window and built up the fire, but I fear I was too late, for now she has become feverish as a consequence of the draft she suffered."

"The sun has made the day milder," Benjamin said.

"It was bitter cold when I arrived. My feet are still ice."

She continued. Although there did not appear to be cracks in the flooring where the boards were visible, she felt something—yes, right through the carpet. She tugged her shawl closer as if offering proof. Benjamin's face burned from the excessive heat of the fire. Mrs. Oglethorpe flirted a handkerchief before her nose. There was, she declared, always such a smell of cooking.

"The girl must prepare food," Priscilla protested mildly.

"Offensive to one in your condition surely. I wish you'd let me find a girl in town for you who is nicer in her ways."

"The one we have will do," Benjamin said curtly.

Mrs. Oglethorpe then wondered at length if Dr. Platt quite understood Priscilla's constitution, if he had fully considered the complications. Perhaps they should have consulted a physician from Savannah, but it was too late now. After all, it was not as if they all had not a great deal to fear. Priscilla had lost two babies and never before endured to the eighth month. Were there not precautions that might be yet taken? She did not want to alarm anyone, but she often lay awake the entire night with the most frightening apprehensions.

That it was familiar made it no less disagreeable. Benjamin bore it the best he could, for he could do nothing else. When he tried to answer her, Priscilla became agitated with nerves. He had begged Priscilla to let him banish her during the last month of pregnancy, but she was clearly afraid of Mrs. Oglethorpe. Benjamin had heard Priscilla defend herself weakly and assure her mother that she was and would be all right; and he had on those occasions seen Mrs. Oglethorpe study her daughter's face with implacable pity, shaking her head in certainty that ill would come. Ill had come, and she was proved right. — Did she not know? Had she not borne four children of her own in pain and sorrow?

Benjamin appealed to Sarah, who told him she could not step between mother and daughter. Jane tried what she might with her natural good cheer and her own happy experience of motherhood. Priscilla appeared to draw strength from her sister-in-law; but whatever comfort she found vanished the next time she met her mother.

Noon dinner was observed, if not shared, by the three. Priscilla ate some of the white meat of the chicken and a spoonful of rice without gravy, which Mrs. Oglethorpe pronounced too rich. Mrs. Oglethorpe refused anything choicer than the back, which she claimed she preferred, having got used to it by deferring all her life to her husband and children. She picked every shred of meat and skin from it and then took the bones into her mouth and sucked them in a way that made Benjamin long to silence her with a shout. She refused coffee, waved aside the offer of cake and observed that it appeared dry. She allowed that, seeing they had left-over cake to finish, it was a good thing she had stopped the girl's making apple tarts. Benjamin did not argue. He knew that it would only end in distressing Priscilla.

After noon dinner Mrs. Oglethorpe put her arm about Priscilla's shoulders and guided her away. They would lie down together and rest, she said. Benjamin saddled his horse and went his round of the fields, marking the progress of the day's work. Late afternoon he found his way to his sister's house, where he put himself into good humor in Daniel's calm, easy company. When Jane pressed him to stay for supper, and he allowed Davy and Bobby Lee to pull his arms and kick his boots and climb all over him begging him to stay, he remembered Freda's apple tarts and went home.

Priscilla excused herself from joining her mother and her husband at the table. She would, she promised, have a glass of buttermilk before she went to bed, but she wanted nothing yet. Mrs. Oglethorpe accompanied Benjamin to the dining room silently. Her eyes grew large when she saw the platter of fried pork chops Freda set on the table, and larger still when that was followed by a bowl of potatoes in cream sauce, another of boiled cabbage, another of stewed tomatoes, a platter of fried sweet potatoes, and smaller glass dishes of pickled cucumber and beet relish. Benjamin urged Mrs. Oglethorpe to serve herself. She asked him to call the girl and tell her to bring the cold chicken remaining from noon dinner. This was done, and when it was set before her, she speared a wing onto her plate. When Freda was gone, Mrs. Oglethorpe delivered a monologue on the subject of waste. Benjamin took refuge in his supper, which he consumed with less enjoyment than he pretended.

"What happens to all the food you don't eat?"

"It is eaten by others, ma'am."

"No wonder your man Zadok can raise such a large family."

"They work with him, for me."

"Fried meat at night cannot be healthy."

"Then I shall die before I'm thirty."

"You please the devil when you mock the Lord."

"It is not the Lord I mock, ma'am, and I eat what I please at my own table."

"Then may the Lord have mercy on you."

"Amen." He took a pork chop he did not want and sprinkled a little black pepper on his fried sweet potatoes.

When he finished the last bit on his plate, Mrs. Oglethorpe scraped her chair back as if to leave. Freda entered from the kitchen bearing a new platter high. "Apple tarts," she said.

5

"Bobby Lee! — Davy!"

The quiet was unnatural. Nell had asked that there be no tiptoeing and whispering; she liked the sounds of the house.

"Robert E. Lee, do you want your bottom blistered? — Jefferson Davis, come running!" She changed tactic. "Bobby Lee, you're the oldest, and I depend on you to act it."

She might have been calling the stars in the sky.

"If you don't both come this instant, we'll leave without you!"

Suppressed giggles guided Sarah through the hall toward the room where soiled household linens were kept. They were washed there on rainy days, although the open yard was preferred when the weather was fair. Outside the door she stopped, and the stifled laughter stopped. She opened the door cautiously, was attacked by two shrouded dwarfs, and screamed. Her great-grandsons threw the sheets back from their heads and, exultant with pity, demanded to know, "Did we scare you, Grandma?"

She protested that she was faint and collapsed into a chair, as they whooped proudly and climbed into her lap, sharply elbowing each other for preferred positions until she pulled both against her.

"Tell us a story," Davy asked automatically.

"There's no time."

"A short one," Bobby Lee coaxed.

"Well," she said. "Once upon a time there was a place called Beulah Land—" They giggled, content. As she began an anecdote she knew so well she could have repeated it in a fever, another part of her mind cried, "Dear Leon, how you would have loved them!" There was no confusion of loyalty in her heart to the two men she married; each held a distinct place.

Finding them, Jane began to scold. "Come along, we're late, and they know all about Lovey and Floyd and Uncle Ezra. They've begun to correct me when I get absentminded."

The boys slipped to the floor, and Sarah stood, smoothing her dress.

"Can we sit on the hay box?" Davy asked.

"If you don't fight," Jane answered.

Zebra had Jane's buggy at the side door off Sarah's office, and they were presently on their way. It was a cold, still morning, and the horse was ready to move briskly, his breath as apparent as the steam from a locomotive. As they drew near Elk Institute, Jane, who was driving, said, "I have four stops to make in town, but none need take more than ten minutes. We'll be back for you in two hours. Are you certain that isn't too long?"

"I could stay two days, two months," Sarah assured her.

Jane halted the horse, and Sarah stepped down. "Tell them all I said howdy," Jane said, and Sarah nodded.

The boys took it up. "Tell them I said howdy."

"Tell Uncle Roman to come see us!"

"Tell Uncle Roscoe to come too!"

"Say howdy to Aunt Selma!"

"Say howdy to Aunt Pauline!"

"Bye, Grandma!"

"Be good!" Sarah called.

"You be good too, Grandma!"

As the buggy turned and headed back to the main road, their continued shouts were lost. Sarah studied the building before her. It was so much like, and so little like, the original house at Beulah Land that had been burned during Sherman's march. The land it stood on was once Oaks Plantation, the Davis home land, but

Benjamin's father James, blinded in the war, decided that he could not manage it and sold it to Junior Elk at the war's end. Junior was the son of Beulah Land's old enemy, Roscoe Elk, long the Kendrick overseer before he became one of the richest Negroes in Georgia. Junior cut Oaks into tenant farms, keeping the largest acreage for himself and building a house on it that copied and mocked the one his father had served and hated.

This was the house she stood before. As she advanced along the wide brick walk leading to the front door, she thought about the ironies of all their lives. The house was now a school called Elk Institute, giving free education to the Negro children of the county, and the third Roscoe Elk was Sarah's friend. By the gift of the school after Junior's death to Junior's half brother Roman, he turned the old Elk dream upside down, for Roman had been fathered by Leon Kendrick eight years before Sarah married him and became Sarah's protégé, the first pupil of what evolved over the years into this school.

She saw no one as she entered and went quietly down the wide center hallway. Following the sound she recognized as Roman's voice, she opened a door to find herself at the rear of a classroom of about fifteen Negro children. Roman was at a blackboard behind the teacher's desk, and his back was to her. He was writing words in chalk in the elegant, ballooning script he used only to teach. Twisting the chalk to make a firm period, he then rolled it between both hands and slowly read the words. "Girls jump rope; boys play ball." Turning, he saw Sarah, and his thin, rather severe face softened. Instantly noting the change, the children turned to see who had come in. "Attention!" Roman said, tapping the chalk sharply on the blackboard. The children faced front. "It's five minutes before recess, and I want everybody to write down on his or her tablet what I've written on the board, as many times as you can but making each letter clear and perfect. I will examine the tablets after recess. If anybody makes a sound while I'm out of the room, Herman will take the names, and he or she will be boiled in oil."

They bent heads over desks, and as Roman came to Sarah, she slipped into the hallway. He closed the door behind them, and she said, "You shouldn't have stopped. I've only a few minutes, but I couldn't resist putting my head in when I heard you."

"I didn't know you were coming."

"Roscoe sent word he'd like to see me."

"Why didn't he go to you?" They entered his office next door to the classroom. "Do you want some coffee?"

"No. — I'll find out when I see him." Sitting, she removed her gloves. "You look tired, my dear. How are you?"

"Sometimes it seems hopeless."

"You keep the best school in the county, black or white."

"If only we had them longer. The older they get, the less willing the parents are to send them. They want them in the fields. They see no reason for them to learn to multiply and divide when they've learned how to add and subtract. I declare we're lucky to get them full time eighty days a year. That's only sixteen weeks out of fifty-two. Next year they'll have forgotten what they learned this year."

"You do a great deal. Everybody knows it."

"Maybe I'm too old to teach," he said wistfully.

"Fiddlesticks. You're ten years younger than I am."

He smiled at her. "When are you going to get old?"

"Never. How are Selma and Pauline?"

"They have colds, but they won't miss their classes, so everyone is going to have a cold."

"I'll stop to see them after I've seen Roscoe. Take a day off, Roman; come and spend it with me at Beulah. It'll do both of us good. We'll walk all over, as we used to, and talk, talk, talk."

"And you'll tell me c-a-t is cat, but it isn't."

"Aunt Nell would like to see you."

"I'll come soon. Is she herself?"

"Some days." Sarah shook her head. "She eats everything, but not as much."

"She was always of a delicate constitution," he said in a girlish tone, mimicking Nell.

She stretched the fingers of her gloves and stood, and he stood with her. Both felt for their backs and, recognizing the gesture in the other, laughed. "Oh, Sarah," Roman said, "we can't be. You sixty-eight and me right behind you."

"We just stood up too quickly," she said. "It could happen to ten-year-olds."

He walked with her into the hall. A bell rang, and the classroom doors opened. The children were orderly, as they had been disciplined to be, but they stepped friskily, and Roman became the fussy principal of the school. Clapping his hands together, he ordered: "Don't push! Slow down. Anybody I see pushing stays *in*side! Ethel, you're too big a girl to act like that—come here to *me!*"

Sarah joined the crowd in the hall. All the pupils knew her, and the ones closest spoke greetings as she made a path through the games they were forming in the school yard.

Roscoe Elk had built his house away from the school and planted a row of japonica to act as a screen of sorts, but he liked hearing the children when they were let out to play. Trained in the law in Philadelphia, he spent his days now managing the affairs of the school and the tenant farms his father had set up. Although he had scrapped original agreements and made terms more liberal, the tenant farms were still that. His housekeeper Geraldine let Sarah in and she was presently seated with Roscoe in his office. As she was most easy in hers, so was he in his; that was one of the things they knew about each other. Geraldine brought coffee and a lemon cake which she said Roxanne had made especially for her. She knew that when he was ready Roscoe would get to his reason for asking her today, so she relaxed and allowed him to pour coffee and cut cake.

Roscoe was a stout man in the late twenties, homely and ordinary enough except for blue eyes and a sprinkle of freckles he had inherited with light-brown skin from his mother.

They talked of Nell Kendrick, and then Roscoe, lacking the delicacy of Annabel Saxon, asked the state of health and spirits of Mrs. Benjamin Davis. They spoke a little of Roman. "Oh, he despairs one day and conquers the next," Roscoe assured her.

"Perhaps he's lonely," Sarah suggested.

"Lonely *here?*"

"Lonely for his dead friend."

"We are all his friends here," Roscoe said softly, understanding her but pretending not to.

"Lonely for himself. We lose ourselves when we do too much."

"Maybe there's nothing private left for him," Roscoe suggested.

"I hadn't thought of that," she said. "If it's so, then he *is* lonely. I've been down that lane."

His hands fidgeted with his cup, and he drained it and set it aside. "How is Miss Jane and her family?"

He never looked at her when he asked about Jane, for she was at the heart of their long friendship, certainly its origin. When Roscoe and Jane were children, each had been taken by the enemy grandfathers, Roscoe and Leon, to watch the miracle of the train's coming in and stopping and leaving. That is how they first grew aware of each other's existence. So much Sarah knew. Later, toward the end of the war, not long before his father sent him away to Philadelphia to be educated, Roscoe had come one night to tell her of hearing Junior Elk and a Union officer named Ponder raise glasses in a toast to the destruction of Beulah Land. The young Roscoe's warning was their only forecast of that destruction. Finally, Roscoe returned to Highboro the summer Jane was being courted by what Nell complained was "every boy in the county with a pair of shoes to put on." Sarah had not seen the truth, but Casey had: that Roscoe Elk loved Jane Davis. Only they knew it. Jane did not. They had never spoken of it after the one time. Good friends though they were, Sarah and Roscoe had never, of course, spoken of it at all, aware that friendship must regard privacies to share confidence.

He smiled now and let her boast about Robert E. Lee and Jefferson Davis Todd, but she knew his mind was moving closer to the reason he had asked to see her. When she paused as if to say, "Well?" he raised his voice to call his housekeeper. "Geraldine! If Claribell and Luck are ready, tell them to come in."

So that is it, Sarah thought.

Roscoe's father Junior had been stabbed to death by his drunken mistress when she discovered that he had taken to bed her thirteen-year-old sister Claribell. Subsequently, young Roscoe had been Claribell's protector, rescuing her from her mother's eagerness to sell her and putting her in the charge of one of the strong-minded women teachers of the school, a Negro from Philadelphia named Mathilda Boland. Claribell seemed to have no mind of her own, but she learned orderliness and obedience and manners, and although shy, she responded gratefully to the kindness of her new protector. Eight months after the murder of Junior Elk, Claribell bore a child. Pliable in other ways, she was an unexpectedly assertive mother. She decided to call her baby daughter Luck. No one had ever before heard such a name, but Southerners are open-minded about names, and so Luck she was called, and at Roscoe's insistence: Luck Elk.

Presently the woman Claribell appeared, neat and plain, bringing by the hand her child. Sarah had seen them infrequently and casually over the years, but she looked at them now afresh, as she knew she was meant to. The woman had bobbed a curtsy on entering. Seeing Sarah, the girl advanced directly. She was, Sarah remembered, between four and five, having been born (why did she remember?) on November 20, 1874. She was blacker than Roscoe. Her hair was tied in pigtails. She wore a pink dress that stood out about her so starchily she could never have sat down in it. Round, intense eyes in a round and shining face appeared to question, even to challenge the visitor, and when she raised her hands, the palms a deeper pink than her dress, Sarah reached to take them.

The moment was achieved. Luck smiled confidently. Sarah smiled admiringly. Claribell smiled proudly. Roscoe's feeling was too strong to be contained in a smile; he laughed, throwing back his head in a great bellow. Luck turned and ran to him. He caught her and stood, turning with her in his arms before sitting down to hold her on his lap. Claribell had slipped out of the room.

Sarah praised Luck's dress, and Luck explained that her mother had made it and showed how the buttons worked and said her mother and Geraldine took pains tying the sash so it was like a butterfly, and now it had been crushed against Roscoe's lap. Roscoe, she called Pa. As eagerly as Roman ever drilled a first class, Roscoe led Luck through a recital of numbers and letters, followed by the days of the week and the months of the year. At conclusion, man and child turned faces from each other to Sarah, and Sarah obliged them with honest applause. Luck was pleased with herself and with Sarah, but when Roscoe told her to leave them and go to her mother, she complied only a little reluctantly, making a firmly executed curtsy before running out.

"She is a joy," Sarah said when they were alone.

"She is the most beautiful thing I know," he said. His blue eyes had never looked at her more intently. "Do you see?"

She hesitated. "Not yet."

"I must have her," he said.

"But you do. She calls you Pa and loves you."

"She must be mine so that everybody knows it."

"What are you going to do?" Sarah asked.

"Marry Claribell."

She thought about it. "Is it wise?" she then ventured.

"I don't know."

"What I mean is—I don't know how strongly you feel about Claribell."

"It will be all right," he said softly.

She paused to consider. Knowing the dangers of frankness, she reminded herself that he wanted to know what she thought; otherwise, he'd not have asked her to come to him. She said carefully, "You are not yet thirty. You may come to know someone you will love very much and want to marry." He shook his head. "I was well into my fifties with no thought of marrying again when I came to love Casey—so much that I don't know how I managed my life without him before he came to me."

"I will not have anything like that." Now it was she who would not look at him, for it was as if Jane had entered the room and stood before them. "I will have Luck—she will be my luck."

"It's dangerous to put so much love into one small object."

"It's already happened."

"Then I am happy for you and her." She put out her hand, and he took it and shook it and let it go. "If there is any way I can help?"

He shook his head. "I'll ask."

They were quiet together for a time.

"What are you thinking?" he said, smiling. "You have an odd expression."

"Of how wonderful we are!" she answered immediately. "Your

happiness means much to me, as you know. Yet I hated your grandfather and your father of all the men in this world."

"You had reason to," he said. "They hated you and wanted to take Beulah Land."

"They had some cause for their hate," she admitted.

"Oh, they were greedy too, eager to be big-rich. But yes, they had. Your first husband was Roman's father." It was common enough knowledge, but it was the first time it had been said between them. "Now let me see—" His tone lightened. "Roman is my half uncle, and we might say he's your stepson; so doesn't that make you and me a little bit kin?"

"It's no wonder outsiders throw up their hands at Southerners," she said. "And now your half sister is to become your daughter."

With a smile he said, "Speaking of someone legitimate, isn't it time one of us had a letter from Abraham?"

6

However disreputable he was considered by the women of the county, their husbands and brothers would once have agreed that Alf Crawford performed a service. At the end of the war, being a practical man and finding himself a widower with five daughters and only a small farm, he looked at what he had rather than what he had not. He made a fair crop of corn, but not much else, so he decided to convert it into whiskey. When men came to buy it, they stayed to admire his daughters. If "going to Crawford's" was a way of saying they sought the comfort of strong drink, then "going to the barn with one of Crawford's daughters to look at the cow" came as certainly to mean another kind of ease. The distiller and procurer may, depending upon the viewer's need, be the welcomest of sights, or the most repellent. Before Benjamin's marriage, Alf Crawford had often enough been a man he greeted with gladness.

Time had altered the circumstances of both. One by one: Alvina, Alma, Annie, Abbie, and Adeline exchanged Crawford for the names of five humble farmers and became wives and mothers of respectability if little consequence. Alf Crawford now lived alone, with only a black woman named Yulee, who was nearly as old as he, to attend him; and when it was put about that his whiskey was not what it used to be, few continued to make the journey to the little farm that had been a magnet for the thirsty and lusty. Feeling no great gratitude for his earlier use of them, the daughters left Alf to fend for himself, and this he did by selling bad whiskey to whomever he could, usually Negroes, and by raising chickens, those of his neighbors when they strayed. In the last year Alf had allied himself with a youth named Eugene Betchley, younger of two sons of another poor farmer, who favored setting traps and throwing seines to tilling the soil with his father and brother.

Early one morning in February, Benjamin discovered Alf and Eugene in the back woods of Beulah Land. Eugene ran when Benjamin hailed them, but Alf, who was old and fat, waited with a smile of fellowship the years had made uncertain. After greetings, civil on one side and hearty on the other, Benjamin began to examine the trap which Eugene had dropped in his haste.

"Don't know why he run off thataway," Alf said, "seeing you and me are old friends. I told him you wouldn't mind us taking a critter or two, or even a *few* of the many crowding your woods. Them as ain't fit to eat will have a thick pelt this time of year, a man can sell for a few nickels or a dollar or two. It's been a hard winter for poor folks."

Benjamin said, "A trap like that broke a dog's leg last week, and we had to shoot him."

"Is that a fact?" Alf exclaimed sympathetically.

"My brother-in-law has found other traps sprung with dead animals. Snares too, and signs of the creek being dragged with seines."

"Now, Ben, you ain't telling me, are you, you own the very

water and the fullness thereof? It flows onto your land and off it, and the fish flow with it."

"When it's on our land, what's in it is ours."

"I never expected you to grudge an eel or an old pike."

"Come fishing with a pole any time you like, but I won't have seines used and the fish not wanted left on the bank to die."

"That must be somebody else, neither one of us, Ben."

"Tell Eugene I'm going to his pa if it happens again."

Alf winked. "He don't listen to his pa, and that's the truth. Kind of goes a separate way, you know. Don't mean a bit of harm. I never seen harm in him."

"Tell him what I say, Alf."

Out of sight, Eugene stopped running. He cursed Benjamin Davis aloud to the woods and swore he'd go back and face him, but continued in the direction that brought him presently to a lane that led to the main road. Eugene was eighteen, with a man's body and a boy's mind. He resented all who stopped him from having his way. He hated his father and brother and refused to work with them. Often he slept away from home, and when he returned for a meal, he brought his own food: a rabbit or possum or fish, with enough over what he'd eat to pay for the lard and cornmeal he took from the family supply. He was a big fellow with loose black hair and beard. His eyes were black too, and his teeth nearly so with accumulation and neglect. He was proud of his sexual powers and had lain with a score of willing females, black and white, since he was fourteen.

Approaching Bessie Marsh's farm, he decided that Benjamin Davis had wronged him, because he'd left a good spring trap behind him on Beulah Land. Stopping in the road, he studied the gray board house. Its small porch buckled and sloped and was supported precariously at the corners by piled field stones. Nothing grew near the house, but Eugene knew the extent of the farm, and he suddenly fancied that he could make it his. That would show him to be his own man; his father and brother could go to hell, for he'd be better off than they with forty-four acres to their twenty-seven. He'd own land. As he thought about it, he smiled. In the boy's mind thought had become accomplishment. Smoke lifted from the chimney as he walked around the house.

Leon stood at the back door and glared when he saw Eugene.

"Where's your ma?" Eugene called.

"Drawing water," Leon said.

Eugene went to find her. "Morning, Miss Bessie."

Bessie made no answer, but she glanced at him as she pulled the rope. The attached bucket came into view, and she poured its contents into the house bucket she'd brought with her.

"Let me tote for you," Eugene offered.

"I tote for myself," Bessie said.

Eugene took the full bucket from her; and when she made no protest but wound the well rope around a nail to hold it in place, he said sociably, "Cold this morning."

"If you worked, you'd warm up."

He laughed long enough to set the bucket down on the hard ground.

"Tired already?" she mocked. As she reached for the handle, he took her and pulled her against him. Twisting her arms, she freed herself.

"Get further and smell better," she ordered. "I won't be grabbed at by no stinking youngun."

"I've got my full growth, Miss Bessie, as some could tell you."

"Go tote water for them."

She went toward the house with her heavy bucket, and he returned to the well to draw more water. There was no dipper, so he lifted the well bucket and drank from the side. She paused at the door beside her son. "Look here, Miss Bessie! I'm washing myself for you!" With that he threw the remainder of the water into the air over his head, wetting himself.

"You crazy youngun!" she cried.

"Can I come in the kitchen to get dry?"

She hesitated. "I'm not asking you to breakfast."

That was his beginning. The next time he appeared in her back yard she was on her way to milk. Again he took the bucket, this time empty, and found the cow in her stall.

"Know your way, don't you?" she said, following. "I'm missing a chicken or two," she added slyly, for country gossip was never far behind events, and Eugene and Alf's small forays were known.

"Does she kick?" Eugene said, slapping the cow's flank.

"When she takes a notion. She's skittish." Eugene squatted, spat on his hands, and began to massage the cow's teats. "What's her name?"

"Got none."

"Coo now, Sooky," he murmured as gently as a lover, resting his head against her warm flank. "Don't that feel good to you, old girl?" When the teats were warmed and beginning to give, he clenched the bucket between his knees and directed the streams of milk into it. She watched him speculatively.

"Shaved off your beard."

He shrugged. "No good to me."

That morning he stayed to breakfast, having assured his acceptance by bringing a freshly caught and skinned rabbit. After she'd fried it, Bessie ate as hungrily as did her mother and son, for they enjoyed little game. Now and then she directed a scornful look at her guest to warn him that his contribution allowed him no liberties. Leon ate sulkily, but he ate. Finishing what had been given her, the old woman dragged her chair as near the cookstove as she could without burning herself and sat in it unmoving. Bessie scraped plates and carried the scraps of bone and gristle that had not been consumed to the yard to throw to the chickens, who came running, not knowing how little there was.

Eugene remained half the morning, wandering and looking. Bessie went on with her work. Leon followed his mother until she told him to get from underfoot and fill the woodbox in the kitchen. When he brought in his first armload, the grandmother stirred in her chair. "Who is it?" she whispered.

"Me," Leon said.

"Afraid it was him."

Bessie came in with three eggs she had found.

"Is he gone?" her mother asked, again in a whisper.

"Yes'm," Bessie answered.

"Who is he?"

"You've known his pa all your life."

"I couldn't see him clear. My eyes are gummy."

"Gene Betchley."

"Gene Betchley." The old woman repeated the name as if she knew him and did not know him. "What does he want?"

He returned every day at different times until they came to expect him and wonder when he would arrive. He seldom presented himself empty-handed, and Bessie guessed that most of his gifts had been stolen. All were useful and none of a personal nature: a couple of cabbages, a half side of salted pork, a gallon of syrup. His face was pale and pimpled where beard had grown, and Bessie could look at him with indifference and think: a boy. Although he made an effort to appear cleaner, his clothes smelled rankly of old sweat and long, continuous wear. One morning he found her at the washtub, and she told him she'd wash his shirt if he left it with her. He took it off on the spot, and when she saw the grime of his drawers, she told him to go into the house and remove them, and instructed Leon to bring them to her. Eugene sat by the cookstove wrapped in a quilt until his clothes were washed and dried, the old granny squinting at him calculatingly, and Leon watching him as if he were a coiled snake. He didn't seem to mind or even to notice them, but spent the waiting time whittling a spoon from a piece of pine he took from the woodbox. He broke it finally trying to make the neck thinner. When Bessie came in to cook noon dinner, his eyes followed her. It was not that he looked at her admiringly, but no one for a long time had looked at her so much, and she enjoyed the attention. When her hands were busy kneading dough for flour hoecake, he sidled over and slipped an arm low around her waist.

Leon said, "Leave Mama alone."

Bessie laughed. "You watch how you talk to grown men."

"I reckon he's jealous." Eugene smirked.

"He's got no cause," Bessie answered him sharply, though looking at Leon. Shifting her eyes to Eugene, she said, "Keep your hands to yourself."

Leon ran out the door and did not return until after Eugene put on his dry clothes and went away. When Leon came in, his mother teased him so merrily he decided he hated her too and told her so, whereupon she slapped him. The old woman, who usually had little to say for herself or anyone else, worried about the reason for their visitor's regular attendance on them as she gummed her soft boiled peas and hoecake. "What's he want? Reckon he's after the farm?"

"It ain't much to want," Bessie said.

"More'n he's got," the old woman said cannily. "What else would he be after? There ain't nothing."

Without being asked, he began to do chores around the place. From drawing water he turned to chopping wood, which gave him the notion of sharpening the ax. One morning he brought a basket of half-rotten apples and fed them to her old sow. He mended harness and made himself acquainted with Bessie's one mule. Bessie didn't talk much to Eugene, but she decided he'd got a bee in his bonnet about her, so she figured to let him help her as long as the fit was on him. The weather turned mild, and he mentioned plowing. She said he'd better go help his pa if he wanted to plow, for she couldn't pay wages.

"Don't want wages," he said.

As much as he could he ignored her son and her mother, although it was plain enough the old woman distrusted him and the child felt threatened. Only when they were by themselves did the young boy and the young man show their dislike. After the early physical advances he made to Bessie, he made no more. Both knew he was waiting for a sign from her. Then ten days after coming every day, he did not come.

Night came, but Eugene did not. Nor was he slouching beside the well next morning as Bessie half expected him to be. The feeling of his absence grew as the sun rose higher. It was a clear, dry day, and Bessie suddenly made up her mind to air bedding. Quilts were thrown over the clotheslines. Bessie's featherbed and the old urine-stained mattress the boy slept on with his grandmother were laid on a slope of pine needles where the sun gradually drew out of them a smell as stale as it was palpably human. Bessie kept busy; she would not admit that she was waiting.

With dinner cooked and eaten, the afternoon passed. Cold supper finished and the weather remaining warm, they sat on the porch, like people dreading bad news. The boy went to sleep when twilight began to blur landscape, and Bessie woke him roughly and told him to go to bed. Her mother went inside with him. The dark deepened, and Bessie sat on. All was quiet inside the house. In the distance—from the Betchley farm? she wondered—a dog barked furiously and subsided abruptly. The night seemed more still and lonely than ever. Bessie sighed and rose tiredly from the sag-bottomed chair. Scratching her arm, which did not itch, she turned her face to the breeze to catch the odors of the night. In a meander she then made her way into the yard and around the house, coming at last to the outhouse beyond the barn. It was black inside, but there was, she thought wryly, nothing for her to look at, as she loosened her clothes and settled buttocks over the larger of two holes cut in the wooden seat. After sitting a time she wiped herself with a dry corncob, although she had performed no evacuation. When the door creaked, she knew it was not the wind. She cried out, but softly.

"It's me."

She was not surprised. She knew she had wanted something like it to happen; but she had not gone as far as deciding how she would behave, for to admit there was anything to decide would have been to admit too much. Her relief at recognizing Eugene hardened her voice. "What you doing here? Where were you all day, and yesterday?"

"Brought you something." He reached for her hand and guided it to his penis, which he had drawn from his clothes before entering.

"I don't want that!" She snatched her hand back.

"You do, Bess."

"Get!" she commanded.

"If I been watching you, you been watching me too."

"Get! Go!"

He slipped to his knees. She didn't know what he was doing when she felt his head burrow under her dress and push upward. His mouth followed hair to her opening, and for a moment his teeth gingerly clenched the fatty mound above it before his tongue entered her. She stood stock-still with astonishment until released by the savagely comic thought: "Won't get a youngun this way!" As shock dimmed to passive acceptance that stirred to vanity, he paused, and after a moment withdrew his head. Rising to his feet, he shoved her so that she sat on the seat. "Now you." She didn't understand. "You, me." He took her head in both hands and pulled it to his penis. She flinched, but he held her.

She allowed it to touch her lips, then to open them. Presently, he drew out, and she waited for him to lead her again. She could not see. She did not know how they were positioned, but everything began to move and meet: arms, bellies, crotches, mouths. In momentary panic she thought his thick tongue would choke her, his penis rend her, and then all eased and gave, and he began a steady, rhythmic motion. As they worked together, she was roused to clutch and groan with pleasure and he to grunt and then to beg, his voice caressing and cursing her until there was only one word spoken over and over to time his movements: "Mama—Mama!—Mama—Mama, Mama, Mama, Mama, Mama—Maaaa!"

He twitched and died in her, his energy seeming to pass to her and become hers. She supported him now, encouraging his collapse and comforting his dying. "There, sh, there, sh, sh, sh—"

She almost slept but was suddenly alert when she heard another voice, her child's, from outside the door, which Eugene blocked with his body.

"Mama! Is that you in there?"

She answered faintly, "Yes."

He had sounded frightened.

"I'm in here," she said, making her voice stronger. "What do you want?"

"I woke up and hollered and you never answered. Are you sick in there?"

"No."

"You sounded funny."

"Go to bed," she said sharply. Each waited, sensing the other's uncertainty. "Leon?"

"Yes'm."

"Go on back to the house. If you want to pee first, pee in the yard but not on your grandma's row of fern." Again she waited. "Have you gone, Leon?" She decided that he had when there was no answer. Eugene stirred. He was on the floor, she on the seat. His head found and rested on her lap. She cradled it with her arms and kissed the dampness from his brows, not caring that his face felt greasy under the sweat or that his hair smelled of swamp and wood smoke.

7

Good timing by coincidence is always more pleasing than its achievement by deliberation, so Sarah was particularly glad to have a letter from Abraham Ezra Kendrick on the morning she attended the wedding of Roscoe Elk and Claribell. Abraham was fourteen years old, the son of Floyd, who until his death had been the only Negro overseer of a large plantation in that part of Georgia. Floyd and Sarah's first husband, born a week apart, had been lifelong friends. Since Roscoe Elk's father and grandfather had been in different ways responsible for the suicide of one and the murder of the other, Roscoe and Sarah shared the guardianship of the boy. Judged to be more than ordinarily quick at school, he suffered from overindulgence until Roman had the idea of sending him to Philadelphia to study. Roman had spent his early teaching career there, and Roscoe had read law there, so it seemed fitting. After their first doubts about letting the boy go so young, Sarah and Roscoe agreed to share the expense of his Northern education. It had turned out a good arrangement. Abraham was doing well; he had wanted just such independence to bring out his best. He wrote progress reports to his guardians alternately, which were shared immediately on receipt, for they were often as entertaining as they were detailed.

Benjamin had brought the mail from Highboro that morning. In his impatience during the time of waiting for Priscilla to give birth, he assumed errands and small chores that would have fallen to others another time. He also practiced to avoid his mother-in-law's company, so when he delivered the day's mail to Sarah, he was eager to accept her commission to carry a bundle of clothes to Bessie Marsh. There were some worn pieces Bessie might adapt for personal use, but Sarah always sent new things for Leon, and she had been disturbed by Benjamin's recent report to her of his ragged appearance. The things she had packed today were stout common goods; Bessie could not claim they were too fine for regular use.

It was late morning when Benjamin turned his horse into the farmyard. Hearing a sound he identified as the beating of wet clothes, he followed it around the house to that area beside the well which Bessie used to do her washing. After presenting the bundle and the message Sarah had charged him with, he asked about the boy.

"He's bound to be somewhere," she answered. "He was here a while ago. Little as he is, he has his uses. Takes the cow to forage and totes wood and slops and is pretty good about keeping his eye on Ma. She can't hardly see now, and he's her eyes, you might say, when she needs him to be." Bessie continued with her work after offering to stop and being told that Benjamin could stay for only a few minutes because it was getting on to dinnertime.

"How is Mrs. Ben?" this prompted Bessie to say. "I know she's not had it yet or I'd have heard."

"Her time's overlong," Benjamin said.

"Poor thing. I remember how tired I got carrying that youngun of mine." Beating wet clothes again on a stump, she glanced at him and was gratified to see him turning his head and looking about. "Would you like to see the boy?" She lifted her voice. "Leon! You, Leon! Come and say howdy!" When there was no immediate response, she smiled. "Kind of bashful with folks he don't know. Not that you or Miss Sarah are exactly strangers. Why, most of what we wear on our backs was give us by you and her. — Leon! Come running to me when I call you!"

He did so, sprinting around the barn but stopping abruptly when he saw who was there.

"Morning to you, Leon," Benjamin said.

The boy stared and came on.

"Say it nice like I taught you," Bessie ordered him comfortably, "lest Mr. Ben decide you're simple."

"Morning, sir."

"Brought you some clothes to wear, that's what he's done. Say 'Thank you.' "

"Thank you, sir."

Benjamin blushed with embarrassment for him. "How's the—that kitten?" he asked to ease the moment, and was dismayed to see that his question made the meeting worse. The boy looked wordlessly at his mother.

"Well," she said, taking the response, "I hate to tell what happened to that poor mite. He went and got himself into my old sow's pen, and she went for him. She'd go for me if I didn't carry a stick when I went in there. It was terrible. The boy liked to cried his heart out the day it happened. I didn't know what we'd do to shut him up."

"I'll bring you another," Benjamin said to him.

The child's look of apprehension increased. Turning, he fled.

"I told you how bashful he can be with strange folks, and he don't in the everyday way know you, does he? Never mind him."

"I'd like to know him."

Bessie wiped her hands on her dress front and folded her arms. "What give you that notion, I wonder? Here he's been ever since he was born, and good as you and Miss Sarah are about helping out, you never paid any attention to *knowing* him. Reckon it has to do with you about to have one of your own." She corrected herself with a wink. "One you can at last *call* your own. But, hush, Bessie. Nobody wants to dig up old graves. Forget what was and march ahead, has always been my living guide."

"He'll be old enough for school in another year."

"And big enough," Bessie said, "to be some real help around the farm."

"He must go to school," Benjamin said.

She said vaguely, "Well, I don't know. The school's there and he's here, and he'll do more good working on the farm than squirming at a desk, is the way I look at it. I'll see he learns to read and write, but otherwise—" She shook her head.

"I'll send a man over to help you."

"That ain't it," she observed judicially. "The boy'd be learning more here than he would at school, the kind of thing that will stand him in good for the future."

"I want to educate him when he's old enough."

"Out here is going to be his life, this farm. I never remembered

you, Ben—reckon I can call you that, with no one to hear me—you never set a lot of store by schooling as a boy. I've heard you say so."

"Times were different," Benjamin said.

"Well," she said mildly, and turned back to work, as if they'd said all they could about the matter.

"You'll think about it?"

"Yes, I will," she agreed amiably, but in such a way as to show him she was merely humoring him. "Got to get ahead with these things. So much to do and spring practically here."

"When do you want me to send the plowman to turn your ground and help you plant?"

"I meant to tell you," she said. "You won't have to do that this year. I've made a kind of—other arrangement. Don't you worry about us. We'll be all right. Tell Miss Sarah I asked after her health, and Mr. Troy too. She's a well-meaning lady, and I have a lot of respect for her."

"I'll send a man anyway. You can use him for whatever needs doing, plowing or not."

That was the moment Eugene chose to appear, looking slyly surprised to see Benjamin, whose arrival he had observed from the barn, where he was working. "Morning," he called, and approached.

"Morning." Benjamin looked inquiringly at Bessie.

"He's helping me; ain't you, Gene?"

"That's right."

"Being a real help."

Benjamin knew he was being laughed at and didn't understand.

"Morning I saw you last, I come on here," Eugene explained. "Had got myself sopping wet somehow—" Bessie laughed aloud and checked herself. "She let me sit in the kitchen till I dried off. Since then she's done a heap for me."

"No more'n you done for me," Bessie said with a simper.

"That's account I'm sweet on you," Eugene allowed.

"Listen to him!" Bessie screeched with delight.

"It's so and you know it," Eugene declared.

Bessie said to Benjamin, "You tell him I'm too old for him. He

won't listen to me, though I've tried. He just hangs around and won't go home. That's why I put him to work."

Eugene said, "Wasn't I willing?"

"Oh, you were willing enough, I won't deny!"

"It ain't a bad farm," Eugene said. "All it needs is a man."

Bessie laughed and dipped another load of clothes from the black pot in which they had been boiling. Dumping them on the stump with her stick, she began to pound them. "More to wash now, with his too," she complained.

"When we going to get married?" Eugene teased her, as if Benjamin were not present.

"Just hear him!" Bessie appealed to Benjamin again. "Always after me. I had to promise I'd think about it. Only way us women folk can get a man to shut up."

"When's it to be, Bess?"

"Let you know when the plowing's done!"

"I'm good at more'n one kind of plowing."

"Don't talk ugly front of Mr. Ben. I strictly forbid it."

Benjamin said lamely, "I'll be going."

"Glad you come by," Bessie said as if they had enjoyed a casual visit. "Give Miss Sarah my thank-you, bless her heart."

He nodded and mounted his horse.

8

Roscoe Elk attended no church regularly, but he had arranged for a Reverend Curtis Odom to marry him to Claribell because, as he confided to Sarah, "He's the only colored preacher I know who's not a shouter." The ceremony required less than five minutes and took place in Roscoe's office. It was witnessed by Sarah, Roman, Selma, Pauline, and Mathilda Boland, the teacher who had paid early, particular attention to the welfare of the mother-child when

she was more child than mother. Claribell appeared only a minute before the service and left a minute after it. She wore white, as she almost always did. Luck, starched stiff as a tombstone and bribed to silence, was held in check by Geraldine, both of whom entered and departed with Claribell. Roscoe had keyed the occasion to the ordinary; hence the brevity and office setting. Refreshment was token: a glass of claret and a plate of plain cake to be eaten from the fingers.

Roscoe and Sarah drank to each other's good fortune. They were talking about Luck, and Sarah had just produced Abraham's letter when Geraldine returned and whispered to Sarah that Mrs. Todd waited in the parlor and begged to see her most urgently. With a look of alarm, Sarah set down her glass and hurried from the room. Roscoe followed, but paused outside the door of the parlor.

"Is it Aunt Nell?"

"No." Jane appeared surprised at her apprehension. "Priscilla has started, we think. I was there, so I sent for Dr. Platt. Zadok went galloping. Where is Ben?"

"He went to Bessie Marsh's for me."

"He'll want to be at home."

Roscoe knocked and then entered without waiting. "Let me find him."

"You are kind," Sarah said gratefully.

"It's your wedding day," Jane objected.

Roscoe looked at her a moment before he turned and left them.

"He's a strange man," Jane said. "I've never understood him."

They were soon at the house in the Glade, where they found Ann Oglethorpe on her knees at the bedside praying for her daughter while Freda worked around her to render immediate aid and comfort. Sarah lifted the mother to her feet as Jane began to assist Freda, both of them knowing more of what to expect and what would be needed than the older women.

Mrs. Oglethorpe resisted. "I stay with my child."

"Jane and Freda will attend her," Sarah assured her.

"It's my duty."

"Not beside her now—"

"I won't desert her in this black hour!"

"You'll only distress her if you stay."

"My prayers will console her."

Sarah, who was the stronger, led her into the hall. "Your prayers are to the Lord; He will hear them out here as well as in there."

"I must be where I can hear her cries!"

"You would only add your own to them."

"I am determined to share her suffering—"

"You will compound it if you do. Please." Sarah maneuvered them into the sitting room. "Now come and sit down. This chair is a good one for waiting, and it is likely to be longer than we think, for it always is."

Mrs. Oglethorpe pulled away and fell to the floor. "I shall not leave my knees until the ordeal is ended." She clasped her hands as she raised eyes and voice. "O Lord, hear me now!"

"God is not deaf. If you must pray aloud, pray quietly."

"Have Thy will of us, for we know that the punishment of lust is pain and sorrow. Spare my child if it be Thy will, and if it not be, take her from this vale of tears to Thy bosom—"

Sarah stared at her in alarm.

"We know that birth is pain, and life is pain, and death the greatest pain of all, as it can be our only way to salvation. The flesh does not fall into final corruption without final agony, and the smell of birth and death are an equal abomination—"

Thinking of Benjamin, Sarah seated herself in the hope of calming the other woman by example and engendering, if she could, an air of order to the event at hand. "I beg you to come and sit beside me, Mrs. Oglethorpe."

"I cannot rest. My daughter has been sullied by a sinful man. Let her, O Lord, be purified in the fire of Thy wrath. Let her, if it be Thy will, find redemption in that fire and emerge a chastened spirit, no longer doomed to submit to the lust of the wicked—"

Sarah rose. "I cannot allow you to—"

"My voice shall not be stilled! — Blessed Savior, smite the wicked and their granddams!"

Sarah took her by the arms and tried to lift her, but the woman twisted free. "Spare me, Lord, to see the wicked punished on this earth and in this house!"

Sarah delivered a slap to Mrs. Oglethorpe, the force of which shocked her to temporary silence. It was on this tableau the doctor entered.

Looking at them with only mild interest, he said, "I called and no one came. However, I know the way." He went into the hall.

Mrs. Oglethorpe cried after him, "If there is no hope, I must be told! I must be with my child in her dying hour and know that her heart is fixed on her Blessed Redeemer!"

Dr. Platt had as little patience as do most doctors. Further to that, he had experience of Mrs. Oglethorpe in sickrooms. "If you come in, I'll leave the house."

As Mrs. Oglethorpe considered the threat, Sarah made her way to the kitchen to see what she might do there. Food would certainly be needed, and Freda was busy. In the kitchen she found Freda's mother.

"Zadok told me," Rosalie said, "so I'm here."

Sarah felt a wave of relief for the solid presence and good sense of the woman before her. "Thank you, Rosalie."

"Mr. Ben is mine as much as my own children."

"I know it," Sarah said. "I'll help you."

Rosalie was about to refuse her when she saw Sarah's head tremble and knew that she was afraid. "Yes'm," she said instead. "You and me can do what'll be needed."

They set to work—and a good thing too, Rosalie announced when the visitors and messengers began to arrive. Friends meant well, no doubt, but they took no thought of the care they caused, only consulting their anxiety and curiosity.

Mrs. Oglethorpe observed something of this to Annabel and Frankie Saxon late in the afternoon, whereupon Frankie replied, "So true. I remember when mine were born."

"Everybody came," Annabel said. "And when they went home, they still sent servants for news. It is the way when these things happen in the important families. It is like the birth of princes. The child born this day will be the future master of Beulah Land."

Emerging from the dining room, Sarah said tartly, "That child's father is not yet in a position to hand it over; nor has he indicated that he is impatient to be. You *will* try to hurry me off to heaven, Annabel."

Annabel laughed complacently. "You are shocking, Auntie Sarah."

Frankie said, "Miss Sarah, I wish you'd put in a word for me with your husband. Mr. Troy promised to have the portrait done a week ago and has put me off. Now I fear it will not be ready for my little entertainment a week hence."

Benjamin had arrived soon after his sister and grandmother, Roscoe Elk having met him on the road from the Marsh farm. Allowed to see his wife briefly, he was then banished from the room where the birth would take place. For a time he played host to callers, but he was too distracted to keep his temper with either the archly sympathetic or those whose concern was more genuine, and he retreated to the yard, where he found Zadok. When his day's work was done, Daniel Todd came and joined them, and the three men walked and talked of the commonest things, which are matters of life to all farmers.

Casey appeared and went on small errands for Sarah, was everywhere, in fact, and nowhere for long. Sarah thought she had never loved him so well or needed him so much. It wasn't what he said or did that gave her solace, but the love in his eyes reminding her who she was. Priscilla's younger sister Elizabeth came and sat and cried, and her mother told her to go home and give her father supper. Three dozen came and sat and asked the same questions and were given the same answers; and the day wore on to evening.

Daniel went home to take supper with his sons and see that they went to bed, and then returned to wait for Jane, who had no thought of leaving her sister-in-law until the child was delivered. The woman in labor worked on in exhaustion, fainted and woke again. Her groans were low and few, but when they came, they were of such keen distress they harrowed the listeners more than steady screaming might have done. Terror showed in her eyes; she opened them only now and then, as if to make certain the world was still there.

The night advancing, an eerie quiet gradually possessed the house in the Glade. The woman who was the center of all thoughts was attended by Dr. Platt, assisted by Jane and Freda, who had not left the room for more than a few minutes since entering it that morning. Although urged to go home, Rosalie kept vigil in the kitchen with Zadok, the two whispering now and then but speaking mainly with their eyes, ever ready to do anything needed. But nothing was needed, nothing wanted but for the time to be over. Benjamin sat with Sarah and Daniel, a bottle of brandy on the table beside them and glasses in their hands. They seldom spoke, for all had been said, and all waiting is finally silent. Apart from them sat Mrs. Oglethorpe, waking occasionally to look at the others with disapproval.

It was after midnight when Dr. Platt emerged and told them that the child had arrived. There was no keeping them out, nor did it matter, for Priscilla slept. "I have given her opium," Platt said, collecting his tools. "I am going home and have some myself."

Jane lifted the baby as Daniel held the lamp for them to look at her. "She's a girl," Jane had said to Benjamin. The baby's closed and sleeping face was in shadow until Daniel moved the lamp another inch, and they saw the deep, disfiguring harelip.

Mrs. Oglethorpe found her voice. "She bears the mark of Cain, for she was begot by the devil's disciple."

9

Night had been mild, and morning promised fair. Benjamin did not wake until seven. In spite of the long birth day of the child and the short night since, he woke with acute awareness of the new life across the hall from his bedroom. He felt her nearness, savored their kinship, and found that he had accepted the fact that she was flawed. Dressing quickly, he went to look at her. Rosalie sat beside the cradle. There was wonder when he saw the child, but none that she was his. She was a girl, she had a harelip, she looked almost as raw as something yet unborn; but she was his, and his satisfaction was touched with no regret.

Because Priscilla was sleeping, he and Rosalie did not speak until she followed him into the hallway. "You've been up all night," he said.

"Soon as Almeda comes I'll go home. She's better with babies than I am."

He went to the kitchen to find that Freda had breakfast ready for him. Sarah and Jane arrived while he was eating. Although they had breakfasted at home, they sat with him and drank coffee. As they talked, Mrs. Oglethorpe entered the dining room. Her glance acknowledged them when Sarah and Jane murmured good morning, but she greeted no one. She sat down, and Freda placed the glass of milk before her which was all the breakfast she took. After a slow sip of it she declared, "One thing is certain. You cannot call the unfortunate creature Bruce."

Benjamin continued to eat, spearing dripping egg onto a piece of fried pork chop and following it with a whole fig preserve. When he'd swallowed, he said, "That is her name, Bruce Davis."

"It is not a proper female name."

"It will be hers."

Mrs. Oglethorpe shook her head. "Cannot."

In the silence Jane said, "Call her Bruce Priscilla."

"Brucilla," Freda suggested, pouring more coffee. "I woke up with it in front of my mind."

Jane and Sarah smiled encouragingly at Freda, and then at Mrs. Oglethorpe without getting any response. Exchanging eye signals, they rose. "Let us ask the mother, if she is awake," Sarah said.

"I don't approve of made-up names," Mrs. Oglethorpe said. "They always sound niggery."

Benjamin said, "I will call my daughter Bruce, and people will get used to it."

Sarah and Jane left the dining room and went upstairs. Freda returned to the kitchen, where Benjamin presently heard her talking to her sister Almeda. Benjamin was aware that Mrs. Oglethorpe was staring at him and waited for her to make up her mind to speak. "You know why she is malformed," she stated.

"I'm going to Savannah to see what can be done."

"It is the Lord's punishment for your licentious youth. I hope it will weigh on your soul and be a lesson to others. The sins of the fathers are always evident in their children."

He sat very still. "I'll ask Zadok to bring the buggy for you this morning. Your visit is at an end. Please be packed and ready to go with him no later than noon."

"I have no intention of leaving my daughter."

"You will go if I have to carry you."

"You wouldn't dare."

"Try me and see."

She studied him, her face grim. "No. I am one woman you'll not defile with your touch."

"You're welcome to the distinction."

"I shall tell everyone."

"You may visit Priscilla, but for no more than an hour a day until she is well enough to visit you."

"You will live to regret this."

He rose from the table, bowed, and went out.

Sarah had made inquiries before the baby was born about possible wet nurses if one was needed, and it was soon apparent that one was, for Priscilla, when she began to produce milk, did not have enough to nourish the child. Dr. Platt was no help in the matter, considering his responsibility finished when he spanked air into a babe and drugged its mother to forgetfulness. Leaving Jane to calm Priscilla, who was in tears after Mrs. Oglethorpe recited the details of Benjamin Davis's "callous and heartless" command, Sarah took her buggy and went from farmhouse to farmhouse. It was not until the middle of the afternoon that she found what was needed.

Velma would do, she decided, looking the girl over not unkindly but yet with the eye she might have used to calculate qualities, good and bad, of a farm animal. Velma was sixteen years old; her body was mature. She was not coal black, but her white blood must have come into the strain a couple of generations back and combined again with colored. She had borne a child the week before, and the child had died, but not before her mistress reckoned that its father—Velma was neither married nor mated—was her own husband. Velma had been ordered to leave the farm that very day, and she was ready to go with Sarah five minutes after Sarah had offered her wages.

As Sarah drove back to the Glade, Velma beside her with a bundle of clothes on her lap, she told her about Benjamin's household. The girl was not nervous; she seemed pleased with the turn her life was taking. She appeared, if anything, too relaxed, which decided Sarah to say, "They will be good to you, but you must not lie or steal, because if you do, Rosalie will beat the tar out of you."

"Who this Rosalie?"

Sarah explained.

"She bigger than I be?"

"Considerably," Sarah said, although she judged them to be about the same size. "She has a husband and three sons and two daughters, all grown. They are good people, and no one will mistreat you as long as you behave yourself."

"I'll run off if they don't suit me."

"They'll run you off if you don't do your job."

Sarah explained then about the newborn child's harelip and asked the girl if she'd ever seen one.

Velma replied that she had, and that she had also seen albinos.

Sarah asked the whereabouts of her family. Velma became vague about their moving "somewhere down in Lowndes County," and wasn't sure they'd stayed when they got there.

Finally Sarah asked, as if it had just occurred to her, "What is the family name?"

Velma rattled the names of her mother and brothers, there being no living father or sisters.

"No," Sarah said. "I mean last name. The way my name is Sarah Troy, yours is Velma what?"

Velma looked offended and did not answer. Sarah let her sulk for a mile before saying, "Would you like to be called Velma Kendrick?"

"Don't know," the girl mumbled.

"Kendrick was the name of my first husband's family, the old family of Beulah Land, although now we are Troys and Davises and Todds."

"I know about y'all," she asserted with a toss of her head; but the frown she'd worn suddenly faded and her face cracked in two. "Velma Kendrick!" Quiet for a few moments, she repeated the name and began to giggle. "Hee, hee, hee—"

Sarah drove her buggy directly to Zadok's house, where Rosalie took charge of Velma. While she heated a tub of water on the kitchen stove, she ruthlessly inspected the girl's head and body hair for lice, finding none. Velma looked murderous but submitted, remembering perhaps Sarah's threat of a beating. Rosalie then ordered Velma to bathe herself all over. Velma protested that she was clean. Rosalie picked up a stick of stove wood, and Velma stepped into the tub.

Clean and dressed again, she was escorted to the house in the Glade and introduced to the mother and the child. When she saw Bruce, her anger died. "Po' youngun," she crooned, and reached for the fretting baby, who took her nipple hungrily and began to feed. Looking down at her, Velma said, "Your name's Bruce Davis, so they tell me. Well, mine's Velma Kendrick. Howdy-do."

It had been thought to have Velma serve only as wet nurse, while Almeda continued to see to the child in other ways. But Velma was possessive and a quick learner, and she had taken over the nursery entirely before the week was out.

10

"Yes, she may," Sarah admitted. "On the other hand, she may live another hundred years. You mustn't wait on that account. If you can take the time, go now. When you were at the hospital in March, they told you as much as they could without seeing the child; so don't wait. And for what? There's never any knowing." Benjamin appeared to consider what she said. She smiled. "I remember telling you once long ago when you asked my advice that you never asked anybody anything until you'd made up your mind what you were going to do. You were a stubborn boy, and you're a stubborn man."

"And you love me."

"I love you."

He rose from his chair. Hands flat on the desk, he leaned across it to kiss her. "Come to Savannah with us."

She shook her head. "It's not what it was when I was a girl. A lot of fat men looking important and spitting tobacco juice. Jane said she'd go with you."

He paced the length of the office twice, pausing to look out the door, which was open to the broad veranda that wrapped around three sides of the big house at Beulah Land. "Beginning to rain." Whatever else occupied his mind, the concerns of a farmer were always there and weather was remarked on. He returned to his chair. "Bruce is two months old and fat as a kettle. I'll talk to Jane tonight and see when Daniel and the boys can spare her."

"Priscilla hasn't changed her thinking?" Sarah asked. She knew what the answer would be, but much of conversation is taken up asking familiar questions and receiving expected answers.

Benjamin gave a sharp shake of the head. "Mrs. Oglethorpe knows she can't forbid my going, but she threatens never to speak to Priscilla again if she goes with me."

"What a blessing it would be if she went with you, and Mrs. Oglethorpe kept her word, and Priscilla didn't care."

"But she does care."

Sarah shook her head. "It does no good to be facetious. I'm sorry. — Priscilla doesn't actually oppose you in this?"

"She says little. She'll pick Bruce up, but never hold her more than a minute. She hates to look at her."

"It takes some women that way, they say. Hers was a long pregnancy and a difficult delivery. She'll find her way to the child."

Benjamin said, "Her mother comes every day now the weather's fine and takes her for a buggy ride; but she won't set foot in the house. She won't even step down from the buggy, and holds her whip up ready for attack."

"You did forbid her."

"I told her she could visit an hour a day."

"She'd die before she abided by any rule you set, my dear. You know that."

"The more Priscilla sees her, the less she'll talk to me. Sometimes I have to sit her down in front of me and make her talk. Then she cries and says things I know her mother has put into her head. Mrs. Oglethorpe believes it is defiance of God's will to try to change Bruce's lip. She says the Lord punishes vanity, and the mark is His warning to me to repent my sins; that it should always be there for me to see and be reminded of Judgment Day." He traced a figure eight with his forefinger on the back of a closed ledger. "I would verily like to take a pitchfork to that woman."

"So would I," Sarah agreed.

"They'd hang us."

"Not if the judge had ever spent an hour with her."

"I want you to do something for me while I'm gone." She watched him and waited. "Go to Bessie Marsh's and see how Leon is."

"Gene Betchley's still there, last I heard."

"I want to know how he treats my son."

She looked alarmed, but nodded.

And so one April morning they took what the town called the Down Train to Savannah; Benjamin and Jane and Bruce, attended by Velma, whose joyful anticipation of the journey excited such envy in Robert E. Lee and Jefferson Davis Todd that they cried lustily. Sarah said to Jane, "You see how they will miss you."

"Not at all," Jane replied. "They're simply angry at not being allowed to go." By the time the train pulled away, Bobby Lee and Davy had wheedled her into promising additional lead soldiers. Sarah took the boys back to Beulah Land, where they were to spend the day. Later, the three walked to the Glade to tell Priscilla of the party's departure, but they did not stay long because Priscilla found their liveliness wearing. Before leaving, Sarah asked if she would like to accompany them into Highboro the day after, but Priscilla, hesitating and sighing, refused, saying that her mother was coming to the Glade. At three o'clock the next afternoon they stood on the splintery wooden platform to watch the Up Train come in from Savannah, after which Sarah took Davy and Bobby Lee to Sullivan's Dry Goods store to wait until the mail was sorted in the post office next door. They begged for sweet johnnycake and cheese, which they never had at home, and she obliged them with a small order to Mr. Sullivan.

As Benjamin had promised, letters arrived. There were three, one from Jane to her husband and two from Benjamin, for Priscilla and Sarah. Putting the others away, Sarah read hers quickly, standing at the front window of the post office for better light.

Benjamin told of an easy journey: Bruce did not cry, and Velma did not want to get off the train when they got there, partly because she had never before been on one and partly because she was suddenly opposed to the idea of giving "her baby" into the hands of strangers at a hospital. He had settled for Velma to remain with Bruce while she was at the hospital, and she had vowed not to sleep a wink, lest they cut off her leg in the night. Benjamin and Jane had rooms at the boardinghouse where she and Daniel sometimes stayed. Bruce was to have the lip sewn the next day. "Today," Sarah thought. "Already it is done."

She drove the buggy directly to the Glade to deliver Priscilla's letter. Mrs. Oglethorpe was cold and watchful with the boys. In his friendly way of sharing, Davy asked if she would like to hold the snail he'd found in the yard. She told him he was disgusting and ordered him to remove it from the house instantly. Priscilla read her letter in silence and murmured that there was nothing to add to the brief news Sarah had conveyed from her own. Given no encouragement, Sarah made it another short visit. Daniel came to Beulah Land for supper that evening and read his letter from Jane aloud. The boys were disappointed not to hear mention of the lead soldiers and implored their father to remind her of them when he wrote lest she forget them. But Jane had written graphically of the speed of the train, which made them squirm with pleasure and ask for the letter to be read twice again. Then they all had a visit with Nell, who welcomed them eagerly and just as eagerly urged them to leave her shortly thereafter. The boys were yawning, so Daniel put one over each shoulder and went home, Sarah and Casey walking with them part of the way.

In the morning, after she and Zadok had seen the day's work started, Sarah and Casey took the buggy and went to Bessie Marsh's. Sarah had no reason for the visit and did not bother to invent one, putting it simply that she and her husband were driving about the country and decided to stop. Bessie was civil enough and a little amused as she saw Sarah's eyes go toward the man working in the field nearby, who lifted his head once to stare at the visitors. There was no sign of Leon, and when Sarah asked about him, Bessie said he'd gone with his grandmother to graze the cow. There was new grass over yonder after the recent rain. Could they see? This side of the woods. There he was! No, he was gone again, that quick. Old cow wasn't worth much; still, as long as she gave them a splash of milk and a pat of butter—

Bessie was making soap in the black washpot, and she continued with the work. "Stinks, don't it?" she said. "Otherwise, I'd ask you to stay awhile." Casey said they must be getting on home.

Turning in her seat after Casey had picked up the reins and flicked the horse's back, Sarah called, "Is that Gene Betchley helping you out?"

"Yes'm." Bessie was openly amused. "He's a right smart of help too, so *he* tells me. Trying to talk me into us getting married. Beats all, don't it, such a young fellow after an old woman like me? You mightn't agree, ma'am, seeing you married younger than yourself!"

Sarah did not open her mouth to speak for five minutes, but her lips worked busily. Finally she said, "Turn this buggy around."

"Road's too narrow," Casey said. "I'd spill us."

"I want to go back and tell that slut what I think of her."

Casey hugged her with one arm, but she shrugged away.

"She usen't to be sly-uppity. He's put mischief into her. And I didn't find out about Leon for Ben!"

"The boy's all right or you'd have known."

"How would I?" she said crossly.

"Because you know everything." His eyes danced. "Because you're my old woman."

She swung her reticule, landing it squarely on his head. Laughing he drew on the reins, halting horse and buggy. "Sarah," he said, taking her hands. When she tried to twist free, he held her firmly. When she was still, he kissed her. She smiled at last, and he said, "Don't be a fool, girl." He kissed her again more slowly and whispered, although they were alone in the middle of nowhere, "Let's go home and pull the curtains and go to bed." She touched him at the crotch with gentle familiarity, and he caught his breath.

11

The cloud was so low she thought it smoke from a fire in the woods until it lifted and drifted away without dispersing.

"Thinking about me?" Eugene said. "Standing there with your arms folded, dreaming."

"Dreaming of nothing. Would that be you?"

"You're some woman, Mrs. Betchley."

"Marsh," she corrected him. She had been cooking supper, but the kitchen was close and smelly and she'd come to the door for a breath of air. The cloud had given her pause.

"Get used to your new name."

"Waste of time."

"Be plum mean to keep me working and waiting unless you're making your mind up to be good to Gene."

"You're free to go."

"I'm not, as you well know." He honeyed his voice with insinuation. "You're good enough to eat, Bess, and I've a mind to start on you here and now." He watched as the blood rose under her skin and spread its flush up her neck and over her face. Snaking his arm about her waist, his hand caught a breast and then sought buttons to undo.

Leon came around the house and, seeing them, stopped. Bessie shook her head, more at herself than at either of them, and stepped back into the kitchen.

"What are you gawking at?" Eugene demanded of the dumbstruck boy before he followed Bessie. "Your son needs to learn respect."

"Don't mind him."

"Hates the sight of me, and so does your old ma."

"They're jealous."

"A ma jealous of a daughter? A youngun jealous of his ma?"

"Leon's not used to a man here."

"You and me ought to have us a baby."

"You're the jealous one. If you don't like it here, the road's fifty feet from the door."

He scowled and was silent. She lifted a lid and stirred the contents of a pot. Replacing the lid, she wiped steamy hands on her dress front, saying in a conciliatory way, "Spring greens, fatback, pot dodgers. Ought to hold us till tomorrow morning."

The face he turned to her was as accusing and pleading as a child's. "Come tonight," he said.

"If I'm not tired," she half agreed.

"Only time I know what's on your mind is when I got you under me." She looked at him steady and unsmiling, and his were the eyes to give way.

Eugene did a man's work and ate his three meals a day with them at the table in the kitchen, but he slept in the harness room of the barn, and that was where he and Bessie came together privately. It was true, as he said, that Leon and her mother resented him and feared his staying. The boy's hatred was pure and simple; the old woman's included the suspicion that Gene Betchley coveted the farm more than her daughter. Certainly Eugene had first dallied with the idea of making the place his own. Yet if he had roused Bessie to fevers she thought she'd learned to live without, he had in doing so become besotted with her. A few weeks had transformed her from a woman growing old to one in her prime.

Bessie was suspicious too, but she knew her power over the younger man. She would not be hurried, or surprised into anything more than she had already been. There was her son to think of and her mother. Looking at Gene with their eyes, she saw no reason they should love him or he them; but if she decided to marry him—and she saw certain advantages in doing so—then they would have to accept him. Gene was a hard worker now when he wanted something, but she was long acquainted with his shiftless father and brother, and with Gene's own early history. It was hard to accept the fact that the boy she'd never bothered thinking about was a grown man with will and substance, as well as a body that could make her beg like a soul in hell. He was a great worry to her. Even as she acknowledged it, she longed for the hour she could go to him, and she thought: "Aye, God, better a host of worries than to live and die alone."

On the day they were returning from Savannah, Benjamin and Jane settled Velma with Bruce and left them for a while. Jane loved the train and enjoyed walking through it as she rode it. When they came to the dining car, they decided to stop for iced tea and to make conversation with other passengers, although their journey was not long enough for them to require a meal.

As for Velma, she had taken the precaution of packing a basket in the boardinghouse kitchen that morning, for she feared that hunger might overtake her on the way home. As soon as they were out of the station she opened the basket and peeled a banana, then ferreted out a fried chicken leg and took alternate bites of chicken and banana. She had discovered bananas in Savannah, and Benjamin had been good enough to buy her a dozen just before they left.

The man and woman across the aisle were whispering to each other. Velma knew they were talking about the baby, but part of her mind was occupied with the enjoyment of the scenery sliding past the window and the taste of her interesting combination of victuals. They were trying to decide something. *He* shook his head and smiled. *She* shook her head and frowned, then looked thoughtfully over and cleared her throat. "What's wrong with that baby?" she asked.

Banana and chicken consumed, Velma threw skin and bone out the open window before acknowledging that she'd heard by bringing her eyes to rest on the woman's face. "Nothing wrong with this baby," she informed her.

Having made a beginning, the woman was determined not to retreat. "It looks different."

"*Different?*"

"Different from other babies."

"Every baby looks different if you got any eye for babies," Velma stated.

"I mean funny-different," the woman persisted.

Velma's eyebrows went up. She glanced at the sleeping baby on the seat beside her. She looked back at the woman. "Mrs.," she said kindly, "I do not know how many babies you have seen, but speaking for myself who have seen a hundred or more, this baby here is the best I have ever set eyes on."

"Something wrong with her mouth."

"No ma'am," Velma averred stoutly. She looked back at the baby. "You maybe mean that tee-niney red crease. Well'm, I can tell you about that." Velma thereupon did so, with much emphasis on her own reactions to the doctors and nurses at the hospital and her "considerate opinion that the whole business of letting strange folks wearing spook dresses cut you up" was not something she would care to go through again.

Both the man and the woman enjoyed the harrowing recital and at its conclusion, if they were not ready to agree with Velma that Bruce was the prettiest thing they ever did see, the woman was willing to praise her as a sweet, good-tempered little thing to have gone through so much.

Five waited for the train.

Standing on the platform when they heard the whistle blow and straining their eyes to espy the distant smoke, they made a picture. But Sarah's hold on Davy's hand and Daniel's on Bobby Lee's were more in the nature of physical restraint than familial affection. Casey Troy stood behind them holding his own hands.

Benjamin having reclaimed his child, Velma was first to step off the train, and by wedging her empty basket in the doorway and dropping her shawl and tripping over the first step, managed to delay the moment of reunion. But seconds after she regained shawl, basket, and balance, Jane stepped down after her; and her sons were astonished to see their father push past them to crush his wife to his heart, whereas clearly the important matter to be settled was the number and quality of the lead soldiers they had been promised. As Casey attended to their luggage, Jane freed herself and bent to hug the boys, and Benjamin kissed his grandmother. Only then did he present his daughter for them to see.

Studying her, Sarah said simply, "It will be better. That's what they said, isn't it? You wrote and told me that. As she gets older, the scar will fade some. It appears so prominent because it is all we look at now, but that will never be true again. It may not disappear entirely, but we shall note it ever less."

The Todds went home directly in Daniel's buggy, the children longing to inspect their prizes, which Jane declined to show them on the station platform. Casey drove the Beulah Land carriage. Sarah said goodbye when Benjamin alighted at the Glade with Bruce and Velma, promising to come back later. Thus, Priscilla was allowed to greet her husband and child in more privacy than was usually vouchsafed the return of family members. She submitted to Benjamin's embrace, but when he faced her around to see the baby in Velma's arms, he felt her trembling. She looked, and looked away. Turning, she walked swiftly from the porch into the house and to her bedroom, where she was presently heard weeping. Benjamin did not follow her.

Mrs. Oglethorpe broke her vow not to set foot in the house again when her son-in-law was there. She wouldn't, however, go further than the little parlor off the living room, waiting there for the child to be brought to her. Hands clasped as if in prayer, she peered long before delivering herself of two statements.

"God is not mocked," was the first.

Mrs. Oglethorpe would have been surprised and offended to be told that she equated herself with the Lord, and in truth she did not; but she did impute to Him judgments and opinions that, properly speaking, were her own. She called herself a Christian, but her God was of the Old Testament.

Her second pronouncement was: "She will never be a temptation to any man, and that I take as a blessing."

Mrs. Oglethorpe's visit was brief. Priscilla showed herself when Sarah returned, but listened to the sensible words of the older woman without comment. Benjamin ate supper alone and after walking in the Glade for half an hour went to the nursery. Opening the door, he discovered Velma with the child in her lap. She had bathed and fed her and was brushing her soft hair into decorative whorls, which the baby seemed to like, because she submitted amiably. "You is pretty," Velma was saying. "Prettiest baby in the world." For the first time that day Benjamin's smile was genuine, as he stepped forward to congratulate both of them on coming home.

12

By common agreement the most dreaded social event of the year was Annabel Saxon's family supper, which exacted its toll upon those who attended and those who served it on the last Sunday of every April. "Before the hot summer," Annabel explained, although April was frequently marked by high temperatures, if not by that intense heat that would reduce them in August to mumbling, stumbling automatons. Many were the resolves to avoid the affair next time, and the ways considered were as ingenious as they were various. Yet when the night arrived, all who had been summoned attended, even as an execution is a magnet for a crowd.

No one anticipated the occasion more gloomily than Annabel herself. Miser-mean, she grudged the expense. The servants complained a month before and sulked a week after. Something was always spilled, something broken. It meant that Annabel must cease or curtail her usual activities, and she vastly enjoyed a talent for scolding and harrying as she organized the female concerns of the community. With the bleakest of sighs she decided, however, that it must be done. *Rank imposes obligation* was a dictum never far from her mind. Was she not the wife of the town banker and the daughter of Oaks, which for nearly a century before the war had been one of the greatest plantations? She knew her duty.

Each year the guest list grew longer. There were never enough deaths to balance out the births. At last night's supper more than forty sat down at two tables, the young ones better off at theirs on the cool side porch than their elders crowded into the stifling dining room. The young children, attended by their mammies, were included because they were family. They must learn from the earliest age what that meant and accept the superiority and ascendancy of Annabel Saxon. No one was spared, except the dying.

Children who played peacefully together every other day spat and fought and cried, and the mammies quarreled with each other as they tried to pacify their charges. Adult relatives who might ordinarily meet in harmony and even affection were inspired to contradict and accuse. Why the party always went badly might only be guessed. Perhaps it was nothing more than the lack of any desire in the hostess to give or take pleasure.

It was, Sarah said to Jane, the only time she caught herself ready to snap at Casey, the best of men and most loving of husbands. As antidote to the predictably vexing evening, Sarah and Jane had taken to using the day after it for what they called their cemetery drill. This was a sort of work ceremony initiated by the first mistresses of Oaks and Beulah Land, whose cemetery plots abutted as nearly as their home plantations. Although it would be easy to command others to the work, Sarah and Jane enjoyed it, because for the day they were able to forget routine responsibilities, to talk about any and every thing that occurred to them, and to remember their dead with more of speculative interest than grief. It was always a happy day. Shears, hoes, rakes, twig brooms, and gardening tools were tied to the back of Sarah's buggy; and taking a basket of victuals that included a bottle of wine, they drove off to be their own women and no one else's until sundown.

Others were not tolerated: no child or friend or husband. Doreen Davis used to help them but had not since moving to Highboro to live with Miss Eloise Kilmer and her cats five years ago. When Benjamin married Priscilla, Sarah invited her to join in the family ritual, but Mrs. Oglethorpe advised her daughter against it. Mrs. Oglethorpe rivaled Annabel Saxon in her dedication to duty, but only as long as she found it indoors. She was ready to do the Lord's work, she vowed, but ladies did no labor where they might be observed by passers-by.

Ending a long silence as they hoed grass alongside each other, Jane said, "Do you think Frankie has changed?"

"By asking, you are suggesting that she has. I don't know. I don't see her often or think about her much."

"Last night she seemed gentler."

"How?"

"Everyone," Jane said, "knows about Bonard's drinking. Usually, the more he drinks, the harder her jaw sets. Last night she ignored him altogether."

Sarah removed the straw hat she wore against the sun and wiped sweat from her forehead with a dirty hand. "If that is your evidence of a new softness in the lady, I shan't credit it. People are never more typical of themselves than when they surprise you. I am forever being surprised by the people I know best; and when I stop to think about it, it seems to me they are only being true to themselves." Replacing her hat, she wielded the hoe again and caught up with Jane, who had worked a little ahead.

"When you turn the particular to the general, it means you don't want to talk about the particular."

Sarah hit her lightly on the rump with her hoe handle. "Very well, missy. Five years ago I'd have said there was little question that Frankie would make Benjamin unhappy and that Priscilla would be a good wife. The one problem was Mrs. Oglethorpe, and they seemed to be getting around that. I was a little amused when both Benjamin and Priscilla were at pains to tell me how *good* the other was. That should have been my warning."

"Bonard's drinking hasn't kept him from doing his work at the sawmill. Papa says he couldn't run it without him."

"Bonard doesn't have much choice. There was no place for him at the bank. Blair Second is clearly going to get that; he's his father all over again. The way Frankie spends, Bonard would be a pauper if he didn't work at the mill and work hard."

"Frankie seems a good mother."

"Fanny is a pretty child," Sarah conceded, "and Blair Third is more nearly civilized than are most boys of five."

"All children are on their best behavior at Aunt Annabel's, even mine. She scares them."

Sarah laughed. "And yet, think of what her own were. When

you were children, you and Benjamin used to fight them. One day right over there"—she pointed with her hoe handle—"you shinnied up that big angel and whacked Bonard with your Bible every time he tried to untie your sash. Benjamin was at the base doing his best to kill Blair Second."

"Prudence is getting fat."

"I don't imagine anyone minds," Sarah said.

Jane giggled. "I don't think Blair Second minds anything except the bank. He and Blair First both were born to ignore the women they married. The bankers never looked once during supper at the bankers' wives." They were quiet for a little time merely working and sweating, the only sound that of their hoes chopping and prying up the roots of crabgrass. "I saw Ben watching Fanny and Blair Third."

"Benjamin has children on his mind. I wish Priscilla did, but she doesn't. I'm sorry, but I can't love her. I've tried for five years. She defies loving. Maybe Benjamin was thinking last night that Frankie would have given him children, and maybe she would have. Still, he loves Bruce in a way I feared no one would. She's a happy, good baby. I give Benjamin and Velma credit for that, not Priscilla. I've never seen her look at her without frowning."

After a moment Jane said, "I saw Frankie watching Benjamin last night."

"You appear to have spent the evening watching people watching people. It was one way to get through it, I suppose. Millie's cooking is down. The asparagus was overcooked, and the coconut cake had a dip in the middle. Josephine wouldn't have served either to guests."

"I think it was the worst ever of Aunt Annabel's family funerals."

"That's like saying the devil's left horn is sharper than his right," Sarah said. "Casey maintains they are the same every year, even to the overdone asparagus. He claims to be able to predict each remark, who will make it, and at what point it will be made. He knows exactly when to listen for the crash of the first plate at the children's table and the first shouting from the kitchen."

"We're going to Frankie's for supper on Thursday a week."

"Why?" Sarah said.

"When we were standing around admiring Aunt Annabel's portrait again, Frankie reminded Ben that he hadn't yet seen hers. He and I were in Savannah with Bruce when Casey finished it and you all went to look at it. She said we must see it and invited us on the spot: Priscilla and Ben, Dan and me."

"Mm."

Sarah wandered away and stood frowning down at a tombstone. Jane came to stand beside her. It was the grave of Edna Davis, the old mistress of Oaks and great-grandmother to Jane and Benjamin.

Jane picked gravel from a split in her hoe blade. They never brought good hoes to the cemetery drill. "You have a special look on your face when you think of her," Jane said.

Sarah said, "She was my friend. Women need each other, but they seldom trust each other. You and she are the only true friends I've had among my own sex. I get on better with men." They turned from the Davis graves back to the Kendrick ground. Sarah picked up a twig broom from the ground and brushed away old leaves from the grave of Felix Kendrick. "Aunt Nell knew we were coming and said to get her place ready. 'By my beloved Felix,' she said, 'only not too close.' "

"Did she love Uncle Felix, or did she marry him because her sister married the other Kendrick brother? Sisters don't marry brothers the way they used to, do they?"

Sarah said, "She's never talked about it, and she wouldn't. From bits and pieces over the years I've gathered that the intimate side of marriage was not to her liking. Certainly Uncle Felix took his pleasures where he found them, and he found them everywhere. In other ways he and Aunt Nell were devoted to each other. When he had his stroke, she wouldn't leave him until he was past danger. Then she happily turned him over to the Negro woman he'd been taking to the hayloft for years. She's a strange one, Aunt Nell. She loves all of us, I suppose, but eating was her only passion."

"I can't believe she's dying," Jane said.

"She may live forever," Sarah said cheerfully. "She's never been corroded by much pleasure or pain. Taking to her bed means nothing. When the old ones do that, it's the overture to Act Five, but—have you noticed?—that always seems the longest at a play, no matter how much you've liked it."

They smiled and resumed working. They sweated and gossiped, saying things they might never have said in any other place at any other time, and certainly not to any other person. When they put down their tools to go and wash themselves and see what Josephine had packed for them to eat, Sarah said, "No wonder I love this day."

13

The Thursday they were to go to Frankie's was an ordinary day which Benjamin spent in an ordinary way, riding and walking the fields with Zadok to direct and monitor the work of the hired force of Negroes, about twenty of whom lived at Beulah Land and were considered permanently attached to the plantation, their women and older children working alongside them in the fields or employed in housework. The corn was flourishing, having had a proper proportion of rain to sun, and the cotton stretched in neat rows farther than the eye could measure, interrupted now and then by small clumps of trees that had been left to provide occasional refuge from the sun that would weary the hardiest in July and August and September.

Benjamin and Sarah continued to breakfast together, there being no formally laid first meal at the house in the Glade. Priscilla took a tray in her room, and Bruce was breast-fed in the nursery, although she was beginning to be given other food as well. Benjamin often drank coffee with Freda in the kitchen before joining his grandmother at the main house, but he always came home for noon dinner and early evening supper, having asked Velma to bring Bruce to the dining room so that she might be a part of family meals from the beginning. The May sun warmed without burning, and in late afternoon Benjamin and Daniel met to swim in the creek and scrub themselves clean with Spanish moss.

Going home, Benjamin followed what was becoming a new routine by taking Bruce in his arms and walking through the Glade. Velma accompanied them, not anxiously, for she trusted Benjamin with the baby as she did no one else, but there if she was needed. Bruce was content in Benjamin's arms, and he fancied that she would thus learn to love the Glade as he had loved it since boyhood. It pleased him to imagine that one day it would be her first memory. Seeing that Benjamin had dressed for the evening party, Velma followed closer than usual, in order to take the child if she began to wet. She did not, and Benjamin praised her when, their tour of inspection over, he handed her to Velma, who beamed at him and the child, sharing the praise.

Happy with his world, he sauntered to his wife's room. They had not resumed sharing it since Bruce's birth, but he was in and out as he chose. Finding Priscilla as he'd left her at noon, he asked when she would be ready to leave for their engagement. She told him that she was not going; her sister Elizabeth had come in the afternoon with a message from their mother. Mr. Oglethorpe, it seemed, was again unwell.

"You promised Frankie you'd come," Benjamin said.

"I think 'promise' a strong word for an invitation lightly offered and casually accepted. You accepted; I did not."

"I looked to you before I said we'd come, and you did not say no. I believe you nodded."

"I do not think I did."

"Agreed with your eyes, then."

"You took it for granted, husband."

"You did not demur. You heard Jane accept for her and Daniel. I looked at you when you said nothing, and only then answered for us, because you seemed to wait for me to do so."

"What does it matter? Surely everything yields to family illness."

"Has the nature of your father's complaint been settled?"

"Dr. Platt isn't certain, but advises sleep and no solid food for a day or so."

"Then it is no more serious than other such 'complaints' he has taken to bed. After so many years I wonder that his stomach is not proof against your mother's bad table."

Her voice sharpened. "You've abused my mother quite enough on that score in the past."

"Did Mrs. Oglethorpe know we were going to supper at Frankie's?"

"I believe so. I sent word by Elizabeth that I would come."

"That word you will consider a promise."

"I can add nothing to Frankie's party. I do not admire her and should be thought deficient in my appreciation of her portrait. You will make up for me in that respect. If you will just take me to Mama's and set me down, you are then free to go to Frankie's and praise everything enough to satisfy both her and Bonard. I shall be happier sitting with my family, and ready when you return for me."

"It will be thought inconsiderate."

Priscilla smiled faintly. "You exaggerate the importance that attaches. Surely you realize it is you she wants. I should contribute nothing."

"You're jealous," Benjamin guessed.

"It is unkind of you to say so even in pique."

"Is that all you have to say?"

"I assure you Frankie will bear up under the disappointment."

He turned abruptly and stared at the bed. "I am ready to go when you are."

"Now," she said, taking a shawl she had laid out and whipping it around her shoulders.

Following, he said, "You've no wish to speak to Velma or say good night to Bruce?"

"Velma is capable, and the child doesn't understand 'good night' any more than a cat would."

Benjamin entered the nursery to find Velma sitting at the open window, her breast bared to the feeding child. When she saw him, she smiled a welcome. Benjamin watched the baby's contented sucking, taking comfort from the sight. Bending, he touched his lips lightly to the top of the child's head. It was as warm as his lips, her hair softer than a flower. Priscilla waited at the door. "I'll get the buggy," he said.

The anxiety in Annabel Saxon's suggestion that Frankie be painted by Casey Troy "to catch the bloom before it fades" was premature. With the care she took, it was unlikely that fading would commence soon or advance rapidly, and she understood perfectly well that her mother-in-law's remark was prompted by the spite of an old beauty for a young one rather than by fear that the moment be lost. Certainly tonight there could be no concern for her appearance.

"Casey has caught you just as you are," Jane declared as the guests paused again before the portrait after supping.

Daniel shifted his lanky frame and muttered what Jane hoped would be taken by their host and hostess as concurrence. Daniel still distrusted Bonard because he'd once tried to marry Jane, and he was never comfortable in his company. It was worse for him tonight because Sarah was not there. She could make him feel easy anywhere.

Benjamin lifted his glass to Frankie and Bonard in turn. "I'm bound to admit the real thing is more remarkable than canvas allows, but as much as can be copied, Casey has done."

Bonard finished his wine, looking gratified. "Cost me a dollar or two," he bragged. Remembering Casey's relation to Jane and Benjamin, he added, "And worth it."

"And more," Benjamin said, his eyes meeting Frankie's.

"No question." Bonard was refilling his glass. That done, he offered the bottle with a gesture to the other men, who refused it with a shake of the head.

Frankie smiled with pleasure, and when her husband lifted his glass to drain it, said to Jane, "Come and let me show you the new silk I found in Savannah. I don't know how you could bring back so little from your trip. I always return with twice as much as I intended to buy."

"True," Bonard agreed as his wife and cousin left them in the living room. Opening a box of cigars with a pocketknife, he removed one and clamped it between his teeth before holding the box before the other two.

"No, I thank you," Daniel said.

Benjamin accepted a cigar, rolling it between his palms and sniffing the tobacco as it warmed and moistened.

Bonard said, "Better take them to the yard. Frankie won't let me smoke in the house. Claims it gets into her clothes."

Benjamin went after him through a glass door that opened directly into the rose garden which Nell Kendrick had ordered planted when Felix had taken her as a bride to live in the house. Daniel remained where he was. He was content to be alone, but he was not alone for long. The son of the house appeared in his nightgown. Both children had been shown off earlier and taken away by their mammy.

"You're not Papa, you're Uncle Dan," the boy said.

"Howdy, Blair."

"Mama told me to come say good night to Papa."

"He's in the yard smoking. I'll tell him for you when he comes back."

"I'm bigger than Bobby Lee."

"You're a year older," Daniel said reasonably.

"I bet when he's old as I am he won't be big as I am. Davy is a little thing."

Daniel frowned at the boy. "Good night." He seldom liked children other than his own. The boy didn't budge.

"You live in the country," he said. Daniel nodded. "We live in town."

"That is so." Daniel yawned, and in came Fanny, followed by the mammy and Jane and Frankie. Daniel explained where the others were.

"Uncle Daniel is bigger than Papa," Blair said.

Fanny presented herself before Daniel's chair. "You can kiss me," she told him.

Jane and Frankie laughed. Looking back at her as seriously as she gazed at him, Daniel kissed a finger and touched the girl's cheek. Delighted, she kissed her own finger and touched her cheek.

"You can't kiss me," Blair said.

"Nobody could pay me to kiss you," Daniel said which Frankie declared amusing as she helped the mammy shoo the children from the room. "Let's go home," Daniel whispered to Jane.

"Soon," she promised. She went to stand before the portrait again. "She *is* beautiful. In very fact: perfect. I used to be jealous of her, but I'm not any more."

Daniel joined her, frowning critically. "Picture looks realer than she does. She's always so got up. Anyway, she's nothing compared to you."

She grabbed him around the waist with both arms, and he was kissing her when Frankie returned.

"Look at you," Frankie teased, and Jane was glad to see envy in her eyes.

Daniel squeezed his wife quickly before letting her go. "Just an old couple from the country."

The night air was sweet with the scent of roses until the two men strolled from the house and began to puff tobacco smoke into it. When both cigars were burning, Bonard celebrated the accomplishment with a grunt. "Lost any of your hands this year?"

"All mine are signed," Benjamin said.

"You know how little a promise means to a darky. Their touching the pen don't mean a thing, though your Papa makes them do it at the mill if they can't write their names. Some of ours heard the call of way-yonder and went to Kansas, and far as Illinois. Thought they were going to get rich. No money to go on, they beg or steal, live a day on a box of crackers or a can of pork and beans. But soon as they get there, they're homesick for down-here. Like they say, 'Nigger away from home is like a flea in a tar barrel; nobody cares.'"

Benjamin reiterated, "That's truly a fine portrait Casey made of Frankie."

Bonard winked at his guest. "Hope it keeps her tractable for a while. She's pleased with it."

They walked and smoked. Presently Bonard stopped, looking thoughtful. "Ben, you remember what good times we had as young bucks? Money to spend, nothing on our minds, plenty of pussy we didn't pay for, unless you want to count the Crawford girls. Now I pay for it and don't always get it." He walked again.

Benjamin was surprised that Bonard should say such a thing to him, for although they had been friendly in the offhand way of cousins, they had never been friends. "You have two healthy children, Bo."

"Well, yeah," Bonard agreed. "You've had some bad luck that way."

"Bruce is fine now. We've a good girl taking care of her, and she's growing like a hound puppy."

"Glad to hear you say that," Bonard said too heartily. "I bet she'll be all right. Not every girl is a beauty or needs to be." Again he was thoughtful, and when he decided to speak his thought, it was: "I sure am working my butt off at the mill. Have to, to keep Frankie in everything she wants. That woman can spend money faster than a nigger can eat watermelon and spit seeds."

He wouldn't have asked it in daylight or if their conversation had been different. "Bo—after your children were born, how long before you, you and your wife—"

It took Bonard a moment to understand. "Oh, you mean! I waited a couple of weeks, I guess, because she made me." After a long pause for another thought he asked, "How old is your Bruce?"

"She was born in February."

"March, April, May," Bonard counted. "Lord God! — Well, I reckon you been getting it somewhere. Know I did, did and do." When Benjamin remained silent, Bonard said, "Mean to say you've not been doing it atall when your wife was pregnant? You used to need pussy like a horse needs hay to work. Do without a week and you'd go around with that thing splitting your britches. I remember." Benjamin walked, and after a moment Bonard caught up with him. "Forget it if I spoke out of turn, but it ain't good for a man to be without."

"No," Benjamin agreed, and they went into the house, discarding cigars in a rose bed on the way.

14

At sixteen Elizabeth Oglethorpe was pretty, whereas her sister had been as plain a girl as she was now a woman. That plainness had even been part of her appeal for Benjamin, along with what he called her goodness, when he was passed over by Frankie Dollard for his cousin Bonard. Benjamin remembered this when his knock at the Oglethorpe door was answered by Elizabeth. "Come in, Ben."

He shook his head. "Thank you, Betty, but I get up at five, so if Priscilla is ready, we'll go along."

"She's waiting."

He'd known she would be, and she came immediately. They went to the buggy without words. It was not until they were leaving the town that he spoke. "How did you find your father?"

"He is resting now. He asked to be alone, and we hope he will sleep."

"I trust he'll be recovered by morning, but you may want the buggy. I'll tell Zadok, and he'll have a man bring you in whenever you say."

"Mama will send word if I am required."

The town behind them, they crossed the bridge over the swampy creek, its moss-hung sycamores tall on both sides. It was a still night, and the horse's hooves on the wooden boarding waked some of the wild creatures. Benjamin heard a rustling in the brush and then a sound of big wings. Buzzards, he decided.

"Was it a pleasant evening?"

"Most pleasant," he answered. "Frankie has an excellent cook. I made your excuses. Everyone admired your devotion to family and expressed the hope that Mr. Oglethorpe would recover. Not wanting them to live in suspense, I gave assurance that his indisposition was not without precedent, nor beyond the physician's skill. I did not, however, suggest that he merely had a bellyache."

"Your banter is coarse and heartless."

"I beg your pardon. Shall I tell you about the portrait?"

"I have already heard it described as a masterpiece. Is there anything to add to that?"

"Nothing that would please you. The children were brought out."

"We all saw them recently at the elder Mrs. Saxon's."

"Aunt Annabel would not care for your description of her."

"It is not a description; it is to differentiate her from her two daughters-in-law."

"They are lively children. Frankie and Bonard are proud of them."

"I hope they will be good," Priscilla said.

They rode in silence until they reached the Glade, where Benjamin helped his wife down from the buggy before unhitching the horse, not wanting to rouse one of the men. When he had rolled the buggy under shelter and settled the horse in his stall, he returned to the house. Entering the big bedroom, he found that Priscilla had undressed and put on her nightgown. It was a plain white gown, high at the neck and touching the floor when she sat, as she now did before the mirror, brushing out her hair. Though she was not beautiful, finding her so was a reminder of past intimacy between them. He went to stand behind her, looking at her in the lamplighted mirror glass.

"Good night," she said when she saw him, and continued brushing. When he did not go, she added, "It is late, and you will be up early." He placed his hands on her shoulders. Rising, she turned and swept her hair back with both hands, catching and tying it at the neck. It gave her face a vulnerable look.

"I want to sleep with you tonight," he said.

"I'm tired. We will be more comfortable if we continue as we have been, you in your room, I in mine."

"I am not thinking of comfort." As she moved away, he caught and held her.

"I told you: I am tired."

"I need you," he said. "It's three months since the baby was born. I asked Bonard how long they waited—"

"You discussed me with another man?" Her face went red.

"How was I to learn, except from a married man?"

"You should have asked me."

"You never want to talk about these things."

"I am too ashamed," she said after a pause.

"Ashamed, Priscilla? However innocent you were when we were married, you surely knew something of what it would mean. It's a long time since we were together. I need you, Priscilla. Let me love you. Try to love me and let me show you. I want you and I want another child." He kissed her, but she pulled away, and he let her go.

Stepping to the wardrobe, she said, "I won't allow you to force me."

"I never have, I never shall."

"I have submitted." She found a robe and put it on.

"Was it only that?"

"I am not a harlot."

"You don't have to be to enjoy your husband. Some women—"

"Spare me your knowledge of 'some women'—"

"I'm sorry."

"This is not a time to talk, Benjamin. Please leave me so that I may sleep."

"Let me sleep with you. I promise to do no more."

"No."

His voice faltered with the words: "I beg you to let me sleep beside you tonight."

"I should not close my eyes. You make me say now what I'd have said later. I don't want to anger you, but I see no other way." She stopped to consider her words. "I will live with you and do my duty, but I will not sleep with you."

"I don't understand."

She hesitated, sat down again in the chair, and pulled the robe about her legs. "It violates my feelings for you. I cannot respect you as I should when I see you sweating and red and uncontrolled. It must not happen again."

"Tell me why," he said coldly.

"I have prayed, and God has answered me that it is wrong to lie with you. The miscarriages were the expression of God's disapproval. Can you believe them to be anything else? The child's defect is God's last warning—"

"Priscilla!" For a moment he was too saddened to say more.

She hurried on. "If we let ourselves have another child, it will die, and I will die. I know it. That is what God tells me. I have heard His voice in my heart."

"You have heard your mother!" he said, voice and anger returning.

"I knew you would say that, because you don't want to hear the truth. That's why I hoped I shouldn't have to tell you. I wanted you to understand without my speaking."

He said, "You have no love for me."

"If you will let me alone, I will try to love you in God's way. But I cannot love you—if that is what you call it—in your way. I swear I cannot and will not."

Again he said, "You have no love for me."

She shook her head. "Promise me, Benjamin, to pray on this. You don't see now because you don't want to see, but if you pray as I have done, it will be clear to you. Do this not only because I ask but for your salvation. Unless you repent of past sins—"

"What sins?"

"Ask God's forgiveness. He is a stern God, but He will hear you as He has heard me."

"You call my loving a sin?"

"What of Bessie Marsh and the others before her? Is that not sinning? Even now you go to her house—"

"I go to see my son."

"He is a child of sin and doomed as you will surely be if you do not beg God—"

"I'll beg for nothing! — You have no love for me?"

"I am afraid. — You have not borne a child and you can't know the terror of being a woman. I at last understood that all I endured was the result of the things you did, the things you wanted me to do, but always *your* pleasure!"

"I can never hope for another child?"

"It would die. I would die."

"You want me to live a celibate life?"

"You want to make me your whore?"

"You were to be my wife and I your husband. Together we were to be what we hadn't been apart."

"I have said all. I am exhausted."

"I am to have no love—"

"You are like a little child. Go to bed."

He turned and left the room, slamming the door behind him. Next door the baby woke and cried. He stopped dead in the hallway until he heard Velma's voice, murmuring and soothing. It was a warm night, and the door of the nursery was open. He waited until the baby was quiet, and then he went into his room and closed the door.

The windows were open to the air and moonlight. He needed no lamp. When he had undressed, he pulled back the top bedclothes and lay naked on his back. Going over everything Priscilla had said to him, he knew there was no way of changing her. He even began to understand why she felt as she did. He had not wept for a long time, but he did so now, turning on his face as if to hide his grief and his need.

15

"Tell me what you're thinking."

He looked at her and then at the plate from which he had eaten. They were on the west porch, Sarah having asked Mabella to set the breakfast table there because it was a warm morning, getting on for hot even at seven o'clock.

"The cantaloupe," she said, "wasn't ripe, but it's good to have the taste again. They'll soon be better. I don't understand your putting pepper on it, but then some people like salt on watermelon. You ate two eggs and a slice of ham and two biscuits and some honey. I've known you to make a bigger breakfast when you had a fever and could hardly swallow. Something is wrong."

"Nothing, Grandma."

"I would do almost anything for you, Benjamin, short of taking a butcher knife to Casey or Jane."

He was silent.

Sarah sighed. "It's like priming a pump until you wonder if there's water after all. — You went to Bonard and Frankie's last night. Did something happen there?" He shook his head. "Very well. You've just had word that Sherman is coming through again." He frowned; he was not listening. The jokiness left her voice. "What's the matter, boy?" He looked straight at her then, and his eyes misted.

Clearing his throat, he coughed, laughed, clapped his hands, and stood up. "Time for you and me to take a walk, my lady." He reached for her hand and led her down the broad, shallow steps. They walked and he talked. It was not easy for him. After a while they paused at the swing Casey had rigged from a limb of one of the live oaks for Davy and Bobby Lee. Sarah had not spoken or tried to help him. Still listening, she sat on the swing seat, and Benjamin began to push it back and forth, first gently, then higher and higher. The regular movement freed his tongue; he said everything he could say to anyone. When he tired of pushing the swing in the regular way, he caught it and twisted the ropes together, letting it go, spinning Sarah around.

"Stop!" she demanded, braking herself with a foot to the ground. "You make me dizzy. Let's go over there." They strolled in the direction she indicated to a bench circling the whitewashed base of an oak tree, and for a time they sat quietly, considering what he had told her. As if continuing a thought she said, "You have Bruce."

He agreed with a nod. "I want a son too."

She hesitated, knowing that what was in her mind was important not only to them but to Beulah Land, because it carried a commitment she had never before made. "You have a son."

"He isn't mine."

"We must think of a way to get him." Though she said it lightly, her face was serious.

"Take him from his mother?"

"You can't have her too, nor do you want her. I used to think Bessie a simple girl, but that was simple of me; and now the Betchley man is living with her she's sly as moonshine. I've worried about Leon. I didn't allow him your grandfather's name to grow up ignorant in the middle of nowhere. She's told us she's no intention of letting him go to school after he learns to read and write. It's time for me to do something. You'd better keep out of it. Women take advantage of you. They don't take advantage of me."

"What will you do?"

"She'll guess what I want," Sarah reckoned. "I must put fat bait on my hook."

He laughed outright and rose from the bench. "I'd better get to the fields."

"Why?"

"I've got all the men hoeing grass; it took over the cotton after last week's rain."

"Zadok doesn't need you to keep them at it. Go away for the day. Are you certain there's no changing her feeling about you?"

"I am," he said grimly.

"Then forget her," she said.

"I can't; she's my wife."

"I don't mean put her out of your house. Put her out of your mind. Get your pride back. I've seen it drained out of you. I'm not suggesting that you be foolish, but live your life as a man if she won't let you be a husband." Sarah left the bench, and they began to walk back to the house. "She isn't going to be one of us after all," she said musingly. "I thought she would. I wasn't born to Beulah Land either, I married it. — I had a letter from Abraham yesterday. He hates Latin and has been to a play at the Walnut Street Theater. Take the letter to Roscoe for me. That'll start you. Tell him to come see me when he's read it, and if Luck is with him, say I send her a kiss."

"What if she wants me to deliver it?" he said teasingly.

"She wouldn't be the first little darky you've kissed."

An hour later Benjamin had delivered the letter, and Roscoe, swinging Luck into his arms, came to the porch to watch him go.

As he mounted his horse, the child wiggled fat fingers at him and repeated, "Bye-bye-bye."

"Goodbye, Lucky. I'll tell Grandma you're coming to see her tomorrow."

"I've got a new pink dress."

"She'll be jealous," Benjamin said. The girl laughed gleefully.

Down the carriageway he saw his Great-aunt Selma on the porch of the school waving to a visitor in a buggy. The buggy moved off; Selma went back inside without seeing him. She had become nearsighted from so many years of teaching, and Benjamin suspected that she was selective about what she saw, as well. He thought of stopping to visit, but she looked busy, and he was curious to know who was in the buggy. Trotting his horse ahead, he came alongside as the rig turned into the main road and saw that its driver was his hostess of the evening before. She was as surprised as he, and they laughed at each other as they explained. Her errand had been not dissimilar to his own. Annabel, who considered herself the principal patroness of the school, had asked her to deliver a bundle of clothing she'd bullied town acquaintances into contributing for the girl pupils. Because of the heat and the length of the drive, Annabel was disinclined to make the journey herself. A servant might have been sent, but that would have looked cold, and Annabel prided herself on her humanity when she thought of it. Besides, she wanted the message of gratitude to be returned to her intelligibly, not garbled by one of the Negroes, so she persuaded Frankie that the thing she needed after her evening party was a morning of country air.

Surprise and amusement gave way to ease and eagerness to please as they trotted their horses along at an equal pace. Benjamin realized that it was the first time he and Frankie had been relaxed together. Certainly they had not been during the days he courted her; he'd been too much in love. Perhaps it needed accident for it to happen. For once he could think her pretty without feeling compelled to say so. Her complexion fair, her color high, her face shone rosily in the heat, which she appeared not to mind, although there was no breeze except that made by their motion, which was hardly enough to stir her hair or the open collar of the voile dress she wore.

He decided that she was without artifice today because she didn't need it. They were alone together, so she could be herself. This was the way it might have been if they had married each other.

They were delighted with the morning; gaiety sparked between them. At a junction she slowed her horse to a walk, as did he, and she pointed with her whip. "Where does that road go?"

"Through woods for half a mile before farmland begins again."

"I'd like the shade."

"Do you want company?"

"Yours, yes."

As they turned off the main road, she saw a tree full of yellow plums. "Look."

He stopped his horse and without dismounting picked and ate one. "Not yet sweet," he said, tossing another into her lap.

"I want some anyway."

He gathered a dozen and tied them into his handkerchief before following her down the road with woodland on both sides. Benjamin knew it; it was the one he used to take five years ago when he squired Bessie away from the family farm for dalliance. It was Frankie, not he, who decided the stopping place. Was it where he used to leave his buggy? He didn't remember, but it was pretty and inviting with its brown pine needles covering the ground and the pungent smell of green pine in the air.

As he dismounted and tied his horse, she stepped down from the buggy and secured hers. "For a Savannah girl you know your way with a horse and buggy," he said.

"I learned because I like to be independent."

The thought of his situation at home and her closeness here gave him a partial erection, and before he could try to hide it he saw that she was aware of it. She strolled a little way into the woods, and he followed with the handkerchief of plums. "Have you never been here before?"

She shook her head, bending a low, leafy tree limb out of the way. Smiling, she waited for him in the open space beyond. "I don't believe there's anyone else in the world."

He untied the handkerchief and held the plums before her in his open palms. Instead of taking one, she looked directly into his face with an invitation that was clearly beyond flirtation. The plums scattered as he let them go, and she came against him.

At nine o' clock there had been no thought of her in his head. At ten they'd met by accident. Before eleven they were lovers. And now, as they lay side by side on the buffalo robe he'd fetched from the buggy, they became friends.

"That's what we missed," she said.

When he reached for it, her hand met his. "I suppose we mustn't meet again."

"Why?" she asked.

"I'm Bonard's cousin."

"That keeps it in the family," she said. "Very sensible and Southern."

"I've betrayed Bonard's trust," he declared.

"He betrayed yours five years ago, and so did I. Good revenge for you."

"I don't feel that way."

She let go his hand and turned on her side to look at him. "I know you don't. You're a good man, Ben. I shouldn't have let you go."

"You fell in love with Bonard," he excused her.

"I was no more in love with Bonard when I married him than I'd been with you earlier. I was tired of being poor, and I despised my silly family. I wanted a more substantial life than theirs, and the way to get it was plain."

"You weren't in love with me?" he said.

"Ha! I've touched your vanity. — Maybe a little if it pleases you to hear it. But more important: Beulah Land was to be yours."

"You couldn't have been that calculating."

Without apology she said, "I was concerned for the future and didn't allow myself the luxury of swooning over your Adam's apple."

"I was in love with you."

"When did you stop being?" she asked interestedly.

"On January 1, 1874."

"Do you know the exact moment too?"

"It was when I paid a formal call on you and Bonard and found out you were going to have a baby."

She did not laugh, but she was amused.

"Do you want me to fall in love with you again?" he said.

"That would be unwise. I shall always be Mrs. Saxon."

"Why did you decide not to become Mrs. Davis?"

She looked at him with surprise. "Surely you knew. Because of the child Bessie Marsh was going to have. Your child who might one day try to claim what was yours. Cold caution on my part. The crux of the matter, if you remember, was your refusal to deny that the child was yours."

"How could I lie?"

"It's the easiest thing in the world."

He bent and kissed her and kept his face close to hers. "Is that a lie?"

"A sweet one," she said.

"Would it also amuse you to know that it was right here Bessie conceived the child that made you change your mind?"

Lifting her face, she bit him on the chin.

He pulled away and began to laugh. "You're jealous!"

"Vanity," she said. "Never compare women except in your mind." She ran her hand back of his neck. "You need a haircut."

"In five years of marriage Priscilla has never told me I needed a haircut."

"Maybe she doesn't look at you," Frankie said. "You need a haircut."

He put his face close to hers again and whispered, "Don't you love me a little?"

"I'm glad you don't chew tobacco. Bonard does, in addition to smoking those stinking Cuban cigars." She sighed. "At this moment I love you a little, but an hour from now my mind will be on something else, and so will yours."

He kissed her long and fully. "Not if you stay."

She drew away. "That will be all for today."

"I must say you're cool about it," he complained.

"We don't have to count three and drown. We'll meet again."

"Do you think we should?"

"Certainly." She rose briskly from the buffalo robe. "Shake the pine needles out before you put it back in the buggy."

"Do you feel guilty?"

"No," she said. "You do."

"Mm."

"Enjoy it while it lasts; it won't last long." She had begun to arrange her hair and clothes.

"Not guilty about Priscilla," he said. "It's Bonard. We were boys together."

"He's told me about that," she said drily. "But you weren't real friends, were you? Or how do you account for his taking me away from you without a qualm? That was my trump card. He enjoyed cutting you out."

"Did he say so?"

"Did he not!"

"The bastard!"

"You speak, sir, of the father of my children."

"Oh." He blushed.

"Ben," she chided him, "I joke about everything when I trust someone. Let me trust you."

"Yes," he said.

She was ready to go. He shook and folded the buffalo robe.

"I'm not saying Bonard is a bad husband; he isn't. He gives me a house and a position that I wanted and enjoy. I'll not disappoint him much in those areas. I'll be a proper good mother. I'll manage his house and keep him out of trouble. Without me he'd have gone bad, you know. Everyone says I spend too much money and make him work too hard, but what else has he to do with his life? Before me he wasted it on bets on horse races and drink and women. Now he lives a decent life and he's better off. His mother was quick to understand that. We don't like each other, but she knows my value." They began to walk toward the buggy. "I'm not a romantic girl, and you mustn't expect me to be. But I've always liked you, and I'll be your friend if you'll be mine."

"I will be," he said.

"I enjoyed what we did, Ben, and Bonard isn't very good."

"He isn't?" Benjamin said.

"Didn't you know?"

"How does a man know about another man?"

"Women do." She shrugged. "You didn't guess?"

"He always talked like the king buck of Georgia."

"That should have told you. It tickles you now, but later you'll think it was hateful of me to say it."

"Mean, maybe."

"I am mean sometimes, when people deserve it. I don't understand how Bonard instilled such loyalty in you. Because he was older?"

"It's more men sticking together."

"Women can too," Frankie said, "but only in extremis."

"When shall we meet?" Benjamin said as she stepped lightly into the buggy without using the hand he offered.

"Not soon nor often," she answered. "I'll think about it and let you know. We will both be careful. You don't want to offend your family, and neither do I. It's unnecessary and would be stupid. It would be equally stupid for us not to meet if we want to. Do you agree?"

"You know I do."

She took up the reins as he untied the horse. "Stay for a while after I go."

He came around the horse's head to be beside her. When he put out his hand, she took it firmly in hers. He said, "Thank you, Frankie. You don't know how good you've been for me."

"Yes, I do," she said. "Bonard told me what you confided about Priscilla and your having been without anyone for so long."

"The devil he did!"

"He thought it a joke—you, who used to be such a lover of the ladies, reduced to asking him when you might again expect to enjoy the favors of your wife. Oh, he laughed. That's what decided me to seek you today, though I'd had it in mind before. And that's why I was so surprised to meet you at the school. I'd already planned to look for you when I left it. Why do you think I brought along a buffalo robe in this weather?" She turned the buggy neatly in the clearing and set off toward the main road. When she reached it, she lifted her hand for a backward wave, knowing he'd still be watching her.

Body and mind in harmony, Benjamin did not become aware of

hunger until midafternoon. When Frankie left him, he discovered that his horse was standing in the sun, the sun having shifted. He moved him into shade and loosened the saddle belt before returning to the nearer woods where he and Frankie had been together. On his knees, with palms flat, he went over the ground as if to convince himself that it had happened as he remembered it. In doing so he discovered a plum, ate it, found another, another, found and ate them all. Then he lay on his back, knees up and head cupped in hands, looking through spiky pine to sky. He slept, woke thirsty, and thought the horse must be thirsty too. A search revealed a branch of the creek they'd passed earlier, and at a place where the water ran clear over pebbled sand, he watered himself and the horse. Squatting, he cupped hands and drank, then splashed his face. Hunger asserting itself at that instant, he turned his horse toward Beulah Land.

16

His grandmother met him in the hallway, and on seeing him expressed her relief as "Thank God."

"What's wrong?"

"You're not to alarm yourself—"

"Aunt Nell?"

"It's *him.*"

"Who?"

"He's here."

"Leon," he guessed.

"I put him in Daniel's old room. It's near the kitchen but away from Aunt Nell and on the east side of the house. However hot the mornings, the afternoons are worse. He'll be cool at night."

"He's sick," Benjamin next guessed, starting toward the room his grandmother had indicated.

"Dr. Platt has been," she said, following. "It's malaria. An hour after you left, his mother brought him in her wagon and left him."

"It's too early for malaria."

"Bessie says he had it last fall. Platt says he didn't get over it, but kept it in his blood."

It was not one of the guest rooms. When Daniel and Jane married, it was kept as an all-purpose emergency or accident room, for such was useful on a large farm with many workers. At the bedside table Mabella was pouring lemonade into a glass. The boy looked pale as milk, and he stared at the serving girl as if she came from another world. Mabella stepped aside for Benjamin, who first bent over the bed and then dropped to his knees, the better to see and be seen.

"It's me, Leon. Grandma says you're sick. You'll be all right. I had it two years ago." There was recognition in the boy's eyes but no more than that as the eyes closed on a private struggle. He trembled, then quivered, then shook violently. Touching his head, Benjamin found it burning with fever, and the boy's teeth began to click like hailstones on a windowpane.

"Get quilts," Sarah said to Mabella.

Benjamin lifted the child from the bed, swaddling the sheet about him and cushioning the shaking against his own body. Sarah offered two quilts Mabella had fetched from the corner cupboard, and without giving up possession of his son Benjamin managed to take them one after the other and swathe the fevered body in his arms. That accomplished, he sat on the side of the bed as still as he could.

"Freezing to death," the boy said in gasps.

The quilts and the heat of Benjamin's body had no apparent effect. The chill continued for five or six minutes before gradually subsiding, to return twice again and quicken and subside before the boy lay slack and spent. Putting his cheek against his, Benjamin whispered, "He's sweating."

Sarah nodded. "Bring a towel, Mabella, and clean sheets."

Only when the boy's breathing had become normal did Benjamin relinquish him to Mabella and his grandmother. He looked tired; his eyes were closed; and he made no protest when the women stripped the damp petticoat from him and dried him. Sarah laid him naked on the bottom sheet of the bed, and Mabella arranged a fresh sheet over him. His head rested on the pillow, and he slept. Kneeling again at the bed, Benjamin watched him until Sarah touched his shoulder and motioned him into the hallway. "Mabella will call us if he wakes."

He followed her into the office, where Josephine had set out a pitcher of iced tea and a plate of cake. Benjamin took a piece of cake in each hand, but he did not sit as Sarah began to talk.

"I was studying last year's corn figures, but couldn't keep my mind on them for turning over what we'd talked about this morning. Then, lo and behold, Mabella came running to say there was a woman in a wagon in the yard with a sick youngun, and could I come. It was like an answer, for they were the ones I'd been thinking of. Bessie told me he had chills and fever and they were too busy out there to look after him. Would we? Of course, I grabbed him. She didn't come in, said she had to get back and knew we'd see him through and let her know anything, good or bad. I put him to bed. She had that old petticoat on him, one of her ma's, I expect; but we're making him some nightgowns. I've got Dorothea in the sewing room this minute. I sent Wally, because he loves to ride fast, to tell Dr. Platt if he didn't get himself out here within the hour I'd skin him alive. He came back with Wally and said it surely looked like malaria and there wasn't anything to do but give him quinine and calomel and wait. Platt gives calomel for everything the way Mabella reaches for lemons the minute she hears anybody's down sick. I tried to get Leon to eat, but he wouldn't or couldn't, so I stopped fussing over him. I haven't left him for more than five minutes. He's a good boy, never complained or whimpered the way most children do when ailing, though I could see his fever was up and rising. Not knowing what to do, I waited. Then you came. You've eaten every piece of that cake. Didn't you have any dinner? Sit down."

"No'm." He sat.

"Where've you been not to eat?"

"Round and about, the way you said do." He told her of his visit with Roscoe and that she was to expect a call tomorrow from Luck in a new pink dress. First she said she'd send word for them not to come, then that she wouldn't, then that she'd decide later. Both lapsed into silence until Sarah broke it. "I'm ashamed to say it with the poor child suffering, but I'm glad he's here even the way he is. We mustn't scare him by doing too much. Will Priscilla be upset?"

"I reckon; don't you?" Benjamin said. "Why you think Bessie brought him?"

Sarah frowned consideringly. "It was the way she said. Nobody there to look after him. Her mother is near blind; it's the boy who takes care of her, not her of him. Bessie's in the fields from sunrise to sundown when she's not cooking or washing for them. I feel sorry for her, though I don't like her."

Benjamin rose and went to the tea tray. Pressing the remaining cake crumbs into a single ball, he ate it. "Benjamin, do you want Josephine to fix you something? She'd be tickled to death. She's jealous of Freda, I don't know why, except that she fed you for so long and now you look to Freda."

"No, ma'am. I'd better go home and make my peace. I'll just look at Leon on the way. I'll be back after supper."

"I'll send one of the hands to tell Bessie the doctor's been and Leon's sleeping."

Before going home Benjamin saw Zadok and Daniel, both of whom knew of Leon's arrival. Anything of consequence that happened at the big house at Beulah Land was relayed immediately to all who lived and worked there. The youngest child and the oldest granny knew the sick boy had been brought to stay with them, and they knew who he was. Approaching his own house in the Glade, Benjamin unreasoningly expected to find it changed, because so much had happened to him since he'd left it that morning, but all was the same. Bruce was well and happy. Freda had fretted at his not returning for noon dinner and welcomed his assertion that he was close to starvation. He found Priscilla in her room sitting by an open window with a piece of embroidery on her lap. She was the exception to those who knew about Leon's presence at Beulah Land. No one had thought, or dared, to tell her.

Benjamin hadn't seen her since their quarrel the night before. When he knocked at the open door, she glanced up calmly and bade him enter. They exchanged polite greetings, and he told her that "various matters" had kept him from home at noon, an explanation she received without comment or any appearance of caring.

"Did you know that my son is ill and his mother has brought him to Beulah Land?"

Her fingers paused at their work, but she did not look up from it. "I did not know. So that is where you have been."

"Only for the last hour. He has malaria. A chill seized him when I was there."

She said with uninflected gravity, "Her bringing him is an imposition at best and at worst an impertinent reminder of old scandal."

"It was right for her to bring him. She couldn't take care of him."

"You may say so, but you cannot expect me to."

He said sharply, "You take little notice of your own child. I don't ask that you concern yourself for mine."

"It is all unfortunate," she replied, ignoring his reproach.

"Yes," he said.

"It would have been proper for Mrs. Troy to refuse him."

Benjamin stopped the words that came to his mind. "She does not see it so, I'm glad to say."

"She would do anything to please you."

"That says nothing for the goodness of her heart."

"Charity need not be indiscriminate."

"A convenient belief."

She flushed but still did not look at him. "I do not 'believe' anything for 'convenience,' Mr. Davis."

It was the first time she had so addressed him, although it was not uncommon for certain old-fashioned wives to refer to a husband thus in conversation with others and even on formal occasions to so address him. Stung, he said, "I saw Frankie again today." She resumed her embroidery. "She was at the school when I stopped to see Roscoe Elk."

"It gratifies her, no doubt, to enjoy your admiration on two occasions within a day's duration. Will you take supper at home? If not, I'll instruct Freda accordingly. She cooks too richly for my taste."

"I'll be here, and I've told her to cook everything in the house. After supper I'll go back to stay with Leon."

She held her work up from her lap, searching it against the light for flaw. "I shall pray for his recovery. Nevertheless, he is a child of sin, and no amount of your irony against me will change that."

Although she came to the dining room when Freda rang the dinner bell and even ate a little from two or three of the dozen dishes on the table, Priscilla held no further conversation with her husband. He ate hugely and with extravagant compliments to Freda, who basked in his praise. He also maintained a conversation of sorts with Velma and Bruce, who were present according to his fixed request. It was largely one-sided, however, Velma being too bashful to answer freely with Mrs. Davis there.

After supper Benjamin took Bruce from Velma and walked in the Glade, the nurse following. When he gave the baby to her after half an hour and wished them good night, explaining that he was leaving again, Velma said, "I hear your boy's sick, Mr. Ben. If they's anything I can do, you say."

"Thank you, Velma." Benjamin touched the baby's chin with his forefinger. "Do you think she knows me?"

"She *do*, sir. She talk about you all the day long."

At Beulah Land, Benjamin was told that Leon had eaten a gruel Mabella made for him and that there had been no return of fever, no further chill. Sarah accepted his determination to remain the night, doing what she could to make him comfortable and retiring with Casey when Benjamin promised her he would knock on their door if he needed anything.

When they were alone, he tried talking to the boy, but Leon was exhausted, and soon Benjamin turned the lamp low, setting it away from the bed. Leon slept. After a while so did Benjamin in his chair. Leon woke twice to ask for water, which Benjamin gave him from the pitcher Mabella had provided. At five o'clock Sarah entered to find that Benjamin had stretched out on the bed beside the boy. They were both asleep as she tiptoed away.

17

The thing Leon found strangest was the activity and the noise. Not having known anything but the little farm, he was at first astounded by what appeared to him vast numbers of people, white and Negro, coming and going. Kept in bed his first day, he could see his father through the open window with two men he heard him call Dan and Zadok, as well as what he overestimated as "a hundred" Negro men, women, and children, all of whom used each other's names, joking, jostling, working, and idling. He'd never seen so many Negroes all at once. He recognized Mabella, who had been with him steadily since his arrival, and Josephine, who came in occasionally to ask if he liked blueberry pie or to observe scoldingly any arrangements Mabella had made that did not suit her. Sarah was there frequently.

Midmorning, Jane Todd brought him a glass jar of Cape jasmine fresh from her garden and said he was to call her Aunt. With her were Robert E. Lee and Jefferson Davis, who were comfortably younger than he and who had to be restrained from jumping on the bed, which made him feel superior. They were permitted to remain when their mother went off to see someone she called Aunt Nell in another part of the house. When Mabella left them for a few minutes, Davy and Bobby Lee promptly pulled out their penises and ordered him to show his, which he did briefly and with a blush, his mother and grandmother having told him it was a thing to keep hidden. Satisfied that they were alike, the boys dismissed their parts and began to tell him stories about Beulah Land, gratified to find someone who knew nothing of its history.

Benjamin came at noon before going home for his dinner, praising Leon for having had no chill or fever. He returned in fresh clothes at the end of the day after a swim in the creek. With him came the Todd boys and their father, whom he was told to call Uncle Daniel. On their second visit Bobby Lee presented Leon with a few of their toys on the understanding that they were only being lent. There was a tiny wagon with wheels that spun and a wooden tongue that moved up and down and sideways. There were half a dozen marbles, each a beauty in itself and a hazard for adults when they rolled off the bed and two could not be found. There was a metal windup darky, painted like a minstrel man, who danced a jig when set on the floor. Best of all, there was a picture book of lions and tigers, ostriches and apes.

Dorothea had not been idle. A word to the seamstress was like a sermon to another servant. Used to sewing for the Todd boys, she produced three pairs of cotton pants with blouses to match, in addition to the nightgowns Sarah had ordered. He'd need them, she knew, because malaria kept its victim in bed only during the fever and chills. A written description of Leon's condition was sent by Sarah to his mother, allowing him to be feebler than he was, to discourage Bessie's coming for him too soon. She, evidently, had no such thing in mind. He was there; he might stay a while, for he was no use to her until he was well and only another mouth to feed. Such was the verbal message returned by Sarah's courier with an admonition for Leon to "mind them." Every hour, and then every day when he could count the time in days, was felt by Benjamin to be something won.

All was not, however, progress.

On his second full day at Beulah Land, Leon again had fever followed by a hard chill. For six days the pattern was constant: chills and fever every other day. Then four days passed with no active recurrence of the disease, and then, triumphantly, an entire week.

Every hour that he was free of bed was one of new experience. Fetching the mail from town, Benjamin brought gifts: a paper of peppermint sticks, a rubber ball with a good bounce, a picture book of animals that was his to keep, a pocketknife that Sarah took away and said she would give him when he was older, a Jew's harp, and a cloth sack with a drawstring that held two dozen marbles, each different and all as fine as anything Davy and Bobby

Lee owned. He was allowed to visit the venerable Aunt Nell. She announced that he was the image of her beloved husband Felix Kendrick, whose face she had not the faintest recollection of, but Sarah told her it was a nice family thing to say. Casey Troy took his picture alone, and with Benjamin, and with Benjamin and Sarah, and with Mabella. The Todd boys showed him everywhere they were allowed to go, which did not include the woods unless they were accompanied, so Mabella was designated guardian, a role she had already assumed, and kept a lenient eye on Leon most of his waking hours. Josephine grumbled when Sarah told her to use another girl in the kitchen as long as Leon stayed, but she was soon as bossy-kind with him as she was with everyone else, in the way of good cooks everywhere.

No one said what he was to call Benjamin, so he settled for "sir." It was, Benjamin reasoned, better than being called Mr. Davis by his son, but he wanted to acknowledge their relationship and was stayed only by Sarah's cautioning him to go slowly, for the boy's sake as well as his own. He spent time with him when he could, and when there was no time to spare, he set Leon in front of his saddle to ride the fields with him as he checked the progress of work. Leon understood that it was a proud thing to ride so, and for the first time he allowed himself to believe that he was the son of the man he'd been told was his father. Benjamin's arm around him holding the reins was certainty; and now and then Benjamin gave him the reins when he reached down to accept something being shown him by a man or woman on the ground.

The event Leon most looked forward to came in late afternoon when, the sun still hot but work done for the day, Benjamin dismissed the field hands, and he and Daniel called Leon and Davy and Bobby Lee to come with them to the creek for a swim. They carried fresh clothes to change into, for the swim was a way of bathing, and they'd have sweated many times through everything they wore in a day. The boys went barefoot. Neither men nor boys wore underclothes, only cotton shirt and trousers.

Daniel Todd was quiet almost to solemn, and this brought out in Benjamin a humorousness Leon liked. Davy and Bobby Lee were very free with their father and clearly worshipped him. Leon envied them the ease with which one or the other would take his hand when he wanted to. Only now and then would the man pick up and set aside one who had become a nuisance by climbing over him when he sat or lay on the ground, which was enough to sober even the livelier Davy. One day watching them with their father, Leon took Benjamin's hand. Benjamin looked down at him, surprised and friendly, but then Leon didn't know when to let go, so he did it awkwardly. He'd had no experience of touching those he liked and being touched by them.

He couldn't swim. They all taught him with such enthusiasm they almost drowned him, but he learned to dog-paddle and was never again to fear water the way some country boys unaccountably did. Swimming seemed to run, or not, in families. After swimming—and Davy at two was as independent in water as he was out of it—they sat on the bank to dry themselves before dressing. There was a large holly tree they used to drape their clothes upon, because it was known to be free (they didn't know why) of the red bugs that got into seams and bit and were hard to get rid of. Leon learned to hang his things on the holly so that they would neither rip nor be blown into the creek.

Finally they dressed and walked back through the woods, quieter as the creek was quieter too, nothing stirring in it, something thoughtful in the gentle movement of men and water at the end of the day. The boys broke free and ran ahead, or made sorties into the woods on either side of the path. The best part of the day was followed by the worst, when they parted in the yard, his uncle Daniel taking his cousins home, his father sending him into the house to his great-grandmother while he went on to the house in the Glade.

Leon was never taken there, and he knew that it had to do with the woman who was married to his father. Once Benjamin brought down a Negro woman he called Velma and a baby he said was his daughter Bruce. He wondered about the scar on her lip, but no one mentioned it.

Leon did not miss his mother. She had never paid him much attention, and she'd given him none since Eugene Betchley attached himself to the farm. Now and then he thought of his grandmother, who had been his companion more than anyone else and whose bed he had shared. He'd hated it and felt smothered by the sour odor of her through the worn petticoat she never removed. Sometimes he remembered the smell with pity and a stir of guilt at not being there to help her, for how could she get around without him? She had not been affectionate, but a child will love someone if he can, and Leon had attached himself to the grandmother.

One morning when Leon was at the Todd house, Bessie came to Beulah Land. Happening to be on the porch, Sarah saw her approaching and stepped down into the yard to greet her as Bessie jerked the mule to a halt. "Get down and come in," Sarah invited.

"I won't do that, Mrs. Troy, for I'm in a big hurry for town. Got a heap of tomatoes and butter beans to sell. Wondered if you wasn't tired of my youngun. He must have been here three weeks, I reckon."

It was nearer five, as Sarah knew to the day, but she managed to say with a vagueness as unconvincing as it was uncharacteristic, "Long as that? We're not a bit tired of him. Since he's been out of bed, he's never underfoot, usually off with Mrs. Todd's two. We hardly know he's on the place."

"He could be a right smart of use if you told him what to do."

"He hasn't been strong enough to do other than traipse around with the children and watch them play," Sarah lied.

"Look out he don't possum you. You sent word he was over the chills and fever."

"You know how it is with malaria. Free of it a month, then back it can come to nearly kill you."

Bessie said agreeably enough, "Well, I spect you better have him ready to go home with me when I stop after town. That's why I come, to tell you."

With an exertion of will Sarah forced a smile for the country woman, who had taken off her sunbonnet to wipe her forehead. "Let him stay a week longer to be sure. You don't want a sick child when crops are coming in. How's your corn?"

"Pretty good, better later. Big crop of garden stuff; that's why I'm wanting to sell some."

"Gene Betchley still helping you?"

"I owe a lot to Gene," Bessie said, reserve entering her voice. "He's a real worker."

Sarah nodded. "He's better off helping you farm than he was setting traps in our woods."

"Your grandson told you that?"

"Everybody knows what Gene was doing before he settled down at your place. How do you pay him?"

It was Bessie's turn to smile. "You have the boy ready when I come back," she said, but her voice was less assured than it had been. Knowing her advantage, Sarah spent another five minutes coaxing with forced good nature, attacking and withdrawing, her smile as fixed as a smile on a statue. In the end she won; but when she stood on the porch watching the wagon disappear through the orchard on its way to the main road, she wondered if the encounter had not gone as Bessie wanted it to go.

18

When he was not with Davy and Bobby Lee, or asleep at night, he was with his father. Shyness had given way to trust on both sides, and it now seemed to Benjamin the most natural thing in the world to say, "Come on, Leon." The invitation might take them no further than the melon patch or the hog barn, but the boy's eagerness to accompany him no matter where gave Benjamin pleasure every time it happened. Together they rode into the fields, sometimes into town to pick up the mail or to see Dr. Platt, who finally said Leon was cured. Once Benjamin took him to see his aunt Doreen and Miss Kilmer. After a moment's consternation, as much at the idea of "entertaining two gentlemen" as at the identity of the younger, they made a party of the half-hour visit. There was tea and cake and much ado about the several house cats who, usually aloof, took it into their heads to parade and be admired. The ladies were completely won when the usually bad-tempered, all-white Toby sat at the boy's feet for five minutes gazing at him with adoration that would have shamed the shepherds in the manger.

Another time they went to the cotton gin, which Isaac was making ready for the late-summer ginning. And one day on impulse Benjamin stopped at the sawmill where the blind James Davis turned blood red when Benjamin told him, "Papa, I've brought my son Leon to meet you." It was some years before Leon understood what the moment held, for Benjamin had been sired by James's brother Adam, dead of yellow fever when James married Benjamin's mother Rachel. The only quarrel Benjamin and James ever had was on the day Benjamin discovered this, when James had determined to sell the war-ruined Davis plantation, and Benjamin felt that it was his birthright. Subsequently, James married and fathered three daughters, removing himself from his old family by starting a new one.

Benjamin himself could not have said why he followed impulse and stopped at the sawmill. Perhaps he was saying to one man what he could not say to the world: "I claim my son."

Benjamin's taking Leon around with him caused gossip in the town, usually disguised as expressions of sympathy for Priscilla Davis. "Poor woman," it was said, "not only is she afflicted with a marked child, but she must suffer her husband's display of his sinful past." Ann Oglethorpe paid one of her rare visits to the Glade, where she shouted at her daughter and urged her to action. Priscilla grew pale and tempered her mother's fury the best she could, begging that she be permitted to pray over the matter, a plea Mrs. Oglethorpe could hardly deny. That evening Priscilla charged her husband with bringing disgrace upon her and upon himself. He told her that she could stop public comment simply by going with him and Leon to town tomorrow morning and being seen by the promenaders of the main street. She said earnestly, "It would not be right," and doubtless believed it. He then told her she might do as she pleased, but that it pleased him to take his son about with him. Troubled time though it was, Benjamin could not remember being happy before, and this in turn troubled Sarah, for Sarah knew Bessie would use Leon as power over them.

It was a week to the hour she came to take Leon back. This time she got down from the wagon to wait on the porch for Mabella to make the boy ready. She refused refreshment, but otherwise was smiling courtesy, her eyes hard and bright as glass in the sun. Sarah was glad that Benjamin was in the fields with Daniel and Zadok. Mabella was sent to fetch Leon from the Todd house, where he was playing marbles with Bobby Lee and Davy. When she'd washed his face and hands, she brought him to the porch with the carpetbag Sarah had provided for his new clothes and toys.

"I'm ready, Ma," was Leon's greeting to Bessie after not seeing her for six weeks.

Bessie nodded; they did not touch.

Indicating the bag, Sarah said, "Things we sewed for him. I hope you don't mind."

Bessie assured her she did not. "I brought him to you all but naked. You've given so much; how can I say give no more, for I see it's your pleasure to do it, ma'am, as it is ours to receive. Has he thanked you? If he hasn't, I'll cut the blood out of him when I get him home. I've got the best tree for growing switches in the county." Her eyes glittered as her mouth smiled to indicate a jest.

"Having him here has been our pleasure," Sarah said. "I hoped you'd leave him until the Fourth of July. We have a family get-together every year. — That's what it is, more than to celebrate the event." She made the near-apology because observance of the holiday was considered misplaced patriotism by many of those Southerners who had suffered least from the preservation of the Union. "They've talked about it, Leon and Mrs. Todd's boys. The Saxons and Davises will come out from town—and all over," she finished quietly, afraid that her tone sounded like begging.

"Shouldn't think they'd *all* care to eat barbecue with my youngun—no need to nudge you, ma'am, your memory being as good as mine! But if you've set your heart on having him, I'll lend him to you for the day. Not to make a habit, just a favor to you this time. I know how folks can look forward to a thing that don't matter one bit to others. If he's a good boy, I'll spare him from farm work long as he's home by night." She shifted the rockers of her chair so that she faced the boy. "You going to be good?" Leon nodded. "Now say 'goodbye' and 'much obliged' like the little gentleman I can see you've become. Lots waiting to be done at home, and your granny needs you."

Leon went to Sarah. "Goodbye, Grandma, and I thank you."

Bessie chortled. "Calling *you* his granny!"

"It was simpler," Sarah explained. "That's what the other children call me." She kissed him quickly on the forehead and smoothed his hair with her palm, as she'd done his father's a thousand times. "Come back when you can."

"Yes'm."

It was only when he turned to Mabella that he broke down, for Mabella opened her arms to take him and howled her grief. They hugged each other until Sarah said, "Now, Mabella."

Mabella let him go and both wiped their tears and pretended to laugh, which only broke their hearts again and led to another mournful embrace, ended at last by Bessie's relentless good humor. "Mercy, if he ain't plum took to your nigger gal! What's her name?"

"Mabella!" the girl wailed.

"I never seen him carry on so. You must have been mighty good to him one way and another." She turned to Sarah. "You've always been a fool about your niggers, ain't you? — Come on, son," she ordered briskly.

Mabella could not witness the scene of departure; she turned and fled. Leon dried his tears with the backs of his hands and picked up the carpetbag, Sarah helping him and his burden into the wagon. Already seated, Bessie took reins in hand and slapped the mule's rump. "Bye, Mrs. Kendrick—I mean Troy. Always think of you-all as Kendricks."

Leon set his face and did not speak as his mother turned the wagon over the corner of a bed of zinnias and walked the mule down the carriageway, through the orchard to the main road. Sarah watched until they were out of sight. When she moved, she discovered that her hands were clenched. Going to her office, she opened a box in a desk drawer and took out a silver dollar. She found Mabella in the kitchen and gave her the money.

"What for, missy?" The girl lifted her eyes from the coin to stare at the back of her retreating mistress. Shaking her head, she said, "Never understand white folks if I lives to be a hundred and twenty."

Josephine cuffed her on the shoulder. "Won't live to twenty if you don't get the lumps out of them potatoes. You're done playing mammy."

Bessie and Leon did not talk during the journey to the Marsh farm. They never talked in a merely social way. Indeed, Leon had no experience of such a thing before his stay at Beulah Land, where Negroes as well as whites laced the hours with talk for the sake of talk. When they came to the farm and turned into the back yard, they found Gene Betchley at the well drinking water from the side of the draw bucket. He had just stopped work for the noon dinner Bessie had left boiling on the kitchen stove. He'd leaned his hoe against the side of the well, and his naked back was rivuleted with sweat. The still air held his smell, which Leon decided was like that of the soured wet sawdust he remembered from the mill.

Man and boy stared at each other until Gene dropped the bucket, spilling water and laughing. "If you ain't a pretty thing!" he exclaimed. "Clean as a cloud and stiff as a cake of salt."

Leon hopped down from the wagon and then stepped up on a wheel spoke to reach for the carpetbag.

"What you got there?" Gene asked.

"Help me unharness," Bessie told him.

"I want to see what he's got." Gene snatched the bag out of the boy's arms and opened the top of it, pulling clothes out with mock daintiness. "Fitten for the son of the Pres-i-dent!" he joked before wadding a shirt blouse to wipe sweat from his armpits.

"I'll have to wash and iron it," Bessie complained. "Leave them things alone."

Gene reached into the bag again and brought forth a hand-toy cart. He spun the wheels and ran the cart up his sweat-wet arm as if the arm were a path. Maneuvering the cart playfully around the back of his neck to run it down the other arm, he let it slip and stepped on it with his bare feet. Leon had stood quietly; now he attacked, kicking and butting the man. Gene stepped back and slapped him. Leon fell, muddying his knees where Gene had spilled water on the ground. As he retrieved his broken toy and got up, his mother was saying, "See to the mule like I said."

"Learn him some respect!" Gene commanded.

"You act more like a youngun than him."

"If you don't, I will," Gene threatened.

"Take that bag in," Bessie told Leon, and as he reached for it, his grandmother came out through the kitchen door.

"You back, Bessie, I heard you. You got the boy?"

"I'm here, Gran," Leon said.

"There's a heap of things I want you to do for me," she announced. He went past her into the house and through the kitchen. She followed him. "Want you first to cut me a new toothbrush for my snuff. From that sweet gum. I can't find it, and Bess won't bother. Been doing with plain sticks. Peel the bark and chew the end till it's soft for my old gums. You hear? Where are you?"

"Yes'm, I hear." He had hidden the carpetbag as best he could behind the bed they shared.

Finding him by his voice, she grabbed him close and whispered, "Gene wants me dead."

"Why, what's he done, Gran?"

"May not be able to see, but I feel things." She let him go and sighed. "Lord, sometimes I don't care. Go get my toothbrush, so I can push my snuff proper. Your ma brought me a new can."

19

"You'll be sorry."

"I know," she agreed.

"Never interfere in a marriage," Casey said.

"If there's any hope—"

"Do you believe there is?"

After breakfast with Benjamin, Sarah had returned to her bedroom to talk to Casey as he dressed. She rose at five or six o'clock, depending on the season; he rose at seven-thirty the year round. Casey took her hand and led her to the love seat by the fireplace, where they sat down. The love seat was turned to the room because it was summer; in winter it faced the fire. Folding her fingers, he rubbed the knuckles gently with his lips. It was one of his private endearments that soothed her when she was troubled, but this morning it had no effect.

"You see, Casey, I was doubtful about the alliance, but changed my mind and encouraged it."

"Only because Benjamin wanted it."

"I should have been wiser. I have always been unwise!"

He slapped her hand and dropped it into her lap. "If you're going to criticize yourself, I must leave you. You may abuse anyone else as much as you please."

She kissed his cheek. "You are forever surprising me. I think I can love you no more, and then I do."

"Change your mind."

"No. I *must* speak to her."

He rose from the seat. "If you ask me later why I let you do it, I'll take a stick to you."

"What are you doing today?"

"Starting the painting of Jane." It was something he'd thought of doing while working on the portrait of Frankie Saxon. "I've made a dozen sketches without her guessing why. For a beautiful woman, she has little vanity. She thinks I'm sketching the boys, or the goat they play with."

"When he finds out, Daniel will be your friend forever."

Casey said drily, "Daniel will not, and you know it. He'll always be jealous because I married you."

"Nonsense," she said comfortably. "He adores Jane."

"He adored you first. I haven't forgotten the way he looked at you at Lauretta's wedding."

"All of fifteen years ago."

"I see you don't deny it. I want coffee."

She took his arm as they left the bedroom and started for the dining room. "Eat a real breakfast. Josephine worries about you because she can't fatten you up."

"Coffee and a biscuit will do. I do not hew wood and draw water like you and Benjamin, so I do not require great bowls of grits and platters of meat and eggs."

They paused at Nell's door for Casey to say good morning. Sarah had visited her earlier. Nell shrank under the sheet and smirked. "Bianca has promised to curl my hair. She says everyone who comes will want to come see me."

"And so they will if you let them," Sarah acknowledged.

Casey said, "You'll be the prettiest ninety-seven-year-old woman at the party."

An hour later Sarah and Priscilla were seated alone on the porch of the house at the Glade. At a distance Velma played with Bruce on an old quilt spread in the shade beside the brook. Sarah's eyes went to them often; Priscilla's did not.

Sarah had told her she wanted to talk about family matters. "I apologize to begin," she said. "I know it isn't my business, but it concerns me. Benjamin mentioned at breakfast that you'll not be joining the party tomorrow. Will you tell me why?"

"I thought to spend the day at home."

"At your mother's; you don't mean here," Sarah said to get it clear.

Priscilla nodded with a frown. "Papa has not been well."

"He hasn't been well since the war," Sarah said. "I hope it's nothing new or more serious?" She waited, but Priscilla offered no further comment. "I wish you would talk to me."

"It is you who want to talk to me, Mrs. Troy."

"I do, but I need your help. — You appear to be withdrawing from us. We come to see you, and you used to come to see us, but you haven't for some time. Is there any offense?"

Priscilla hesitated. "I am sorry if you and Jane think so."

"Then why?" The younger woman did not reply, and after a moment Sarah, looking toward the brook, observed, "She is a happy child. We seem to have had her always. Have you noticed that about babies? As soon as they come, they belong to the family."

"As I do not." Priscilla looked startled, as if she'd meant only to think and not say it.

"I wish you did. I think you wanted to be one of us when you married Benjamin. You reminded me of myself. When I was a girl, I came here to visit, and then I fell in love, not just with Leon Kendrick but everyone—most of all with Beulah Land."

Priscilla considered what she had said. "With me it was more a turning away from my family."

"Part of the same thing."

"I have seen that I was unjust and come to understand that my mother is the best woman in the world. She only ever wanted what was best for me."

"I think that is the way she saw it," Sarah said. "Did we fail you?"

Priscilla colored. "Mrs. Troy, is this a conversation we must have?"

"Are you troubled about something you don't altogether understand?" Sarah persisted. "It isn't always easy to talk of intimate matters with one's mother. Sometimes an outsider—"

Priscilla shook her head. "It is you and Benjamin who are troubled, not I any longer."

Sarah said, "I know intimacy is not a thing that can be asked for. Forgive me if I seem to do that, but—have you never enjoyed 'the night side' of marriage?"

"Can any woman?" Priscilla answered coldly.

"I for one of many."

"I have God's love. Benjamin's love is the devil's."

"I won't argue God and the devil with you, but you are wrong."

Priscilla looked about them. "This place you call the Glade has always seemed to have something evil and cursed about it, as if terrible things happened here in days gone by. Have you never felt that?"

"I love it as I love Beulah Land," Sarah said simply.

"I hate it," Priscilla said evenly, "as I hate Beulah Land."

Sarah struggled to control herself. "It must be a hateful life for you then, to live here and not feel one of us."

"I accept it as my punishment."

"Is it not also a punishment for your husband?"

"If it is, so be it. I am the Lord's servant and instrument. I cannot question His wisdom."

"There was a time you questioned the wisdom of your mother."

"I was wrong, and I have suffered for it. I shall endure what I must, but not debauchery."

Sarah's eyes stung with outrage and pity. She got up to leave. "I'm sorry. I beg your pardon for coming today."

Priscilla's voice stopped her at the steps. "You made the Marsh bastard welcome at Beulah Land."

Sarah turned in surprise. "Benjamin's *son*. You knew about him before his birth, long before your marriage. You cannot accuse anyone of deceiving you."

"Where that child is welcome, I cannot be. They say in the kitchen that he comes tomorrow."

"Yes."

Sarah went down the steps and only waved to Bruce and Velma before taking the path down the hill. She found Otis where the fields met her back yards. He was stretching wire over the pit a younger man had dug for the barbecuing. Otis was Beulah Land born and had lived there, slave and free, his whole life. He and his twin sister Lotus had been among the first pupils in the cabin school Sarah started at Beulah Land when she was a young wife but not yet the plantation mistress. Lotus had married Floyd and died soon after giving birth to Abraham. Sarah talked to Otis a little now of his preparations for tomorrow, and he showed her the wood he had cured to make the right kind of ash for barbecuing the meats. She felt better by the time she continued to the house.

Leon was looking forward to tomorrow, but he did not talk of it except to Granny Marsh, lest he be forbidden at the last to go. He had been ridiculed by his mother as well as Eugene Betchley for the manners he'd adopted at Beulah Land, and he had found that life was easier if he pretended to be unchanged from the old days. That he was different he knew, but he understood that he must not show it. Only to Granny Marsh did he speak of the plantation. She did not always listen, but now and then she would ask a question, usually about food.

As he watched the cow graze and she sat on a log with the cow's halter rope around her ankle, they speculated on the food there would be tomorrow. When he quizzed her about looping the rope so, she told him Gene had taught her to do it. "Said I was good for nothing, but I can tend this old cow so she don't stray. If she gets wandery, I know by the tug."

"Davy doesn't remember," Leon said, "but he says he does. Bobby Lee remembers last year, though. He says there'll be barbecue, pig and goat. They've a man, Otis; he watches the meat all night while it cooks slow. Josephine is to make something called Brunswick Stew."

"I've had Brunswick Stew," the old woman said. "It's got corn and tomatoes and okry and butter beans in it, and ham and chicken shredded fine with the fingers so you don't hardly know what you're eating. Brunswick Stew can be good."

"Yes'm," Leon agreed, although he'd never tasted it. "There'll be fried chicken on top of the barbecue. Pickles and beets and roasting ears. A washtub of potato salad! Mabella's making that, she told me." He paused to marvel. "Watermelons cooled in the creek, all kinds of pies and cakes. Chocolate and lemon and peach and blackberry. Devil's food cake and angel's food cake. Funny names."

They sat on the log together thinking of the good things he might expect to see until Granny Marsh said conspiratorially, "They good to you there?"

"Yes'm."

"Tell you what you do. Ask Miss Sarah to let you bring me some Brunswick Stew. None of the barbecue, for I can't hold it; it pure turns my belly to knives. But I bet if you ask her, Miss Sarah will let you have some Brunswick Stew in a quart jar for me. Say it's your notion; don't tell her I put you up to it."

"All right, Gran."

"Now go get me a toothbrush.. I've wore this'n out." She showed him the old one he'd cut for her, blackened with snuff and hard use.

20

Every soul on Beulah Land woke to the scent of the peppery, vinegary sauce Otis had developed over the years and with which he basted the slow-cooking meats through the night. Otis himself would smell of the stuff for a week after his vigil; so pervaded were his senses as well as his clothes, he could neither smell nor taste it, and it was by guess and gumption that he applied it from the end of a stick swathed in rags.

Whereas Annabel Saxon's dinner party at the end of every April was as welcome as weevils in the cotton, Sarah's annual celebration of family ties on the Fourth of July elicited good-tempered expectations. The horses trotted more eagerly, it was said, and the wheels of the carriages spun more speedily toward Beulah Land than they ever did toward the banker's house in Highboro. They came from country and town, and Sarah's notions of family were generous—Annabel said ridiculous. Everyone in the county who could make a claim to a connection with Beulah Land would put himself forward in the hope of an invitation, and Sarah had a hospitable heart. She even asked the Oglethorpe family, but they always refused her.

From Elk Institute came the teachers black and white, led by Roman and Selma and Pauline. Roscoe Elk would come too, this year bringing bashful Claribell and bold Luck. Annabel shared the sectional feeling about separation of the races socially, but this was a family affair, and the land where the school stood had once been her family's plantation. Most of the guests would eat standing; it was important that black and white not sit down together. And besides, Roscoe was rich; and wasn't she herself the chief patron of his school? She chose to look on the presence of Negroes as a compliment to herself, and told everyone so, in just the way Sarah had counted on her doing.

From the Todd farm, which everyone except the Todds considered still a part of Beulah Land, came Daniel and Jane with Robert E. Lee and Jefferson Davis running ahead of them. Doreen Davis arrived early with her friend Eloise Kilmer, who was by now declared to be an honorary aunt. Before closing the door on their house in Highboro they would have kissed all their cats, admonishing them to be good (especially Toby) and promising them tidbits of goat on their return. From Highboro too came entire families, all tied together and allied to Beulah Land: Annabel and Blair Saxon; Blair II and his wife Prudence with their daughters Belle and Anna; Bonard and Frankie with son Blair III and daughter Fanny; and James Davis with his wife Maggie and their three daughters, Cora and Beatrice and Rebecca. Counting the servants these brought and the occasional house guest who had lingered beyond a planned stay, they would all together number seventy or eighty.

The only vehicle that rolled against the general tide that day was the buggy bearing Priscilla Davis to her mother's house in town. Benjamin had watched her go, agreeing that he would not expect her home until the next noon. As soon as she left, he threw Bruce into the air, kissed her when he caught her, handed her to Velma, and mounted his horse. Riding to the Marsh farm, he found Leon ready and waiting on the gray, splintery porch that looked the same as when Benjamin had taken Bessie for buggy rides the year before he married. Old Mrs. Marsh was with her grandson, who had dressed in blouse and trousers made by Dorothea during his stay at Beulah Land. Bessie and Eugene were out of sight, she in the kitchen, he in the barn. Benjamin got down from his horse to pay courtesies to Mrs. Marsh, but he did not tarry when he saw Leon's nervousness. The boy would not look at him; his old shyness had returned, causing a renewal of Benjamin's. As they said goodbye, the grandmother whispered a reminder to the boy that he understood; and after setting Leon on the horse in front of the saddle, Benjamin mounted again. When they were on the main road out of sight of the house, Benjamin halted a moment in the shade of a tree. "You all right, boy?"

"Yes, sir," Leon said without turning his head.

Benjamin's arms tightened around him in a hug that had nothing to do with managing the reins. He felt his son relax against him, and they rode on to Beulah Land. "Bobby Lee's been practicing. Says he can beat you at marbles now."

"Maybe so," Leon said. "Maybe not." For no reason they could have explained, they laughed together, easier.

First they went to the Glade, which Leon had never seen, and Benjamin walked with him over the place, happy with his exclamations of discovery, remembering how it had appeared to him when he was a boy, although, in truth, his feelings about it had never changed. Freda had gone ahead with Zadok and the rest of her family, and when Benjamin called Velma to bring Bruce, the four went down the hill. Approaching the big house, they observed the orderly hurrying about of all who were part of that day, whether as servant or host or guest, and the roles were often blurred. Sarah was everywhere. Casey fussed quietly with his camera on the shady side of the porch; he would record much of the scene in photographs. Bianca had spread a light counterpane of exquisite crochet on the invalid's bed and was heating tongs on the chimney of an oil lamp to curl Nell's hair. Nell watched her with lips pursed critically.

They had begun to arrive before ten o'clock, Zebra managing the traffic and assigning a place to every carriage and wagon and buggy. Two stableboys stood by him to unhitch horses and mules for those who had not brought their own servants. Josephine commanded the kitchen, and by eight o'clock Mabella had cried twice, once when Josephine slapped her and again when she praised her potato salad. However, between them they marshaled the wives and daughters of the field hands into a staff of workers and runners. Even the smallest girls were employed to wave palmetto fronds over platters of food to keep flies from lighting.

The long porch around three sides of the big house was always thronged, though guests continually wandered in and out of doors. In the house several rooms had been prepared for the use of the party, two where the females might rest when they felt like withdrawing; two for the children and their mammies, well stocked with beds and pallet rolls and a variety of chamber pots.

There was a smoking room for the men if they chose to come in from the sunshine, but one of Sarah's few house rules was that no one might chew tobacco under her roof.

As soon as she arrived Annabel paid a duty call on Nell, as did everyone during the morning. They had never liked each other, Nell considering Annabel a vain, overbearing woman, and not slow to say so. Today Nell observed that Annabel's neck was beginning to look like a lizard's. Annabel countered by remarking that she certainly hadn't expected to find the old lady alive another Fourth of July. Satisfied that they had drawn blood, each turned her attention to others. Sarah and Annabel too were old adversaries and would have a few shots to sling at each other as the day progressed, but a balance was usually struck between them, and they knew pretty well how far to go and when to stop, each enjoying the illusion that she saw through the other like spring water.

"I do love an old-fashioned country party," Annabel said benignly. "Everything slapdash and no trouble to the mistress."

Sarah, who had worked early and late for a week, observed obliquely, "Doesn't Maggie look young?" She knew that Annabel found any compliment to her sister-in-law irritating. Annabel considered that Maggie had twice betrayed their girlhood friendship, by marrying her brother James and by conniving to get Prudence, the daughter of her first marriage, married to the elder Saxon son.

Sidling toward them at the sound of her name, Maggie Davis said with gushing insincerity, "Miss Sarah, you are a walking angel and everybody says so."

Annabel yanked the sleeve of Maggie's dress to suggest that it required adjustment. "Voile doesn't suit the Junoesque figure," she pronounced.

"James likes the feel of it," Maggie said with twinkling rancor. "The sense of touch is so important to the blind."

Sarah said mildly to Annabel, "What's that you're wearing?"

"Pongee. It's new."

"Is it?" Sarah said with unflattering surprise. She studied the material briefly. "Well, it's better out here in the sun. Indoors it made you look yellow as a Chinaman."

Maggie laughed heartily and ambled away. Watching her go, Annabel said, "She must weigh two hundred pounds."

"Maybe James likes the feel of it," Sarah said.

Blair Senior, Blair Junior, Bonard, and James were discussing business, that of both the bank and the sawmill. Benjamin joined them under the oak tree where they stood watching two Negro men set up trestle tables to accommodate the vast quantities of food being prepared in the kitchen. The talk went to predictions of crop yields, and from that to more general predictions for the future of the family, the county, the state of Georgia, the South, the country, and the world. They alternated the grim and the hopeful until Bonard told the first dirty joke of the day. He had a talent for collecting and telling them, and never repeated himself. As one led to another and they became dirtier, the men drifted automatically away from the main party, until they were joined by other men and some of the older, bolder boys who were attracted by their frequent laughter. They decided during a pause to make their ritual inspection of the livestock and nearer fields. All men were supposed to be knowledgeable about such things, although none on the present occasion, not even Benjamin, knew as much of what they were pretending to examine as Sarah did. For the most part, men talked to men and women to women, but there was considerable mingling too, as affections and disaffections eased and sharpened.

The women talked ailments and remedies, servants and food, children and the old, fashions and flower gardens. Each knew the prejudices and vanities of every other. Compliments and barbs were exchanged about "my begonia" and "your crepe myrtle." Flat contradictions were followed by warm statements of support. Jane said that she found used tea leaves good for the top of fern pots, and Prudence begged anyone to advise her how to rid her yellow rose bushes of lice. The prompt answers ranged from applying vinegar and tobacco juice to picking them off by hand. Frankie, absently fingering the lace at her throat, was remembering the hour she'd spent yesterday with Benjamin in the wood they had gone to their first time together and once or twice a week since. When they appeared to be waiting for a comment from her, she sighed and said everyone knew she was a Savannah girl and couldn't grow jimsonweeds. Miss Kilmer, smoothing her shirtwaist, reminded them of the trouble she had with her garden because: "The dear kitties *will* go marauding."

"Drown them," Annabel suggested, and when the cat lover gasped, added placatingly, "You know I don't mean it, Miss Kilmer, but you'll admit you let those creatures do too much as they please. You'll wind up having no garden at all."

"My sweet peas have never been better than this year," Miss Kilmer announced with more acid in her voice than anyone had ever heard. Sarah frequently made the comment to Casey that Annabel brought out the worst in people.

Annabel yawned and smiled, and as Sarah joined the group, she challenged her with "Auntie Sarah, everyone admires my pongee. Take a look at Frankie in this light. Isn't she a wonder? I declare she is the image of me when I was her age. Everyone says so. It's like having my youth again. I vow you'll have been sorry many a time for letting her slip through your fingers! I thank the stars Bonard had the wit to steal such a treasure from under your grandson's eyes! You may say I fancy it, but I mark an even rosier glow on her these last few weeks. You see how happy Bonard makes her. Isn't it so, my dear?"

"Indeed, ma'am," Frankie agreed demurely.

Annabel considered her remarks a double scoring, for not only had Benjamin and Frankie been very near marrying; at the same time Sarah had violently opposed an attempt of Annabel's to marry Jane to Bonard. Continuing the attack, she said, "I don't much approve your allowing Bessie Marsh's youngun here among us."

Sarah said, "Both his father and I wanted him. He is one of the family, and you may as well get used to him, Annabel, because he'll be with us in future whenever we can manage it."

"You see how wise you were to avoid such a marriage," Annabel said to Frankie as if the others were not there. She sniffed. "I don't wonder that Priscilla chose not to come today."

"She's with her father," Sarah said. "He is ill."

Annabel shook her head as one who knows better. "That union isn't turning out well, is it? And to think 'twas I who put Ben up to it."

Sarah said, "You must allow something to free choice."

"Law yes, but these things are always a matter of suggestion, and it was I who put it into his head or he'd never have thought of her. She wasn't the sort of girl a young man like Ben looked at, nor the other young men thought of marrying. I remember his laughing when I told him how good she'd be for him. Ah well, one of my rare pieces of bad advice."

"I can think of hundreds," Sarah said, "although I don't allow that it was bad in this instance."

"You don't mind my talking so, surely? We're all family here, and you can say what you like to family." Annabel smiled good-naturedly, satisfied that she had avenged the pongee.

Sitting with Nell, Doreen, who had no gift for light society, asked if she would like to hear a hymn. Nell said she would not, but Doreen obliged anyway with verse and two choruses of "Beautiful Isle of Somewhere." Doreen had a strong voice for praying which she enjoyed exercising, but an unreliable one for melody. Nell pretended to go to sleep, and then went to sleep, but when she was ready to leave her, Doreen shook her awake and begged earnestly, "When you get to heaven, Aunt Nell, ask God what He's done with Pharaoh, and when He tells you, find him and say I'll join him in the sweet by-and-by."

"Who is Pharaoh?" Nell asked.

"My beloved horse the Yankees killed. Don't you remember?"

"Yes," Nell said softly. "I'd forgotten, but now I remember that day."

The children, with country space at their disposal, ran free, although their gossiping mammies kept watch over them, ready to attend at the first sound of crying. There was little trouble, however. Davy dropped a curly leaf from a tomato plant down the neck of Anna Saxon's dress and told her it was a spider. Anna squawled, refusing to sit on the ground the rest of the day and promising Davy that if he came near her again, she'd bite him. Blair III stepped on a pretty piece of blue glass, cutting his big toe in a new-moon arc, the scar from which would be with him until he died. He cried a little, because it bled copiously, and was bandaged and petted by his mammy until inactivity bored him, whereupon he quickly mastered the trick of hopping and even running on one set of toes and the other heel.

The plantation carpenter, a man called Scudder, had set up two extra swings, a seesaw, and what they called a spinning jenny, which had nothing to do with spinning cotton but was a center-balanced, center-fixed thick board that could be pushed in a circle at moderate speed carrying at each end a child who weighed about the same as his partner on the other end. If the weights of the two children differed, then the lighter passenger kept to the far end of his side while the heavier sat closer to the center. The problem was in stopping once speed had been achieved, and a child had to be nimble to find the ground with his feet before he landed with a hard bump. The daughters of James and Maggie Davis were twelve, thirteen, and fourteen and would not on other than a family occasion be playing with the smaller children. When they kept the contraption to themselves for what he considered too long a time, Bobby Lee told them it was his and Leon's turn to ride. Rebecca pushed Bobby Lee over backward when he tried to unseat her, whereupon Leon struck her on the arm with both fists. As she set up a wail, her sister Beatrice told Leon he was a bastard, because she'd heard her papa tell her mama so. Bobby Lee, recovering his legs, shoved Beatrice one way and Rebecca another, although they were each three times his weight and double his height. Cora, the eldest of the three sisters, kicked Leon on the behind when he tried to push the spinning jenny around. Fanny Saxon and Luck Elk, who had been chummily sharing a swing seat a little distance away, left it and joined the battle on the side of the boys, simply because it looked to be Big against Little. Davy, who had been watching the proceedings with growing outrage, began to butt everyone his head could reach without regard to the target's being friend or foe. As the clamor grew, mammies came running, and the combatants were soon pulled apart and shaken or hugged, depending upon the disciplinary technique favored by the several women.

It was a happy day. Sarah called Doreen to ask God's blessing on the gathered family before they began to eat. Then as everyone moved and milled about the trestle tables under the trees, they said how good everything looked and then how good everything tasted. Gaiety gave way to sober appreciation, and when the largest mouth and the greediest eye had been filled to surfeit, a quiet time followed. The women withdrew to their resting rooms, and the children were bedded down in theirs, most of them on floor pallets, because children always preferred them to beds for their novelty and because they allowed more scope for mischief. For a while they giggled and nudged each other and changed places and accused each other of breaking wind, and then they went to sleep.

The men and bigger boys wandered into the woods, and when they came to the old Kendrick swimming place on the creek, they propped their backs against stumps or slumped under the trees, and most of them slept. Eventually, when all were again awake, they undressed and swam, only the Negro men not going into the water when Benjamin urged everyone to "come on in." Late afternoon, they trooped back to the big house bearing on their shoulders long, stripy watermelons they had cooled in the creek.

The women had revived and found new energy for conversation, although the topics of discussion were unchanged. Reconciled to waking as they had been to sleeping, the children played. Although they protested that they were not, all were ready to eat again, this time of the red, sweet, mealy flesh of the melons, and to spit the black seeds playfully at each other as they swatted flies and cursed mosquitoes. Now and then they managed to sit quite still as Casey made more photographs. Thus the day's party drew to a close; but its end was accomplished gradually. Horses and mules had to be hitched, hands had to be shaken and promises made in answer to a hundred requests to "come see us soon." And Sarah and Josephine had to fill plates and baskets with left-over food and press them on departing guests for their supper when they arrived home. Last to go was Benjamin, taking Leon to the Marsh farm with a quart jar of Brunswick Stew in a hamper that included barbecued pig and cucumber pickles and three kinds of cake. As man and boy rode slowly along the darkening way, they sang "Yankee Doodle," not because it was the Fourth of July, but because the words amused them. ". . . stuck a feather in his cap and called it macaroni!"

21

From the dignity of the messenger and the bowed heads of their mistresses the cats concluded that gravity was in order and composed themselves in a semicircle, looking as glum as deacons. "Something must have told me," Doreen said to Eloise. "I'm so glad I sang her a hymn. Do you reckon she's had time to get her bearings and give my message to Pharaoh?"

Brought the same news on the same morning, Annabel Saxon burst into tears and abandoned the breakfast table, leaving her husband to stare as he went off to open the bank and to marvel that there was never any knowing another human heart.

Two women who shared the same mile of earth died on July 4, 1879, both called old, although Mrs. Marsh of Marsh Farm was half the age of Nell Kendrick of Beulah Land. Their circumstances at death could hardly have been more different, the one cherished by family, the other despised; yet the subject of food, indeed of the very same dish, was by no remarkable coincidence near the mind of each in her ultimate hour.

Through the window Nell Kendrick saw Benjamin ride away with Leon in front of his saddle, and then she went to sleep. It had been a long, satisfying day. She had spoken pleasantly to everyone (except Annabel) who stopped to render respect. She had eaten with enjoyment—too much, it was true, but that had been her way. After the clamorous day, silence and peace settled over Beulah Land with the coming of night. There was only an occasional murmur of gossiping voices and tired laughter as servants cleared house and yards of the marks of family celebration.

She woke a scant hour before midnight to hear Bianca snoring on the floor pallet beside her bed. She thought of throwing her bedside Bible at her, but belched gently and closed her eyes, remembering the taste of Brunswick Stew. And so she sighed and died. Her death was not discovered until Sarah entered the room at five-thirty the following morning.

Mrs. Marsh's end was less gentle and occurred a dozen hours earlier.

She had tied the cow's rope to her left ankle and was sitting on the edge of a copse at the side of the cornfield. There wasn't much grass, and the cow had several times turned to the standing corn. Although nearly blind, the woman was alert, and she yanked the cow every time she tried to pull toward the corn. Woman and cow were annoyed with each other, the one wanting the corn leaves and the other to sit quietly and think about Brunswick Stew. — Would the boy remember? If he didn't, would Miss Sarah not think of it anyway? She was a kinder woman than most and had been thoughtful of them in their past need. It was getting on for dinnertime and she was hungry; she'd mash her peas and pot liquor together so they'd go down easier.

Eugene Betchley approached the copse carrying a live frog in his hand. He had first thought only to play a trick, knowing the cow's skittishness; but then it occurred to him that more than laughter might be got from his fooling. Mrs. Marsh's ears were sharp enough to hear his hard feet crunching the stiff earth rows as he came along. "That you, Bessie?" she said. There was no answer, and she was suddenly alarmed. "Bessie?" she called. When there was still no answer but the sound of footsteps coming on, she screamed for her daughter. "Bessie! Where are you?" She froze, her nose having told her who was there.

Eugene set the frog on the dry grass before the cow. The frog leaped. The cow shied. The frog leaped again; the cow bucked. Eugene yelled and slapped her hard on the flanks, and she went running, dragging the woman into the cornfield. Eugene picked up a rock and followed, coming to the cow, which had slowed to take a few corn leaves, their underside rougher than her tongue. The dazed woman was trying to untie the rope as it dragged her, but before she could manage it, Eugene struck, bashing in the side of her head.

When the dinner of boiled peas and corn bread was ready and the sun told her it was noon or nigh, Bessie stepped from the kitchen to the back yard and rang the rusted hand bell that had been used all her life to summon anyone at work in the fields. Eugene joined her presently after stopping at the well to slop water down his throat and over his hands, which he wiped on the bib of his overalls. Bessie thought briefly of her mother when he came in, but she thought of her only as being late, and no one at the Marsh farm waited for anyone else when food was on the table. With a shrug she sat down opposite Eugene and filled her plate after he'd served himself.

Both ate heartily, but when Eugene made as if to empty the last of the peas on the last of his crumbled corn bread, Bessie said, "Save that spoonful for Ma. She mightn't have heard the bell." She knew by the mockery in his eyes that something had happened and jerked the pea bowl away from him. "Where is she?"

Tilting the chair back to balance on two legs, he sucked his teeth and studied her face. "Ain't it nice, us here by ourselves?"

She rose and clutched him by the hair of the head. "Tell me."

"Don't do that!" He struck her hand away and stood up. "In the field," he said sullenly. "Cow dragged her, looks like."

"You seen her and left her?"

"Might have been sleeping for all I knowed. I wasn't that close."

"Where?"

"Cornfield, by that clump of sassafras. — Hey!"

Bessie was running, Eugene after her. When they came to the place, the cow was eating contentedly, disregarding the body of Mrs. Marsh, who lay on her back, blood drying darkly where it matted her gray hair, her eyes sightlessly open to the hot sky.

Bessie saw and understood. She wouldn't look at the man, for to do so would have made her his accomplice. She was afraid of him, but she knew she must protect him.

Eugene said, "Musta been sleeping to let the cow do her thataway. Way it happened, I spect. I'll take her on to the house."

"You sure she's dead?" Bessie asked unnecessarily.

Eugene squatted and examined the head, eager now to cooperate. "Oh yeah. She's gone, all right." He untied the rope that bound her ankle. "Never should have done that. Not much good to herself and none to nobody else. Have to think on it that way, like she's better off and so are we. I'll fetch her home. You bring the cow." Bessie took the rope from him when he handed it to her. He lifted the worn, soiled body to its lifeless legs and held it to look at the lolling head before slinging it up into his arms. "Heavier than she looks." Bessie followed with the cow.

After bathing her and putting a clean dress on her, Bessie laid her on the bed she'd shared with Leon, throwing a sheet over her to keep flies and gnats off. Eugene walked to the country church a half mile away and brought back the preacher's wife, Miss Ona, who said she'd sit with the corpse so they could finish the day's work. Bessie and Eugene returned to the fields, coming in at sundown to send Miss Ona home with word for Reverend Paul that he could do the burying in the morning and they'd be there early to dig the grave.

Bessie and Eugene had eaten a supper of flour hoecake and fried fatback by the time Benjamin arrived with Leon. In a flat voice Bessie told them that Mrs. Marsh "got killed by letting the old cow drag her." She'd seen it happen from a distance, she related, but when she got there, it was too late. Leon confirmed Eugene's remark that Mrs. Marsh was in the habit of tying the rope to her ankle. Seeing Benjamin touch their son with concern, Bessie glared. "If you hadn't been off having a good time today, you could have saved her."

Leon's eyes owned the truth of it.

"You want to see her? I got her laid out and ready."

She led them in and turned the sheet back from the face. After she explained when and where the burying was to be, Benjamin said he would bring a coffin from town.

Bessie accepted without thanking: "She'd appreciate that." She covered the face and led them to the porch, where they found Eugene lifting the cloth on the hamper. "What you got there?"

Eugene handed her the hamper.

Bessie looked over the things under the cloth. "Pity we've eat. Well, won't none of it go to waste, will it, Gene?"

"Sure won't," Eugene said, picking up the fruit jar of Brunswick Stew and uncapping it to sniff.

"That's Gran's!" Leon said sharply.

Eugene smiled at him dolefully.

"Don't you take it bad," Bessie warned Leon, and then put herself in Benjamin's way when he moved a step toward the boy. "You go along," she said. "We'll expect you early as you can make it in the morning."

The funerals were as different as the lives and deaths of the two women.

Mrs. Marsh was put down in earth as hard as her lot had been. The rural church with its dozen splintery benches was on a hill that afforded no tree, no flower, not even a weed or blade of grass. The ground was dead, and summer had baked it as if it were clay. Sarah had planned to go but could not with Nell's funeral to settle, so Benjamin and Zadok arrived at the Marsh farm soon after eight o'clock, having roused the storekeeper in Highboro at six-thirty to sell a coffin. Watching them carry it to their wagon, he told them it was good luck for a coffin to be his first sale of the day.

Bessie waited impatiently and offered no refreshment. The long summer days, she said, were not long enough for all there was to do. Eugene was in the fields; he would not go with them. Benjamin and Zadok carried the coffin into the house, where Bessie helped them to load it and return it to the wagon. Then Leon sat between Bessie and Benjamin, who drove, while Zadok knelt in the body of the wagon, his hands steadying the coffin over the bumpy road to the church. Benjamin and Zadok dug the grave, and the others waited, blind in the sun. Miss Ona tried to lead them in singing, but gave it up after shrilling solo through all the choruses, which she prided herself on knowing, of "In the Sweet By-and-By." Reverend Paul, when the grave was ready and the sweating men who'd dug it stood aside, lifted his hands and bowed his head. In a voice that begged without hope and threatened without power, he consigned body to earth and soul to heaven. The ceremony was as bleak as its setting. Throughout it Bessie farted quietly, having eaten largely of the Brunswick Stew the night before on top of her early supper. Benjamin and Zadok filled in the grave, and nobody cried. Benjamin gave Reverend Paul a dollar before they left.

The funeral of Nell Kendrick was the next morning at St. Thomas's in Highboro. The church would not hold all who came, and those unable to enter waited in the graveyard to witness the burial. There was good singing from the choir and bad from Eloise Kilmer and Doreen Davis, each trying to keep her companion to the pitch and failing, like panicked swimmers drowning one another. There were two long readings from the Bible in addition to the words of the burial service, which the Reverend Horace Quarterman intoned with soaring awareness of the magnitude of occasion and congregation. Nell, had she not been dead, would have slept through it.

There was no weeping on the main floor, but upstairs in the section reserved for the Negroes of Beulah Land, there was. Mabella's familiar wail rose high. Josephine itched to give her a slap. In truth, Josephine grieved more than any, perhaps, except Sarah. When Josephine, who had been head laundress, became cook at Beulah Land on the death of Lotus, Nell complained that her biscuits tasted of soap; but that had been at the beginning of Josephine's reign in the kitchen. They had long since been each other's admirer, Josephine loving Nell for her appetite—what cook can altogether resist greed? — and Nell loving Josephine for her unfailing ability to satisfy both appetite and greed. Josephine would never again wake with the certainty she'd enjoyed in Nell's lifetime of how *necessary* she was; and to be needed is all.

Downstairs, Sarah's mind wandered. She came out of a study aware of the smell of the old hymnals. They had endured all weathers, and even in this driest heat of midsummer conveyed a memory of the chill of December devotions and wet Sundays in February. Heavy on the air too was the smell of flowers mingling with the too sweet scent of face powder. For a moment Sarah, knowing where she was, could not remember why she was there.

She brought herself back to the present moment. *Aunt Nell.*

Sarah smiled. Beside her, as if he followed her thought, Casey smiled and squeezed her hand. Sarah loved Nell Kendrick and would love her as long as memory held, but she understood that Nell had not been, nor wanted to be, a lovable woman. She was selfish, first to last. She'd lived entirely to suit herself insofar as she could. She had lied to herself about almost everything and everyone around her. She saw no fault in the people she approved, no virtue in those she disapproved. By denying love to her husband, Felix Kendrick, she had denied him the children he wanted and turned him into something of a libertine; and she had done it all persuaded that she loved him. But Sarah would not forget that when Felix became ill, Nell nursed him day and night until danger of death was over; nor would she forget it was Nell who insisted, since Felix could not, that every penny they possessed go to saving Beulah Land when it was threatened with bankruptcy; nor that it was Nell who, begging and praying, had tried to save Lotus and Nancy from being raped by the Union soldiers, and that when she could not, she had hidden Jane from them. Nor would she forget Nell's dedication to besting Annabel. How she would miss her old ally there! And beyond these reasonable claims on love and memory, there was the further one, the all but incredible yet undeniable fact that perfect selfishness such as Nell's not infrequently generates the purest affection.

There was singing again; it was nearly over. Then brief silence and general rustle told Sarah the church service had ended. She took Casey's arm, and they walked up the long center aisle, followed by Benjamin and Priscilla, and then by Jane and Daniel and the Todd boys. In the graveyard there was another prayer, and the coffin was lowered into the ground—"by my beloved Felix, only not too close," as she had wanted it.

They turned away with that quick release of tension all ceremonies produce. Voices rose cheerfully, filling the bright July morning.

"The last of her generation—"

"A great lady—"

"A loss to us all—"

"Her fine Christian spirit—"

"Too bad she couldn't live to be a hundred."

Again Sarah smiled as she and Casey waited for those who wanted to speak the words they'd saved until now. There was little that anyone could regret in Nell's death, and so the suggestion was made a number of times that it would have been fitting had she lived to be an even hundred. It was like Southern hospitality, Sarah thought: no one allowed to go home without its being said that his stay had been too short.

Here was Annabel at last, touching her handkerchief to the oily sweat of her chin. "Well, Auntie Sarah," she said brightly, "with Aunt Nell dead, you become the family elder."

Among the attendants and witnesses was one who did not deplore the brevity of Nell's earthly exile. Ann Oglethorpe, attended by husband Philip and daughter Elizabeth, took her turn before Sarah. "I pray the Lord to forgive her greed and snatch her from the flames in time." She turned away, leaving daughter and husband to bow and smile amends.

Shortly after, as Sarah accepted the more conventional comfortings of others, she saw Priscilla leave Benjamin to join her mother; and the two walked soberly among the graves with their heads close. Elizabeth left her father standing statue-lone among the carved tombstones and went to Jane's side, where she was immediately joined by Thomas Cooper, the only one of Jane's old beaux still a bachelor. Benjamin was with Frankie and Bonard. Bonard's usual flush deepened as he began to laugh and then to cough, lighting a cigar. Frankie ignored him to look at Benjamin as if, Sarah suddenly realized, she owned both of them. Was Jane right that there was something between them now? Annabel commanded the attention of James and the ebullient Maggie, whose cheer was undimmed by the occasion. Nell's maid Bianca was at the graveside watching the filling in. Casey caught Sarah's eye; it was enough to induce him to move off to Bianca, who had no special friend among the other house women at Beulah Land. She had served Nell all of her adult life and was considered "stuck-up."

The last consolation acknowledged and the graveyard empty of all save family, Sarah went to Casey and Bianca. Casey was saying, "She looked very pretty, Bianca, our thanks to you."

Tears trembled on the old one's eyelids, slipping into the wrinkles of her cheeks. "What's to become of me?"

"You're to do as you please," Sarah told her. "If there's anything of Aunt Nell's you'd like to have, except her jewelry, which she said was to be Miss Jane's—"

"I want her clothes," Bianca said promptly.

"They're yours."

"And her walking cane?"

"Yours too."

"Can I have her bed?"

Sarah hesitated only briefly. "Everything in her room will be moved to your cabin. I'll tell Wally this evening to attend to it."

Bianca nodded with satisfaction. "I want to see Josephine's face when she finds out."

22

Sarah was not a patient woman, but she made herself wait more than a week before going to see Bessie. It was a busy time at Beulah Land anyhow. With the corn being harvested, everything bent to seasonal expedience. Fodder was pulled when the corn was mature but the leaves still green. These were stripped from the stalk, twisted, and hung on a standing ear, later to be gathered and tied together with a strong green leaf before being loaded into wagons. It was hot dirty work for the men. Their arms and backs ached; and sometimes their hands, used though they were to rough labor, bled from the cutting leaves. When the corn was harvested, the cotton would be ready for picking and ginning. The picking was easy on hands, hard on knees and backs. Taking the cotton to gin was like a holiday after the long weeks of toil that had gone before. The house women were busy too, pickling and preserving and drying the fruit and vegetables from orchard and garden.

But beyond these occupations and preoccupations of the day was Sarah's resolve to have Leon at Beulah Land, if she could. She and Benjamin talked about it, and when he continued to put the natural question "How?" she could only say she didn't know how, but means would be discovered. On a Sunday afternoon when others were sleeping or wishing it was Monday, and others were loving and wishing Monday would never come, she hitched her buggy and drove off to see Bessie. She had no plan; she trusted to luck, and luck, as sometimes happened, was with her. She found Bessie alone in her kitchen boiling tomatoes to put up for the winter. They were already overcooked, Sarah noted on entering, and the kitchen was steamy. At Bessie's invitation Sarah set a straight chair on the back porch outside the door so that they might talk while Bessie watched the tomatoes.

"Smell of these things has brought every fly in the county," Bessie declared.

Casual interchange established after opening amenities, it was easy enough for Sarah to express regret at not having been able to come when Mrs. Marsh died, and for Bessie to say she'd wanted to go to Mrs. Nell Kendrick's funeral—"but there was just no way, ma'am."

Sarah agreed. "Both coming together like that. Strange it should happen so."

"The ways of the Lord." Bessie shook her head.

"Mm."

"Still, I don't know," Bessie tempered, "both of them being so old. Mrs. Nell was rich old, and Ma was poor old, and that evens their ages, you might say. In numbers Ma wasn't as old as you, Miss Sarah, but she was wore out. Hadn't happened the cow dragging her, it'd been something else. She was ready."

Although the tomato odor was so strong as to be stench by now, Sarah said, "Don't they taste good in the winter? Open a jar and whatever you've got on hand becomes a meal."

"Yes'm," Bessie said curtly, with a cook's concentration as she tested the consistency of the tomatoes. "Now."

"Let me help you." Sarah left her chair, and the two women worked quickly with a dozen scalded jars. They did not talk at all until they were done, by which time Sarah as well as Bessie had sweated through her clothes.

"I'm going to leave everything to clean up later," Bessie said. "Got to get out of this kitchen." So saying, she led them through the kitchen doorway, carrying a straight chair in either hand. In the back yard she set them under the leafy chinaberry tree near the well. Upending the dried-out draw bucket to dislodge a cluster of dead chinaberries, Bessie dropped it into the well with a clatter and a bang, letting it sink and cool before giving it more rope and drawing water from the coldest depth. She offered the first dipper to Sarah, who drank it gratefully. Bessie then drank two dipperfuls, wiped her mouth on her apron, and joined Sarah in the shade.

"Where's Eugene?" Sarah asked, building upon their work intimacy.

Bessie laughed. "*Eugene* sounds like somebody I don't know, but *Gene* is in the woods with his traps. Not your woods, ma'am, I hasten to add. Him and old Crawford still like to seine for fish and kill animals."

Sarah nodded absently, as if all men did and she understood it to be so. "Is Leon off with them?"

"Oh, no'm. Leon don't go. Not that Gene ever asked him to, but Leon wouldn't step on a moth if it was a gold piece. Don't know where Leon got to, actual fact. Since Ma died, he's broody, roots around by hisself ofttimes. Thought first he was up to boy mischief, but I reckon he's too young for it, if they ever be." Bessie winked at her guest.

Sarah made herself smile. "Jane's boys are always asking for him, wanting him to come spend the day."

"I spect he misses them too," Bessie admitted. "No younguns near here to play with."

"Set him on the road one morning to catch a ride over," Sarah suggested. "Lot of wagons back and forth from now to November. We'll take care of him and send him back safe and sound, as we've done before."

Acknowledging this reminder of favors done, Bessie said, "No fear you wouldn't. He was fat as a pumpkin after staying with y'all that time."

"I'll take him today if he wants to come," Sarah offered.

"Reckon not," Bessie responded drily. "Another time maybe."

Knowing that most women enjoy gossiping about themselves and that Bessie had few opportunities, Sarah took a deliberate chance. "What are you intending about Gene?"

Bessie frowned. "Don't know how you mean." Before Sarah could admit defeat and get up and go, Bessie said, "Yes, I do. Well, I've got kind of a problem." Sarah waited, not daring to look encouraging. "Thisaway: put a man and woman together and you-know-what is going to happen, no matter their ages. I reckon anybody can figure that far. Ma used to say he coveted the farm. Maybe he did, but it's not only that. Sometimes he's more man than I want on the place, and others he's like a youngun I must take care of. I know how to manage him, and he's been good, sure enough has." She sighed impatiently. "I got to make up my mind. He's after me to let's get married. — I'd find it hard to tell another woman, but you know the past and won't blame me: I'm going to have his youngun by the end of the year."

Sarah could have shouted, she could have sung, but she put on a sympathetic frown as she appeared to consider the problem. "You're in something of a fix."

"Yes, ma'am." Bessie tried to smile and grimaced instead. "One youngun the wrong side of the cover is enough for a woman. Another and I'd be done in this county. Every man with the itch would be scratching hisself at my door thinking I had to let him in."

There followed a contest of silences. Sarah let hers lengthen almost to rejection before commenting, "Maybe marrying is best." A moment later she added, "We did what we could, Bessie, but I never thought it was enough."

"I didn't expect you to dance for joy and hitch me to your grandson. As for him, another might have denied the whole thing."

"If you marry Gene," Sarah said, "you won't lose us as friends; I promise you that." She paused, knowing that she must take the next step boldly or not at all. "You've never been anywhere, Bessie, except Highboro. That's everywhere to us in the county but nowhere to the rest of the world. How would you like to go to Savannah and you and Gene get married there?"

"Leave my farm?" Bessie looked alarmed. "I never slept a night away from it my whole life."

"I don't mean for good," Sarah amended. "I said it wrong. I mean like taking yourselves a wedding trip."

"You're talking like we're rich, Miss Sarah. Gene has made a difference on the farm, but we're just getting by and barely." Sarah waited, and the words came that she wanted Bessie to say. "It's a pretty notion though."

Sarah had seen excitement behind Bessie's surprise, if only for a moment. She spoke firmly. "You must make up your mind to marry Gene or not; but if you do, I'll give you and him fifty dollars to make a trip to Savannah for your wedding."

"Who'd look after things here? Leon couldn't go with us."

"You wouldn't want him either, a time like that. I'll send Otis to take care of your stock. He's the best of our older men. He can sleep in the barn, or if you don't want him to, he can come back and forth every day."

Bessie laughed and declared with more truth than she knew, "You got it all figured out!"

"Something to think about." Sarah knew better than to press. The idea had been given and accepted and she knew it. She rose from her chair. "I've about dried out, but I must smell of tomatoes. Better get home to Mr. Troy before he wonders if I went to join the gypsies."

Bessie followed her to the shaded horse and buggy. "You been a help, Miss Sarah, as always."

Sarah adjusted the bridle and straightened the reins. When left to stand where there were flies, her horse was a head shaker and tail switcher. Climbing into the buggy with her back to Bessie, she observed as if it were an afterthought, "Leon can stay with us while you're gone—if you decide you want to go. Jane's boys will be glad to have him." She took up the reins.

As the horse maneuvered the buggy across the shallow depression between yard and road, Bessie called, "Did you mean that fifty dollars, Miss Sarah?"

"I did."

23

Cant notwithstanding, it is as wholesome to eavesdrop as it is unnatural not to; and if the talk is about oneself, it may also provide instruction in survival. Leon had been asleep for an hour when his mother's voice and Eugene Betchley's laughter from the kitchen woke him. They were talking about Beulah Land and Sarah Troy. He knew she had been to the farm that afternoon; his mother had teased him at supper for missing her visit by going to the creek. He did not very much enjoy swimming by himself, but he did so every day because he knew that Eugene had never learned how and resented his doing it. He would do anything to aggravate Eugene, including calling him Eugene instead of Gene, which he preferred. He was drowsing again when he heard his name spoken. A few minutes later Eugene came into the bedroom with his mother, and their low voices indicated that they believed him asleep on the bed he used to share with his grandmother.

"You know you don't come in here," Bessie said.

"That was before I heard about my youngun. — Fifty dollars! Never expected a Kendrick to pay me for my fucking."

"Better go."

"He's asleep."

"She's not a Kendrick, she's Troy. Before that, Kendrick; and before that, I don't recall her family name."

"Don't matter," Eugene said. "Females are whatever their menfolk are. Like you'll be Bessie Betchley."

"Haven't said, have I?"

"You better, after I've give my back to this farm—"

"Give your front somewheres else, didn't you?"

He snickered with her.

Leon's eyes were closed and his back was to them, but presently his mother said, "Now stop it and go to your bed in the barn."

"Not unless you come with me."

"I like my own."

"You like mine sometimes," he wooed her.

"I'm tired and got things to think about."

"You got nothing to think about," he said, "except fifty dollars and my baby in your belly. — She's a fool giving us fifty dollars now because she didn't do right when you had *him*."

Leon lay rigid under the coarse gray sheet.

"She's not giving fifty dollars to us; she's giving it to me."

"I still don't know how come."

"Him."

"Him?"

Leon figured them to be looking at him. He wanted to turn over or rub one foot with the other, but made himself lie still.

Bessie said, "Looks like Ben ain't going to have any boys he can call his. Makes Leon special to them, don't you see?"

"That little dirt dauber," Eugene said in exasperation. "You tell me—"

Bessie yawned loudly. "You go to bed like I said."

"If they're willing to give fifty dollars to keep him for us to go to Savannah, how much you reckon they'd give to keep him forever?"

"I'm not giving him to them," Bessie said.

"I didn't say give. How much would they pay?"

After a moment Bessie said tersely, "Good much, I expect, and you can forget about it."

"It's something to wonder. No need to spring the trap yet, is there? Wait for them to come beg. Of course, if old Ben put another youngun into that Sunday girl he's married to, it might turn out a boy and they'd stop wanting this'n."

"I said forget it and go on to your room."

"I got a right here now we're to marry."

"You got no rights I don't give."

"I'm going nowhere."

No one spoke until Bessie whispered, "He'll wake up."

"He's just a youngun."

"I don't care, I don't want him hearing us."

"Maybe he'll learn something. Has to find out somehow. Way I did hearing Ma and Pa. Remember waking my brother up to listen, and he tried to do it to me between the legs."

"Sh. I don't think he's asleep." His mother's whisper was betrayal, and he hated her even more when she continued in a coaxing tone, "Leon, are you awake?" There was a sound of cloth ripping. "Look what you done."

"Take it off."

"Won't you go like I said, honey?"

"No."

"I wish you would."

"Naw, you don't."

"Yes, I do," she crooned coyly.

Leon longed to be a grown man. He would kill them both.

Eugene murmured, "I like knowing my sprout is in here. Let's wake him up." Bessie giggled and was quiet. Then she drew her breath hard, and Leon heard bed motion and knew what they were doing. He wanted to holler at them to stop, but he began to cry, keeping as quiet as he could. By then it wouldn't have mattered to them if they'd known he was awake.

24

With a nod to propriety, but mainly for her own convenience, Bessie March married Eugene Betchley the day before they were to travel together to Savannah. Having long and sometimes bitterly considered the subject of marriage, Bessie viewed it now only as a thing to get done. On the last Sunday of September, between hot noon dinner and cold evening supper, the couple went by wagon to Preacher Paul's country church. The only witnesses were Leon, Sarah and Casey Troy, and the preacher's wife, Ona.

Eugene did not want his father and brother, and Bessie did not want anyone at all; but she could not bar Miss Ona, and Sarah had insisted upon being present with Leon. Bessie would not allow Casey to photograph them because her pregnancy showed, but said he might pose them at the station before they boarded the train, if he was intent on it, and she would hold her cloak in front of her.

After the ceremony, which was as plain as the funeral of Mrs. Marsh, Sarah asked if Leon might go to Beulah Land with her and Casey. Bessie said that tomorrow was soon enough. Sarah had not yet given her the money; until it was in her hand she would withhold the boy. He wasn't, however, obliged to hear the raptures of the wedding night, for there were none. When Eugene reached for her as his by right, she slapped him away, declaring that she had no intention of getting sweaty again after her bath. She had not bathed for the wedding, but as soon as supper was over, she filled a washtub on the kitchen floor and sent Leon out of the house. She then took off her clothes and scrubbed herself. When she was done, she ordered Eugene to wash himself in the same water and then to pour the dirty mess over the bare floor, which, she said, needed a douse as much as he did.

The three rose early next morning, and Otis arrived on foot before they'd finished breakfast. Sarah had sent him over the week before to learn his duties. It had been settled that he would stay at the farm while they were away, sleeping in the barn. Bessie had agreed to the arrangement reluctantly and only because she was afraid lightning would strike in her absence and burn everything down. Eugene thought he would like being able to say in Savannah that they "had a nigger on the place tending to things." By eight o'clock they were dressed in their best for traveling, and Bessie packed their other clothes in the carpetbag Sarah had given Leon. Leon put his own things into a basket to carry to Beulah Land.

Eugene hitched mule to wagon, and off they rode in silence. Otis had nothing to say, for Benjamin had warned him that Mr. Betchley and his bride might be uneasy with colored people. Leon was content to think of Beulah Land. To be sure of two weeks there was like a promise of life everlasting. Bessie and Eugene were mute with anticipation of their train journey and determination not to bend before the Negro man. Eugene drove the wagon, Bessie beside him. Otis sat with Leon behind them on the floor of the wagon.

Dreaming of tomorrow and tomorrow, Leon became aware that Otis was studying him in a friendly way. He smiled. "How've you been, Uncle Otis?"

"Tolerable," Otis replied. "How 'bout you?"

"Tolerable, I thank you."

His eyes on the child's face, Otis said with artless admiration, "You sure remind me of Mister."

Leon's finger went to his lips in a silencing gesture.

"Oh-oh." Otis was chastened for only a moment before he smiled again. Smile broadened to laughter without sound. Infected, the boy copied him. "You mawking me!" Otis accused. Man and boy shook their shoulders and rocked on their haunches with conspiratorial laughter as the two in front of them sat stiff as fence posts.

They arrived at the station long before the train was due, but Sarah and Casey were there before them, as was a substantial representation of the families of the town and county. A modest crowd was a feature of the hour before train time twice a day in Highboro. Even if no letter, no visitor, no returning relative was expected, it was thought that someone should be there to observe and to relay what he had seen. If the crowd this morning was larger than usual, it was because word had spread of an additional diversion that might be expected, and of Sarah Troy's part in it. Eugene had told Alf Crawford, who had told everyone else. The day was fair; the mood of those promenading cheerful and curious. The only frown was that of Brian Sullivan, who had enjoyed the favors of Bessie Marsh in exchange for shopping credit. He came out of his groceries-and-dry-goods store to glower and shake his head and to ask what the world was coming to when pigs were encouraged to fly. It happened that the only one in earshot was an idling Negro woman, who looked startled at being so addressed but laughed heartily to show her agreeableness. Mr. Sullivan retreated to his barrels of flour and bolts of calico, leaving events to go forward as they would.

On the station platform Sarah's eyebrows lifted as she recognized the carpetbag, but she greeted Bessie and Eugene with the kind of brisk kindness she used to keep a distance between herself and people she did not care about but was determined to treat fairly. Casey presented train tickets to Eugene, who put them into his pocket and bowed as importantly as a senator. Benjamin appeared to congratulate the couple, not on their marriage, which might have seemed tactless, but on their imminent journey, which he was certain they would enjoy, recommending particular sights to their attention and the names of eating houses that had given him satisfaction in the past. Summoned by Bessie, Otis returned to the platform to promise again to honor the instructions given him many times over concerning the farm and the care of its creatures. When he had done, Sarah told him he might go back to the farm with mule and wagon. — If Mrs. Betchley had no further errand or use for them? Bessie allowed that she had not, and Otis went his way with a sigh of relief.

Against her instincts, which were always to relieve and reassure, Sarah waited deliberately until Casey had posed the nervous couple and taken their photograph. By then a number of the strollers and idlers had paused on the platform to observe the central group. Sarah decided that was the moment to open her reticule and bring out the rolled bills she had counted when she took them from her office desk. With no reticence, as if she were merely an honest woman paying a debt, she said, "Here you are, Bessie Betchley. I said I'd give you fifty dollars, and I'm going to. I assure you *these* greenbacks are good as gold. Hold out your hand."

Bessie did so, as matter-of-fact as the donor. Of those watching, none watched more closely than Eugene Betchley. "Ten, twenty," Sarah counted, "thirty, thirty-five, forty, forty-five, forty-six, forty-seven, forty-eight, forty-nine, fifty dollars. Just as I promised. Do you want to count it back to me, or are you satisfied?"

"I counted with you," Bessie confirmed, "and I didn't miss, though I never counted so high since I learned in school."

The little crowd laughed with the appreciation they might accord a sally by a favorite in a play, which encouraged Eugene to guffaw with sheer pride in having a wife who, although old, had brought him a farm and fifty dollars.

Annabel Saxon and her two daughters-in-law had been parading the platform awaiting the train they expected would bring them letters. They paused now as Annabel proclaimed archly to Sarah, "Some fools and their money are soon parted."

"While others and theirs are never cleft," Sarah replied in a parody of archness. Prudence giggled; Frankie smiled.

Annabel shook her head as if at so many gnats, saying to Bessie, "There are wicked people in Savannah ready to snatch the purses of ignorant country folk."

"They'll not snatch mine, Mrs. Saxon, for I shall sew it to my dress every morning with stout thread."

"See that you spend your dowry wisely," Annabel advised.

"A dollar is as slow leaving my hand as it is coming to it."

There were titters from the nearer women.

"That's all I have to say to you, Bessie Marsh."

"Betchley now," Bessie corrected her.

"To be sure," Annabel agreed, "and not too soon either." She stared at Bessie's belly before turning to Leon, who stood between his mother and Sarah Troy. "You, boy. Will you be known to us hence as Leon Betchley and call him"—she nodded toward Eugene—"Pa?"

Sarah opened her mouth to protest, but before she found words, Frankie Saxon said, "You forget the boy has a papa; haven't you, Leon?"

"So he has," Benjamin said, emerging from the background where discretion had drawn him after his earlier words to the couple.

Far from feeling embarrassed, Leon was glad to hear himself acknowledged publicly. Nor had he been shamed at the notion of being bought and sold; it was rather as if his freedom had been paid for. The exchange of money demonstrated that he had a value in all their eyes, and when the whistle sounded, it seemed the most natural thing in the world for Benjamin to lift his son to his shoulder to watch the train come in.

Although it had long been part of their lives, no one considered that the train had become common. They came every day to look

at it as they might marvel at any other wonderful thing, except that the train was unique in being personal to each of them. There was always the possibility, however unlikely, of its bringing a message from the bigger world, an item of wear or amusement with one's name on it to indicate that far away it had been so intended. Those not leaving or arriving, nor there to say hail or farewell to others, yet felt that another time might find them the object of the conductor's attention, the focal point of eyes on both sides of the train windows. Steam hissed, to vanish in air; pistons churned and the great wheels slowed. Tomorrow or next week any of them might step up and aboard, to step down again in the great world of Savannah, and from there go anywhere.

When the train stopped, passengers and mail and barrels of goods were given up and collected. Casey Troy helped to settle the Betchleys in their seats, and Leon stared through the window as if an ocean now divided him from them. The train started again with a creaking of iron and a leaking of water. Sarah Troy moved with it along the platform and waved; so did others. Those on the train, all strangers now and united, waved back; and then it was gone, leaving the crowd lonely for it, without reason to linger, and so they dispersed. (Perhaps another morning would bring, since this one had not, the waited word, the gift from the world yonder to surprise and delight one alone and particular.)

"Let's go home," Sarah said with satisfaction.

25

Mabella was at the door when the family group returned from Highboro, Sarah and Casey in their buggy, Benjamin trotting his horse alongside them, Leon in front of the saddle. With arms wide and a royal curtsy, Mabella welcomed her favorite; but as he slid down the horse's side and acknowledged her greeting, Jose-

phine appeared to tell her to get her uppity butt back to the kitchen. Sarah commended Josephine with a nod, because she wanted the boy's stay at Beulah Land to be treated as a normal occurrence, not an event for celebration. For the same reason Benjamin went to his house in the Glade to take his noon meal, and Jane had warned her sons to stay at home until Leon came to find them. However, an Indian raid could not have prevented Mabella's making Leon a chocolate pie, because she knew he preferred it to all other desserts. It was perfect, with thick, black chocolate and an egg meringue so high and golden it made Josephine's eyes narrow, particularly as Mabella had made a secret of it and chose to present it immediately after Josephine had brought into the dining room her own offering of walnut cake. Setting it before him, Mabella whispered to Leon to share it with no one. Noting by his expression that he was disposed to follow her advice, Sarah cut a quarter of it for him and set the remainder on a shelf of the screened food safe for him to request as he pleased, which he was to do at the end of supper that evening and again before he went to bed, when he drank two glasses of milk. He took the last quarter at breakfast after consuming a piece of fried steak, three biscuits, and a helping of grits and gravy. He was like his father in more than the facial resemblance Otis had remarked.

When he went to see Bobby Lee and Davy after noon dinner, they took him around to show him how everything had changed since he'd been there. That was four weeks ago to spend a couple of hours while his mother drove the wagon to town and back. Paths will waver, however slightly. Flowers fade or come on new. Last month's frying-sized chicken, having escaped the skillet, flutters to the fence to practice his crowing. Everything on a farm grows or dies; nothing is constant. Bobby Lee knew two new riddles, but before Leon could try to guess them, Davy told him the answers. One thing had not altered. The weather was still sunny and hot, and the three boys and their two fathers enjoyed a swim in the creek toward the end of the day. Returning to the big house, they discovered Jane and Sarah in rocking chairs on the shady side of the porch.

Watching them approach, Jane lifted her voice to them. "Dan, have you noticed how Leon has grown since the Fourth of July?"

Daniel, who hadn't, said agreeably, "Sure has."

"Haven't I grown?" Bobby Lee wanted to know.

"Maybe," Jane said. "I see you so much I don't notice."

"How about me?" Davy pled.

"No bigger than a flea," Sarah said.

"I'm going to Savannah a whole month by myself," Bobby Lee threatened, "and when I come back home, I'll be a foot taller, I bet you, and you'll say, 'Hooee, look how big he is now!' "

Davy hissed derisively.

Sarah said, "I'll hear no nos; everyone is staying for supper. Josephine, not me, says so. There's no going against her when she makes up her mind. That includes you, Benjamin; and I want you to insist on Priscilla's coming down too. You tell her I want her specially."

"She won't come," Benjamin said.

"Try her."

"I'll go help you persuade her," Jane offered.

"All right."

As the two set off, Davy said he wanted to go, and Bobby Lee ran to join them with his brother. Compelled to look around, Benjamin found Leon gazing at him, so he said, "Come on, boy." The brother and sister and their children disappeared into the shadows of trees that followed the old trail up to the Glade.

Daniel came and sat down beside Sarah. After a moment he said, "It's like old times. Remember Aunt Nell and her rocking chair?" She smiled. "I wonder if God kept a record of her number of rocks; must have been a million or two." They rocked to and fro with no further exchange until Casey came out on the porch and surprised them. Their heads were almost hidden by the high backs of the chairs. He tiptoed behind Sarah's and caught it at the height of its rock. Pulling it to him, he kissed her on top of the head. When she turned her face to him, he exclaimed, "Good gracious me, I thought you were Jane!"

Daniel whipped his chair around and started to rise, only to find Casey laughing at him. Resuming his seat, he said, "You're only funning, Casey."

Casey said to Sarah, "I'm going to show it tonight. Yes, madam. Months in the doing, it is finally done."

"Casey!"

"That's why I put Josephine up to the party."

"I wondered what got into her. She loves a party more than ants do, but never thinks one up. You've been secret about it."

"Sneaky as a hound sucking eggs," he admitted.

Sarah smiled in anticipation. "You like it."

Casey nodded. "I finished it two weeks ago; I've even varnished and framed it. But I was waiting for things to settle down."

"Why didn't you tell me?"

"You wouldn't have let me wait, and I wasn't having people traipse in for a glance one at a time, between the cotton picking and the wood chopping and the hog slopping and the chicken feeding. No, sir and ma'am. It is to be unveiled. It is covered with a sheet at this minute, safe from chance intruders."

"What the devil are you carrying on about?" Daniel asked mildly. "Some kind of picture?"

Casey said, "One that will have you bowing your head and wiping your eyes and blowing your nose."

Daniel grunted. "Picture of somebody with a bad cold."

Casey said, "Why, you're funning, Dan."

At the same time Priscilla too was being surprised on her porch, but less happily. Velma was out by the brook with the baby after bathing and dressing her to show her off to her father when he returned from his day's work. As the walkers from Beulah Land came up the hill, Benjamin took the child from Velma and kissed her chest through her muslin frock to make her laugh. Then he squatted so that the boys might see her. Jane went on to the porch, joining Priscilla.

"She smells like vanilla," Bobby Lee volunteered.

"Milk," Davy said.

"You want to hold Bruce?" Benjamin asked Leon.

Leon poked out his arms as if they were to be loaded with stove wood for the kitchen fires. Benjamin gave his daughter to his son. Bruce lifted fat fingers to investigate the face she did not know.

Velma said flatteringly, "Never see her do that with nobody; did you, Mister Ben?"

"Milk," Davy repeated decisively.

Priscilla called sharply from the porch, "Benjamin! Give that baby back to Velma!"

Velma looked to Benjamin, and when he nodded, took Bruce from Leon, who looked relieved.

"She don't smell as bad as most babies," Bobby Lee said to Davy. "You smell your own lip."

"*Sour* milk," Davy insisted.

Benjamin left them. As he stepped up to the porch, Priscilla was saying to Jane, "The last several Sundays after church Betty stops to talk to you, and when she does, Tom Cooper comes and joins in. Mama wants to know what they talk about—if there's something peculiar about it."

"How could there be?" Jane said coolly. "They've always known each other."

"She means special and particular."

"I can't say as to that."

"It wouldn't be suitable."

"You mean because he's older?" Jane smiled. "He was one of my beaux before I married, but not a very earnest one, and that doesn't make him elderly."

"He's a farmer," Priscilla said. "Mama doesn't want to lose Elizabeth."

"His farm is little further from town than ours."

"It would break her heart to have us both living in the country."

"It hasn't anything to do with me, has it?" Jane pointed out.

"If you would watch her and let me know what you think—"

Jane said shortly, "I shall not do that."

"Elizabeth is young and unsteady—"

"Think what you're suggesting," Jane said.

"Mama is anxious," Priscilla said, "and asked me to ask you."

"She'd do better to ask Betty."

"She's done so, but she doesn't trust her to tell the truth."

"Then she shouldn't trust me either." Jane looked to Benjamin for help, only to see that he was looking to her the same way, wanting her to present their grandmother's invitation. Welcoming the deflection, she said, "I came up with Ben because Grandma wants all of us to have supper tonight with her and Casey. Especially you. It's a family party, a family evening."

Priscilla laughed uncertainly. "I couldn't even sit down before one of Josephine's gargantuan meals. It's been so hot again today."

"I want you to come," Benjamin said.

"I'm sure you do," Priscilla said blandly. She hesitated, as if considering going for Jane's sake. "Better not. Freda has already—she wouldn't like it, I know."

"I'll speak to Freda," Benjamin said.

"I know how well you manage her, but don't," Priscilla said, "for I'm not going with you." Priscilla shifted her eyes from them to the children at the brookside. "Your boys are surely—oh, look. The big one pushed the little one in."

"Bobby Lee!" Jane called. "You stop that, you hear, or I'll make you learn the names of the books of the Old Testament by next Sunday."

Priscilla said, "Is it wise to use the Bible as a threat?"

"It's the only way I can get him to mind," Jane said unrepentantly. "He hates it worse than washing his feet before bedtime. — Davy! Are you wet?"

Velma answered for him. "Just his legs. I felt him and the rest of him is dry as a pine cone."

"Change your mind," Jane coaxed. "You don't have to change your clothes. Look at me wearing what I had on."

Priscilla said, "Mrs. Troy must excuse me from the welcome for her visitor. I'm surprised you approve him as a playfellow to your children."

Jane made herself smile. "They like him as much as they do each other. Perhaps more."

"Why won't you come?" Benjamin said to his wife.

She looked directly at him. "You know good and well."

Pretending not to notice the bitterness in Priscilla's voice, Jane smiled again and strolled away to the brook.

Priscilla said, "Take that boy out of my sight. How dared you bring him up here?" Benjamin continued to look at her a moment longer before leaving the porch to rejoin the group below. Priscilla picked up the sewing basket she had set on the floor when Jane came. Then she turned her chair deliberately so that it faced away from the visitors.

26

Daniel's head was bowed, his eyes wet. He then did what they would later say was an extraordinary thing. He went to Casey and embraced him. Everyone applauded. Although he himself had come to Beulah Land a Union deserter in the last year of the war, he had resented Casey as an outsider Yankee and grudged Casey's admission to Beulah Land as Sarah's husband; and he had been jealous of every man Sarah or Jane smiled upon.

Casey was a clever and accurate portraitist, and sometimes more, but all were agreed that his painting of Jane was his finest work. It realized every feature; no finger or eyebrow was in question, not the angle of an elbow wrong. It showed the blooming beauty of the woman, and it showed what she was. Her directness and calm were there, her humor, her capacity for love, her strength that could occasionally become impatience and pride. There too were shadows of the past, acknowledged but not allowed to predominate.

So, when the normally reserved and distrustful Daniel Todd, seeing the portrait for the first time, was surprised into making his feelings known, Casey thought that he had never had a better compliment to his work, or one harder earned.

"I wish," Sarah said to Benjamin, "Priscilla had come."

"You think people alter, given the right impulse at the right moment." Benjamin shook his head.

She considered him. "You don't seem unhappy."

"No."

She looked a question, but he offered no answer.

It was a happy evening. They ate heartily of the supper Josephine and Mabella set before them, and talk ran free, from recent harvesting to speculation on next year's prices, from the day's town gossip to family stories, most of which were known to all except Leon. Funny incidents and grim times were recalled, and every one was true, or had started so and still retained basic truth, whatever shading the teller imposed. The lighter recollections were not favored over the dark; all had a place in the family heart, and there seemed nothing incongruous in remembering the hunger at the end of the war as they enjoyed the present rewards of their labors.

After supper Jane went to the piano and played for the others to sing, and when she complained of their being lackadaisical about it, they blamed Josephine for feeding them too well, and gave their attention to the albums of photographs Casey brought out to show them, one leading to another and taking them back to the wedding pictures of Sarah's sister Lauretta to the Union Colonel Varnedoe. That had been in 1865. They paused longest over the collection of family poses Casey had made on each January first after his marriage to Sarah.

They went back to the portrait; they could not have enough of it. Even Jane, in whom there was little of Narcissus, stared long at it, coming to her own terms with what had been set down of her. There is no face stranger than one's own.

When Davy began to doze, Bobby Lee kicked his foot. Josephine came to ask if everyone wasn't hungry again, and everyone said no; but Mabella followed immediately with a cake tray and teapot and a pitcher of milk for the boys. It was then Leon enjoyed the third quarter of his chocolate pie. Bobby Lee and Davy watched him soberly as they swallowed more walnut cake. They weren't resentful of his not offering them a share; they understood each other's rights and ownership. Davy began to yawn again when he finished the cake, and Jane said they would be heading home, but no one got up to go until Mabella returned to say a last good night and to announce that she had never seen such a moon as was in the sky and she wished they would all go out and look at it.

They did so and praised her for bringing it to their attention. They'd never known such moonlight, and wondered why it was so bright and if it *meant* anything, and lost themselves in admiration of it. "It's not even full," Benjamin commented.

"As near as nevermind," Sarah decided. "It's the harvest moon, the same every year, only we forget and it surprises us."

They went their ways at last, Casey promising Daniel he'd deliver the portrait tomorrow morning after he doubled the wire on the frame. He wanted to hang it himself when they decided where it was to go. Daniel carried a son on either shoulder, for they claimed they were unable to walk a step. Jane declared they were simply lazy and administered a couple of slaps to their behinds to let them know that was the end of indulgence for the night. When Sarah kissed Leon and told him to go to bed, he shook hands formally with Casey and Benjamin. Sarah had settled him in the room that had been Nell's. All her furniture had gone to Bianca's cabin and the room had been refurnished with a piece borrowed from here and another subtracted from there. Nothing at Beulah Land was thrown away, merely shifted or set aside until someone discovered a new use for it. The room was already being called Leon's. His clothes and toys were there, and Sarah and Benjamin had decided in brief consultation to take him to town tomorrow to buy him new ones.

Benjamin took his leave, and Sarah and Casey went to their room, where they would dawdle over undressing in order to savor the evening again by recounting bits of it to each other. Benjamin was tired but not sleepy. He lingered in the side yard enjoying the cool night until one of the barn cats ran past him, making him start. As if that were a signal, he turned toward the Glade. He had gone only a few steps when he heard Leon's voice. "Good night, sir." Benjamin went to a window to find the boy leaning on the ledge. "I blew my lamp out and got in bed," Leon began to explain, and got no further.

"You're not hungry, are you?" Benjamin asked.

"No, sir," Leon said, and they both laughed. In spite of the brightness of the night Leon could not see Benjamin's face clearly because it was toward him, away from the moon. That made it easier for him to say, "Can I go with you tomorrow?"

"Where?"

"Anywhere."

"I don't know what I'll be doing."

"I won't get in the way."

"Are you sure you hadn't rather play?"

"I can play with Davy and Bobby Lee any time."

"All right."

Benjamin started to say more and then thought he'd better not. Instead he said, "Go to bed now. I get up early."

"I'll be ready."

Benjamin turned away, hesitated, and turned back once more. "Good night, son."

"Good night, Pa."

Leon rose early next morning, as he was to do every morning of his stay at Beulah Land. He woke to the sound of crowing and wings flapping. He saw from his bed by the window the first stretching and yawning of the farm dogs as they set out on tours of the grounds, which darkness and dew had made mysterious and new. When he heard Mabella in the kitchen starting the cooking fires, he dressed to join her, enjoying the sound of her talking to the stove, flattering the wood into catching, scolding the smoke, and adjusting the damper. Josephine allowed herself "not best pleased" to find him in the kitchen a quarter hour later when she arrived to begin her day. Josephine liked a quiet time in the morning, followed by a muttered monologue concerning the flaws in Mabella's character and her shortcomings as a kitchen helper. Instead, she had to listen to Mabella's being appreciated and thanked again for making the chocolate pie. The stove fired, Mabella began to set the table in the dining room for breakfast, Leon following her back and forth as they chattered until Josephine found herself, as she was not slow in telling them, "nearly distracted." Distraction did not, however, keep her from pounding steaks and sifting flour and mixing in lard and beginning to roll dough. When the new milk was brought from the barn, Mabella strained it and set it to cool and then skimmed the cream from last night's milking to churn butter.

Sarah appeared soon after, and when she'd had some words with Josephine and Mabella, she and Leon visited the back yards and the nearer barn, where they found four kittens lapping milk from an old blackened pie tin that had been set down for them. The mules and horses were stamping in their stalls and whisking their tails, as much to announce that they were awake and restless as to discourage flies. The hogs were lined up before the dry troughs of their pen outside the barn grunting metronomically as they waited for the first feeding of the day.

Benjamin met them in the yard, having already spoken to Zadok about the day's work and holloed to Daniel across a field. The three went in to breakfast, ready by then for steak and biscuits, grits and gravy, peach preserves, and for Leon the last of the chocolate pie. After eating, the man and the boy walked to the pasture where Zadok had started three of the men digging postholes for new fencing. When Benjamin continued talking to Zadok, Leon climbed a pear tree to examine a bird's nest and was pleased to find that his fist fitted exactly into its soft deserted cup. When he came down, Benjamin and Zadok were counting in unison as they paced off a section of earth in measuring strides; and then Leon and Benjamin walked down to the lowest, wettest field, where the sugarcane grew. There, half a dozen men were busy cutting it for grinding into juice to make syrup. Benjamin took a knife from his belt and cut off a section of a stalk, stripping away purple rind and notching pieces of the cane, which he and Leon then broke off to chew for the sweet juice.

It was midmorning that they went back to the big house and found Sarah ready to go with them into Highboro. Brian Sullivan was glad to see them, and as he fitted Leon with "the best navy blue all-wool cassimere reefer suit a boy can have," he consoled himself for the loss of favors from the boy's mother by reflecting that he should never, at any rate, have to pay for the clothes of the brat she was carrying in her belly. Let the high and mighty of Beulah Land do that, if it pleased them to acknowledge their transgressions. He sold them two pairs of shoes, two pairs of knee pants, and another suit, a four-piece combination consisting of jacket, two pairs of pants, and matching cap. Their next stop was Mrs. Bascom's candy store, where Leon was allowed to choose peppermint sticks for himself and the Todd boys. Then they went to the post office for mail. Finding no letter from Bessie, they all breathed a sigh of relief.

27

If the first day seemed long with its various events and occupations, the ones that followed were not, for Leon, long enough. He dreaded every nightfall, knowing it brought nearer his return to the poor farm that had been his birthplace. For minutes and even hours he might feel suspended in time and believe the golden days would last forever; but then shadows would lengthen, a bell ring, a voice call him indoors to remind him of time passing, winter coming, his mother's return.

He walked with his father and he rode with him, at first in front of the saddle on Jupiter, then alone on gentle Minerva, the mare Sarah herself rode occasionally and considered suitable for his learning to ride. Every day or two Benjamin and Leon went to see how Otis was getting along. The first time he saw the farm again he was ashamed of it, and of himself for being so. He wouldn't get off Minerva until Benjamin reached up and pulled him down. Even then he would not enter the house, afraid its mean spirit would catch and hold him if he did.

There hadn't been much for Otis to do, so he showed them over the barn for them to see how he had got the loft in order, and mended old hanging harness and chain, and cleaned the stalls of the cow and the mule. The pigs and chickens were thriving, and Leon guessed that Otis fed them more than his mother did.

There were mornings and afternoons with Davy and Bobby Lee, playing marbles and hide-and-go-seek, or merely climbing, skipping, running, falling and pretending to fall, to roll on the ground like the hounds rolling on their backs in loose dirt. They spent an hour one day trying to ride the Todd goats, called simply Billy and Nanny; but those amiable creatures avoided their attempts to sit astride by stepping smartly sideways. When Bobby

Lee finally secured a seat on Billy's back, the goat froze, would not lift hoof or horn despite Bobby Lee's entreaties for him to run. They cut poles and tried to fish in the creek, without luck, and the two older boys blamed Davy's noisiness. Although the days were warm, Leon would during the night wake and pull up the quilt Mabella had thrown loosely over the foot of his bed. One morning there was frost. Everyone protested that it was too early for it, but there it was on fields and pastures until the sun melted it.

Sarah took him with her one afternoon when she paid visits to Roman and Selma and Pauline and Roscoe at Elk Institute. She was surprised to discover Frankie Saxon there on an errand for her mother-in-law and to learn that her daughter Fanny was at Roscoe's house, where she had demanded to be set down to play with Luck. The children, having taken a liking to each other on the Fourth of July at Beulah Land, had confirmed their friendship. Frankie strolled back to Roscoe's house with Sarah and Leon. Leon was at first snubbed by the girls, but they were too curious to be exclusive and before long he was removing the bandage from his thumb to show them how he had pierced it with a fishhook. They vied with each other in admiring shudders while Leon boasted that it hurt only when he washed with soap. After that they chased each other about until Sarah concluded her visit with Roscoe and was ready to go. Although Sarah did not ask Frankie, she found that she and Fanny were accompanying her and Leon to Beulah Land, the two buggies rolling side by side as their occupants called remarks to each other. Benjamin saw them arrive and joined them on the porch for tea.

There were country dances both planned and improvised which entire families attended. If a child grew sleepy, he was laid down on a big bed of the host's house alongside other sleeping children, close as the kernels of an ear of corn by the time mothers and fathers collected them to go home. Sarah and Casey, Benjamin and Jane, even Daniel—all loved dancing. Only Priscilla stayed at home. She used to dance, but said she would no more. The dances were not only for the farming families; townspeople came too, just as country people went to events in town. It was from such a party that Elizabeth Oglethorpe ran away to marry Tom Cooper.

The autumn days were always a time for marrying, and there was usually no reason for a couple to run away, as it was called more romantically than realistically, because the bride and groom's parents were seldom surprised at a union, and by the time it was accomplished had reconciled themselves to it if they could not be enthusiastic. For Elizabeth, though, to run away seemed the best, perhaps the only way. Ann Oglethorpe declared herself against dancing, but so generally accepted and enjoyed was the diversion that she did not forbid it. That she might soon do so, however, was suspected by Elizabeth. There is no mind quicker than a young girl's when she sees her advantage at risk.

Where everyone knew everyone, no chaperon was thought necessary, and when a single girl was not escorted to a dance by a father, mother, brother, or married sister, she went with whoever else was going. Mrs. Oglethorpe was suspicious of this relaxed custom, but on the night of her younger daughter's elopement, she would not have considered that she had reason to fear.

Having invited herself to spend a couple of days at the Glade, Elizabeth proceeded to visit Jane Todd and have herself and Priscilla and Benjamin asked to come back for supper that evening. For once Priscilla did not discourage a social proposal, although she would later blame herself and be blamed for her seeming acquiescence in the affair. In good time and in excellent order—cheerful, clean, combed and brushed—the young Davises and their sister presented themselves at the Todd house, where they were welcomed to a festive supper. It was hardly finished when Tom Cooper appeared, happening, as he said, to be passing. Shortly after, an itinerant fiddler stopped and wondered if his services might be needed, whereupon Elizabeth looked so eager, Daniel told him to wait a while in the yard if he had nothing better to do and they would see. Almost on his heels came another musician with a banjo, and behind him a wagonload of young people who declared merrily that they were looking for a party and had heard there might be frolicking tonight at the Todds'.

If Daniel doubted the spontaneity of developments, still, such things did happen, and one hesitates to question the opportunities of pleasure. Word of such gatherings always spread with mysterious speed, and an hour after supper two wagons and several buggies had brought other friends and neighbors ready for dancing. Hearing sounds of jollification across the few acres that divided her from the Todds, Sarah powdered her face and, taking Casey by one hand and Leon by the other, joined the party. At the first squeak of fiddle and pluck of banjo, Priscilla murmured to Jane that she would slip away and to Benjamin that he was to make himself responsible for Elizabeth for the rest of the evening.

Sarah was not one to assume a grandmotherly pose and superintend the children. She told Leon to find Bobby Lee and Davy, and if he got sleepy to go home and put himself to bed; and when the first set was formed after more casual dancing, she and Casey were ready. Elizabeth Oglethorpe stood up with Tom Cooper and Jane with Daniel, but Jane had to drop out to welcome newcomers, and before she could rejoin Daniel, Elizabeth took her arm and said she must speak to her privately and immediately. More amused than alarmed, thinking no more at issue than the mending of a strap or pinning of a hem, Jane led Elizabeth to her sewing room, where Elizabeth quickly confided her plan for elopement and admitted that she had devised her visit to the Glade for just that purpose, and Tom had plotted the surprise party, putting several young farmers up to arriving in groups and paying fiddler and banjoist to appear as if they were idling by.

However busy her mind during this recital, Jane found herself speechless at its conclusion and could only gape at her guest until she was saved from protesting by Daniel's entering the room. Daniel never lost sight of Jane when they were with others, and he had wondered at her abrupt withdrawal. Jane told him to fetch Tom and Benjamin. This done, two minutes were not gone before the party of five in the sewing room were laughing, if with some nervousness, at the scheming of the young lovers. Daniel was reserved and cautious, but Jane and Benjamin were soon persuaded to lend their support to the event.

Nothing much beyond complicity was asked. Elizabeth and Tom were to go to his father's house, where a preacher already waited to marry them to each other. Benjamin and the Todds were to continue the dancing party as if nothing untoward was happening. When he went home, if he found Priscilla awake, Benjamin was to tell her as little as he could, no more than that Elizabeth was safe and happy and married and that she and her husband would appear before her family as soon as they received word that they were welcome. This agreed, the couple, who were after all eloping merely to what now was to be their permanent home, left by the back way while the others resumed their social roles for the evening. Sarah was aware of something afoot more than tripping to tunes, but after Benjamin turned aside one or two indirect questions, she let him be. The evening ended as all such evenings did, with tired feet, a dozen new crosscurrents of attraction and jealousy, and a chorus of good nights.

Carrying a sleeping Leon in his arms, Benjamin walked back to Beulah Land with Sarah and Casey, and when their good nights had echoed each other, continued alone to the Glade. The house was dark, and he crept into his room without waking his wife and having to provide explanations. Next morning, after having his first coffee in the kitchen with Freda, he knocked at Priscilla's door. She was awake and called permission to enter, thinking it Freda bringing a breakfast tray. It was many months since Benjamin had seen Priscilla in bed in disarray and the sight, perhaps surprisingly in the circumstances, amused him.

"I'm on my way to Grandma's for breakfast," he said, "but you must know that Betty married Tom Cooper last night. They are at his father's, where they plan to live. After you've told Mr. and Mrs. Oglethorpe, they would like to visit you-all and get your blessing. I'll have the buggy ready to take you to town whenever you want it." She could only stare. "You would do well to persuade Mrs. Oglethorpe not to act like a fool for once in her life."

28

It was not in Priscilla's power to heed her husband's advice; nor was she much inclined to urge a course of forgiveness upon her mother. Thoroughly vexed with her sister, she condemned and hanged her a dozen times over as she drove the buggy into Highboro. She considered that Elizabeth, in betraying her trust, had offended against honor and duty; yet what most disturbed Priscilla was her junior's setting herself up as an independent woman. How dared she so presume beyond the state of childhood? Priscilla had, too, an awful suspicion that her sister looked forward to the night side of marriage with no great alarm, indeed with anticipation rather than that apprehension any good woman might be expected to bring to such an occasion. She reminded herself of Elizabeth's unhealthy curiosity. She was no more than ten when the two came upon stray dogs attempting to mate in the public road, and she asked if a boy's thing was anything like that she saw before her. And only a year ago the inconstant creature had confessed to kissing a young man other than the one she had now married and to enjoying the experience. Priscilla had been shocked and disgusted and had said so, since when Elizabeth had kept her own counsel.

Sisters do not always cherish one another with that tender regard society expects in such a relationship. The eight years that separated Priscilla and Elizabeth made for gaps in their interests and attitudes only emphasized by the difference in their natures. Priscilla was a plain, sober woman of twenty-five. Elizabeth was a lively and pretty girl turned seventeen who had refused to take her sister as model. She'd had to survive without much sympathy and encouragement from any of her family. She could hardly remember a day her mother and sister had not scolded her, whatever she did or said, with the hope that she "would soon grow out of it." When at last she began to answer that she did not wish to grow out of being her own self, she was pronounced vain and pert. Her father was not susceptible to the charm of his daughters; however unfair, he would never forgive them for flourishing after his beloved sons had been slain in battle.

Elizabeth might have responded cordially to any young man who wooed her, but so formidable was the reputation of her family, none had ventured to do so before Tom Cooper. Ten years her senior, Tom had put off marrying until he'd helped his father back to prosperity after the lean postwar years. Then one day he saw Elizabeth as if for the first time, fair and waiting to be loved. He was not long in deciding that her family presented no impossible barrier; and Elizabeth soon knew, if they did not, that she had been lucky in attracting the affection of a man superior to the general run in character and every eligibility. Discovering his kindness, she determined not to submit him to the humiliation of begging her hand of her mother. Elopement was dictated not by frivolity but by reason.

At the Oglethorpe house Priscilla presented the few facts of Elizabeth's defection without elaboration or comment. The rage of Mrs. Oglethorpe was initially private, her husband and elder daughter being the rocks upon which it broke. Was ever Christian mother so wickedly served by erring daughter, or wife offered such frail support by husband? She called upon Heaven to witness she was distinguished for misfortune. She expressed gratitude that God did indeed chastise those He loved; but that she might bear her precious burden, she asked for strength. She prayed to know the grace of resignation, but hinted that it might wait until the sinners had been discovered and wrenched apart. Mr. Oglethorpe was to whip both publicly with that instrument customarily reserved for the disciplining of horses. When the poor man lifted one empty sleeve as plea of his inadequacy for the assignment, Mrs. Oglethorpe scorned it as the excuse of an indulgent parent who had never shown proper authority.

Priscilla offered to take her to the Cooper farm.

At the time mother and daughter were making their way thence to accomplish the ends of righteousness, Benjamin Davis was drawing on his trousers for the second time that morning in more cheerful spirits than he had the first.

"A shame to cover that noble behind," Frankie teased him.

Appearing to study the construction of his belt buckle, Benjamin smiled. Slipping the belt around his waist, he said, "What are you up to, visiting Roman's school, making Grandma give you tea at Beulah Land? Leon was saying at breakfast this morning—"

"He is Fanny's hero. She says he can whistle and cross his eyes at the same time." She looked about the little room and laughed. "Bedded in the cotton gin! How have I come to it?"

"The trail is long and winding," he said. She arched her back and stretched her arms, yawning. "By God, Frankie, you are a sight."

"Come and tell me."

Rejoining her on the bed, he held and kissed her as she shifted her body to accommodate them.

"Your shirt is scratchy."

"I'll take it off."

"I must go and so must you. Why do you always dress right after?"

"Because you tell me to!"

"When I don't, you start again. Don't you ever feel: 'enough and done'?"

"No."

"Don't unbutton yourself."

Knowing she meant it, for she turned to reach for a petticoat, he took her and kissed her again. "You want me to tell you how you look?"

Slipping the petticoat over her head and swinging her body to sit on the side of the bed and so rise, she said, "I know how I look. You leave me red, almost raw. I have to use more and more face powder. I'll be known as the snow maiden."

He circled her waist with an arm and kissed her back through the petticoat. "But not the ice maiden."

"Benjamin—"

He let her go.

Standing, she continued to dress herself. "You're certain your man is safe?"

"He asked no questions when I brought the bed and chairs and told him to clean out this space. Nor will he."

"Where are his quarters?"

"They're hardly that. One room where he sleeps and cooks and talks to his cat. Down a flight of rickety stairs and on the other side. You won't see him coming or going, unless there's some danger to us. You're safer with Isaac than with me, I promise you."

"I'm safer with any man than with you; but will he not wonder?" She examined her face in a hand mirror.

"No. You agree this is a good place to meet now that cold weather is coming? It's out of the main way. No one ever thinks of it during the winter."

She nodded and began to dress her hair with quick skill. "I never thought to enjoy it in the morning."

"I wake up hungry for everything—food and work and love."

"Well," she agreed temperately, "it's a practical time of day for us. No one is going to suspect us of infidelities in the morning."

One arm folded across his chest and chin cupped in the hand of the other, he watched her ready herself for the eyes of others. "Frankie, you've saved me."

"Just remember that isn't why I meet you."

"Why do you meet me?"

"That sounds coquettish or begging. No need for you to be either. I meet you because we are loving friends."

"I'm glad to hear the word 'love.' "

"You didn't. I said 'loving' deliberately. How is your famous conscience?"

"Asleep."

"Don't say so; it doesn't please me, and it isn't true."

"Do you want me to complain to you even as we're making love?" She smiled and picked up a cloak. "When we're together, my conscience sleeps."

"And bothers you when we're not," she said with another smile, impatient but helpless.

"What about you?" he asked.

"Benjamin," she said firmly, "no woman who leaves you to rust is worth a twig of my conscience."

Ann Oglethorpe ordered Priscilla to wait in the buggy and

stepped down into the Cooper front yard. It was big and bare of grass or flowers, shaded by three large oaks. Approaching, they had seen Ford Cooper raking leaves and adding them to one of the fires smoldering in the ditch that separated his front yard from the public road.

"Morning, Mrs. Oglethorpe," he said, strolling to meet her.

"Mr. Cooper, put aside your rake and lead me to my daughter, if she is here."

Ford Cooper dropped his rake and left it where it fell, but it was a courteous rather than an obedient gesture. "She is, ma'am. Your daughter and mine since last night. I'm happy to have her and only sorry it happened in a secret way." He lifted his voice. "Mrs. Ben, leave your horse and buggy and come in with your mama. You're both welcome today and any day, though I don't recollect your coming before, even when Mrs. Cooper was alive to receive you." There was in his tone something of warning, not to Priscilla but to her mother, that she must not rely overly on his good manners.

"Thank you, Mr. Cooper," Priscilla answered. "I'll just wait in the buggy."

"As you will. How is your good husband?"

"Tolerable," Priscilla answered coolly.

"Miss Sarah and hers?"

"Well, I believe."

"The Todds well too, I hope."

Mrs. Oglethorpe turned on him impatiently. "Mr. Cooper, it's not a time for your old-fashioned courtesies. You know why I've come. Please take me to Elizabeth at once, or tell her to come out to me. Perhaps that will be best."

"I can only offer you my hospitality," Ford Cooper said slowly. "Elizabeth is my son's wife and not one for me or any other to order: do this, do that. If she wants to see you, I expect she will. I know she does, if you come in the right spirit."

Mrs. Oglethorpe marched past him, across the wide yard, up the steps, across the porch, and through the front doorway without a knock or a call for permission to do so. "Elizabeth! It will do no good to hide from me! I have come to have it out with you and in no mood to—" She paused, finding herself in the living room and face to face with her daughter and Tom Cooper. "Elizabeth, tell me what you have done."

The girl giggled involuntarily. Tom blushed but spoke up clearly. "Elizabeth and I were married last night, Mrs. Oglethorpe. We are husband and wife and ask your blessing. We'd have come to you as soon as we heard we'd be welcome."

Ignoring him, Mrs. Oglethorpe fixed her daughter with a grim look. "Is it so?"

Elizabeth nodded and was breathless when she spoke. "We came straight here from Beulah Land last night. Papa Ford had the preacher waiting, and we were married in five minutes. Then everybody drank a glass of peach nectar, and it was good."

Ford Cooper had followed his guest. "May I offer you a glass of the same, ma'am? It's made by me, and I vouch for everything made or grown by Coopers, father and son."

Mrs. Oglethorpe's eyes had not left Elizabeth. "You are married?"

"Mrs. Tom Cooper," Elizabeth whispered.

"The preacher's name."

"Reverand Bob Stewart."

"Methodist," Mrs. Oglethorpe said as sourly as if he had been a Mohammedan.

"You spent the night here with this man."

"We are married; this is our home," Tom Cooper said.

"You are ruined."

"I am happy, Mama. I wish you'd understand that."

"I will not call you daughter again. Whether you are what you call happy, I do not consider. You have misled, deceived, lied, sinned against your mother and father and sister. We do not forgive you, nor shall we ever. Can you speak of happiness when I tell you that you have broken your father's heart? He will not allow you into the house or speak to you again. He would have come himself to say so but that he is so overcome by the wickedness of your behavior. You may have your clothes, but wait for me to send them to you. Do not come to us now or ever."

29

While it afforded some reward, her visit to the Cooper farm was not an event Mrs. Oglethorpe might reflect upon with unqualified satisfaction. There had not been the guilty cringe or remorseful tear she had anticipated. She considered stopping at Beulah Land. The time of day should find Benjamin Davis out of doors and she could depend upon herself to put Mrs. Todd and Mrs. Troy out of countenance for their negligent chaperonage, at the same time suggesting complicity in her younger daughter's path to perdition. Yet there was ever something unpredictable about the response of Sarah Troy, and she did not want another half success. She would return home to ponder matters.

Doing so, she found Mr. Oglethorpe in the crowded, small room he called his library, in which he kept war mementos and books, letters and journals, and the swords that had belonged to his sons. To have discovered him lost in a book would have ill pleased her. She found him instead so far capable of forgetting their present trouble as to be dozing benignly in front of the modest fire he had made, snug in his worn velvet chair, beard touching his chest, eyes closed, his one hand cradling on his lap the kerchief that had been taken from the corpse of his younger son where he had fallen at Sharpsburg. Such was the poor man's only comfort: to love and dream of the dead. Seeing him so, Mrs. Oglethorpe's outrage at his peaceful escape from disappointment exploded in a barrage of censure.

Mr. Oglethorpe woke, stared at her first blankly and then with sad comprehension. He made no effort to defend himself. His eyes filled with tears of abhorrence, and he died. It was the ultimate act of denial, and no wonder it infuriated Mrs. Oglethorpe. She continued cursing him until her daughter, alarmed at the violence of language, intruded upon the room and saw the state of things. She called out to their one general servant who came and provided during the next half hour all the clichés of comfort in calamity anyone could want. But Mr. Oglethorpe had escaped, and Mrs. Oglethorpe could not follow him into Valhalla.

Challenged by fresh tragedy, she rose to meet it with all the considerable strength at her command. News of Elizabeth's runaway marriage was being enjoyed when word of her father's death circulated to thrill the town further. A sigh alone from the doubly bereaved Mrs. Oglethorpe would have been enough to link the two events forever in the minds of the townspeople, but she did not satisfy herself with anything so modest as that. It was immediately put about that the old soldier had died of a heart broken by his youngest child. A moment's sensible reflection would have shown such to be unlikely if not impossible after what he had endured, but sudden marriages and even more sudden deaths do not stimulate the exercise of reason. Eager relays sped the information that Mrs. Oglethorpe disowned Elizabeth and forbade her to see her father in death or to attend his funeral. When the news reached Beulah Land, Sarah and Benjamin and Jane set out immediately to the Oglethorpe house. Having exiled himself from his mother-in-law's company since Bruce's birth, Benjamin waited on the porch while his sister and his grandmother entered.

Sarah told Ann Oglethorpe that Benjamin had commissioned her to include his condolences with her own and that he was at the door to be commanded by her and his wife. Whatever a man might be needed for, he begged to be allowed to do. Mrs. Oglethorpe stared at her visitor briefly. "Nothing," she said. "You may tell him nothing is required of him. Now, ever."

Sarah turned to Priscilla. "Perhaps you would go to the door and speak to him yourself."

"I pray you," Mrs. Oglethorpe said with a glower, "leave me *this* daughter, as she is my single comfort and support."

"As you will." Sarah shifted her eyes slowly back to the mother. "I shall go now to Elizabeth, who will surely be much distressed. May I take her word that you'd welcome her comfort too? — I beg you, ma'am!"

"You may not interfere in that way, madam."

Leaving Benjamin in town to offer his services discreetly to the Reverend Horace Quarterman of St. Thomas's and Jane with Priscilla to supply what practical aid she might, Sarah drove the buggy directly to the Cooper farm. Having heard that her father was dead and that her banishment was to continue, Elizabeth was weeping. Her husband and father-in-law had tried to console her, but so unused were they to having an intimate female relation, they welcomed with relief the appearance of Sarah. Sarah's sympathy was simple and unsentimental, and Elizabeth soon recovered her balance and surprised them all by saying, "My poor father. Do you think Mama killed him?"

"It may indeed be so," Sarah replied with a calmness that astonished the two men, and with more truth than she knew. "Mrs. Oglethorpe possesses an excitable temper not generally appreciated, but I well remember her several tantrums at the time Benjamin and Priscilla were contriving to marry. I can believe that she might today have expressed herself to your father in intemperate terms on the subject of you and Tom. Mr. Oglethorpe was a gentle soul. His experience on the battlefield did little to prepare him for violent family exchanges."

"Still, I am to blame." Reassured, but ready to deny that she was, she wept again, but not for long. Withdrawing after a moment or two from the embrace Tom offered, she dried her eyes and face and produced a smile to thank the three for their patience with her.

Ford Cooper looked more cheerful. "I'll go to the kitchen and tell Mercy to boil some coffee!"

"No need, Father," Elizabeth said, "if you will allow me."

She stepped briskly out of the room.

"She is a good young woman," Ford said to himself as much as to his son and neighbor.

Sarah responded warmly, "She is, Mr. Cooper. I have always found her as sensible as she is pretty. I regret Mrs. Oglethorpe's attitude toward her daughter's choosing to marry and should like to say, since there has been no time to say it before, that I think Elizabeth has done an excellent thing for herself—as well as for you, Tom. I am sorry she is to be kept from the funeral. It is not right."

"As to that," Tom said, "she won't be. My wife is subject to no one's dictates but her own. If she wants to go, I'll take her. I consider her claim to be there as a daughter equal to her mother's claim as a wife."

Ford Cooper said, "I knew the man long if not well, and nobody will keep me away, though it's not my church."

"You will do me honor," Sarah said, "if the three of you share our family pew for the funeral."

Priscilla went to the Glade for an hour for clothes she needed in town, but she did not see Benjamin, since he was attending to a working party at the time. She left some lines to let him know she would return in a few days and to say, "If you think it fitting to attend, the funeral is at ten o'clock day after tomorrow. It would be best for me to sit with Mama and you with whoever comes from Beulah Land, as I imagine someone will feel obliged to do."

Revealing naught but black backs, Priscilla and Mrs. Oglethorpe sat stiffly alone in the foremost pew, the coffin within an arm's reach. A few rows behind, Sarah and Casey flanked Tom, Elizabeth, and Ford Cooper; and further along were the Todds. Between Jane and Daniel were Davy and Bobby Lee, and between the brothers sat Leon, commissioned to pinch either if they squirmed. Children commonly attended funerals, which thereby became a recognized part of their social requirement. Leon had not, however, been to a large town funeral before, and being present gave him a further sense of belonging to Beulah Land.

The service was standard and brought forth no stronger emotion in the attendants than to wonder whether there would be an encounter between Ann Oglethorpe and her alienated daughter. When the church service ended, the congregation broke for those who were interested in making their way to the graveyard for the final ceremony. Sarah Troy was seen to address a few earnest words to Mrs. Oglethorpe during the transition, but the widow shook her head vigorously, and Elizabeth made no further effort to be reconciled with her mother.

As usual when all was over, people drifted among the graves recollecting their own dead and reminding each other when there were lapses of memory. Leon had learned to print his name and therefore recognized it when he saw it. Benjamin found him staring at a tombstone. Taking the boy's hand, Benjamin told him, "Leon Kendrick was your great-grandfather. And it was *his* grandfather, whose grave is over there, who planted the first seed and harvested the first crop at Beulah Land."

30

Sarah handed the short letter to Benjamin and waited as he read it. "I knew it was time," he said as he handed it back to her.

"Tomorrow." She watched as he went to the window of her office and looked out.

"I'll go tell Otis to be at the depot with the wagon, and I'll see everything's in order. I've no doubts of Otis, but I won't have complaints of him from Bessie or Eugene."

"Why should they complain?" Sarah asked.

"Because they think that's the way you handle Negroes."

"I suppose you're right." She relaxed a little. He had taken it better than she expected. Although he was upset, his voice revealed little beyond a reluctance to be resigned.

Having so decided, she was caught unawares. "Grandma, I can't let him go back to them!"

"There's nothing else to do."

"I'll pay Otis or another to help Bessie work her farm."

"Has Leon said anything to you?"

"No, ma'am, he just looks; but he wants to stay with us, you know he does. This is home to him."

"He was born a Marsh on the Marsh farm. We weren't so eager to have him then."

"I didn't know him then." She almost smiled. They lived and worked so closely together as equals, it sometimes surprised her to be reminded that he was young. "He just meant trouble to me.

Frankie turned me down because I told her he was coming." He sat down facing her across the desk, as they had sat together so many times to talk of so many things. He crossed his legs one way and then the other before setting both feet on the floor and leaning back. "I despise myself when I remember I didn't want him."

"But you did," she said. "You and I sat just as we are now, and you told me how, in spite of everything, you were happy at the idea of being a father."

"Did I?" he said as if he doubted her.

"It's not the first time you've forgot your own virtues."

"Then I'm lucky to have you remind me."

She said drily, "If I didn't, I expect somebody else would."

He stood up. "I'm going to meet the train tomorrow and tell Bessie I have to have him."

"Don't."

"I'll ask her what she wants from us."

"No, Benjamin."

"I won't let him live out there with Eugene."

"Leave it alone for a while."

"She knows he'd be better off here. Bessie's pregnant again; it's not as if—"

"She's not a bitch who forgets her last pup when she has a new one."

"I didn't mean it like that."

She paused and spoke with more deliberation. "Benjamin, don't meet them when they come. Let me take Leon in my buggy. It'll be easier for him. He loves you, and it would be harder for him to leave you and get in the wagon with them than to leave me. Besides, I won't prompt him to feel anything, and just the sight of you would. You talk about his looking. You ought to see yourself."

"Does it show?"

She rose and went around the desk to him. "Everything."

At his bedtime Sarah told Leon that his mother and Eugene were returning from Savannah the following day. Although he had prepared himself to hear her or Benjamin say it, his shock was nevertheless severe. She kissed him quickly and left him to put himself to bed, knowing he would cry but that he would then sleep. It was better, she'd thought, to tell him at night than to spoil his last full day at Beulah Land. When he woke, he would remember, but a night's sleep would ease him into the difficult day ahead.

Sarah was up betimes to go to the kitchen before Leon's customary early visit, for she wanted to warn Mabella against any display. Yet Mabella took the news of Leon's leaving equably enough, making only automatic exclamations of desolation, whereas it was big old Josephine who turned her back and whose shoulders Sarah observed to be heaving in silent distress. How and when it had happened, she didn't know, but it was evident that Josephine had taken the boy to her heart.

At breakfast Benjamin presented a calm demeanor, speaking easily to Leon of his pleasure in having him at Beulah Land, but not of his regret at Leon's leaving. He said he wouldn't be going to the depot with him to meet his mother because Zadok wanted him to look at the potato mounds. He wasn't certain they'd used enough straw against the wet weather to come. Josephine brought in sweet cinnamon rolls and they talked of how dear Aunt Nell had loved them.

The wagon with Otis and the buggy with Sarah and Leon waited at the depot for the Savannah train, but there was no festive air about the occasion as there had been when the Betchleys were going away. It was cool and inclined to rain, and those who had come to observe the ritual of the train's arrival and departure had taken shelter in the baggage office, where the clerk had built the first autumn fire in his stove. The train stopped, but they had misjudged their place, so Bessie and Eugene descended behind them. However, the two little parties were soon joined, exchanging plain greetings followed by questions about the trip and comments on Savannah. Bessie wanted to know if her farm was all right and if anything had died while she was gone. Sarah noted that she looked tired, whereas Eugene had imposed on his country coarseness a suavity of Savannah manners and a new quickness of gesture and alertness of eye. The wagon was loaded and set off for the farm bearing Bessie and Eugene and Leon with their receptacles of clothes; and Sarah drove the buggy home with Otis beside her, his roll of clothes on his knees. "Sure glad to be getting home," Otis commented. "Lonesome place out yonder." Sarah patted his arm to thank him and allowed herself a few angry tears.

As the wagon creaked through the familiar and arrived finally at the most familiar sight of all, Bessie's confidence and good humor returned, whereas Eugene grew sullen and taciturn. Leon stood behind them on the floor of the wagon, looking as hopeless as a duke in a tumbril.

By nightfall the three had resumed their old roles. Bessie commanded the house, having gone over the barn and examined the livestock with Eugene as soon as they came home, grumbling at the way the level of corn had gone down in their absence. Leon tagged along beside his mother, but when he asked if he might sleep in the barn where Eugene used to sleep, Bessie said, "No, you may not. I won't have you out here with a candle; you'd forget to blow it out and burn up my stock."

Leon went to bed after supper without waiting to be told, eager to shut his eyes against the surroundings and to have that day over. Tired more from the things he had felt than the things he had done, he soon slept; nor did he wake when Bessie and Eugene came in.

"Be quiet as you can," Bessie cautioned as they began to undress.

"What for? There's nobody within a mile."

She looked at him quickly but said nothing, making the bed ready for them and then herself ready for it.

"We ought to stayed in Savannah."

"Takes money," she said.

"I could have made some if we'd stayed."

"You tell me how."

"If I had a stake to start, I could build it up, a place like Savannah." He kicked his shoes to the wall and squirmed out of his trousers. Hopping on one foot to keep balance, he said offhandedly, "How much you spect we could get for the farm?"

"I don't plan to sell," she said irritably, but her face softened as she looked at him in the lamplight. "Whatever, it wouldn't be enough for what you want. It's piddling to think about, and a waste of time to imagine I'd let go the only thing I'm certain of."

He didn't dispute what she said. "What about getting more where we got the fifty dollars?"

"They're not fools."

"They are about him, you tell me." She blew out the lamp and got into bed. "I'm not ready," he protested.

"Find your way in the dark."

They lay silently on their backs for a time before he turned to her. She pushed him away. "I don't want to."

"I do."

"It ain't comfortable for me no more with all this."

"What am I supposed to do?"

"Wait till after I've had it."

"Two months?"

"Maybe not so long."

"I ain't gone that long since I learned how to do it."

"You can stop acting like a youngun that has to have everything he wants."

Presently he said, "I got to have me some. If you won't give it to me, others will."

She reached to touch him. "I reckon you are hard up."

"You right. Hard and up." He snickered.

"Sh."

"Your hands are rough as a grater. Use some spit." He waited a minute and said, "That ain't a lot better. Use your mouth. — Now, that's it. That's better. That's all right. That's good. Good. Good. That's good. Go slow. Slow. Stop. Just wait a minute. Again. That's it. Hold it tighter. Fast. Faster. Keep it going. That's it, that's it, oh. Oh, I'm coming. Oh, here I come!"

When they settled themselves for sleep he asked curiously, "Did you swallow it?"

"I forgot where the slop jar was in the dark. I couldn't let it run on the sheets; only have to wash them again before time."

"Remind me not to kiss you for a while," he said.

"You don't much anyhow."

"Are you complaining?" he said, then again with increasing anger, as if his own question stoked his displeasure. "I said: Are you complaining about me, old woman? For if you are, I can find some that won't, and don't forget it neither. Godalmighty."

"You and your peter," she said bitterly. "I reckon that's about all you got to be proud of."

"Well, I sure ain't proud of marrying you. I had me a nigger gal before I come here that could suck better than you can fuck. Now what are you going to say to that?"

"That you're low-down. Go to sleep. There's work tomorrow."

"If you think I'm going to work my ass off forever on this one-mule farm, you're wrong; you're mighty wrong. I got other things on my mind; can't you see that?"

"Reckon you won't speak to us all when you're Mr. High and Mighty. What you figure doing, trapping critters again with old Crawford? Making moonshine? Or just plain stealing?"

"There's ways and ways."

"You can forget about selling my farm from under me."

He was silent for a time and she began to be sorry for him because he was young. She remembered well enough the feeling she'd had when she was young, of its being the end of the world out here with no one to turn to. "Are you 'sleep, Gene?" she whispered.

"Leave me alone."

31

James Davis owned three quarters of the sawmill, but Bonard Saxon, whose father owned the other quarter, managed it. This had come about naturally enough, because James was blind and everything had to be read or explained to him before he could make a decision. Bonard now made the routine decisions, although he was meticulous about consulting his uncle on important matters. Bonard worked early and sometimes late, to keep up with the extravagance of his wife, he said, although that was more a matter of brag than of fact, Frankie being only about as self-indulgent as other wives of her position. And for all his steady application to the sawmill's business, Bonard still found time for his own indulgences in women and drinking. Alf Crawford was an old acquaintance who, if he didn't have a thing himself, usually knew where it might be got; and he had often been the means of supplying Bonard's needs. So it was that when Eugene Betchley turned to Alf to advise him how to make money, Alf sent him to Bonard, the only man of any substance he might call upon for a favor. Bonard was alone in the office on the October morning Eugene pounded at the door.

"Gene!"

"Alf Crawford said come."

"Well, come on in then. Hear you been playing the dude in Savannah. How you like it, hum? Not much like little Highboro. More eyes watching but not all of them on you. – Alf tells me you're worried about something. Sit down."

"Not so much worried as wanting," Eugene said. "Wanting a job to work."

"You?" Bonard looked amused. "Thought you'd turned respectable farmer and settled down—"

"'Down' is right. I'm looking for 'up.' Like to rise a little by doing a week's work for a week's wage and hoping for even better if I show some worth."

"How's married life?" Bonard winked.

"She's got a baby on the way. You must have heard."

Bonard nodded. "Quick work, or was the cart before the horse? Never mind, never mind; happens ever' day, don't it?"

"Not much to a farm in winter, and with another mouth about to open and squawl for victuals—"

Bonard laughed. "Don't sound much like the old Gene, no sir! Used to be ready to grab gun or girl, never mattered which, long as there was game in it. Well, don't give up your fun. When you try to get it back, you won't find it easy. I tell it from my own experience."

Eugene affected relaxation, sprawling in his chair before slowly fanning his knees in and out. "Never heard of you stinting on your fun. Fact, Alf tells me you still—"

"Well, you know, have to keep my hand, so to speak, in. A job, you said. Do you mean it?"

"I mean it."

"Women do drive men to it, don't they? Damnedest thing. Reckon the sight of Savannah ladies opened the eyes of your missus and now she wants you to buy her a little of this and a lot of that. Don't I know! Tell you what, I'll think on it some and talk it over with Uncle James. Don't make a decision without his say-so. Might be. Uh-huh, you might well do. — We been taking on more niggers, you see, because they come cheaper than white men; but the trouble is making them work. Tell a white man to do a thing and leave him to do it. Leave a nigger and he sets down on his ass. Keep 'em on their feet or they go to sleep. How you like to be nigger watcher for me, see to it they don't stop pulling and pushing my saws 'cept to tear off a piece of chewing tobacco twice a day?"

Eugene started to work at the mill the following day, as Bonard told him with a wink, "After I talk it over with Uncle James. He's the real boss; rest of us just draw our pay." Eugene proved himself immediately. That he lacked experience working with Negroes was an advantage, because it made him edgy. The men took his tension for meanness, which it presently became. They didn't like him, but they no longer idled over their work; and Bonard soon understood he had hired a useful man.

Early in November, Sarah went to see Bessie. She found her and Leon at work in the barn, the woman with a pitchfork, the boy with a rake, their knuckles red and cracked with the cold. When Sarah made it clear she intended to stay a while, Bessie put down the fork and led them to the warm kitchen, where she made a pot of coffee. After praising Eugene for the way he was applying himself to his work at the mill, Sarah observed sympathetically that it must leave everything for her to do on the farm.

"Well'm, I'm used to it, ain't I?"

"Not so near the time you'll take to bed."

"Leon's a help."

"Leon'll be starting school one of these days. You need somebody to shoulder the heavy, now Gene's doing so well for you-all at the mill. You know what a lot of hands we keep at Beulah

Land. Try to hire by the month but wind up taking them for the year, because we have to have the best and that's the only way to get them. Then they stay on and on, and it's not much different from the old days, is it?"

"That's because you're too easy with them. Gene tells me—"

"They earn their keep, only there's not so much for them to do now. I'm going to send a man over tomorrow and from now on to do whatever heavy work you tell him needs doing."

"That's kind of you, Miss Sarah, but Gene won't like it."

"I'll be in Highboro this afternoon, and I expect to stop at the mill. It used to be ours, you know, before I sold it to Mr. Davis."

"Yes'm, I remember."

"I still act bossy when I go around there, and people do what I tell them. Gene will be no exception; you'll see."

32

Crossing his back porch in a leap, Benjamin burst into the kitchen, shaking himself like a wet dog. "Raining ice water, I'd swear before God! Never known it so cold and not freezing. It'll freeze tonight."

At the stove Freda said, "I recollect a freeze one September, oh, back some years. September! With summer another month to go."

"Well, we're nearly into December, and if it freezes and stays frozen a day or two, I'm going to butcher a few hogs." He sat warily on a wobbly-legged, cane-bottomed chair to remove his shoes.

"Won't they taste nice!" she exclaimed approvingly.

"What're you cooking that smells so good?" She lifted a pot lid as he stood again. "You mean that's just chicken and dumplings? Heaven never smelled so sweet on Easter morning."

The shifting of her eyes warned him before she said it. "Mrs. Ben is home."

"Where?"

"You better go up there, Mr. Ben. Give me that wet coat." She kicked his shoes under the stove to dry.

At the top of the stairs he met Velma, crying and wringing her hands. "Is anything wrong with the baby?"

"Her's all right. *Other* her, *big* her, *she* say to fotch my clothes and hit the grit, for Velma not needed no more!" Overcome with her revelation, she wept with fresh vigor.

He took her hands and shook them roughly. "Don't cry. It'll be all right. I promise you'll stay. Go to the baby."

Leaving her, he went to Priscilla's room and knocked on the closed door, entering without waiting for permission. Priscilla had dragged her biggest trunk to the center of the room and was on her knees before it.

"Traveling or going somewhere?"

She swiveled her head to acknowledge him with a frown. "You make a joke of everything."

"A pleasantry only, from surprise. It's a while since you were here, and you've sent no direct word. What are you doing?"

"I should think it obvious. I'm going to be at Mama's for a few weeks."

"You've been there now for a few weeks."

"A few more then. Maybe a few months. She's alone, with Elizabeth married and Papa dead. She needs me."

"You're needed here."

"Not in any way I can permit myself to be used," she asserted.

"The Glade is your home."

She looked about the room slowly before shaking her head. Going to the wardrobe, she removed two cloaks, one light, the other heavy, shook them out and began to fold them. "It never was, and when I came back today, I felt more lost than ever. Mama's house is home."

"You mean to stay there."

"For the time being."

"For the indefinite time being?"

"If you like to put it that way."

"It's not what I like. It never is with you."

"It pleases you to abuse me." The straight stare of her eyes belied the mechanical quirk of her lips. "Very well." On her knees again, she placed the cloaks carefully at the bottom of the trunk. "At least I satisfy that need."

"You're angry because of what Elizabeth has done. That's it, I see. You think *I* should go to your mother and apologize, beg forgiveness for your sister's deciding to make her life with a man instead of rotting away in that female piety and mortification of the flesh your mother calls 'goodness.' And you'd like to blame me."

"You cannot claim innocence."

"You blame Grandma and Jane as well, and you've decided to punish us. By leaving, you show the world that you withdraw from the contamination of Beulah Land. You and your mother have settled on this way to mete out punishment."

"My absence cannot be much punishment to you."

"You hope it will shame me."

"I have given up expecting anything to shame you." She busied herself opening doors and drawers, transferring small items of apparel to the trunk, pushing all down gently when she had completed a layer.

"It's your mother's revenge."

"How dare you accuse her?" she said without inflection, as if determined not to show anger.

"I'm to have no wife."

"You've told me I'm none already."

"I begged you to love me once, but I'll beg no more, and I'll not make apologies."

She opened and stretched a shawl, examining it with exaggerated care before folding it again. "You have evidently discovered someone to gratify *that* need. I only hope it isn't one of the Negroes, Velma or Freda."

"It isn't like you to speculate on such matters," he pointed out.

"Earthly love, if love you can call it, does not concern me. I am not a soulless animal."

"When I think of your mother," he said, "I wonder how your poor father managed to sire four children."

"You are disgusting," she said as a sad fact.

"What did you say to Velma?"

"That I don't want her to nurse my daughter, whom I intend to take with me when I leave today."

After a pause he said, "You shall not take Bruce."

"Yes, I shall. A child, a female child in particular, belongs to a mother."

"She's done without you since she was born. You hardly handle her even when you are here."

"If I've seemed to you to neglect her, it is because I shared the humiliation of her deformity, the mark she bears as witness to your sins. Henceforth, I shall do my duty and raise her as she should be raised, to fear God and hate the devil. I shall pray for her, and with her, for salvation."

"I have never touched you in anger—"

"No, you have done worse."

"Understand this: Bruce stays with me. If I must say it: I am stronger than you."

She looked at him intently, as if measuring the degree of his strength. "Will you force me to apply to the Reverend Quarterman?"

"I am also stronger than he."

"Even you would not strike a man of God."

"When you go to him, tell him what I say, and let him judge how brave he is."

"You risk damnation."

"Without a qualm."

"I shall tell people, you know that."

"There are always fools to listen."

"I know why you are determined to have her; don't think *me* a fool. However many bastards you sow and reap, she'll be your only legitimate child. You cannot marry again."

"Why did you come today in a freezing rain?"

"Mama hired a wagon to take Elizabeth's trunk to her. It brought me and will pick me up with my trunk as it returns. I am not dependent on you."

"What of your mother's means?" he asked after a moment's thought. "I'll arrange for you to have whatever you require."

"I'll send you accountings. As for Mama, she will not need your charity. Papa had railroad shares and never sold them, as so many others tried to do after the war."

At the door he paused. "I hope that in time you will want to return to the Glade and to your child."

"If I am without my child," she said, "it will be her loss and upon your soul, which is already heavy-laden."

He left the room without a word and went to the nursery to reassure Velma, which took a little while. When he left her, he told her to lock the door and to open it to no one until he came again. Returning to Priscilla, he watched as she finished packing and closed the trunk. When she stepped back and nodded, he lifted it to his back and carried it down the stairs so carefully it bumped neither wall nor banister, setting it down in the hallway beside the front door. Coming after him, Priscilla took a narrow chair under the wall clock, folding her hands on her lap. Benjamin stood on the porch until the livery wagon drew up to the house, whereupon Priscilla came out to give the Negro driver instructions on the loading of the trunk. When he had secured it to her satisfaction under the canvas hood covering half the wagon body, she joined him on the driver's seat. From the doorway Benjamin called to her to take shelter with the trunk. Without turning her head, she replied, "I intend to be seen by all." The driver picked up his reins and turned mule and wagon toward the road that followed the curve of the hillside down.

33

When he entered the office, he knew they were talking about him by the way they turned without surprise, as if he had been one in their discussion and they now sought his concurrence in what they had decided.

His sister said, "I need Freda, and I've had a talk with her this morning. She's willing to come to us, but only if you tell her to."

His grandmother said, "You are to bring Bruce and Velma down here."

Jane continued, "She's always been wasted in the Glade with no one but you to care about her cooking, and you away half the time. That kind of treatment drives a cook insane. I'm surprised she hasn't run amok with a butcher knife."

Sarah added to her previous thought. "It isn't as though the Glade alone is your home. This is your home. All of Beulah Land is your home."

"I wish you'd move in with us," Jane said. "Bobby Lee asked me if you were going to, and Davy asked if we had to take Bruce too."

Sarah said, "Don't be silly, Jane. His place is here with Bruce, and Bruce *must* come; there's no question about that. Otherwise, she'll grow up peculiar like your great-aunt Selma, seeing no one but you and the Negroes."

"I don't know why it took you so long," Jane said, "to understand that Priscilla wasn't coming back except to get her clothes—"

"*And* her Bible!" Sarah injected triumphantly.

"She probably has half a dozen, one for every weekday and a special, illustrated, indexed, morocco-bound edition for Sunday."

"Does she, Benjamin?" Sarah asked in astonishment, as if she had just discovered a secret they had kept from her.

"Now you will let me have Freda, won't you?"

"You see what I mean about Bruce."

He looked from one to the other and said to one after the other, "No," going out and slamming the door after him. But in five minutes he returned. They watched him in offended silence as he took a chair, set it at an angle facing them, and straddled it, folding his arms on its high back. "Did you mean it when you said you knew all along Priscilla wasn't coming back to me?"

"I guessed," Jane said.

Sarah said, "I'd have been surprised if she had, given what that foul mother of hers surely considered the excuse of a lifetime. She never liked it out here, never tried to be one of us. I've made allowances—"

Jane patted her grandmother's hand. "Lord knows, you have. And the way she's always stuck her nose up at Dan because he was a Yankee, I could wring her neck."

"As if a man can help what he's born," Sarah said spiritedly. "Yankee or not, Daniel Todd is as good as anybody and better than most."

"You said when he came to us we'd make a Southern gentleman out of him. You overstated the need. Dan was born a gentleman."

Sarah nodded agreement. "Why, it was he who insisted on naming your first child after our General—"

Benjamin held his hands up in the air until they were both silent. "Now," he said quietly, "what about Bruce, Grandma?"

With more consideration than she had spoken earlier, Sarah explained why she thought he should bring Bruce and Velma down the hill to live at the big house.

"Well," he answered finally when she paused, "I think you're right."

Sarah looked relieved. "It really will be better for her."

"Safer," Benjamin said. "Her mother can't come and get her when I'm away in the fields."

"I'd like to see her try it," Sarah said. "I'd have her head on a platter."

"On a pole," Jane proposed.

"About Freda," Benjamin said.

Jane was suddenly shy. "She really is too good a cook to be wasted, Ben, and my old Poppy, though I've tried hard to teach her, isn't worth knocking over the head with a piece of stove wood. She'd have suited Priscilla. Neither knows a hard-boiled egg from rice pudding. Even the boys complain privately, and they'll eat anything. It's no wonder they swarm over Josephine like flies on fresh chitterlings."

"I didn't know Freda was dissatisfied," Benjamin said.

"Ben," Jane said, "Freda would—well, any of Zadok's family would crawl to hell and back twice a day and twice times that in leap year if you asked them to. But to tell a good cook to put her meal on the table and then take it away uneaten is more than flesh and spirit can bear."

"Amen to that," Sarah said.

For the first time that day Benjamin smiled. "Take care of the body, and the soul will take care of itself."

"I'm not a hedonist like you and Aunt Nell," Sarah said, "but a little balance is a good thing."

Benjamin got up from his chair, taking it and setting it back in its usual place. "All right, Jane, you can have Freda. I'll tell her."

"Even Dan may give you a hug."

Benjamin laughed. "I'll help Velma bring Bruce down with her things, Grandma."

Sarah stood. "Million things to do. I'll turn out that big corner room upstairs, the one facing our little cemetery. You won't mind looking out on dear Floyd's grave."

"I wouldn't," Benjamin said, "if I was going to be there, but I'll stay in my own house in the Glade, Grandma, I thank you."

"Stubborn," she declared. "You can't be by yourself up there."

"I'll be here for meals," he said, "since Jane is stealing my cook, but it's my house up there, Grandma. Don't you get too bossy and carried away."

"Don't you either," she said tartly, but when he kissed her cheek, tears came into her eyes. She didn't try to hide them but wiped them away matter-of-factly. "I'm going to drive my buggy over to Roscoe's this afternoon. Me and him have got a lot to talk about. Did I tell you I had a letter from Abraham? He's taking the boat from Philadelphia, and Roscoe will meet him in Savannah and bring him home for his holidays. I've agreed to let him stay with Roscoe. Roscoe wants him, and Abraham wants to be there. I thought I'd take Roscoe a mess of backbone and a yard or two of sausage today too. They won't be killing any hogs, he told me, till just before Christmas. They always like to wait. I wish you'd ride over to see him with me. He has this idea he wants to talk to you about. It's to build our own cotton mill here in Highboro. He says the boys and girls who come to Elk Institute then go off to Augusta or some other where to work in the mills. They make them work twelve hours a day, he says. They don't see daylight all winter. He's going to make an estimate of what a beginning will cost and hopes we'll go shares. What do you think? It might be something for Abraham's future. I've done a lot of thinking about it. Benjamin, I wish you wouldn't fidget. You make me rattle when you edge off like that. Just wait a minute, if you please."

"I have a lot of things to do."

He had moved to the door, but her next question stopped him, hand on knob. "How serious are you about Frankie Saxon?"

He looked at her amazed but answered calmly enough. "As serious as a married man can be about a woman married to another."

"I'm glad you remember that you're both married. Adultery is never a simple matter, and it can turn out to be most painful for people around, as well as the two themselves."

"How did you know about Frankie?"

"Jane and I have noticed you together. Oh, there's nothing anyone would see who wasn't looking for it, but be careful. I don't condemn you or her. How could I, since I was an adulteress myself? I just feel profoundly sorry for you both."

"Grandma!" Benjamin and Jane said together.

"Oh, I married the man later. You're young, and there's so much you don't know. I'm afraid you won't be marrying Frankie, though. Priscilla will outlive Methuselah."

34

It was an unhappy time for Benjamin. Married, he was without wife. A father, he was without children. He saw Bruce, but she was no longer his in the way she had been at the house in the Glade when her mother avoided her and Velma wove the child's day life around Benjamin's comings and goings. At the big house there were many people, and although Velma conscientiously and even jealously followed her duties as mammy, she made friends and began to share her charge with Sarah and Casey, Jane and Daniel, and the frequent visitors who stopped at Beulah Land for conversation, a meal, or a week. Bruce thrived on the attentions of a large household and was so good-tempered that even Jefferson Davis Todd was heard to admit that she wasn't the worst baby he had seen, although she still smelled of milk.

Benjamin did not miss his wife.

He did, however, miss his son. Every day or so he went to the farm to see him, knowing Eugene would not be there and having the excuse of checking on Zebra, the man Sarah had assigned to Bessie's work; but he did not see Leon alone, except the time he took him to town for a haircut. Afterwards, to take him back to the farm and leave him was almost worse than not having him at all. He wanted renewal of their easy companionship, a continuation of the feeling that he was passing on to his *son* some of the things he knew.

Sarah visited Bessie often as the time drew near for her to give birth, and she rarely came empty-handed. The small gifts were part of an accumulative bribe. She knew it and Bessie knew it. She so reiterated the theme of Leon's going to school, and the convenience to everyone of his staying at Beulah Land when he did so, that Bessie was close to giving way.

For Leon it was as bad a time as it was for his father. Both Benjamin and Sarah studied to pay him minimal attention on their visits, not wanting Bessie to perceive the extent of their feeling for him. However, Bessie was occupied with her concerns and did not give the boy much consideration. Eugene ignored him as much as he could, for which Leon was glad enough; but to be present and feel unseen, or to be seen only to be damned and told to keep out of the way, was eroding to the spirit. Leon began to look as furtive and unwanted as he felt. His conviction grew that he was being thought nothing of by anyone at all. He became awkward and clumsy, dropping things, forgetting to do what he was told.

Priscilla settled down with her mother as if she had never left her. All was reconciled between them. One was never seen out of the house without the other. They sat together, sewed together, slept in adjoining rooms, walked the town side by side, and shared prayer book and hymnal at church. They absented themselves from no religious service except weddings and attended funerals as if they were paid mourners, whether or not they cared about the family concerned. The Reverend Quarterman became a little wary of them, wanting them to evidence some frailty he might correct. Only once did he, at the behest of Mrs. Oglethorpe, command Benjamin to give poor Bruce into the care of her mother and maternal grandmother. Benjamin instantly and not over-politely refused. Mrs. Oglethorpe complained that Reverend Quarterman had not urged their claim insistently enough; but, in fact, Priscilla was content to be without her daughter, for she had the virtue of being said to long for her, the pity of being deprived of her, and the comfortable certainty that she would not be required to answer a child's need in the night for milk or love.

Benjamin made no attempt to see Priscilla. There is nothing appetizing in an empty plate, and he knew she had nothing for him. When they chanced to meet in passing, as they did before or after church on Sundays, and occasionally on a sidewalk in the commercial part of town, they gratified the colder expectations of their acquaintances by bowing to each other without a word.

So matters stood when on the seventh day of December, seven weeks after the Betchleys returned from Savannah and reclaimed Leon, Bessie Betchley bore another son. She was attended by young Dr. Rolfe, who had recently been taken on as country assistant to the aging, lazy Dr. Platt. The baby was called Theodore Aquinas after a character in a play his father had seen in Savannah and thought very grand. Preacher Paul and his good wife Ona came to pray. Sarah and Jane drove over to speak words of comfort and admiration as they spread before the mother their gifts of caps and long dresses and bootees. Alf Crawford knocked on the back door on the evening of the birth day, and he and Eugene sat at the kitchen table and enjoyed a pint of whiskey he had just drawn from his still. Eugene strutted through town and wore the purple suspenders Bessie had bought him on their wedding trip. Bonard Saxon celebrated the event by raising Eugene's pay two dollars a week and giving him a cigar out of his best box. The new father wore it between his teeth all day before lighting it and parading down the main street on a sawmill mule. If any thought him a fool, none said so in his hearing, whatever jokes they made behind his back, for Eugene had in a month's time acquired a fearsome reputation as a man easy to offend and quick to attack. He used his fists on white men and the club he had carved from seasoned oak on the few Negroes at the sawmill who were slow to know his supremacy. Most of them had learned that it was easier to flatter and obey than to lose teeth, or in one instance an eye and the hearing in an ear.

It was little wonder that Eugene felt himself beginning to be an important man and no wonder at all that he looked on Leon with darker frowns and damned him with quicker curses than ever. One night, the tenth in the life of Theodore Aquinas, the family were sitting at the kitchen table over their supper. Bessie's breast was bared to the nursing babe even as she ate her meat and bread. Eugene had been alternately jocular and testy since coming home from the mill, but no one spoke at the table.

No one had spoken to Leon since Eugene's return that evening. It was often the way. Leon and Bessie might be tranquil enough with one another all day, but when her young husband came in, Bessie flattered him by taking his side against Leon, usually in ways no more marked than mild ridicule. Bessie did not hate her older son, but she had always resented him for the fact that his father had not wanted to marry her, and she had never tried to love him. To her mind it was only paying him back, particularly in light of recent attentions paid him by Sarah Troy and Benjamin Davis, for the trouble and shame he'd brought her. If ridicule discomforted him and pleased Eugene, where was the harm?

Leon decided he would like syrup on his flour hoecake because the fried sow belly was salty. Like his father, he fancied sweet and salty together. He didn't want to ask for the syrup, and when he reached for the pitcher, which was near Eugene's plate, his hand jerked and the pitcher grazed Eugene's cup, tipping it and spilling coffee over Eugene's plate of food. If Bessie hadn't laughed, the moment might have passed with no more than a curse and a slap. But she laughed, and her laughter shook the nursing baby from her teat and made him cry. Eugene struck out with his wet hand. The blow knocked Leon from his chair. The shock of it ran through his body as he rose to accuse—he did not know why the words came—"You killed Granny!"

The room and all in it were dead still except for the baby's whimper. Bessie and Eugene stared at Leon. Eugene said, "I'm going to take you to the barn and whip you."

Bessie nodded, frightened. "Yes, hon, you better. You better do it."

"Mama!" Leon kicked as Eugene reached for him.

"No use crying for me, for you deserve it for saying such a lie! You can stay out in the barn all night, no matter how cold it gets!"

Grabbing the boy by the hair of the head, he dragged him along the floor and out the door. Bessie guided the baby's mouth back to her nipple. He took it and was quiet.

35

Eugene rode a sawmill mule to work every morning after Bessie gave him breakfast, and he was gone when Zebra arrived on a Beulah Land mule before daybreak. Entering the barn in the dark, Zebra found his lantern and lighted it, expecting to enjoy a pipe of tobacco before milking the cow. When he lifted the lantern over his head to look about, he saw the dark, small heap on a mound of hay and went to see what it was. The figure was just recognizable when he held the lantern close. Setting the lantern down, he touched the boy's cold hand and then his bruised and swollen face. Gripped by fear, he blew out the lantern.

Zebra and Sarah were old friends, and she'd chosen him to work for Bessie because she could trust him to watch the way Leon was treated. She'd warned Zebra of Eugene's temper and reputation for using brute strength, and he had seen for himself the bad feeling between man and boy, so he did not even consider carrying the boy into the farmhouse. Gathering him up as carefully as he could, he remounted his mule, and by constantly kicking the animal's fat sides made quick progress back to Beulah Land, not knowing whether his burden was alive or dead.

Benjamin and Sarah were at breakfast when they heard Josephine scream. Running, they reached the kitchen before Zebra had time to hand over the child. Benjamin took him and followed Sarah to Leon's old room, where he laid him on the bed. Mabella was there with a lamp, her eyes big as eggs. Benjamin made exclamations of rage and reassurance as he removed the boy's bloodstained clothing, and Sarah told Josephine to send Wally for the doctor as quick as he could ride.

It was Rolfe who came before the hour was up, by which time Leon was lying quiet after being gently cleansed with warm wet cloths Josephine fetched from the kitchen. Rolfe asked no questions and answered none directed to him until he finished his examination. He worked slowly and methodically, those in the room falling silent and gaining confidence in him as they watched. He had never been to Beulah Land before, Dr. Platt having reserved its illnesses and accidents for his own attention and reward. When Rolfe had done with his bottles and bandages and the boy was covered again with a sheet and the softest old quilt they had, he motioned everyone to leave.

Josephine would not move from the bedside, but the others, including Zebra, followed Sarah to her office. Zebra was asked to repeat what he had told them of finding the boy. Rolfe listened and said, "He's alive because he's young. The cold was a bad thing for him in that condition." He looked from Sarah to Benjamin. "I'd say he was beaten and left to live or die as he would." Mabella brought in coffee and poured it out. When he had been given a cup, the doctor continued, "My counting is two broken ribs, a broken finger—I think he was thrown and fell on his left hand and side, for the wrist is sprained. The eyes are swollen shut but not put out, as I first feared. Four loose teeth, one or two of which he will lose. You saw the cuts on his back and legs. They might have been made by a piece of leather harness, considering where he was found. I've done what I can, but he's going to hurt considerable and for a long time. I don't like to soak a child with laudanum. If he doesn't get pneumonia, he ought to come around. I'll be back this afternoon—unless you want me to ask

Dr. Platt to come. I know he generally sees you-all. He sent me because he—was on another case." Sarah, who had never favored Platt, shook her head. Rolfe finished his coffee and stood. "If he wakes, somebody be there."

"Somebody will," Benjamin said. He thanked the doctor and led him out of the house, seeing him on his horse and away. Returning to Leon's room, he found his grandmother. Gray daylight now came in at the windows, and the lamp had been extinguished. Mabella tiptoed about, and after a little argument replaced Josephine at the bedside, her eyes never leaving the child's sleeping face. Benjamin stood for a minute at the foot of the bed with Sarah, but when he turned to go, she followed.

In the hallway, they met Casey. "Josephine just told me."

Benjamin said, "I'm going to the farm to find out what happened."

Sarah nodded. "I'd better stay with Leon."

"I'm coming with you," Casey said to Benjamin, who looked surprised but made no objection, and half an hour later they trotted their horses into the farmyard, where they found Bessie emerging from the barn. She stared at Benjamin suspiciously as he swung down from his horse. "Zebra hasn't showed up. I had to milk the cow, and I can't find Leon."

"He's at Beulah Land."

"So he ran away to you!" Her tone was both exasperated and relieved. "He slept in the barn last night. He's been wanting to ever since me and Gene got married, and last night we let him." Neither man spoke; Casey remained on his horse. "Well, what did he tell you?" Bessie demanded. "You can't believe what younguns say; they make up things to excuse themselves. — Slipped off, and me beginning to worry! — He don't always turn up for breakfast. Boys go about their business same as men do, both expecting you to be there when they come. All this time at Beulah Land without asking! Sly—wait till I get my hands on him—"

"Nobody is going to lay hands on him again," Benjamin said.

"I sure don't have to get your permission—"

"Don't you *know?*"

"I know he misbehaved himself and got corrected for it. He

threw coffee all over Gene and said a mean, ugly thing. Gene's put up with a lot of his sass, but I told him he'd better take him to the barn and—I reckon he's repeated to you what he said. Actually accused Gene of killing Ma!" Misreading Benjamin's astonishment, she went on. "Actually said that! And me an eyewitness to the very accident that killed her." She slapped her side in disbelief.

"It *was* Gene that beat him?"

For a moment she looked defensive and tried to cover it with a show of anger. "Ben, don't tell me how to raise my youngun!"

"He's mine from now on."

"He is like mad-itch! — What have you done with him?" She frowned at the bare ground as he then told her the injuries the doctor had diagnosed. "Like I said, him and Gene had a set-to, and I have to say Gene was in the right."

"Is Eugene at the sawmill?"

"Where else would he be this time of day?" Benjamin got back on his horse Jupiter and turned him into the main road, Casey behind him. Bessie ran after them. "You send him home when you get him well! *Idea* you saying he's your'n! He ain't! I had the care of him till you took a notion you'd like to have him—and you wouldn't have if your woman hadn't been dry! — You hear me, Ben Davis?"

Benjamin and Casey did not talk about Bessie as they followed the road that would bring them to the mill before it entered Highboro. Casey spoke of the frost that lingered on the fields, although the sun was well up. The clay road was hard and rang with the horses' hooves because there had been no rain for a week and the temperature had remained near freezing. At the sawmill Bonard told them they would find Eugene stacking lumber and invited them to stop in the office where it was warm when they had done their business with him. Turning a corner amid the stack of lumber, they saw Eugene at a little distance, watching half a dozen Negro men setting freshly cut planks in overlapping triangular formations to be seasoned by the weather. Benjamin stopped and called: "I want to see you private, Eugene!"

Eugene nodded but continued to watch the Negroes a minute longer to be certain they kept to their regular rhythm of walking and carrying and stacking. Strolling over, he handled the club familiarly, not in a threatening way but out of habit, his fingers busy with it as a musician will touch a silent instrument. "What you want?"

"You beat my son."

"I reckon you mean Bessie's oldest boy." He cocked his head back and said it a little rudely but without challenge. "I hit him a time or two for being uppity."

"Doctor says you might have killed him."

"Doctor?"

"He's at Beulah Land where he's going to stay."

Eugene shrugged. "Nothing to me. Between you and Bessie. You want him? I don't. Got my own, one I made. I don't ask another man to do it for me. Tell you: maybe I'll talk Bess into selling him to you. What you say to fifty dollars? A month, I mean, for as long as you want him. You can get a good nigger for fifteen and the best for twenty, but you'd want to pay more for your own flesh and blood, I reckon, if he's yours as you claim."

Benjamin gave no warning word, but his face was warning enough, and Eugene deflected the blow with a quick swing of his club. Casey stood aside but alert. The Negro workmen froze in their tracks as Benjamin leaped upon Eugene, bearing him to the ground. The two struggled and rolled, their clothes collecting leaves and wood shavings until they came to a rise of ground and could roll no more. On their knees then, facing, each strove to overpower the other. They looked an even match at first, neither able to land a solid blow, their hard grunts and red faces the main evidence of conflict. They were not practiced fighters. Benjamin hadn't struck another in anger since he was a boy, and Eugene was used to getting his way with one blow of fist or club without his opponent's fighting back. Eugene had dropped the club, but it rolled slowly after them, and he stretched an arm to reach it. Benjamin saw and kicked the club away, pressing Eugene to the ground and setting one knee on his chest. He then quickly straddled him. Eugene kicked up, but Benjamin's thighs held him down. Eugene grabbed Benjamin's head and cracked it against his own, trying again to buck free of his rider; but Benjamin clung and presently began to deal blows that found Eugene's face and neck. Eugene strained to break free as he was beaten on the face, but he grew weaker and presently gave up resisting, whereupon Benjamin continued to land blows on him until Bonard arrived and wrenched him off the man beneath him, who was now senseless.

"What in hell? — How come you pick a fight with my best man? — What'd he do? — Godalmighty, Ben, that man is worth money to me!" Bonard turned to the little crowd of Negroes who had gathered to stare as the hungry might gaze upon food. "One of y'all come and help me get him to the office yonder!"

Casey guided Benjamin back to their horses, and Benjamin slumped against Jupiter until he could breathe more evenly. Then he carefully set foot in stirrup and swung himself onto the horse. Casey got back on his, and they rode away without looking back.

Leon was able to eat nothing that day but a bowl of gruel Josephine made from the stock of a wild turkey Daniel had shot. That night Benjamin kept a log burning in the fireplace and slept in a chair beside his son's bed, waking when Leon began to cry protests in a dream. Dropping to his knees, he roused the boy with sounds of comfort.

"Pa?"

He touched the boy's forehead with his lips. "I'm here."

Part Two

1886

1

Annabel Saxon took the occasion of funerals, the most recent being that of Margaret-Ella Davis, to remind the women of the family they were getting older. It was never "we," but "you." "You are all getting old," she would say firmly, looking at Sarah Troy. She might then proceed to tick off on the fingers of both hands the ages of various female relatives, close and not so close, present and absent. Often she ascribed more years to them than they honestly claimed, but if one complained, Annabel fixed the objector with such an incredulous look as to cast the matter into everlasting doubt. On her good days, which predominated, Sarah was pleased to correct her briskly, allowing no "But surely—" no wink, no indulgent concession.

"Annabel, you are wrong," Sarah would say. "Your sister is fifty-five. I remember when you were happy to keep her younger than you; but you've always been mean about Doreen."

"I am the soul of Christian charity," Annabel assured her.

"Jesus will be pleased to hear it."

Annabel uttered one of her joyless laughs. "Anyway, you are seventy-five. I don't imagine you will debate that point with me? Nineteen years older than I. A grown woman when I was born."

"That event sinks deeper into history with every breath we draw. — Is that Miss Kilmer behind the fern? I must ask her about Toby. He's getting old too and had a sore paw the last time I saw him."

Sarah's seventy-five years compelled her to surrender few of her activities. "I can do anything," she boasted, although admitting to Jane, "only a little less. I work until I'm tired and rest. Then I work again. It's something you learn." She would never think herself old. She'd learned to behave at times as if she was aging, because it disconcerted the young to see her disregard the limitations that time imposes, but even as she remembered to walk a little more slowly, to bend a little less supplely, she could say to herself: "This is Sarah pretending to be an old woman." Oh, there were days enough she felt coffin-ready, but that was not the same as feeling old.

One of the activities she vowed never to abandon was what she called her cemetery drill, although she no longer insisted that it be exclusive of children, even male ones. Jane had been an easy convert to leaving their families for a day, suddenly and deliberately, two or three times a year. Such a day was this mild and cloudy one in late January.

"It won't rain," Sarah had assured Jane when proposing the excursion that morning in the kitchen of Jane's house. "There's no feel of rain."

Jane agreed there was not; and Bruce was all eagerness when Sarah returned to the big house and told her she might go with them instead of attending school. Sarah had admitted Bruce to participation in the cemetery drill two years ago, when Bruce was five. She represented the youngest generation and must be initiated into the meaning of being a woman of Beulah Land. Children are more ready for responsibility than their elders are to share it. And so after breakfast, when the men had gone about their plantation chores, Leon and Davy and Bobby Lee gathered books and climbed into the wagon to ride into Highboro with their great-grandmother and mother and sister-cousin.

During the passage from home to school the boys veered from mutinous to wheedling, finally extracting from the ladies a grudging permission to join them at noon for an hour when school broke for dinner. Josephine and Mabella and Velma had packed a basket of victuals with generosity and ingenuity. There were ham and pork roast slices between halves of buttered biscuits, watermelon rind preserves and cucumber pickles, baked sweet potatoes to be peeled and eaten from the hand, boiled eggs, sausages stiff in a film of congealed grease, apples and fruit cake and a jar of toasted pecans to be savored with a bottle of blackberry wine.

After leaving the boys at school ("The insult," they declared to each other. "Having us carry a note to Bruce's teacher explaining her absence for the day!") Sarah drove the wagon to the grove of trees behind the church, where she unhitched the horse. Gentle Minerva would be content to wait, shifting her feet, dreaming of soft summer grass, and dropping perfectly round balls of dung to shatter and steam on the hard, bare ground. Jane collected tools from the back of the wagon as Sarah unbuttoned her sweater and Bruce ran ahead to open and close the double wrought-iron gates between churchyard and graveyard.

Together they made the first survey of the Kendrick and Davis burying grounds to decide what most needed doing; separately they set to. As the work went forward, each finished bit gave satisfaction. In the two years Bruce had helped her aunt and great-grandmother she'd learned to make a favorite of a particular grave on each visit. Today she elected Benjamin Davis, comfortable in the reminder that her father's name had first been borne by this man whose date of death was July 17, 1831, and whose stone also carried a legend hardly traceable from the years' accumulation of mold and ground moss: *Over in the summer land.* Of what she'd been told of him, she remembered that he'd been crippled by a stroke of paralysis and carried about during the last years of his life by a great slave named Monday Kendrick. That Benjamin Davis had been her father's great-grandfather. Pitying him as if he'd died yesterday, she made his grave her tender concern.

Glancing at the child, Sarah guessed some of her thoughts. The lip scar shone brightly pink as Bruce sweated with the exertion of repairing and resetting a brick border. She never complained of the scar or asked why she wasn't like other girls. If most of the men and women under the gravestones were unknown to Bruce and a matter of hearsay, many were familiar to Jane as flesh and blood, and to Sarah not merely familiar but family, loved or not but all accepted. She was not unhappily aware that one day she would lie here and that Jane, then Bruce, and those who came after them would perform something like this day's duty to her own mound of earth.

Bruce had never asked before: "Why isn't Aunt Selma here?"

"She wanted to be with Lovey and Ezra in our cemetery at Beulah Land."

Hesitantly, Bruce said, "We owned them, didn't we?"

"They were ours, and we were theirs," Sarah said. "Abraham's father and mother are there too, and Pauline will be one day."

"Why did Aunt Selma want to be with the Negroes?"

"They never hurt her, so she loved them."

Although there was no rule, they generally started at the edges, working apart until the progress of their tasks drew them toward the center, in the way women gradually contract a quilting frame. They might call back and forth a joke or genial complaint, but their exchanges were brief during the first hour or two. There was one grave Sarah avoided until Jane began to work at it, brushing leaves away, pulling a weed, trimming grass as delicately as she would cut a baby's hair. Without looking around she knew that Sarah was watching and that presently she would speak. "You're good to be so careful." Jane would not know she had been tense until she felt her shoulders relax. Bruce had learned not to join them there. Once she had done so; overwhelmed by love, she had touched her great-grandmother, and Sarah had wept wildly. When Sarah spoke behind her today, Jane's gestures became at once more casual. Sarah joined her in the work, and soon they were chatting about any and every thing under the sun except the man whose body lay beneath their hands and out of the sun forever.

Sarah said, "I think Velma's going to marry Zadok's youngest boy."

"Hollis?" Jane asked unnecessarily. Sarah nodded. "Freda hasn't said anything. Is Rosalie happy about it?"

"Rosalie wouldn't consider Princess Alexandra good enough for Hollis, but Velma is terrified of her, which is the next-best thing."

"I didn't know they'd ever looked at each other."

"Nor I until Bruce told me. Velma told Bruce. I can remember when something that happened in one of the cabins could change our lives, and what happened to us could change theirs. Now we all go on not much caring, though we say we do, but that's manners. The old feeling is gone. Perhaps it's better."

The day warmed, and Sarah took off her sweater and hung it on an angel's raised hand. Bruce fetched a bucket of water from the well beside the church, and the three talked as they refreshed themselves. Now and then someone would enter or leave the church. Doreen and Eloise Kilmer came through the gates to greet them, but soon left. Others were content to wave, knowing Sarah did not want company on her workdays at the graveyard. Two who did not come, although they were frequenters of the church, were Ann Oglethorpe and Priscilla Davis. Sarah regularly took Bruce to their house, but there was no ease on those visits, and neither side encouraged closer congress. Mother and child were as cool and correct as oriental envoys.

The morning's peace was shattered five minutes after twelve by the panting arrival of Leon and Bobby Lee and Davy, who had run all the way from school. Jane set them to work. Leon went to give Minerva water and hay and talk to her a little, while Bobby Lee drew another bucket of water for drinking and washing hands, and Davy lugged the basket of food to the wide flat stone covering the grave of Edna Davis. When they were two or three, they ate in the wagon or buggy they'd come in. Today they would want the amplitude of Edna's memorial stone. "She'd be the first to insist on it," Sarah said as she flung and adjusted the tablecloth. Before they could set out all the dishes and jars, they were joined by Fanny and Blair Saxon, who had evidently followed the other children from school.

Seeing Sarah's frown, Fanny said quickly, "We're on our way home to dinner." She clasped her hands behind her to show they did not expect to be asked to join them.

"How's your father?" Sarah asked the girl, and Jane smoothed her hair to make up for lack of hospitality.

"Worse," Blair said for his sister.

"We'll stop by on our way home," Sarah said. "Do you think your mother would mind?"

"No'm, she won't mind," Fanny answered promptly.

"What way does he appear worse?" Sarah inquired.

"It's hard to specify," Blair said importantly, "but Mama said if he wasn't better by dinnertime, she was going to have the doctor again; and Dr. Platt was there yesterday too."

"Well, you'd better run on," Sarah said. "Tell your mother we may stop for a minute—just for a word at the door, not to bother her with a visit."

"Yes'm."

Hungry, the family set to eating, sharing and passing whatever was wanted, the boys behaving well to show their appreciation at being allowed to join the outing. But when Sarah and Jane sat down on old Ben Davis's clean gravestone to enjoy the last of their wine, Davy began to slurp water from an empty pickle jar, pretending to be drunk. Bruce kicked him in a dignified way, which he ignored. "Jody Rountree has to stay after school today and get a whipping."

"What did he do?" Jane asked.

"Let loose a turtle during the arithmetic test."

"That doesn't sound so terrible," Sarah said.

"No, ma'am, but he'd used chalk to print a bad word on his shell."

Sarah smiled, whereupon the three boys whooped and hollered with laughter. It was upon this scene that Annabel Saxon made her appearance, opening and closing the wrought-iron gates with a double clang to silence them. "I never saw or heard anything so sacrilegious!" she declared. "Eating on poor old Granny's grave—laughing as if you were all at the circus."

"Would you like a pickled peach?" Sarah said, unconcerned. "I'm afraid that's all that's left, and it looks a little soft."

Annabel shook her head. "I would not. Fanny said you were here. I was at Bonard's when the children came home for dinner."

"I'm sorry to hear he is less well," Sarah said.

"It doesn't appear to have dampened your spirits. The doctor has been and says it must be pneumonia—exactly what carried away Mr. Troy last winter, at just about this time."

2

Of the various responses to death, surprise is perhaps the commonest, however much the event has been anticipated. Annabel Saxon had little more regard for her younger son than she had for his wife, but surprise and the reiterated declaration of surprise sufficed for the occasions consequent to his demise. Bonard was not yet thirty-seven; nor had he been long or seriously ill, although there were many to remind each other after the fact that he had been unwell for half a year. There was nothing fearsome to warn them like consumption of the lungs or that decline attending a noxious growth; he had only been "poorly," with chills during the last summer of his life and low but persistent fevers commencing with the cool rains of autumn and wasting him to a January grave. Poor Bonard was puzzled but not frightened to find that he no longer wanted cigars and spirits, only wanted to want them. And then pneumonia, sometimes called the old man's friend, became the young man's destroying angel. His death was pronounced a tragedy, but few tears were shed, for Bonard was not someone people needed to cry over. The deaths of others his age were remembered and these challenged by reminiscences of the passing of those even younger, until it seemed that no very remarkable thing had happened.

So long had they been cautioned to tiptoe, Blair and Fanny were more relieved than not when, another noon, they were met at the door by their grandmother and told they were poor orphans and did not have to go to school for the remainder of the week. Although everyone vowed they should not starve, no one actually opened his purse and closed his eyes. James Davis arrived at the house a scant hour after receiving word that death had claimed its head and asserted to the pretty widow that he had lost his second gift of sight. Bonard had been his partner in business and none calling him husband or father need fear hardship while he, James, was able to sell a foot of lumber. "Did he not first develop chills after sleeping a week in the swampy stand we cut below Sharon Hill last August? You may depend upon me, not forgetting that my own mourning, which I have not yet put by, warms my heart further to your grief and need."

Frankie murmured that he was a good man, a kind uncle. Then voice faltered as hands molded air to say what words evidently could not. Realizing the idleness of gesture with a blind man, she asked in a more collected way what there was for her in the line of definite expectations. James coughed and considered: as to that, the share of the sawmill controlled by Bonard had, in fact, never passed from his father's hands.

Later the same day Annabel relishingly confirmed that Frankie was poor, explaining that "the Bank" owned the quarter of the mill that had provided her living.

"I did not realize," Frankie said coldly, "that matters still stood that way."

Her mother-in-law replied, "And why should you have, as long as allowance was made for your every extravagance?"

Frankie said, "The Bank is only Papa Blair, is it not?"

Annabel qualified the definition: "And those who advise him." Her wink left no doubt that she herself was her husband's chief mentor.

"Bonard was promised and surely earned a quarter share in the business. He told me so more than once, and Uncle James has said a hundred times he could not have kept the business up without my husband."

"Now he will have to, won't he?" Annabel sighed. "It was thought not best to give it to Bonard outright. My devotion to my sons' interests—and I think no one will deny me that—did not let me forget certain indications of irresponsibility in my youngest. For an instance: we could not disregard his using sawmill funds which were not his at the time he made his sudden, surprising marriage."

"You have a long memory. I must speak to Papa Blair." As soon as she said the words, Frankie knew they were a mistake. Annabel would not forgive the suggestion that her husband represented higher authority.

"Your pretty ways persuaded him to make over this house to you in the early days when we were all relieved that Bonard had not done worse, but we are accustomed to your charms now." Annabel stamped her right foot. "It's gone to sleep."

"Get up and walk on it," Frankie advised.

"It does me no good." She stamped the foot again.

"You don't take any exercise."

"How can you say so? I am doing something every waking moment. I haven't time to take the extended rambles you indulge in. One of the servants—it must have been Fox and Millie's grandboy; he's an idler but he has a quick eye—observed you coming out of the cotton gin the other day, or was it week? He wondered what you could have found to do there with it closed for the winter. I meant to ask you." Frankie picked a yellow thread from the black silk velvet of her lap. "Your traipsing around does, I grant, keep you in good figure, though you eat like a plowman. Of course, it will catch up with you. I've seen it happen with others. You'll get fat as Margaret-Ella one day. She hadn't seen her feet for five years when they buried her. I always told her she was digging her grave with her teeth."

"She had a weak heart."

"They'll say what they think sounds best. — As to the funeral. When I heard, I sent to the bank for both Mr. Saxons to attend me. I've discussed it with them, and they feel as I do—" She broke off, rising from her chair. "Do you suppose they've finished dressing him? They never think to tell you until they want praise and pay. Which cravat did you give them to use?" She left the dining room where they had been sitting and crossed the hallway to the bedroom, returning a few minutes later. "That blue one won't do at all. There was a spot on it that looked like dried egg yolk somebody had tried to scratch off. I picked a black one, more suitable anyway. They're changing it. Both Blair One and Blair Two agree with me that the funeral must be at three o'clock day after tomorrow. A morning funeral looks as eager as a Yankee peddler."

Frankie shrugged.

"I'll let Quarterman know and tell Doreen which hymns she and Eloise are to get up on. No need for you to do so. It doesn't look well for the widow to interfere in arrangements; it's as if no one cares for her. You musn't go outdoors at all until after the funeral, or show yourself at a window. No more of your walks, mind. I'll see to everything."

Frankie nodded her head. "It's good of you."

"What's a mother for? And don't worry overmuch about the future. I shall help you however I can, seeing how dependent upon us you must now be." She looked about the long, oval room, frowning at the rich curtains and polished wood and silver candelabra. "It will be best to dispose of this house, for you'll have nothing incoming to keep it up. When you sell, the bank will use the proceeds to pay your and Bonard's debts. There are always debts after a death, no matter how well things have been managed. We'll hope there is some small substance remaining to set by for your son's future career. You're to move in with Mr. Saxon and me until we all decide what is best for the future. If you care to make a long visit with your family in Savannah, I'll take charge of the children. I don't shirk my duty, you know. Poor waifs. They are not to suffer for the misfortunes of their parents, if I can help it. Bonard looks just like himself, by the way. That's always a comfort, though I shall never get over the cruel surprise of his going."

The funeral was perhaps less noteworthy for what it mourned of the past than of what it suggested for the future to some of those attending. There was, of course, a general sympathy for the young widow and her fatherless children. There always is in such cases, or there is said to be.

For a dozen years Annabel and Frankie had shared a seesaw; suddenly Annabel believed herself in command. The temptation to use her advantage was assured by her natural arrogance. While keeping a firmly bereaved expression on her face, she allowed her thoughts to dance with future possibilities.

James Davis in his pew was still erect and handsome at fifty-three, his blind face showing none of his feelings as he listened to the words of the Reverend Quarterman and the music made by his sister and Miss Kilmer. He was, in truth, at the boil with randiness, his folded hands on his lap serving a purpose beyond repose. For the two years before her death his wife Maggie had provided fewer rewards than responsibilities. After husbands were found for Rebecca, Cora, and Beatrice, Maggie gave herself happily to gluttony. James grudged her the pleasures of the board only to the degree they inhibited his pleasures of the bed. He was a sensual man. Never a womanizer, ever faithful to his current mate, he nonetheless carried an aura of sensuality neither missed or misinterpreted by the more susceptible of his female acquaintances. Blindness only added salt to his appeal. Maggie's fatness had finally rendered her incapable of indulging her husband's needs, and James suffered a lonely sexual hell. Since her death he'd had enough kindness from Cora, Beatrice, and Rebecca, whose solicitude had become mere bossiness. As he sat surrounded and feeling smothered by them and their dull husbands and foolish children, he wanted to sweep them aside and be his own free man again. He wanted a woman, one woman warm and willing in his arms and in his bed.

Half a dozen rows behind him sat Eugene and Bessie and Theodore Aquinas Betchley. After his fight with Benjamin Davis, Eugene had been sent to Savannah to engage in the shipping arrangements for timber cut by the Davis-Saxon mill. There he had given useful service and been given useful opportunities, achieving a name for cunning and reliability to balance his continuing reputation for quick and harsh response. Traveling by train as he often did between Savannah and Highboro, he had lost the sense of adventure first provided by the calculated munificence of Sarah Troy on the occasion of his marriage. Eugene had become respectable, his past escapades with Alf Crawford forgotten. Alf himself had abruptly decided to become senile and lived with the family of his daughter Alvina in the next county to the north. He was said to spend his days whittling and to show no interest in catering to others' needs for alcohol or fornication. Bessie kept her farm and her second son, Eugene providing for them, although he could no longer be said to live with them. He lived nowhere. A rooming house in Savannah, another in Highboro for an occasional night's lodging when a return to the farm was impractical—these served his needs for food and shelter. If he enjoyed other satisfactions than those offered by his good wife, so did most of the men who dealt with him find such diversion away from home.

During the half-year period of Bonard's gradual disintegration Eugene spent more and more time in Highboro, as James Davis found his presence more necessary in the day-to-day running of the sawmill. He had achieved the advantages of respectability without being required to lead an entirely regular life. If he did no more than his duty by Bessie, had she not been lucky to marry him? She was a woman older than he and mother of a bastard. No one suggested that Eugene neglected his wife, not even Bessie.

On the morning he fled the woods of Beulah Land leaving his traps and, although he did not know it, his boyhood behind him, he had looked upon the Marsh farm as a piece of property to acquire and had worked to get it. He was not lazy. He worked for Bessie before and after he married her and her farm. Now he worked for the sawmill. If the death of Bessie's mother had cleared his path earlier, the death of Bonard Saxon now presented him with matter for speculation.

The funeral over, there were many to press declarations of regard upon the widow. Eugene spoke his platitudes clumsily, merely looking at her. James, with the excuse of blindness and family connection, massaged her hands in the warmest way. Frankie was thinking of neither, for her mind was consumed with the question that had not left it for two days: What is a poor woman to do?

3

"What *is* a poor woman to do?"

They lay close for warmth, not passion's sake; they had already made love, and they were as used to each other's bed habits as a married couple.

"I wish you could be my wife," Benjamin said.

"I shan't feel obliged to thank you for an offer you're in no position to make. Priscilla will live to be old. No matter how long you live, Priscilla will live an hour longer."

His smile was brief. "And they'll say she died because she couldn't live on without me."

"How do you like not feeling guilty?" Frankie asked.

He pretended surprise and mild offense. "I never did." After a moment he amended the assertion. "I haven't for a long time, years."

"I think you miss it."

"No."

"Something was different."

"You talk too much."

"I like to talk, and so do you."

He had been thinking over what she said. "Maybe it was different. It's the first time since he died and a long time since the last time."

"Thirteen days," she said.

He stroked her foot with his own for the compliment of counting the days since they had met privately.

"This is luxury." She sighed.

"A narrow bed in a square room of a cotton gin," he teased her. "Not even a stove to warm you."

"You're my stove," she said. He rubbed himself against her. "Too hot."

"Burn." His arms and legs went around her.

"I've burned enough for one day." He relaxed his arms and legs to make it easier for her to free herself if she wanted to. When he relaxed, she relaxed. "Luxury," she repeated. "I am luxury, you are luxury, we are luxury. — It's like a class at Roman's school. I wish I had already got up and dressed; I'd be warm. I wouldn't have to get out of bed now and shiver while I dress and wait for my own body to warm me." His arms and legs moved to hold her again. Submitting but not succumbing, she observed him as he idly nuzzled her breast. His lips were at first soft as her own flesh. Then they firmed as he opened them to taste her. "I enjoy you," she said. "Not merely *your* enjoyment of *me*. I enjoy *you*. I don't think women find men very interesting. I can amuse myself wondering what it would be like in bed with this or that one; but usually I'm thinking of their response to me, not mine to them. Now, you. I'm pleased but also puzzled why that part of me makes you concentrate so. What is there about it? I don't think of a part of you as particularly appetizing. I like your hands, but it's what they do to me, not the hands themselves. — Ow! You bit me—"

He wiped his mouth on her hair. "I can bite harder than that. I could bite you in two."

"What happened to that girl you told me about?" He lay still. "You know, the one you dream about sometimes."

"You mean Nancy?"

"Yes, that Negro girl you grew up with and then found in a whorehouse in Savannah."

"Nancy," he repeated.

"Yes."

"She was born on Beulah Land and stayed with us all through the war. I wish she'd stayed forever."

"You used to meet up at the Glade and do it, you told me. Don't you know what became of her?"

"I don't know where she is now," he said. "Abraham thinks he saw her on the street in Savannah one time, a year or so ago; but when he called, the woman hurried on, and he decided he'd been wrong. She was Abraham's mammy when his own died, so he had a feeling for her."

After a moment she said, "Was she better than I am?"

"Yes."

"What way?" she asked interestedly.

"All."

She slapped him hard on his naked shoulder and then on the face.

"That hurts."

"I mean it to." He caught her hand when she raised it again, and she let it go limp until he dropped it. "Did she enjoy you the way I do?"

"Yes," he said.

"You're hateful."

"You asked me," he said.

"Did she like any special part of you?"

"She thought every part of me was special," he boasted to rile her.

She yawned elaborately. "I must get up."

"I was joking."

"I have to go. I was about to get up, truly. It has nothing to do with your bragging." His hands smoothed and soothed her into tarrying. "You've been twice lucky, with Nancy and me. Once unlucky, twice lucky. Most men never have even one. They have to be satisfied with their own feeling; they never know a woman's."

They were still for several minutes.

He said, "What about—him? You know who I mean."

"I don't." She sounded pleased. "Do I?"

"You do."

"Oh."

"Yes!"

"My cousin."

"When you were both eleven and he came with his mother and sister to stay with your family in Savannah."

"They visited relatives a lot," she said. "They were poorer even than we were."

"Early one morning he tiptoed into your room. You saw him open and close the door, but pretended you were asleep, and you still pretended when he got in bed with you."

"I wanted to find out what he was up to."

"And you found out," he said.

"Fred was his name."

"I don't want to be told his name! The thing is, he had you when he was *eleven!*"

"Well," she said reasonably, "I was eleven too. You've told me you started around then too. Maybe most children do and never talk about it, don't even remember it."

"I think they'd remember it," he said.

She said, "We were together more completely than I've ever been with anyone, with any *body* since. Even you. Only with him have I not known where one of us ended and the other began."

"You mean that?" he asked coldly.

"I always tell you the truth."

"What happened to him? You never said." He could feel her thinking, but they lay so close he could not look at her directly without changing their positions. "Have you seen him since?"

She almost laughed, and sighed and turned her face to his chest. "Oh, yes. Once. Once only. Just before I came to visit here that first summer, I saw him. The summer I met you—and everybody. He married young. He and his wife came to Savannah for her to meet the family, really just to go somewhere away from home and call it a wedding trip. He married the plainest woman in the world, and she hadn't one single, solitary thing to say for herself, or him, or the cat for that matter. They live in Augusta and have three children now. That was the only time we'd seen each other since the time we were eleven and everything happened, not once but twice. He came and got in bed with me two mornings. Well, he did nothing but fidget and fiddle with his watch and chain. He never looked at me. I mean, he didn't see me when he looked at me. I thought at first he was nervous, and then I realized he had forgotten!" Benjamin began to laugh, and she pressed her face into the gap between his arm and chest. After a minute she raised herself to rest on an elbow and look at him. "I wasn't telling the truth when I said I loved no special parts of you the way you do me. I love it under your arms, and the damp, salty hair." Her hand slipped down under the covers. "I turn to ashes when I touch the smooth—skin—here." He grabbed her and rolled her over. "See!" she laughed. "You have to grab and hold me and try to put me under you. You can't bear letting *me* make love to *you!*"

He let her go. In the pause, both went still. Over the past year they had drifted into such teasing ways, to avoid monotony, and sometimes they were warmed into further engagement. But today when she moved to rise from bed, he did not stop her. Nor did he watch her dress. She was hurrying, and he knew she would not want him to watch. When she had put on her shoes, he said, "There's no reason you have to decide anything right away. Remember: you're Mrs. Saxon too, as much as Aunt Annabel. Your bills will be paid."

"Ah, buy by whom? I think your Aunt Annabel will make me work hard for her charity."

"I wish I could make everything right for you, Frankie." He sounded almost sullen.

Her laugh was against herself, but he was not to know that and pulled the covers up tight around him, shifting in bed so that his back was toward her. She left without saying more. His mind returned to Nancy, at first happily and then with such sadness that he was caught by surprise.

4

Jefferson Davis pounded his fists on the door of the privy farthest from the big house. "What are y'all doing in there? Let me in! I bet I know what you're doing, you're fucking your fists!" He pounded again.

After whispers inside, the door flew open and a hand reached out and grabbed him by the hair, yanking him in and slamming the door behind him. "Now, you shut up," Robert E. Lee told him.

Davy was not inclined to pursue debate; the scene he found himself part of was too interesting. His brother and cousin had removed their trousers and both had erections. Mute with respect, he watched them return to their masturbating. Presently, he unfastened his own trousers and joined the activity. Leon, red of face and penis, suddenly gasped, "I think I'm coming! Yes, I'm coming! Here I come!" And with the last word a jet of semen flew from his organ. His motion ceased; he merely held and squeezed, head tilted like the Dying Gladiator, a proud expression on his face. The other boys stared at him with awe. "I told you I could," he said, his voice natural again.

Davy and Bobby Lee resumed masturbating, Leon watching them with mild interest after he had cleaned himself. Presently, both brothers writhed with completion of the act, but neither, alas, achieved the result of their cousin.

Davy said furiously, "I don't know why *he* can do it and I can't!"

"I've told you," Leon said in a kindly but superior tone. "You're not old enough. I'll be twelve in April."

"I'm eleven," Bobby Lee said quickly. "I ought to be doing it soon, don't you reckon, Leon?"

"Surely," Leon agreed.

"I think I almost did that time. There was a little something, but it wasn't white."

"You won't have to wait long," Leon said encouragingly.

Bobby Lee turned to his brother viciously. "You're just nine, you little shit-ass. It'll be a long *long* time before *you* can. We'll be doing it for years and years before you can even hope to."

"It's not fair!" Davy wailed.

"Hush up," Leon said. "I thought I heard Uncle Dan."

They straightened their clothes and hurried out of the privy as Daniel Todd's voice came to them from a little distance. "Davy! You, Bobby Lee! — Leon? Where are you all?"

Running toward the sound, they found Daniel on the board seat of a wagon drawn up outside the cow barn. "Come on; want you to help me load a cord of wood and take it to your aunt Doreen and Miss Eloise—" He started the mule without waiting, turning the wagon into a road that followed the side of a field into the woods. The boys ran after him, nimbly swinging themselves into the open back of the wagon.

It was a mild Saturday morning in late February. Watching them leave from the window of her office, Sarah decided that she wanted company. She knew she would find it in the kitchen. Their voices reached her before she reached them: Velma's complaining complacently as Josephine and Mabella and Bruce attacked her about her coming marriage to Hollis Davis.

Josephine shouted jollily, "No use you running to me when Miss Rosalie start giving you a bad time—"

Mabella, giggling, added her barb: "You think our *Josie* a mean old thing, you *wait!* You *just wait!* Miss Rosalie so particular she make you learn how to cook all over again *her* way. Say: otherwise, how her Hollis know whether he eatin' peas and corn bread or lye hominy!"

"What you mean *I* a mean old thing!" Josephine thundered joyously. "You call me mean, you feel my fist side your head!"

In and out sounded Bruce's high laughter and Velma's parrying comments, laced with fears and forebodings that were mostly affected for politeness' sake, for she had long ago won Rosalie's approval by her care of Bruce and her own modest deportment. It had been a lucky day for Velma, and she knew it, when Sarah Troy found her and brought her to Beulah Land to wet-nurse Benjamin Davis's daughter.

Before reaching the door Sarah changed her mind, deciding not to join them. Instead, she returned to the front of the house and was in time to see Benjamin trotting his horse up the carriageway. While Casey lived, there had never been time enough for all she wanted to do. Now she might find herself idle and uncertain how to use an odd half hour. There was in the ordinary way plenty for her to see to, but Saturdays had come to be half workdays, made up of miscellaneous small jobs on the plantation. The holiday mood seeped into the house; and although Josephine saw that all was done that needed doing, the routine was less rigid than on ordinary days. Hence, the laughter and teasing of Velma in the kitchen and Josephine's easy acquiescence that morning after breakfast when Bruce asked her if she had time to teach her to make the candy called peanut brittle.

Glad to see him, yet a little ashamed of her need, Sarah took a tart tone with her grandson. "Benjamin! Wherever have you been? I've been looking all over for you—"

"What's wrong?"

"Nothing wrong like the sky falling, but there's something on my mind I haven't had time to go into with you."

"Be back in a minute, Grandma." He continued to walk his horse along the carriageway toward the barns.

He sometimes understood her better than she understood herself, she realized. She called after him, "Only when you're ready. There's no hurry—" He gave no sign of hearing her, for the grateful note in her voice made him feel sorry for her, and pity was something he never wanted to feel for her. It would not have occurred to him before Casey died. He gave her a little time, but not too much, examining a mended harness with Clarence, the boy who took care of his horse, then pausing briefly at the kitchen to share the amusement his grandmother had forgone and to hug Bruce and let her scold him for taking a handful of her shelled peanuts. He was eating them when he joined Sarah.

"I'm worried about Abraham."

His mouth full, he nodded.

"Give me some." He leaned across the desk and shared the remaining peanuts about equally. "Since he's been back he's learned more than you and Roscoe both knew about running the cotton mill."

Benjamin swallowed, cleared his throat, and swallowed again before he could speak. "He's smart, no question."

"And he's a good boy," Sarah said. "He gets on well with everybody, doesn't he?" She watched him carefully. Benjamin did not answer, but he appeared to be thinking about it. "Oh, he jokes," she went on. "That's always been his way, to make a joke. Remember how he kept us laughing when he was a youngun? I don't know where he got it, for Floyd was never like that, and his mother was solemn as a setting hen."

"Nancy, maybe."

"The Negroes at the mill understand he can be playful and still mean what he says for them to do. I don't worry about that." She paused and looked at him, wanting him to say more.

"What you worry about is him and the town people."

"Exactly," she said as if he had discovered the truth for her. "We've spoiled him; everybody that knows him has. We loved him from the time he was born because of his father. Then after he went off to school and came home—" She hesitated.

Benjamin said quietly, "He'll be all right, Grandma."

"He talks different from Negroes down here, and people in town think he's uppity, don't they?"

"Some do."

"There. You see."

"They'll get used to him. Give them time. He sounds brash because of the jokes and because he's twenty."

"Twenty-one. He was twenty when he came home and went to work at the mill. I wish I had some more of those peanuts."

"Want me to get some?"

"You *do* think he'll be all right?"

"We'll have to see, won't we? Is it Gene Betchley that worries you, Grandma?"

"He always has," she admitted, "ever since he went to work at the sawmill and got to like pushing people around." He said nothing, but continued looking at her. "You know he hates us." Benjamin sighed. "Our giving Bessie a thousand dollars to make Leon a legal Davis only made him hate us the more, though he was the one behind it all, egging her on to it. I never bought or sold anybody in my life, black or white, and I wouldn't have agreed if Leon himself hadn't begged us to. It made him feel safer from Eugene. But I didn't like it." All of this Benjamin understood, but he let her say it without interrupting. "Well, Gene can't get at us directly, but he may try to do it through Abraham and the Negroes."

"There's been no real what you could call trouble," Benjamin pointed out.

"Bonard has always been there to step in front of Gene. Up to now."

They sat without talking for a little while. At last Sarah said, "I've tried to be friends with Gene, but I don't get on with him. I used to think I could manage any man alive." He smiled. "Well, you know how I get on with most of them. I like men and boys, and they know it and trust me."

"It's because you flirt with them."

"I do no such thing!"

"You make every man you talk to think he's the only one alive. You could get the devil to lift his hat to you. Oh, what a rounder you'd have been if it hadn't been for Casey and Dan and me keeping you in line!"

"Benjamin, you're making fun of me—"

"Yes'm."

"I've a mind to turn you over my knee, big as you are—"

"Now, you see? What grown man could resist you when you offer to take him on your lap? — It's all right, Grandma. I'm watching Gene, and Abraham too."

5

With normal rainfall, the widest branch of the creeks flowing through the area of Highboro was as full and strong as a river, and it divided a stretch of land still sometimes called the Campgrounds because troops had been quartered and trained there during the war. When James Davis and Bonard Saxon sought a permanent site for their sawmill, the township, nudged by its leading banker, put up the land for sale and the partners bought twenty acres. The creek provided a water supply as well as transportation for the pine and cypress they cut, and the sawmill prospered.

At the time Roscoe Elk conceived the idea of a cotton mill for the district, he bought five acres of the Campgrounds on the opposite side of the creek, knowing he would need power and water. Nothing came of it until November 1881 when he and Benjamin Davis attended the International Cotton Exposition in Atlanta and came home to act on what they had seen. Benjamin made improvements and additions to the cotton gin. No longer was the seed discarded to rot and stink in the rain; new machines housed alongside the gin converted it into oil and fertilizer and cattle feed.

Signing a contract of agreement, he and Roscoe Elk put up the first building of the cotton mill. It was, and remained for a time, a simple, almost primitive operation, nothing on the scale of the mills in Augusta and Columbus which employed hundreds of people. It was started to give employment to such graduates of Roman's school as did not have a mind to pursue life on the land for wages or shares. In the larger mills of those larger towns Negroes had not been found suitable for the work, the transition from field to factory demanding too great an adjustment, and poor whites were used almost exclusively. But for the Beulah Mill, as it was soon called, the workers had been to school and grown accustomed to working indoors. The poor whites around Highboro were not encouraged to come to Beulah because of the complexion of its dual ownership. They also shied from working alongside Negroes who had been to school, elementary though Elk Institute was, telling each other, "If there's one thing I can't stand, it's a educated nigger." But they were jealous of the wages paid, a dollar a day for males, three quarters of that for females.

Without the sawmill's or the cotton mill's making a strict policy of hiring by color, the workers facing each other across the creek were nonetheless predominantly white on one side and black on the other. They were not in competition; there was work for all, and they shared the water supply amicably. Beulah Mill was patronized as a pokey poor relation of the thriving sawmill, a minor interest for its owners, who were content to keep it so. It served the purpose it was meant to serve. No armies waited to be clothed and tented from its spindles and looms; no ships at Savannah fixed sailing schedules to its rate of production. Abraham Kendrick, however, had an itch for expansion; and across the creek another ambitious young man, Eugene Betchley, was watching him.

On the evening of the Saturday that Sarah Troy expressed certain anxieties to her grandson, Frankie Saxon received a caller whose identity and errand surprised her. Supper was over and her daughter Fanny practiced a piano piece in the living room, making the same mistake at the same point and then beginning the piece again. Frankie did not understand her daughter; and the patient way the daughter sometimes behaved with her mother, as if their roles were reversed, was not conducive to intimate friendship between them. Her son Blair, Frankie reflected with satisfaction, was more like her. Handsome, conceited, selfish, and charming—he was all that a son may be to warm a mother's heart and make her complain of a sensible daughter.

It had been an exasperating week and month for Frankie, the shock of widowhood unameliorated by any reassurance of financial security. Her mother-in-law lost no opportunity to remind her how poor and dependent she now was. She came in and out every day at any hour, having decided that since the house was to be sold, it had become common property. Frankie's appeal to her father-in-law for a month to collect herself before the house was taken from her was granted.

"Two, three, six months, my dear; there's no hurry," said the man whose exacting wife made him an easy mark for a soft smile and a teary eye.

Taking heart, Frankie suggested that, since Bonard had not enjoyed possession of the quarter share of the mill he had been promised and that everyone agreed he had more than earned, his spirit might rejoice in heaven if that share was now settled upon his earthly dependents.

Annabel had anticipated just such a request and forbidden her husband to listen to the widow's sly importuning. And so, even before Frankie completed her plea, Blair Saxon was shaking his head as if there were bees inside it. "No, no, no, my dear. My wife, Mrs. Saxon—you understand."

Morning, noon, and night Annabel advised and bullied both of them. If Frankie had resented her before, she now loathed her as much as she dreaded a future under her rule. If only, she thought, forgetting the embroidery in her lap, Priscilla were to be trampled by runaway horses, struck by lightning, *etherealized* by her own goodness—anything!—oh, anything to hasten her into the fold of that Blessed Shepherd she was forever bleating about.

"Mama?"

"What?" She was startled to see her daughter before her.

"You were dreaming."

"You've stopped playing."

"I went to answer a knock at the door. It's Mr. Betchley from the sawmill wanting to see you. I asked him to wait in the hall."

Glad of any distraction, Frankie dismissed her daughter and invited the caller to take a chair in the little alcove parlor generally reserved for her use. He took his seat; he cleared his throat and looked around at the room he'd never seen. When she sat, he rose, and then reseated himself. Clearly nervous, he smelled of whiskey just taken, but his redness of face was due to agitation of mind, not drink, she surmised from the experience of her husband's toping. She smiled in a manner intended both to put him a little more at ease and to remind him that she was a lady.

He worked his hands and swallowed and frowned at the floor, like an anxious suitor. — What would her answer be if he were? She studied him without altering her polite expression, enjoying the sensation of having someone uneasy before her. He had put on a suit for the occasion and was freshly shaved, but dark pinpoints of bristle still showed through the barber's dusting of powder. His short, uneven fingernails were black; his hands looked as hard as pine bark. She knew his reputation as fighter, worker, and lover and felt something of his vitality as he sat quiet and seething before her; but he was crude, and coarseness in a man did not appeal to her. Deciding that they would become ridiculous if they continued to sit in silence, she said, "Is it something to do with the mill, Mr. Betchley?"

"Yes, ma'am," he admitted in almost guilty relief that she understood him. "It is that—about that I have come. Your husband, Mr. Saxon—" He stopped.

To avoid another silence Frankie put on a warmer smile. "I believe you and he used first names. His death does not cancel your friendship, I hope."

He looked at her suspiciously. "Well, Mrs. Saxon—Bonard and me talked a lot of times about the mill."

"That does not surprise me." Frankie wanted to laugh, but she kept her voice sympathetic. Country men were as wary as creatures in the brush; in spite of a town layer Eugene Betchley was still country. A pale discharge began to slip from his left nostril, but he did not notice it.

"What I mean—me and Bonard pretty much ran the mill. — No disrespect to Mr. James Davis either." He paused again, but Frankie did not move to help him. "I know Mr. Davis has been showing you through the books—as much as a blind man can. Him and Mr. Blair Saxon from the bank."

"Yes, they have," Frankie agreed, watching the gradual accumulation of snot on his upper lip. "I understood my husband was a true partner. It turned out that he was not, and they—Mr. Davis and Mr. Saxon—have been explaining to me how things were arranged. That has progressed to my becoming really interested in knowing the way the mill operates, and so they explain more things to me, one thing leading to another, you see. It's easier to comprehend than I'd have believed, not nearly as difficult as embroidery or crochet. Of course, Mr. Davis could not actually show me, but he knows what's in every ledger. I seldom have to correct him as we go through them. He has a wonderful mind."

"Yes'm, wonderful. He doesn't have to be told much, or more than once. He's got the memory, as they say, of a Mississippi mule."

"Do they?" Frankie laughed. "I like that, Mr. Betchley, without knowing quite what it means."

Again he looked at her suspiciously, and she resumed a more formal attitude. A woman of her level did not make jokes with a man of his.

He set his face to pursue his purpose. "Bonard and me had done a lot of thinking about that mill and a lot of talking." Again he halted.

"Yes, Mr. Betchley?" she encouraged him.

"He would have brought me into things if he'd gone on living, as we all expected. I promise you that."

Frankie felt herself at a loss. "I'm certain he had the highest opinion of your abilities, Mr. Betchley, and the highest expectation for your prospects. But perhaps Mr. James Davis is the one you should be talking to."

"Mrs. Saxon, are you familiar with the cotton mill across the creek from us?"

Thinking at first he meant the cotton gin, she blushed, and then her mind corrected itself and she replied, "I'm aware it's there. I cannot say more than that."

His face hardened as if to match his thoughts. "The boy that runs it has a lot of ideas, I can tell you."

"Abraham Kendrick?"

Suddenly aware of a tickle under his nose, he grabbed it with his fingers and blew, wiping his hand on his trouser leg. "Him. He's got his mind on doing things big."

"I've never heard Mr. Benjamin Davis say so, or in fact anything about it."

"He might not have. No, ma'am. But he's the owner, you see,

or one of two owners along with rich-nigger Elk—" She felt that she should make some objection to his attitude, but she was beginning to be interested, not in what he had so far said, which meant little to her, but in his intensity. He was a man with something on his mind, and in a way she did not yet understand, she was involved in it, or he thought so. "That boy with his Yankee-nigger way of talking wants to make it a bigger cotton mill."

"Does he?" Frankie waited, and when he did not continue, said, "Well, why not?"

"Rich niggers means hungry whites," Eugene said as soberly as if he were repeating Bible wisdom.

"I don't see what you expect me to do about it, Mr. Betchley; I declare I don't."

"Nothing, ma'am. That's for me. But you can put me in the way of a stick to fight him with."

"How?"

Frowning at the floor again, he said, "You say you've heard Bonard speak well of me."

"I have."

"He trusted me."

Frankie nodded without conviction.

"I want to do what he'd have done. I can do it, Mrs. Saxon, if you'll— Mr. James won't listen to me. He says I'm out of turn and shooting at logs I take to be gators. The cotton mill can't grow without land. Well, Bonard owns the land on the good side of them. Other side is swamp fit for nothing but snakes and mosquitoes."

Frankie looked at him searchingly. "I'm afraid you're wrong, Mr. Betchley. I too thought my husband owned a share in the sawmill, but I discover that he did not—to my distress, I confess."

"I'm not talking about the mill itself. I couldn't say about that, not knowing; I took it all to be family. I mean across the creek. Bonard owns the land next to Beulah Mill, and I've come to buy that land from you. I've got cash money, and I'll pay you what Bonard paid and a tenth more to boot. I figure that will be a good profit on your sale."

"I'm sorry, Mr. Betchley, there's some mistake—"

"Thirty dollars a acre he paid. I know because he told me so, the way he told me a lot of things and to keep them to myself. I'll give you thirty per acre and a tithe of that, making three hundred and thirty dollars."

"I never heard of such a thing!"

Misunderstanding her, he said, "A lot of money, Mrs. Saxon. Nobody will offer you more."

She rose from her chair and stood waiting in a way he could not misinterpret. He flushed more deeply and got to his feet. In an effort to resume courtesy, she thrust out her hand, but he looked at it with such surprise that she withdrew it just as he was deciding to take it. They stared at each other.

"Good night, Mr. Betchley. Thank you for coming."

He nodded stiffly and left without another word.

6

It was customary to pay extra attention to those recently bereaved and to make them little gifts, at the same time respecting their grief and pointing a hope for the future. After his wife's death, James received from thoughtful spinsters and widows many a cake and custard, enjoying them when they were worthy but reflecting little on the dreams that had been baked into them. He did not bother to respond when Annabel, critically nibbling a pinch of crust from such a gift, observed, "I don't imagine you will care to marry again, having tried it twice." Whatever his private thoughts, he had never confided them to his sister, and he was not about to do so now.

James was comfortable in the house he had acquired along with his second wife. Old Tenah, whose cabin was at the bottom of the kitchen garden, continued to cook and clean for him, while her simple nephew Enoch possessed wits enough to guide him about the town. He required no guide at the sawmill, familiarity as well as smell and sound telling him where he was and guarding him from dangerous work at hand. If during his hours at home he was lonely and sometimes deviled by lust, still he managed; and he had begun to wonder if Frankie Saxon considered him very old. He was fifty-three to her thirty-two, not such a difference as there would have appeared had she been nineteen to his forty. He remembered, of course, that she had once been courted by Benjamin, but that was long ago, and they had both married others. Advantage was on his side: she was poor and loved ease and had two children to provide for.

He had never seen her but he knew she was beautiful, and not merely from having been told so. Her scent was to him the most womanly fragrance; her hands were shapely and supple to his touch; her voice, of the middle register and nothing out of the ordinary, had come to sound unique to his ears, no matter what others might be speaking in a room. On a recent stop at the barber's, James had asked that particular care be taken with the trimming of his hair and beard, and wanted to know exactly how gray he was. He was told, "Hardly at all; a man of thirty would be proud to look so fine." James could not see the mockery in the eyes of the barber when he gave the answer he knew was wanted, and cheered himself by supposing that, although a friend or relative might flatter to console, this man of scissors had nothing to gain or lose by telling the plain truth.

Of those who had taken special notice of him since he became a widower was Sarah Troy. Herself a widow, she had no design other than to comfort an old friend and onetime neighbor. Indeed, James's father had proposed marriage to *her* long after James himself had made her daughter Rachel his first wife. On the first Sunday in March, James was engaged to have dinner at Beulah Land following church services. So too were Frankie Saxon and her children, and James had ordered a four-seat rockaway from the livery stable to convey them into the country and home again. As they left the church, Enoch driving, they made a touching appearance to some who observed them, for was not the middle-aged man still in mourning for a wife and had not the black-appareled woman beside him recently suffered the loss of a husband? If the sight of them brought a sweet pang to some hearts, however, it did not to Annabel Saxon's as she watched them from the churchyard. More deeply in thought than she had been at any time during Mr. Quarterman's sermon, she put on her gloves and took them off and put them on again, until her husband Blair, who seldom ventured a complaint, said to her, "Whatever are you doing? Come on, I'm hungry."

Frankie had thought much of her conversation with Eugene Betchley, but without mentioning it to either James or the senior Blair Saxon, although she saw them frequently. She did not know why she hesitated when she was determined to ask for a more detailed and precise accounting of her husband's affairs than she had yet been offered. They had appeared to be open with her, but neither had made mention of what might, what must by right be hers. All they spoke of was "the estate," and she had assumed that it consisted of nothing more than the house and the land it stood on. Perhaps there was other property. If Eugene Betchley knew what he was talking about, and however crude he was the man was no simpleton, that property included half the land now used by the sawmill and ten acres across the creek from it beside the cotton mill. Poor she might be, but not a pauper to beg scraps at the back door. She would wait for the right moment to ask her questions.

On the seat behind James and Frankie the boy and girl gossiped of teachers they loved and hated, and tried to sing a song that had recently gone the round of their school fellows; but when their disagreement over the wording of a verse became a quarrel, they were silenced by a sharp glance from their mother. Blair said he saw a rabbit, though it was gone when Fanny looked where he pointed. If he'd had a rock he could have hit it, he boasted. Fanny told him he was wicked to want to do such a thing, additionally so on a Sunday. Blair pulled a long face in what he thought was a semblance of the Reverend Quarterman, and when she ignored him, untied the sash of her dress, whereupon she jabbed an elbow into his middle and he whined, "Stop it." This brought another look from their mother, who said, "Fanny, dear." Blair smiled at her and Frankie reached to pat his cheek before facing front again and saying to James, "My boy is such a comfort. I look to him to make our future. We are turning in."

"I thought it was time," James said. "There's a dip in the road a hundred yards before the carriageway. Have you never noticed it?"

"No."

"I never did when I had eyes." James raised his voice without turning his head. "What do you want to be, boy—a banker like your grandpa? Doctor, lawyer—or to follow the footsteps of your papa to the sawmill?"

"No, sir," Blair said. "I hate the sawmill. I feel sticky every time I go there. I'll be a poet or maybe a senator. I saw a senator one time in Savannah. He looked rich and Mama said he was."

"And have you ever seen a poet?" James asked drily. The boy did not answer but made motions as if he held a slingshot in his hands and aimed at the back of the man's head.

The rockaway rolled through the orchard and came in sight of the house at the end of the double row of trees. Frankie was thinking for the hundredth time that it might have been hers, had she accepted Benjamin Davis's proposal of marriage a dozen years ago—Beulah Land with its fields and woods and houses and people, hers. Instead of which, she was fretting about ten acres of creekside beside a tacky little factory. Leon and Bruce, Bobby Lee and Davy were watching for them and ran to meet them. By the time they came to the porch the others had come out too, Sarah and Benjamin, Jane and Daniel. Although they had been together at church, conversation was lively in a way it seldom was in the shadow of religious duty. The children raced together around the corner of the house as the six adults adjusted rocking chairs in a semicircle to pass the time until Josephine rang the dinner bell. Interrupting the familiar exchanges, Benjamin said as if bursting with it, "Now, Frankie! What is it I hear about Gene Betchley coming to see you and asking to buy the land next to the cotton mill? You must sell it to us, you know!"

The general exclamations of surprise gave Frankie time to collect herself. She had mentioned the matter to no one and considered it unlikely that Eugene Betchley had done so; certainly he would not have to Benjamin Davis. "How did you hear such a thing?"

He shook his head. "You don't deny it."

"It's true he came to see me. A week ago Saturday."

"I could hardly believe it," Benjamin said, and because he laughed, so did the others, although not with amusement. "Yet it is just the sort of thing he might do: think of a scheme and jump before he thought further."

James said, "He can be clever enough when it suits our book—"

"What did you say to him?" Sarah asked.

"I said I had no notion Bonard owned such a piece of land," Frankie replied.

"Nor did we, I confess," Benjamin said. "It came as a surprise to Roscoe and Abraham, I assure you—"

"When did you hear this?" Sarah asked Benjamin.

"I stopped to see Roscoe before church. We both understood the town was holding the rest of the Campgrounds. Did you know about it, sir?" he asked James.

"How in heaven would Roscoe learn of Mr. Betchley's visit?" Frankie marveled to herself and the air. A door began to open in her mind, but not very far, and she hadn't time to push it further.

"I knew about the land," James admitted, "and so did Bonard's father." He turned his head to where he guessed Frankie was sitting. "It is part of the estate, ma'am. There are two or three such small acreages to be dealt with in time."

"I did not know," Frankie said. "If there are enough of them, I shall perhaps not feel compelled to give up my house."

"They are of trifling value, I must tell you."

"To you, sir, not to Gene Betchley," Benjamin said. "Well! And what do you imagine he hoped to do with it?"

It was Frankie who answered. "He wants to keep you from expanding the operation of the cotton mill."

"He's well informed; we've only begun to talk about it!"

Sarah said, "Abraham is given to speaking freely and hasn't a thought that is secret."

"In any event," Benjamin said good-humoredly, "I want you to sell the land to me and Roscoe."

"What is your offer?" she challenged him.

"A hundred dollars more than Gene's."

"The price is rising. Perhaps I should hold it for auction to the highest bidder—"

James said gravely, "You will surely sell it to the cotton mill, Miss Frankie."

Frankie smiled. "Mr. Betchley was first to ask me, and if I dispose of it to others, will he not be disappointed, perhaps angry?"

Benjamin said, "Leave me to deal with his anger."

"We don't want to offend him, do we, uncle? He is too valuable to the sawmill. But I am forgetting. The sawmill is nothing to me now, is it? Nothing is as it was while Bonard lived."

"I don't want us to offend Betchley," James said temperately.

"Do you trust him?" Sarah asked.

"I must, for there is no other way."

"Surely another might learn to do his work," Jane suggested to her father.

Frankie reached to put a hand on his arm. "Why not I, uncle? You and Papa Blair both say I have a mind for the business!" She shook her head. "And yet you left me to discover the extent of my estate from the man who works for you."

"I wish," James said, "you would not make a joke of these things, ma'am. It pains me to have you believe I have anything but your best interests at heart."

"I know that, sir, and am grateful. Maybe, Ben, you will decide not to expand the cotton mill; I should then feel compelled to sell to no one. — But there is no profit for me in such a course, and I am deplorably poor. My mother-in-law is forever telling me so."

Daniel, who had listened quietly, now said to James, "Benjamin and I know sawmill work, Mr. Davis. — We have good reason to, don't we, brother Ben? — One or both of us could surely help you for a time, should you want to run the mill without Gene Betchley."

James colored. "As a matter of true fact, though I had no plan to announce it—but we are all family, and it will go no further—"

"Look at what happened to my little secret!" Frankie said.

James continued uncomfortably, "I have been talking to Gene about his becoming a partner—in a gradual way. He came to me. That would be after he spoke to you, Miss Frankie."

Benjamin said, "Do you mean to let him have a share of your interest?"

James shook his head. "I've discussed it with Blair and Annabel. Since Bonard died, they see no reason to hold on to their quarter part. I've offered to buy it from them and allow Gene to pay me for it as he can."

"Well, Papa!" Jane said. "It is a day for revelations. Do you really mean to take Gene Betchley as a partner?"

"I know no better way to keep him and to make him feel responsible to the sawmill. It's true when they say if you want a man's loyalty, you must buy it."

Hands tense on the arms of her chair, Sarah pushed herself up as she saw and heard a wagon coming along the carriageway. "Here are Tom and Betty with their brood—Josephine is in her glory with such a party, saying it is like the old days."

The group on the porch began to rise to greet the new arrivals. The Coopers were man and wife and five boys, all laughing and shouting and seeming to fill the wagon to overflow. Tom's father had died, but the young family now crowded the old Cooper house and farm. Attracted by the general din, the other children returned. As the two parties converged in the front yard, Frankie drew her daughter aside. "Did you listen to my conversation with Eugene Betchley the other Saturday?"

"I could not help hearing."

Frankie gripped the girl's wrist. "Who did you tell?"

"Only Luck when she brought me the violets yesterday."

"Luck Elk! And she went directly and told her father and Abraham. So that was the way of it."

"Luck is my friend, Mama."

"But only a Negro."

"What Mr. Betchley said was against her papa and Abraham."

"You might have left it to me to do what is right." When Fanny's only response was a stubborn look, Frankie let go her wrist and slapped her. It happened and was over so quickly that no one saw except Leon. Frankie immediately pulled her daughter against her so that they moved forward together.

Kissing Fanny on the cheek, Elizabeth Cooper complained

laughingly, "Why was I not given one pretty girl to dress up and keep me company? Look at my scamps and scalawags!"

Such was the clamor that when Josephine rang the bell, no one heard it, and Velma came running to tell them dinner was ready. Two tables had been set in the dining room. As dinner progressed, they were alternately gay with talk and silent with appreciative eating. Sarah sat at one end of the main table and Benjamin at the other; between them were James Davis and Frankie Saxon, Jane and Daniel Todd, and Tom and Elizabeth Cooper, who held her youngest, Jeremiah, on her lap. At the other table a few feet away Leon sat at one end with Bruce at the other; between them were Robert E. Lee, and Jefferson Davis Todd, Fanny and Blair Saxon, and the four older Cooper sons: Jesse, Jacob, Marvin, and Garvin.

Their nineteen mouths had been fed and their nineteen voices heard in various degrees of eloquence and foolery. Hunger satisfied, the young ones were sleepy or restless, while their elders grew more studiedly polite with satiety and boredom, for everything had been said that would be said, and more than once. Josephine and Mabella and Velma had come and gone unnumbered times. Sarah, who had attended to everyone and everything, wanted suddenly to be alone, or rather to be alone with Casey until, remembering she never again could be, she allowed herself briefly to hate everyone present for living and smiling and chattering while her dearly beloved was lost, lost forever.

Even as she fixed her face to listen to Elizabeth Cooper tell how well her dried peaches had lasted through the winter without molding, she was aware that Josephine had come to the door wearing her important frown. She hesitated, turned away, and returned almost immediately. Sarah's eyes met the woman's and invited her to come and say whatever was on her mind. Josephine came, leaned, whispered.

"Benjamin!"

At the sound of his grandmother's voice Benjamin rose from his chair and Jane from hers, alert to crisis. Without asking leave or pardon, they hurried with Sarah and Josephine out the door, leaving the guests to stare and murmur. Daniel started after them, but stayed to calm the children instead.

Opening the door to the office, they entered to find the thin figure of a woman crouched, almost cowering in a chair. She raised her head when Benjamin said, "Nancy?"

Trying to smile, she wept instead. "I've come home to die!"

7

Trying to rise, she fell to the floor. Benjamin picked her up and carried her directly to the room they still maintained for farm accidents and minor illnesses. Josephine surged ahead to uncover the bed; together, she and Sarah undressed Nancy and put her into it. Benjamin left to fetch Dr. Rolfe, and Jane, seeing that she was not needed, remembered the houseful of guests her brother and grandmother had forgotten. Returning to the dining room, she found only Velma clearing the tables and was told by her that Mr. Daniel had herded everybody out to the front porch when they commenced to mill around. It was there she found them a minute later.

The adults had been scraping their rocking chairs restlessly into and out of the sun and wanting either to face the light wind to cool off from the dining room or to put their backs to it to avoid it. Grouped on the long shallow steps, the children giggled themselves through the game of changing places in order to sit beside this one or to escape that one, finally settling to tease Davy. Jane appeared just as he realized he was shunned by all and raised his voice to tell them they needn't be so hateful, for he didn't have the itch and hadn't pooted. Daniel gave him a light passing kick as he turned to his wife; and when everyone was looking at her, Jane explained that a woman loved by all at Beulah Land and many years absent had just come home and was, they feared, ill.

Frankie said, "We wondered why Benjamin rode away in such a hurry without even a wave."

"Can you mean Miss Sarah's sister?" Elizabeth asked. "Miss Lauretta—that was her name, although I was no more than born when she married the Yankee colonel and went up North to live. I've always thought she must have been jolly because Mama disapproved of her."

Jane shook her head. "This one went no further than Savannah. She was born here, one of our people, and stayed with us through the war and after."

Tom Cooper said, "A slave, you mean?"

"You've all heard about Nancy," Jane said to the children on the steps.

But it was Frankie who replied first. "Indeed we have." Her quick laugh surprised Jane into a questioning look, which Frankie ignored.

Bobby Lee said, "I have!"

Davy said, "I have too!"

Jane smiled at them and then at their seniors, as if that ended the matter. "Bobby Lee, you and Davy and all the rest of you, run out now and play. Otherwise you'll have bad dreams tonight after those rich victuals you stuffed yourselves with. Greedy-guts, that's what you are. Scat. Scoot."

They went, Davy first, racing toward a cedar tree as if he intended to smash himself to smithereens, to miss it by an inch and continue around the house and into the farther reaches of the back yards. Leon and Bobby Lee gave chase from habit, and the Cooper boys charged after them, Blair Saxon dawdling along with Fanny and Bruce until they began to skip. He paused to pick up a feather from the grass, pretending to examine it, convinced because he wanted to be that he was watched by every eye on the porch. Then heaving such a sigh as might have served a saint renouncing the world, he dropped the feather and skipped out of sight after the others.

He found them on a fence enclosing the pigpens, the girls just climbing up to join the boys, some of whom were perched on the top board like roosting chickens while others twined arms and legs in and out lower boards as if they were growing vines. Blair stared at them with disapproval. As the girls reached the top where space was made for them, he said, "Bruce, you're ugly."

Bruce looked down at him and said, "I know it."

Unsatisfied by her easy answer, he continued, "That old scar of yours gets worse every time I see you."

Leon said, "You shut your mouth before I throw you in the pen to that big mean sow."

Blair put his hands on his hips to jeer. "You know what *my* grandma says *you* are? A bastard!"

Quick as gravity, Leon fell on him, not bothering to fight him, content to hold him to the ground and sit on him. Blair pretended great hurt. "Ooey, ooey, ooey, you've broke something! I think my arm is broke, look how limp it is. I think my ankle's broke, I can't move my foot!" Leon got off him, and Blair made as if to stand, hopping and hobbling. "Ooey, ooey, ooey, ooey!"

"You sound like a pig," Jacob Cooper said.

"Mama!" Blair wailed commandingly as he went off. "Send for the doctor for me—Leon tried to kill me!"

They forgot him instantly. Davy said, "Mama wanted to get rid of us so they could talk about Nancy."

"I reckon so," Bobby Lee agreed.

"*I* never heard of Nancy," Bruce protested.

Davy looked at her, incredulous.

Bobby Lee said, "She saved Mama from being ravaged by the Yankee raiders when Sherman came through. Nancy laid right down on the floor and let them ravage her instead, so they left Mama alone. But they dug up Uncle Ezra's grave looking for silver and gold, and they killed poor Lovey with an ax."

"I hate a Yankee worse than anything," Jesse Cooper said.

"You never saw one," Jacob said.

Familiar with stories about the war, Bruce only said, "What does it mean, 'ravage'?"

"Means they fucked her," Davy said.

As the Cooper boys giggled, Bobby Lee hit his brother on the arm with his fist, but it was so common a blow between them Davy hardly blinked. "You don't say it in front of girls."

"They're only cousins," Davy pointed out.

"They're girls," Leon said severely.

"Girls know what it means," Davy insisted, and his brother hit him again.

Fanny said, "I think it was brave of Nancy to do that."

Bobby Lee said, "I remember Aunt Nell asked for Nancy to come hold her hand one day before she died. She sure loved Nancy."

"What you reckon she's sick with?" Leon said.

"I don't know," Bobby Lee said angrily, as if he had been unreasonably expected to.

"I bet a rattlesnake bit her," Marvin Cooper said.

"That's right," said his twin Garvin.

"Yellow fever," Jesse offered.

Leon said, "Wrong time of year. Besides, she couldn't have come all the way from Savannah with it. Haven't you heard that old saying about the fever? 'After twelve hours a body is ready for his cook or his coffin.'"

Davy, who had been plunged in thought, surfaced. "I'm mighty glad nobody ravaged Mama! God bless Nancy!"

Marvin said, "Let's play. I'm tired of hanging on this old fence."

Garvin said, "We got fences at home good as this one."

The Todd boys hinted to Bruce and Fanny that there were a lot more games boys could play with boys than they could play with girls and maybe they'd like to go sit on the porch and rest. Fanny and Bruce shook their heads, so it was decided to play hide-and-go-seek. Davy was elected to be the one to close his eyes and count to a hundred while the others hid. Instead of protesting, he began to count so rapidly the others scampered away in all directions.

Presently, as if by accident, Leon discovered Fanny behind a door in the cow barn. "I reckon I better go hide some place else," he said with unconvincing surprise.

"Maybe you had," Fanny said.

"I hope you're not mad because I sat on your brother."

"You didn't hurt him," she said.

Leon looked exaggeratedly relieved. "I sure am glad you're not mad. Do you know why?"

"Well, why?"

Leon blushed. "I want you to be my sweetheart."

"Why do you?"

"Because I love you."

"You do?"

He nodded.

"Well," she said, "all right." She put out her hand, and he shook it.

8

Since the near-fatal beating of Leon brought him there seven years ago, Rolfe was the doctor summoned to Beulah Land for illness or accident. He spoke his mind directly when he was certain, and he wasn't afraid to say, "I don't know," when he was not. About Nancy he was in no doubt.

"Consumption," he told Sarah and Benjamin after his examination.

"Can she get well?" Benjamin asked.

"I don't know her strength, never having treated her. She won't say how long she's been sick, and maybe she doesn't remember. You saw the pox scars?" They nodded. "She had that five years ago and has worked as a washwoman since."

Sarah told him something of her history.

"I'm glad you engage to take care of her," he said, "for she'll surely die if nobody does, and she may anyway."

Although they sat with her when Mabella spooned food into her that evening, Benjamin and Sarah said nothing of the future until the next morning. After breakfast they went together to see her. Sarah told her the truth, but less than Rolfe had said at the end of his first visit.

"Shut the door and let me die here. That's all I want."

"We aren't going to let you die at all if we can help it," Sarah said.

"I never thought about children. I shouldn't have come."

Benjamin said, "They won't get it. They're strong as bulldogs. In a few days I'm going to move you up to my house in the Glade." Nancy looked alarmed, but Sarah nodded to assure her it was already decided.

"What of Mrs.?"

"Mrs. lives in town with her ma, and I live here with my boy Leon and my girl Bruce."

"Mabella told me about them."

"The Glade house has been empty," Sarah said. "You'll be quiet when you want to be, but Rosalie will take care of you. Now her children are all married, she doesn't have enough to do, and it will stop her grumbling. We'll be in and out."

Nancy's eyes were closed, but her frown registered protest.

Benjamin said, "You'll do what you're told, for once."

"The main thing," Sarah said, "is rest." She patted her hand. "We'll leave you now. Try to sleep, and ring the bell on the table if you need anybody."

At the door Benjamin said, "You're home, Nancy."

Frankie Saxon had been thinking about Nancy that Monday morning as she waited for James Davis to come to her. When Jane revealed yesterday whose arrival had claimed the attention of host and hostess, Frankie's mind had gone back to the morning she and Benjamin had last spoken of Nancy in the little room at the cotton gin where they met. It was their first time together after Bonard's death, and they'd commented on the fact that it was different for them. They hadn't realized how different it was to be, she mused, wondering if it could have happened then. That was the earliest it could have happened, she calculated. They had lain together on four occasions since that meeting. She asked herself with exasperation: Why, after being together so many times over the years, had she become pregnant now?

She must have a husband, and soon. However sympathetic the town customarily was to widows, they would not understand Frankie Saxon's having a baby ten months after her husband died following a long illness. So she would get a husband, and she knew who he would be and how she would get him. She had long been aware that James Davis wanted her. She might regret the loss of Benjamin, and he would never be reconciled to her marrying his father; but there were advantages to such a match, and not a little amusement. She would never again have to worry about money, and Annabel Saxon would be outraged.

The moment she heard the knock at the door and hastened to answer it, the hallway clock struck ten. She had told her one remaining house servant, Molly, to keep to the back of the house, where she was washing clothes that morning. When she and James were seated alone in her private parlor, they spoke of the fine weather. She told him how reluctant the children had been to go to school after their pleasurable visit to Beulah Land. He asked her if Annabel had yet paid her usual morning visit.

"No, sir; nor will she. She is embroiled in a meeting with other church ladies about the proposed memorial to our Confederate dead. There are conflicting viewpoints as to what form it shall take."

"Why are you not one of them? I fear that I am keeping you at home—"

"For which I am grateful."

He smiled. "What are the conflicting proposals?"

"Miss Doreen and Miss Eloise lead a faction that is in favor of representing General Lee with a drawn sword in the very act of slaying a stone dragon clearly lettered on its side 'The Union'!"

James's smile broadened. "Has no one told them the outcome of the war does not accord with such a monument?"

"I believe so, but they were unswayed."

"And Annabel's idea, what is it? It is she, if we are to believe her, who insists that we have a statue like other communities."

"And she will get her way," Frankie said. "No doubt of it, but after a fight, which I expect she will enjoy. For once I can say she has reason on her side. She points out that while we are all of us devoted to the memory of the General's leadership, the town of Highboro has no claim to the distinction of being noticed by him. He was not born here; he did not even find the occasion to ride his horse through town. She is in favor of a simple figure of a Confederate foot soldier. It is dignified, and it is cheaper than the other."

"What have you given as your opinion?"

"I have not been asked it. I am not quite one of them, you

know. But I believe our hearts hold the memory of the past, and that is the best any of us may do."

"That is too true to be debated. You might be a much older woman for the sensible head on your shoulders."

"Pray do not make me older than I am, sir, for that is quite old enough!"

"You are a child beside me."

"Age does not signify with a man," Frankie said. "You are in the full vigor of your manhood, as anyone may see."

Indeed, anyone might have seen one evidence of such condition at any rate, for James, all his life subject to sudden erections over which he had little control, proceeded now to have one. Frankie smiled; it was all so very easy. James made an effort to shift his mind to prosaic matters. "I hope you did not share the disapproval of the others yesterday when I revealed my plan to allow Eugene Betchley a measure of partnership in the sawmill."

"I did not," Frankie said soberly. "It appears to me admirably reasoned. As you so truly said: if you want a man's loyalty, you must buy it."

"Such is not the case, however, with a woman's."

"No," Frankie agreed. "Not a woman worth having."

He sighed. "A man is a fool to try it, I suppose."

"For you there has been no need," Frankie said. "Miss Maggie was a saint."

"God rest her soul," James concurred.

Frankie allowed a pause, her eyes on the slack, wrinkled trouser crotch of her visitor. "I fear that my own marriage was less idyllic than yours. I would speak of it to no one else—" She paused again.

"I am your friend."

"I have always believed so; now more than ever. Misfortune draws me to your strength, for you are a very pillar. It is reprehensible to say ill of the dead, and I could not bring myself to do so; but my husband did not always understand a wife's needs. Is that dreadful of me to confide? Yet I feel better for it. You will comprehend, sir, I was aware of my husband's philandering. I never let on that I knew. After our children were born, he turned to others as if he had grown tired of me."

"Impossible," James breathed.

"As to that, sir, it was surely open knowledge that he strayed—"

"I did not mean that. I meant that it was impossible any man ever could tire of you, my dear Miss Frankie."

She smiled gratefully, as one starving for any grain of praise. "If I had married such a one as you, strong and good, how happy I might have been." She was not surprised to observe that the trouser crotch was no longer slack and wrinkled.

"Miss Frankie—" James's voice was thick. He paused, swallowed, and licked his lips.

"I have said too much. You think me vile—"

"No!" he said joyously.

"I have longed for affection and not had it, affection that is tender and true—"

James groped the air blindly. Frankie allowed her fingers to touch his sleeve. He grasped her hands and then her arms. She stood. He stood. She was in his arms. Holding him tightly to her, which he considered all his own doing, she turned her lips aside for a moment. "I am mad—"

"And I with love of you!" he declared.

"What would the world say of us?"

"Are we likely to be interrupted?" he asked hoarsely.

Her answer was to give him her lips again. She led him across the hallway to the room she had once shared with Bonard. An hour later, as James rested from his second ejaculation, he said, "We must marry."

"Beloved," she murmured, and his penis rose again as hopefully as a flower lifts its head to the sun.

9

"I've waited near an hour," Benjamin complained as Frankie turned her buggy into the grove of trees and halted the horse.

"I was delayed," she said shortly. "I'm sorry." She secured the reins and sat looking at him.

Unable to gauge her mood, he continued, "I wondered why your note said to meet here."

"I didn't think about the cold."

He put his impatience to the weather. "It ought to be warmer, almost April. Everything will be late this year."

She made no move to join him on the ground but looked beyond him into the pines. "It was here we came together first." He smiled and held a hand to help her from the buggy, but she shook her head. "I wanted a place we wouldn't be seen or interrupted."

He gave her a puzzled look. "The cotton gin is always safe, and there's a bed. It's too damp, and I'm too old, for pine needles on the ground."

"There won't be any of that. I want to talk to you. Come and sit with me out of the wind."

As he joined her, she reached behind them for the buffalo robe and spread it over their laps and legs. He took her hand under the robe, and finding it cold, began to knead it. She allowed her head to tilt toward him as his eyes asked her to, and he kissed her on the lips, but in the light, dry way a couple long used to one another will touch in greeting.

"That's better," he said comfortably. "You've been worrying too much about the future."

Her laugh was involuntary. "I shan't any more."

He held her hand still, surprised.

"I've come to tell you the future."

"Like a fortune-teller?" he teased her. "If we were able to marry, you could forget next year and the next century—"

"Hush, Ben."

When she did not go on, he frowned. "You laughed funny."

"That's what a laugh is—funny."

"Not that way." He waited.

"I oughtn't to find it hard. What I'm doing is best, but you won't see it so. — You admit there's no future for us."

"No more than we've had, I suppose."

"I've decided to marry," she said. Having looked away to give him a moment, she now looked at him again. "I have to marry."

"Bonard's been dead only two months," he protested.

"If he'd been dead only two minutes," she said irritably, "it would be permissible for me to marry again."

"Who?"

"I can't beg my bread and clothes from Annabel Saxon. She's polecat-mean."

"Don't make excuses, just tell me—"

"I'm not making excuses! You'll hate me."

He made himself breathe evenly and said carefully, "I can't imagine who I'd hate you to marry most. I'm sorry it isn't me, but how can I blame you when I can't offer to be your husband?"

"I'm going to marry your father. Today." He stared at her and shook his head as if she'd waked him from sleep. "I'm going to be James Davis's third wife. He's going to be my second husband. — God, Ben!" When her voice broke, her will broke with it, and she cried passionately. He sat still, not looking at her or touching her, until presently it occurred to him to set her reticule before her. Taking it gratefully, she fumbled a handkerchief from it, wiping her eyes and mouth.

"Why him?" he then asked.

"He's wanted me the longest time—"

His quick nod mocked her. "So you made it easy for the poor old man. Let him into the house when you were by yourself, and put on perfume because he can't see how pretty you are, and sat close and talked low and—"

"Don't be so damn noble!"

"All right, Frankie. I see your reasoning. You don't want to be dependent on Aunt Annabel. Who would? So you've decided to marry him. But why *him?*"

"He's a good man. You've always been against him because he sold Oaks plantation instead of holding it to pass on to you. Well, you've got Beulah Land, and he needs me."

"Your logic isn't clear. Aunt Maggie hasn't been dead long, and you're the greenest widow in town. Couldn't you have waited a while?"

She started to answer but shrugged instead. "Would that have made any difference to you?"

"Does Aunt Annabel know?"

Frankie shook her head. "I haven't talked to her yet."

"I'm the first you've told?"

Again she shook her head. "The children, this morning, before they went to school. I didn't want them to come home for dinner and be surprised."

"How did they take it?"

"Fanny was embarrassed. Girls are like that. Blair just laughed and asked if we'd be rich again."

"He's practical like his mama. Wait, Frankie. For your sake, not mine or anybody else's. Think what a lot of talk there'd be. After a few months, if you want to and he does—oh, I've no doubt he will, but it'll be good for him to bide his time—"

"Have you ever enjoyed waiting?"

"Be engaged, have an open understanding, let people get used to the idea. That'll be enough to put Aunt Annabel on notice to watch her manners, and it will give Fanny time to be reconciled."

Breathing more quickly, she stared at him, and her voice trembled with anger when she spoke. "Wait?"

"Neither of you is in the first bloom of impetuous youth."

"Exactly. And I can't wait because I'm going to have a baby. Yes, yours and mine. Do you understand now? I don't know why it didn't happen before but is happening now. — You say there'll be talk. Think how much there'll be if I have a child ten months after my husband died. James doesn't need to know anything. When the time comes, I'll see that he thinks it's his. He'll want to, so it will be easy. Ben, are you crying?"

"I won't let you do it."

"Ben, I have to leave; I've so many things to do today. I'm meeting James at the rectory at twelve o'clock. Mr. Quarterman promised to marry us. Then in the morning we're going to Savannah for a week to give everybody a chance to get a straight face. Mr. Quarterman told us to wait too and agreed to marry us only when we said we'd go to Savannah and marry there if he didn't."

"How can you let him think my baby is his?"

"It's all the same blood. Yours, his—what does it matter? Men are so particular; I'll never understand them. It won't be his or yours; it'll be mine because I'll have the trouble of it!"

He stumbled out of the buggy and had to pick himself up from the ground before he could head into the trees.

"Ben, come back here and tell me goodbye and wish me well!"

He turned around to look at her. "Goodbye, Frankie, and I damn the day I first set eyes on you!"

"You *are* silly." Her voice rose in alarm. "You're not going to the woods to hang yourself, are you?"

"No!" he called back furiously.

"That's a relief. — Ben, I can't see you, can you hear me?"

"Yes."

"I've got good news for you—you don't have to worry any more about that piece of land! I meant to tell you so many things—James says I must let you and Roscoe have it and not Gene Betchley. — Why don't you answer me, aren't you glad? — James paid me five hundred dollars for it and said we'd give it to you as our wedding present. Isn't that good of him? You've misjudged him, you see. Ben, come back and talk. I don't have anybody to talk to—nobody knows me except you. Ben!"

He was gone.

Frankie had not expected the day to be an easy one, but she was of no mind to suffer more buffets than necessary; so after a brief fit of weeping diminished to an uneven heaving of the breast, she took reins in hand, drove home, changed her dress, and met James at the rectory as they had arranged it between them to do, not wanting to rouse speculation by going there together hand in arm. The Reverend Quarterman performed the ceremony with a fine balance of Christian disapproval and beady-eyed excitement, after which the couple repaired to Frankie's house for a private wedding luncheon. The children had already returned to school from their noon dinner, and Molly served the pair with cheery deference, knowing the ruddy-faced blind man would henceforth pay her wages. After bringing in the wedding cake she had baked as a surprise, she watched Frankie cut it and bent her plump body nearly in two for James when he put a silver dollar of appreciation into her hand. She had just returned to the kitchen when Annabel Saxon marched into the house by way of the front door, and without otherwise announcing herself, demanded to know of the very walls around her: "Frankie! You, Frankie! What have I been hearing?"

James grunted. "Quarterman has lost no time reporting. I knew he was afraid of her but not that afraid."

"Her bite is worse than her bark," Frankie said.

Arriving at the dining room, Annabel stopped in the doorway to gaze at the man and woman eating cake. "James, you disgusting lecher!"

"Is it our sister?" James said to Frankie.

"Frankie, tell me exactly what you have done!" Annabel thundered.

Frankie replied circumspectly, "We were coming to ask your blessing when we'd finished here, Miss Annabel."

James said, "It's an excellent cake Molly has made us, and I gave her a dollar. You'd better take a chair and have a slice, Annabel."

Annabel advanced into the room as one in the grip of dread anticipation. "Doreen and Eloise saw you through the window of the rectory. As soon as you'd gone, they got it out of Quarterman that you'd made him marry you to each other. They naturally came directly and in all haste to tell me."

James said to Frankie, "I wronged the poor man," and to Annabel, "I'm glad you and Doreen have made it up about the Confederate memorial. Sisters should never quarrel in public, lest they be thought common."

"Won't you sit down?" Frankie suggested amiably. "It *is* good cake, as my husband says, and Molly will be so pleased if you have a taste."

Annabel rolled her eyes. "Husband! God preserve me. He has

been husband as many times as he was brother. Have you no decent feelings, either of you?"

"Yes," James answered. "That is why we decided to marry instead of indulging our love without benefit of clergy."

"The disregard," Annabel mourned, "the callous disregard of my son's memory—"

"I don't think Bonard is in any position to object," James said.

"To see you sink so low, James. Of course, you, Miss Minx, do not surprise me. I have not forgot the sly way you snared my innocent boy."

"Your innocent boy was more times the lecher than Don Juan both before and after their marriage; and well you know it, Annabel, so let's have no more of that." James put down his fork with a bang.

"How can I face the town? What shall I say?"

"That you have lost a daughter and gained a second sister," James advised. "That will give you a reputation, however undeserved, for both wit and good temper."

Annabel addressed herself to Frankie. "I have forgiven you much, but this I shall not forget. Had you no thought of your children?"

"I had every thought of them," Frankie replied honestly.

"I offered my house to them!"

James said, "That is very fortuitous, Annabel, for we are going to Savannah tomorrow morning and will be obliged if you look after them while we are away."

Frankie offered a conciliatory smile. "You said once that you would keep them if I decided to pay a visit to my family, Miss Annabel."

"Poor waifs!"

"We'll reclaim them in a week," James promised, "before you can take them to the state orphanage."

"James, you are beyond redemption. It is evident that you live for naught but sensation. Very well, I forsake you. After using up two noble women—"

"Neither of whom you could abide."

"One my dearest friend, the other the very jewel of Beulah Land, the daughter of Auntie Sarah, friend and neighbor to our sainted mother and martyred father for half a century—what can your intention now be?"

"To live happily ever after," James answered.

"Where?" Annabel asked quickly.

"Here," Frankie said.

"It's my house," Annabel told her.

"Mine," Frankie said, equally firmly.

Annabel sneered boldly. "How well I recollect the manner in which you persuaded Blair to put the place in your name. Now we can all see why. Let that be a warning to you, James. Take care. I wash my hands of both of you. You'll see the town will follow my example, for I am held in high regard. You'll have no respectable friend, no acquaintance you do not pay for. I shall go directly to the school and take the children home with me, telling them they are twice orphaned within the year, and the year but three months old!"

They sat still until they heard Annabel slam the front door behind her. Then James took Frankie's hand. "That saves us a visit. She means it about taking the children home with her. In which case, we might spend an hour or so in bed, hm? I feel myself in need of it."

Annabel was wrong in her prediction that the town would ostracize the new couple. The depot had seen many gatherings in its history, and even a routine arrival or departure commanded a modest attendance; but next morning at the hour of the train to Savannah, a veritable mob, or as near such as the town of Highboro might produce, was there to call congratulations and say farewell. We are always a little grateful to those who keep us from tedium, and there is comfort in recognizing the base impulses of our fellows.

10

There had been warm days, but not of the continuous sort to be relied upon. In April it stayed warm at last, and one morning Nancy carried a hide-bottomed chair down to the brookside and sat with her hands loose in her lap and her eyes closed against the sun. She may have slept a little, but mainly she thought and dreamed, thought becoming dream and changing back again, mind turning up disconnected bits of the past and setting them in meaningless juxtaposition that was neither nightmare nor farce but contained elements of both. It was what she had learned to call her "sick mind," a part of the illness she suffered.

"Whatever you're thinking, I hope it isn't me, with such a frown on your face."

Her eyes opened to Abraham smiling at her. "What you doing up here, middle of the workday?"

"Brought you a fishing pole," he said. "Luck says tell you she's coming tomorrow morning to take you fishing, rain or shine."

"I never been fishing in my life," Nancy protested.

"You don't have to work at it; anybody can do it. Everybody's born knowing how, like breathing and—let me see—"

"Never mind what it's like."

"I was going to say swimming. You still treat me like you're my mama."

"I *was* your mama after your mama died."

He squatted beside her, friendly, then dropped to his behind on the ground at her feet. "How come you didn't answer me when I saw you that time in Savannah?"

"Don't know what you're talking about."

"I saw it was you, Miss Stuck-uppity. Wanting nothing to do with her old pickaninny—"

She reached to tap his head at her knee. "Coarse as a burr," she told him.

"Who's that gazing at us yonder?"

She followed the line of his eyes to the liver-colored hound who, halfway to them from the house, had lowered her hind-quarters to pee. Even as she peed, she wagged her tail and smiled, the soul of amiability.

"Rosalie's hound dog. They call her Old Mama."

"Not hard to reckon why."

Still wagging her tail, Old Mama waddled forward, teats low and swinging side to side. Nancy scratched the dog's head when she stopped and was paid with a look of adoration. "That's enough," she said after a minute, slumping back in her chair. "Wear me out. Coat's rough as this boy's head."

"You're looking better," he said without the teasing tone characteristic of his speech with almost everyone.

She frowned. "What you doing away from the cotton mill? Thought they'd started building on."

"Ever get lonesome up here?"

"Rosalie's in and out all day long. Miss Sarah, Miss Jane. The children, they come too. I try to run them off, tell them I'm 'catching,' but they slip back."

"That leaves you a lot of time."

"Not so much."

"What do you think about?"

"Old times."

"Old times here or Savannah?"

Her sharp look dismissed his question. "I also make up stories: what'll happen to you and Luck and Bruce and Leon."

"What's going to happen to me?"

"One day you'll get grown, I hope."

"I was legal grown on my last birthday."

She roused herself. "Then start learning to be a credit to your pa and not such a smart-Alexander."

"I'm polite to everybody."

"Not nigger-polite. That's all right with Miss Sarah and them; they're your people. But I've seen you in town with others. You walk and stand before them like *you*. Learn to *edge*. Guess they didn't teach that in Philadelphia. Watch your uncle Roman; he knows how. Most dignified man you ever did see, and everybody has a good word for him, but it wasn't always so. He had to learn to walk slow and talk low when he got back from Philadelphia, and he never looks white folks in the face, for it's not genteel. Always keeps his head down, and he edges. Take a lesson from this old dog, the way she's niggering up to me." Old Mama had not left them when Nancy stopped scratching her. Instead, she waited, not in the way, but there to be noticed if they remembered her.

"You mean," Abraham said, "if I act like her and show myself accommodating, I'll grow tits that sweep the ground?" She kicked him and he rolled over on the ground out of her way. "How about you? What's going to happen when you grow up?"

"I'm all over. Nothing going to happen to me. I'll die one day."

"Need a man in your life."

She moaned, mocking ecstasy. "Used to be girls, the house I worked in, said they just couldn't stand menfolks. I'd tell 'em, 'All right, ladies, wasn't for them, you'd have to work with your hands.' "

She laughed, and he did too, and she began to cough, and Benjamin arrived.

"Confound it, Abraham, I heard nothing out of you for six months except 'Let's expand, build onto the mill!' Here I find you making Nancy cough and the work going on without you—"

Abraham jumped to his feet. "Yassah, boss man, didn't see you coming, sah! I'se movin' fast as my po' old feets kin carry me! — This the way, Nancy?" Still laughing, he threw the fishing pole at her feet and left them, fetching his horse from the back yard and riding away down the hill with a goodbye wave.

Watching him, Nancy said, as if continuing an earlier thought, "And another thing. He oughtn't to ride that horse. A nigger on a mule is one thing; a nigger on a horse is something else."

"I think you're both crazy."

"I was trying to talk sense to that boy so he won't get in trouble. I don't forget what happened to Floyd."

"You're still trying to be his mammy. You and Grandma worry the same way. He'll be all right when people know him better and get used to him. The only ones— Never mind Abraham. I came to see how you are."

"I'm all right," she said glumly.

"I heard you coughing."

"Everybody coughs."

"Not blood."

"Who are 'the only ones' you started to say?"

He looked at her carefully before answering. "The poorer whites that work across the creek at the sawmill. They hate everything about him: the way he walks, way he talks, way he wears his clothes, way he looks at them."

"White trash."

Benjamin shrugged. "I got to get on. Everything was late; now everything's in a hurry to grow with the good weather. Grass taking over the world—"

"Be growing over me pretty soon."

"You reckon?" She waited for him to object, and when he did not, she frowned, which made him smile.

"Get on," she ordered him, and watched him go. When she was alone, Old Mama edged closer and began to wag her tail. "Me and you," Nancy said to her, and reached to touch her head.

11

Having had a husband and a lover who were passionate, Frankie did not consider herself innocent in sexual matters. She had managed Bonard, giving and withholding herself as she pleased. With Benjamin she was better matched; they were nearer equals than often happens in such a relationship. But nothing in her experience or her imagining had prepared her for James Davis. A sense of security, of having leapt safely over the yawning chasm—relief approaching triumph—saw her through the first week in

Savannah. She was even proud of the demands of her new husband, finding it a compliment to her womanliness that he wanted her two and three times daily. James had, she reminded herself, been without wife for some months; and when she thought of fat, red-faced Maggie Davis, she could only pity and indulge him. Besides, he was good to her, encouraging her to buy whatever she fancied in the stores, insisting upon their eating in the finest places, providing her with a carriage every hour of the day. She remembered her mean childhood in the same city; and she reflected on what her life would now be had she continued dependent upon Annabel Saxon. The moments her mind was thus fixed she was able to answer James's needs with something more than tolerance.

But by the time they returned to Highboro, her nerves were as sore as her flesh, and she looked to the future with foreboding, for there was nothing she might do but submit. She was well enough acquainted with her husband's character to realize that he would not be put aside or controlled as Bonard had let himself be. What he wanted he would have; he wanted her, and she was his. With Bonard she had never lost a sense of herself, and for that matter, of him. She may seldom have enjoyed him and never loved him, but he was always recognizably Bonard, and she was able to remain herself in their encounters. Thinking of Benjamin, she had to restrain herself from weeping that she should ever have quarreled with him. Had he not been a true lover in every way? As considerate as he was eager, gentle with himself as well as her, he had been alert to each nuance of response.

With James she ceased being herself, and she had no inkling who he was or how he thought of her. He was always tumescent and went at her with an urgency that might be spent but was never satisfied. Even when they were not actively engaged, he would not let her alone. She would wake in the night to find his sticky hardness pressing and smearing her naked thigh, his blunt, dry fingers prying and probing. His blindness seemed to include his whole body.

She longed for privacy, but there was none for her. He wanted her to be with him all the time, day and night. In the presence of others, he must hold her hand to be certain she was still beside him. (Acquaintances were touched by his devotion and dependence and congratulated her.) He had dismissed the boy Enoch as attendant; she became his guide. With Fanny and Blair he was either silent or impatient, and they learned to avoid him when they could, which left Frankie even more alone with him. And when they were alone, he was capable of taking her anywhere and at any time—on a sofa, on the floor of his office at the sawmill, on the ground, once in the buggy as they rode through the country and, not minding the horse, presently found themselves in a ditch. She went to sleep in apprehension and woke with dread. What drove him, she could not say and did not care. The memory of her early pride at his attentions now chilled her heart. He was inflamed by a joyless, implacable desire to consume her.

She minded least the time they spent at the sawmill, and in doing what she could to prolong the hours there, began to learn about the working of the mill as she had only imagined knowing something of it before. Eugene Betchley was now a quarter-share partner as he'd been promised, and he seemed to have forgotten the interview in which he urged her to sell him Bonard's land across the creek adjoining the cotton mill. He was courteous in a stiff way, having no instinct for good manners but meaning to behave correctly with her. When he saw that she was determined to take a serious interest in the operation of the mill, he tried to ignore her efforts but gradually accepted what he could not avoid. She knew that he was watching her; and it did not take her many days to understand that it was he who ran the work, that it was to him the men looked for hour-to-hour and day-by-day direction and control. Decisions might seem to be made in the office with James speaking the final word; but that Eugene Betchley was brain and brawn of the sawmill, there was no mistaking.

James decided to be pleased with his wife's interest in business and was presently boasting to all that he had found the ideal partner. Galled by such praise, Annabel said sharply to Frankie, "You mustn't overextend yourself, for you are looking quite haggard, I declare you are." After a few weeks of marriage Frankie "discovered" that she was pregnant, and her pale looks were ascribed to her condition. Although James professed himself delighted, in his heart he damned as a nuisance the child that would eventually put a pause in his pleasures.

Gazing at Casey Troy's painting and then at its model, Annabel marveled, "How much you've changed, Frankie! You mustn't expect a pregnancy at your age to be an easy one. You were comparatively young when you carried Blair Three and Fanny, and you know what they say: 'A baby makes a young wife bloom, an old one wither.' Never mind." She patted Frankie's hand. "You've done very well for yourself and mustn't grumble, must you?"

There was, of course, joking among acquaintances. The husbands made mild, envious sallies about old men with young notions, while their wives indulged in cruder gibes about old fools and flatterers. James had been popular with the women of the town; he was so no longer. To marry twice made him interesting, evidencing his appreciation of their sex. To take a third wife, and such a one as Frankie-Julia Dollard Saxon, exposed him as a sensualist. At his age, they opined, a man should be pondering his fitness for the next world. James clearly was not.

Much as there was to exasperate her, Frankie kept busy, did not mope or complain. She carried ledgers home from the sawmill to study. She verified or challenged addition and subtraction. If she was to be her husband's guide, she would be so in ways other than leading him about the town as young Enoch had done. She was more than a walking cane. As she came and went every day, the men at the mill grew used to her and no longer bothered to alter their attitudes in her presence, which pleased her. She had her share of vanity, but she knew she would learn little of the routine if the laborers treated her like a lady on a visit. Now they continued working and talking as she passed among them, and along with other things revealed their dislike and resentment of the Negroes who worked at the cotton mill. The discovery did not much concern Frankie; she merely noted it.

One Saturday she surprised Eugene Betchley staring over the creek with an expression that prompted her to say to herself: "Of course. He is white trash like his men. They think the same, and where they don't, he will always lead them his way." She felt a thrill of danger with the discovery. Eugene was not aware of her presence until his eye caught a wave from the other shore from Benjamin Davis and he turned to find Frankie behind him. It was the first time she had seen him off guard. As he walked away, she called to Benjamin, "Come over! I want to see you!"

Hearing the invitation, the men on the sawmill side did pause over their last work of the day and exchange looks, for the Davis father and the Davis son were rare visitors to each other's mills. Benjamin exaggerated a shrug as people will at a distance to ensure that they are understood. "No bridge! I'll see you in church tomorrow morning!"

"Frankie?" Her husband was beside her. "I wondered where you'd got to. Who are you speaking to?"

"Why, your son Benjamin across the creek. — He seems to have gone away now."

James took her by the hand. Since their marriage he'd been jealous of any man she spoke to, and he had not forgotten that Benjamin and Frankie were once very nearly engaged to marry. He was as aware as others that Priscilla had long chosen to live with her mother and not her husband. He had no idea of how Benjamin found sexual gratification, but he was wary of Frankie's speaking to him in such a free and casual way, for it suggested intimacy.

"It's time to go home."

"Is it?" Frankie murmured. "May days are so long."

"Day and night are one to me. Isn't there something you have forgotten?"

They were strolling back to the office, and Frankie observed the workmen forming a loose line. "Payday!" she exclaimed.

"The money box is ready," he told her. "Blair Two brought it from the bank."

It had been one of James's conceits early in the marriage to allow Frankie to hand their pay to the men at the end of the week. It was now regular practice. As they sat down side by side at the pay table, the line of men shuffled forward. Frankie handed each one the money he had earned, checking his name on the list before her and setting the sum down neatly in another column as having been paid out. It was a task that gave her satisfaction, for she understood perfectly well that poor men had a regard amounting to awe for those who actually handed money to them. Had she not been poor herself?

When the last had claimed his due, Frankie shut the box and handed it to her husband. James locked it and lighted a cigar, another part of the ritual. Frankie said, "What of me, sir? Am I not worth a wage?"

Placing the box under one arm, James rose and took her by the hand. "You have me," he said before he kissed her palm.

12

The sun of summer and the winds of winter affected her more acutely every passing year, and Sarah had gradually given over the management of Beulah Land to Benjamin. She seldom ventured into the fields nowadays, and when she did so, she rode Buster, a gentle and uncharacteristically tractable mule she preferred to any of their horses for both saddle and buggy. Meeting always at meals and in the evenings, she and Benjamin talked over all that happened, but she left decisions on the working of land and livestock to him.

If he was now master of Beulah Land, she was still its mistress, however. She might not have been so ready to hand over authority had a wife hovered at his side to challenge her position in the eyes of the inhabitants of Beulah Land, for she was determined to live out her life as mistress there. After Lovey's death at the end of the war no servant had risen to the requirements of managing the great house, and so Sarah did it herself. It was not simply a matter of beds and barrels of flour, but of lives. "I can't leave for half a day," she boasted with as much truth as pride. Things would have gone along, she knew, but she favored supervision to momentum. She who had never borne a child was a mothering woman. Both Floyd and Casey used to tell her, only partly in jest, that Beulah

Land was her child, although she considered that she had many others. Roman, when he was a boy and she little more than a bride, had been her first adoption; and since then there had been Rachel, daughter of her husband Leon and her sister Lauretta; Rachel's children, Benjamin and Jane; and now their children; as well as Floyd's son Abraham and Roscoe Elk. All were hers in a way they had never belonged to their blood mothers.

Two of the duties she least enjoyed were the visits she made with Bruce to Priscilla and with Leon to Bessie, but she was conscientious about them. Only to Benjamin and Jane did she admit that she never left the Oglethorpe house in Highboro without anger and the Betchley farm without sadness. Yet once a week she attended both, varying the day and time so that the visits would appear to be less the obligation she considered them.

On the June morning she turned Buster into the road from Bessie's front yard she sighed her usual relief, and when they made the first turning of the road that put them out of sight of the farmhouse, she settled herself to enjoy the drive and began to hum. Sarah never hummed a tune; the sound was rather her equivalent of a cat's purring. The sun drew out the mellow leather smell of harness and buggy seat. Red dust rose from Buster's hooves on the clay road. The week had been a dry one, but the air was clear, and the breeze carried scents of the country morning. She had all but forgotten her great-grandson until he spoke words that told her he was of uneasy mind.

"I feel sorry for her, but I can't love her."

"You ought to."

"Well, I don't," he insisted mildly.

"She's your mother."

"Yes'm," he agreed, "but she sold me to Pa."

"Your father was always your father; there was no buying and selling about that." The mule set his pace, the red dust rising and floating away as the wind took it. "It was to give you the Davis name legally; the blood was always yours."

"Was it as simple as you make it sound?"

She smiled. "No. But one day Beulah Land will come to you, and there can be no question about that now."

He was thoughtful again. "It was so Gene Betchley couldn't get at me, wasn't it?" He put his hand into hers but withdrew it immediately. When he'd first come to live with them at Beulah Land he'd often needed to take his father's or Sarah's hand, but now as he went from boyhood through the long years that would bring him to manhood he avoided such gestures except at moments of special need or emotion. His love for Benjamin was absolute, but he'd got it into his head that a show of it was childish.

"What did you and Theodore do while I was visiting your mama in the kitchen?"

"I don't like him much."

"You're as full of judgments this morning as a Baptist preacher."

"He's sly."

"Maybe just shy. He doesn't see other children now school is out."

Leon shook his head in disagreement. "If I wasn't older and bigger than him, he'd try something on me. He tripped me while ago and said he didn't, but I knew he did." Leon was quiet a moment. "He showed me a nest with five baby birds in the pecan tree. The mother made a fuss when we climbed up, so I wouldn't let him touch the bough the nest was on, and he got mad about it."

A bend of the road brought them face to face with a buggy driven by Eugene Betchley on his way to the farm they had just left. "A beautiful morning!" Sarah called in greeting when the buggies passed. Eugene jerked his head in a kind of bow without answering, and Leon stared into the blackberry bushes bordering the road.

Eugene found his wife drawing a bucket of water at the well in the back yard and thought briefly of the morning he had found her so, after running away from Benjamin Davis and leaving his traps in the woods of Beulah Land. Bessie paused at her task to stare at him, but neither spoke while he wrestled a barrel of feed mash from the back of the buggy into the barn. Returning, he wiped grease from his hands onto the weathered barn door and said he wanted some coffee. Carrying the full bucket, she followed him to the back porch and into the kitchen.

When she'd boiled the coffee and he'd drunk two cups of it, she asked, "Will you be staying the night?"

He looked at her and sucked his teeth. "Don't see a thing to tempt me."

Bessie pulled at her dress. "I don't sit around combed and powdered, waiting for you to happen in."

"May stay for dinner. Anything fit to eat?"

"I'm cooking some butter beans with a chunk of fatback."

"Ain't there no lean meat?" She shook her head. "Then kill a chicken and fry it. I don't eat here every day." She nodded as if glad of something to do. "Where's the nigger at?"

"Hoeing grass out of the corn." Removing one of the iron eyes of the cookstove, she set a kettle of water directly over the fire.

"Seen old lady Troy and your bastard. They been here, I reckon." Bessie nodded. "Why didn't you say so?"

"Didn't get the chance."

"What did she want?"

"Visiting as usual. Nobody comes except her, and I don't go nowhere."

"Don't start about wanting to live with me in town, because I ain't going to let you. Did she bring anything?"

"Pair of stockings too big for her. Nothing secondhand. She'd only tried them on and didn't like to send them back, she said. Her legs are losing flesh as she gets old, but she don't want to admit it."

"Burn the stockings. I won't have even you wearing their castoffs."

She set her lips.

"You hear me, woman?"

"After I kill the chicken."

He started to the door. "Going to check on the nigger. If I find him sitting down gazing at his feet, I'm going to kick the shit out of him."

She followed him into the yard to see where the chickens had wandered to do their morning scratching. When she'd caught and wrung the neck of one of frying size, she went back into the house to see if the water was hot enough to scald him for plucking. Finding that it was not, she went into the bedroom. After examining them and holding them briefly against her face to feel their softness, she hid the stockings Sarah had given her in the toes of a pair of shoes. Then she slyly put a ragged scrap of an old petticoat into her dress pocket. She'd pop that into the stove when she heard Eugene returning, and he'd think the smell was that of the stockings.

She had browned the chicken pieces and put the lid on the skillet so that they'd cook through when she heard the voices of her husband and their son from the yard. When they did not come in and she had burned the scrap of cloth, she went to the porch to see what they were doing. They were busy with something over by the barn, and she couldn't tell what it was until she shaded her eyes from the noonday sun. Spying her, Theodore called, "Pa brought me a slingshot one of the millhands made."

She saw then, clearly. Theodore had taken the bird's nest from the pecan tree and set the featherless baby birds on a board propped on two old bricks in front of the barn door. Frantic, the mother bird fluttered about them until Theodore shooed her away with his hands. Eugene fitted stones into the leather pouch of the slingshot. Taking careful aim, he said to his son, "This is how," and splattered the infant birds one after the other against the hard barn door.

13

The hot summer days were upon them and there would be little respite until October other than the occasional storm of thunder and lightning that would astonish their senses and clear the air for only an hour. Everyone complained of the heat, but the young minded it hardly at all and the old kept to their houses with doors opened front and back or set a chair under a leafy tree. Except for the sick, they continued to eat heartily, for the work to be done each day was arduous. The young of both races and sexes went barefoot from April to October, as did many of the adult Negroes, while the adult whites envied them their comfort but did not take their example unless they lived in remoter country areas. There was visiting year round, but in summer it became epidemic, for someone was always claiming that it was cooler here than there and "Why don't you come see us and stay a few days?"

Fanny and Luck had maintained their friendship, but since it was not acceptable for them to stay overnight with each other's family, Sarah asked Fanny to be Bruce's guest at Beulah Land for several weeks of June and July. Fanny was grateful, for she loved the country, and she wanted to get away from her mother and stepfather. Blair Three stayed at home because no one asked him to visit, and he was content to flatter James into giving him bits of money and to be spoiled by Annabel in exchange for spying on his mother.

The three young girls often used the Glade as a shady shortcut between Beulah Land and the Elk house, stopping to idle an hour with Nancy if she gave them encouragement. They had been cautioned not to tire her, but they liked her and were curious about her and were sometimes able to tease her into confessions, albeit selective ones. They were much entertained by her manner of talking, which could make the ordinary lively and droll. The boys came to see her too, but less often than the girls, for most of their time was spent in the woods swimming and climbing trees and vines and fishing and exploring. No matter that they knew the woods as well as they knew the barns; there was always something that had changed overnight.

Rosalie had taken regular care of the house in the Glade against the day it would be used again, but she and Nancy left most of the dust-sheeted rooms closed. Because of its convenience to the kitchen, the center of activity for the two women, they turned the dining room into Nancy's room, Benjamin himself helping them furnish it with a bed and wardrobe. The front and back porches came alive with plants in tubs and boxes. Nancy rescued the flower beds, wanting occasional work to pacify the restlessness of returning strength, and someone or other frequently brought her a root to set, a cutting or shoot to stick into the ground and water.

On a trip to Savannah, Benjamin bought a covered hammock, and Zadok rigged it between two trees. Nancy spent many hours there resting and thinking, listening to the wind in the leaves and observing the sociability of birds and squirrels. There was even a family of rabbits that grew tame enough to feed on the farther grass beside the brook in the cool of morning and dusk. Old Mama would appear to be scratched and talked to, and one day a cat named Revelation followed Rosalie from her house, tired of the noise and hazards of living with Rosalie's grandchildren. After carefully examining the Glade and its inhabitant, Revelation decided to stay. He fancied the hammock as much as Nancy did and, when allowed to, took a position on Nancy's lap or stomach. Together they were so reclined on an afternoon late in June when Priscilla Davis and Ann Oglethorpe drove their buggy up the winding lane to the Glade house.

Revelation was first to hear their approach and indicated disapproval by flicking his ears and flexing his claws, which brought Nancy awake and to a sitting position. Slipping out of the hammock, she advanced to the buggy, guessing who its passengers were, although it was many years since she had seen Mrs. Oglethorpe, and she had never taken notice of Priscilla. With a polite curtsy she asked if they would get down. Not replying, they did so. Mrs. Oglethorpe slapped the buggy whip which she retained from driving against the top of her shoes. Priscilla said to Nancy, "Where is your master?"

"Mr. Davis, if you mean him, lives down at the big house, not up here, Mrs."

Mother and daughter exchanged looks. "Who lives here then?" Mrs. Oglethorpe asked abruptly, facing Nancy. "Someone does, from the look of things." She pointed with the whip, saying to Priscilla, "Look at those petunias, every color you can name. I don't mind a fern; a fern is quiet and dignified. But petunias! Isn't it just like a Nigra to have so many colors? Why, there's a dog. You never used to allow dogs here, and I certainly saw a cat run away when we drove up."

"You did, Mrs. Oglethorpe," Nancy said. "The cat's mine, much as a cat is anybody's, named Revelation from the Bible."

"I know where Revelation is, woman. So you know who I am?" She rested the whip on her shoulder, as a soldier shoulders arms.

"Yes, ma'am. Used to see you in town and thereabouts when I lived here as a girl. You were a few years younger too, if you don't mind my saying so, but take a lady like you, she don't change much over the years." To Priscilla she said, "You'll be Mrs. Ben Davis, I expect."

"I was—yes, I am."

"Nobody lives here but me," Nancy said, "and I live in just a room or two. Rosalie and others are in and out, and Revelation; and that old hound dog that turned away when she saw you is called Old Mama. That's on account she must have had a hundred or two puppies by now and is old in body if not in spirit. From the look of her dugs she might have mothered half the hound dogs in this county, and it's a county full of hound dogs."

"Are you telling us," Mrs. Oglethorpe said skeptically, "you are allowed free run of the house as if it's yours?"

"I don't go poking around in other folks' things, ma'am. Just in my own room or two."

"What do you call *your* room or two?" Mrs. Oglethorpe asked, raising brows to her daughter.

"Well'm, I reckon nothing belongs to me but the air I breathe, and I give that right back again to where it came from."

Mrs. Oglethorpe studied Nancy as she spoke. "You're a peculiar woman," she informed her.

"To some I might seem so, but to me I'm only me. Don't you feel that way about yourself? If somebody was to come up to you and say, 'You're a peculiar woman,' I bet you wouldn't be too quick to agree, though there's some might find you more peculiar than me." Nancy winked.

"They told us you were sick and dying," Priscilla said, as if she suspected that fraud was being perpetrated.

"They told a tale."

"You don't deny that you are diseased?" Mrs. Oglethorpe asked.

Priscilla began, "Dr. Rolfe's wife says—"

"Still am," Nancy admitted. "Consumption. If I commence to cough, you'll want to stand away from me, for I never know what pus and corruption will be churned up. What we all got inside us is enough to give us bad dreams, and that's the truth. Times, wouldn't surprise me to see splinters of wood, way my throat grates. I get better and I get worse. And better again. Today I'm better, but so it goes."

"All those pockmarks," Mrs. Oglethorpe observed thoughtfully, "must come from something else. Did you have the fever? They say you were once a— Women of that kind often— Punishment of the Lord." She turned to confer with her daughter but without lowering her voice. "I find it hard to entirely credit the reports. Surely no man, however depraved, would want such a creature as this one here. I know it is the curse of some men to possess a low animal nature. Even your poor father had an element of it. I had to battle it most earnestly. When it threatened to dominate him, I would pray to our Lord and Savior loud enough to lift the roof and reach His ear. I am thankful to say I was heard."

"We all heard you, Mama," Priscilla said without meaning to be facetious. "Elizabeth used to cry and wonder."

"She should have been proud to hear her mother wrestle with the devil. But I fear she is lost. You, however, have confided some of the horrors of your own marriage bed, so you understand that I am talking about sin and wickedness." She turned back to Nancy, scrutinizing her face so earnestly that she bent the whip in her hand double. "What have you to say?"

Nancy bowed her head. "I'm only what you see, ma'am, a sickly darky living by myself with a scaredy cat and a hound dog of frail character."

Priscilla said, "I wonder if she's a little touched in the head."

"It may be so," Mrs. Oglethorpe agreed, smoothing out the whip.

Nancy giggled foolishly, then covered her mouth like a schoolgirl abashed.

"A loony, or putting it on?" Mrs. Oglethorpe speculated.

"They say she gave good service to the family during and after the war. Mrs. Troy was over-tender to her Negroes. She may fancy a reason to show Christian charity where none is deserved."

"It would not be the first time her actions sprung from bad

judgment," Mrs. Oglethorpe observed sourly. "Mrs. Rolfe says it isn't certain whether this woman will live or die. With consumption they'll seem better only to be put to their eternal rest a month later. It's possible that it affects their minds." She frowned ruthlessly upon Nancy. "You have an uncouth appearance and an ignorant manner of expressing yourself, but, whatever your past misdeeds have been, and I do not imagine they have been insignificant, I cannot believe you offer temptation now to any man." She pointed to the ground with the whip. "Go down on your knees and ask the Lord to forgive your sins. Then we go, but not until then."

Nancy sank to her knees, closing her eyes and folding her hands beneath her bowed head.

Benjamin had crept along through the trees intending to surprise Nancy in the hammock, but paused to listen when he heard her in conversation and recognized the others present. His mother-in-law's words, however, compelled him to step forth from the foliage that concealed him. "I am amazed to find you here," he said to his wife.

Mrs. Oglethorpe started at sight of him, but collecting herself, addressed Priscilla. "I knew something was not right—it was the Lord trying to tell me. They saw us coming and decided upon a ruse. He was to hide and she to put on this crazy behavior to disarm our queries." She nodded firmly. "That is how it is; mark my words. What we've heard is true. If there is one man in the world depraved enough to keep such a creature about him for loathesome purposes, that man is your husband, Benjamin Davis!"

Priscilla said to Benjamin, "They've told us in town of this woman living here. They say she was one of the low, selling herself to any who would buy her in Savannah. Is it so?"

"She is a *whore,*" Mrs. Oglethorpe declared, bringing out the final word triumphantly. "And you, sir, should be whipped in public. By giving her the shelter of your house, you admit yourself to be the whore's monger!"

"Get into your buggy and go—or I'll take the whip out of your hand, Mrs. Oglethorpe, and thrash the pair of you. That will give the town something new to gossip about."

From the ground Nancy begged, "Just let them go, Ben—"

"You see how she calls him?" Mrs. Oglethorpe marveled eagerly even as she hurried after her daughter to the buggy. When they were safely seated, the older woman took reins in one hand and lifted whip in the other. "May the Lord have mercy on you if He dare, you son and daughter of Lucifer! I shall have none!" She landed the leather smartly on the horse's rump, and the buggy jolted away.

When they were gone, Nancy got to her feet. "Laws, Mr. Ben, don't know what I'd done if you hadn't come when you did! — Dem women's been calling me bad names! — Thankee, Mr. Ben!" He stepped back in surprise until she continued in her natural voice. "I don't care what they say about me—I'd have sent them off satisfied if you'd kept your big feet off this place another five minutes! Now they'll do everything they can to cause trouble." She stumbled to the hammock and fell into it wearily, closing her eyes.

He watched her for a minute from where he stood and then went and sat on the ground a few feet away from her but with his head at a level with hers. When she opened her eyes and saw him, she turned on her side. The gesture told him to go, but he remained; and when she looked again and found him there, he said, "I'm sorry. I ought to have let you do it your way, but when I heard what she was saying, I got so mad—"

Her stern expression relaxed into sadness. "They only say true."

"Will you make me fight you too?"

"No use, Ben. I won't get better, for I've no reason."

He took a breath like taking a decision. "I'll give you one. Get well so I can go to bed with you."

"A pretty way to talk to a dying woman—"

"I'll tell you when you can die, and don't you do it before."

"Listen to bossy you." Her smile was weak.

"I mean it, Nancy."

"Look at me," she said. They studied each other before she continued. "The first time we messed around you were—ten or eleven? I was thirteen. I've always been older than you. Now I'm a hundred years old. I'm marked with the pox. I worked in that house in Savannah till I was too ugly for even what they call 'the most depraved.' Nobody got drunk enough to ask my price the last few years."

"You were my first girl," he said.

"You were not my first boy, nor my last. I didn't drift into the business. I knew what I was doing and I enjoyed it when I could. Now I've got no feelings left. I'm what they see, if you don't: a worn-out whore dying of consumption."

"Shut up, if that's all you can say."

"Look at me until you see the truth."

"I'll give you a truth," he said softly. "Don't you know I've been aching to fuck you ever since you got home?" She stared at him. "I'm going in the house and upstairs to what used to be my room. I'm going to get in bed. Come up soon, because I'm going to wait until you do." He rose from the ground and crossed the grove to the house.

In his old room he opened a window and turned back the dust sheet before stripping his clothes off and lying down on the bare mattress. It was half an hour before she came, but she came; and when she reached the door, she entered directly and closed it behind her. He watched her as she undressed, and when she came to the bed, his whole body rose to claim her. With a groan she closed arms and legs about him, and they loved each other as if bent on self-destruction. When they came, their bodies were wet with sweat and their faces wet with tears. Exhausted, she slept. He kept watch, and she woke an hour later to the tickle of his forefinger under her chin.

"Long time," he said.

She turned, a bone snapped. "Years for me," she said ruefully.

"I meant since we've been together."

"Didn't imagine it was a long time since you'd had a woman."

"That's been a good while too."

He told her about the affair with Frankie, and about her becoming pregnant after Bonard died, and about her marrying James Davis.

"Godalmighty. You're in worse trouble than I am."

He shook his head. "I've got you again. The happiest time in my life was the days we spent together in Savannah when I was nineteen."

"That was good," she agreed.

"I didn't want anybody after you sent me away."

"For a week or two?"

"More like three." She slapped him on his naked shoulder. "Ah, Nancy—what mistakes you'd have saved us both if you'd only come with me the way I begged you."

"It would have buried you as well as me."

"Don't talk of dying and burying now."

"I'm not going to die yet," she conceded. "But don't expect me to be a muley-cow, always waiting for you."

He stroked her back and thighs, and after a minute she pressed against him. "Your feelings are over and done. That's what you said."

She lifted her face to look at him. "You've got a gift." He smiled, and she marveled how a smile could light the world.

14

Two decades after the war the all-day party at Beulah Land on the Fourth of July was still thought of as a family affair rather than a celebration of the birth of the Union. Annabel Saxon considered challenging Sarah's claim on the day by selecting it for the unveiling of the new Confederate memorial; but realizing that no one connected with Beulah Land would attend the event if there was such a choice, she settled upon July 2 to harangue fellow citizens with a speech extolling her efforts on behalf of their common heritage. Annabel got her crowd, even Sarah deciding that it was unpolitic not to go. Elk Institute, because of Annabel's occasional sponsorship, provided a contingent of its Negro pupils enthusiastically waving Confederate flags and singing "Dixie." Annabel enjoyed her day in the sun, and Sarah enjoyed hers in the shade, the old trees of Beulah Land providing a thick cover to the annual feast and feasters.

Benjamin escorted Bruce and Fanny Saxon to Annabel's program in Highboro, Leon and Sarah going separately in her buggy and the Todd family in theirs. Afterwards, on impulse, Sarah stopped at the Betchley farm to ask Bessie if she would join them at Beulah Land two days hence. Bessie declined, but Sarah promised to send her a sampling of the victuals. So that it would not have the appearance of leftovers, she made up a basket early in the morning of the Fourth and deputized Leon to deliver it. The prospect of driving the buggy only partially overcame Leon's disinclination to see his mother alone. Bobby Lee and Davy scorned his invitation to share the adventure, for there was much of interest going on at Beulah Land. On visits to the farm Leon was ill at ease because he didn't want to be there; he had not been alone with his mother since he was carried unconscious to Beulah Land after his beating by Eugene. If Theodore was with her instead of in the woods or fields, he could hand over the basket and leave, saying he was needed at the plantation to help with other matters. But when he arrived, he found Bessie in the kitchen washing a greasy skillet from breakfast. As she dried her hands to accept the basket, both were dumb until she cleared her throat to say, "Miss Sarah didn't come?" She provided her own answer. "Too busy, I expect. I don't know where Theodore—he's somewhere."

"Well'm." He stepped back to the door. "I have to get on."

"Dipper of water? Early though it is, it's a day to scorch your hide. I don't reckon you'd be hungry?" She was not eager for him to stay but resented his look of wanting to escape.

To reply, "No, ma'am," seemed not enough, so he added, "I had a big breakfast," and then unnecessarily, "on the porch with Grandma and Pa."

Taking his elaboration for brag, she hardened her voice to mockery. "Did you? Waited on by a whole gaggle of niggers, I'll vow."

He gestured toward the basket she had placed on the table in the middle of the kitchen. He would never see the table without remembering spilling coffee and Gene's slapping him. "There's some of everything," he explained. "I watched Grandma pack it. Barbecued pig and goat—"

"None of us'll touch goat."

"A whole cake, a gallon of Brunswick Stew, and a jar of—"

"You're good as the bill of fare in a dining room in Savannah; but I don't have to be told Miss Sarah spreads a rich table."

"Well'm. I just better go now."

She repeated the motion of wiping her hands on her dress front, although they were dry. "I'll walk out with you. I have to go to the privy. How'd you come—nigger bring you in a wagon or did they make you tote that basket all this way?"

"Grandma let me drive her buggy. Buster's used to me. He's a good old mule."

She eyed Buster critically as they approached the buggy. "Fat as lard from eating too much and working too little. You tell Miss Sarah I'm obliged, you hear, and she needn't fear for her dishes, though I don't imagine she sent her best. They'll be safe till she comes for them."

"I'll tell her."

She laughed shortly. "Brunswick Stew 'minds me of the time—" Color rose under the coarse skin of her neck. "I was going to say when you went first to their family party and come home with a basket of victuals for your Granny Marsh, Lord rest her soul."

"That's some while ago," he reminded her, fiddling with Buster's harness merely to be doing something. He knew it was all right; Wally had watched him hitch the mule to the buggy and said so.

"Expect it seems longer to you than to me. Time don't mean a thing to me, because I don't go nowhere, just set here ignorant of everything but the past."

He longed to leave but knew her tempers. "I take flowers and put them on Granny Marsh's grave."

"Lord, I miss her so. You and Miss Sarah have time to think of doing them things."

He pulled himself into the seat of the buggy and took reins in hand, moving deliberately to show no haste.

She smiled tightly, reading his mind. "Think you're grown sitting up there, don't you? You're a lot like your pa. He was a good-looking boy when he used to sneak around here after me." His embarrassment fed her anger. "Just wait a minute, boy, for I haven't said you could go. Got a thing to ask you been on my mind. It's about that night long back, you know the one. What made you accuse Gene of doing what you said?"

"It just came into my head." He hesitated. "When we were by ourself once Granny Marsh told me she was scared of him because he wanted her dead."

"The imagination of the old—and the young! I reckon you're making that up."

"I'm not. But you claimed you saw it all happen and it wasn't that way."

"That's right," she agreed flatly. "Want you to hear something else I never had the chance to say. Reason I sold you was your pa's folks could do better for you than me." He lifted the reins. "Don't drive off till I say! You're telling yourself what you've all told one another, that I done it 'cause Gene made me. That's a story. You're still the burden I toted in my belly for nine long months while ever'body laughed. Nobody on this earth wanted you. Not till Ben Davis decided he couldn't get a son no other way than taking you from me. That's how you got the name I wasn't good enough for. Don't think it was you he wanted. To my dying day I'll remember the look on his face when I told him I was going to have you. If you'd seen that, you wouldn't think he wanted you." He started the mule and managed to turn the buggy in time to conceal his tears of mortification. "No matter whose fat mule you drive, you're common as the dirt farm you was born on, and don't you forget it, little bastard!"

On his way from Beulah Land that morning he had thought to ride back up the carriageway with head high as they exclaimed over his easy handling of mule and buggy; but when he got home, the large party had begun to assemble and spread indoors and out, populating the porches and yards. Sarah saw him but paused only to ask if his mother had been pleased with the basket before hurrying to the kitchen to cajole Josephine into allowing some of the servants brought by family visitors to help her serve. Josephine did not want people in her kitchen talking and laughing, or even smiling until she said "smile;" and anyone with heavier tread than tiptoe was banished when meringue and custard were in the ovens. Entering, Sarah cried, "Josephine, you are my best friend, so I know I can count on you to be good-natured about something!" Josephine scowled at her suspiciously.

Leon found Wally and the stableboy comparing the horses and mules brought by visitors, so he unhitched Buster and wheeled the empty buggy into its stall. Davy and Bobby Lee, who often gave the impression of being everywhere simultaneously, were nowhere to be seen, having sworn to ignore their cousin's privilege and elevation. As Davy put it to his brother, "Bad enough he can come and we can't. Now he's took Grandma's buggy out, he'll act like King Shit. I wish to God I was eighteen years old and had curly hair and wasn't freckle-faced. I'd come a hundred times a day, I bet you!"

Bobby Lee corrected him automatically. "Hush your dirty talk. If you say 'shit' in front of Aunt Doreen and upset her, I'll skin you like a rabbit and drop you in a barrel of brine. I reckon he's strutting like a banty rooster learning how to crow."

In truth, Leon was glad not to draw attention, for he was certain that if anyone looked at him, they'd see no more than his mother saw: a no-good, dirt-farm, boughten bastard. He slumped, he slunk in the shadows; and when any called his name that day, his heart shrank in apprehension. Finally becoming aware that their cousin was in no fettle to play cock of the walk, Bobby Lee and his brother sought him out. "Did you run it in a ditch and crook the wheels?" Bobby Lee asked.

"No!" Leon retorted furiously.

"You musta done something," Davy observed, "else you wouldn't skunk around looking so dumpsy." His eyes brightened. "Did you try to come and couldn't?"

Leon stamped away in his misery, leaving the cousins puzzled and pondering the mystery.

So occupied was everyone, he managed to avoid more than brief contact with guests for most of the day; but at noon when he was glumly consuming a plate of barbecued pig, Fanny's voice broke his isolation. "I pure despise that old man."

Curiosity made him search around to see who she meant, and

when he discovered the object of her glare, she nodded confirmation.

"He's my grandpa," he objected mildly.

She shrugged. "You all at Beulah Land are so mixed up in your relations I don't try to sort it out. All I know, and that's enough, is he's my stepdaddy. You ought to see how Blair shines up to him, hoping to get a quarter, and he usually does. I hate men and boys. Luck feels the same. We aren't going to have anything to do with them from now on." Lured out of self-absorption, he studied her determined face. "I wish there was another war. I'd go be a nurse like Clara Barton."

"Then you'd have to have do with men," he pointed out.

"Only when they were dying," she said with satisfaction. "Why are you feeling sorry for yourself today? You've got a face as long as Buster's, and I haven't heard you laugh once, even when Abraham told his story about the goat in Philadelphia that could trot backward. I think goats are smart, unlike some people. Just remember: *you're* lucky to live at Beulah Land."

"You mean I don't belong here," he mumbled.

She sighed impatiently. "Where else do you belong? I mean I don't, and I wish I did." She brooded, watching him eat. "I don't like Mama much better than I do him. Do you like her? If you do, just say so. She thinks everybody in britches ought to, so go ahead if you can't help yourself."

"Why should I like her or not? She's just Aunt Frankie."

"That means you like her."

"You're crazy with the heat today."

Deciding not to take offense, Fanny continued, "She's stuck-up and greedy, and now she says she's tired all the time. She blames it on this baby she'll have. I think it's all disgusting, but I bide my time. When I get old enough, I'm going to shake her till her joints squeak and then I'm going to throw her powder puff and all her jars of stuff in the creek. Then she'll look like everybody else, and we can all relax. Grandma Annabel says you eat enough for a dozen darkies picking cotton fourteen hours a day. Wherever do you put it all?" She let her gaze wander back to James Davis, who managed to sit so that one knee bore into his wife's thigh as they ate side by side in the shade. "He's dirty."

Leon's eyes followed hers again. "Maybe he misses places when he washes because he's blind."

"I don't mean dirty like that, I mean dirty-dirty." Looking at his grandfather, Leon blushed, telling himself he must never touch his own peter again except to pee. "Mama says I have to go home in a week or two or I'll outstay my welcome."

"Nobody cares how long you stay," he said, meaning to comfort her.

"I don't want to go home. I hate it at night, because I can hear him through the halls and walls."

Memory and sympathy stirred in Leon. "Some people haven't any gumption," he said placatingly.

"If that's all you can say, I'll find Bruce and talk to her. She's got more sense for her age than anybody I know anyway." She flounced away.

He took his empty plate to one of the long tables laden with food. Mabella greeted him with a friendly smirk. "You back? You'll grow a belly big as Sandy Claus."

"I'll have that pulley bone," he said with dignity, "and some potato salad, if you please, and a spoonful of roasting ears."

Serving him, she warned, "You'll pop like a cotton boll one of these days. Hope I'm not around to see you do it."

"I don't care," he said, and found a place under a tree where no one else was sitting.

If the day was less joyous for Leon than he had anticipated, few present saw any difference between it and Fourth of July celebrations of other years. It was true that Sarah had taken little pleasure in parties since Casey's death, but her sense of hospitality was strong, and only Benjamin and Jane knew that her heart was less than whole. After the successful presentation of the memorial statue to their glorious Confederate dead, Annabel was inclined to enjoy herself. There was much to cheer her. Frankie was looking "very poorly," Annabel whispered, further confiding to intimates her "hope that we are not to lose her." James's daughters by his second marriage were still unreconciled to their father for desecrating their mother's memory. Prudence, Annabel's remaining daughter-in-law and "child of my beloved friend Maggie's sensible *first* marriage," was unexpectedly and uncomfortably pregnant again. Annabel had the satisfaction of believing she had bested Sarah today in their running conflict; and she had succeeded in giving her "frank opinion" to all members of the family gathering who had not managed to avoid her on their apparel, looks, state of health, and the handling of their parental, marital, and financial concerns. She took further satisfaction in the flattery of Blair Three, who, unpopular with other children, played the part of "Grandmother's boy," as Annabel persisted in calling him, ever at her side when not engaged on her errands and commissions.

As was usual, Sarah had flung her net wide enough to include such non-family favorites as Tom and Elizabeth Cooper and their five sturdy sons. Roscoe and Luck and Abraham were there, although not Claribell, whose shyness was indulged by her being allowed to stay at home from big gatherings. Roman and Pauline were there from the school and had quarreled about geography, although Pauline spent most of the day sitting in a chair between the graves of her brother Floyd and her life's friend Selma. As the day passed, the Negro members of the reunion wandered to the Glade to pay calls on Nancy, and finding themselves diverted by her company as most did, remained. Nancy also had her share of white visitors, the older ones having valued her one way or another since she was born a slave.

After the big eating—there would be a lesser one later in the afternoon consisting of watermelon, tea, and cake—there was a general breaking up into groups. The younger children were dragged indoors by mammies to endure their naps. The men and older boys drifted away to the barns, and then to the woods, where they might go to sleep on the ground as they talked, waking to swim, returning finally to the big house in high spirits, bearing on their shoulders watermelons cooled in the creek. The older girls and women were made comfortable with fans and opened beds and gossip as they took their afternoon rest. Frankie had managed a quick plea to Benjamin when the men began to separate themselves for their exodus. "For pity's sake, take your father with you—I must have an hour of peace!" Alarmed by her agitation, he did so, placing an arm around James's shoulders and steering him along after the others.

Frankie did not, however, seek refuge with the sweating, fanning, giggling, yawning women who crowded the resting rooms. After Sarah had done her duty as hostess, leaving Jane to answer the further needs of their female guests, she excused herself and slipped onto the shadier side porch for a quiet hour. Heavy wisteria vines made the place almost dark, and she had pulled up a rocking chair to sit down before she discovered Frankie in the one beside hers.

"My dear Frankie—"

"You wanted to be by yourself," Frankie guessed.

"No." Sarah faced her chair toward the younger woman as an indication that her company was welcome.

"I get no privacy myself, and you must find little."

Sarah smiled politely. "We may, if we like, sit without saying a word."

"I only want to be away from James."

"He is surely a loving husband." She did not intend the statement as a reprimand, but as a withdrawal.

"Yes, ma'am, he is," Frankie replied in a whisper.

"Not many wives would complain of that." Sarah began to rock her chair in the way Nell used to soothe herself to sleep after eating. Her eyes were closed when Frankie said despairingly, "I have made such mistakes, Miss Sarah!"

"We all do that."

"You never have." Frankie evidently wanted comforting, but Sarah had never trusted her, and decided to keep her peace. "I always made wrong decisions," Frankie continued presently. "When I consider that—" She shook her head. "I might have married Benjamin and lived here untroubled all my days."

"Life at Beulah Land is not so simple as that," Sarah said drily.

"One mistake after another, each pointing to the next," Frankie insisted, "when all I wanted was to be one of you. I know you will think it wrong to talk this way."

Sarah considered excusing herself to consult with Josephine, but saw it would appear deliberately unkind. If she was to remain, however, she could not allow the younger woman to pity herself so indulgently. "Maybe you went about it too determinedly," she suggested briskly. "We are easy, you know. If we have a fault, and I do not own that we do, it is that we are easy. Love us and we surrender everything. Only, no one may try to manage us, or say what we must do, for we are stubborn and proud. My Casey understood that so well." Mention of Casey was natural for Sarah, for he was always in her mind, but it was the first intimate reference she had made to Frankie, and Frankie caught it quickly.

"What a thing," she said, "to have loved a husband so. I've cared for neither of mine in that way."

"I think I know why you chose Bonard," Sarah said calmly, "but why James? You might have arranged things with Annabel. She's contrary, and she'd have made life difficult, no doubt, but she adores your children, and she prides herself, God help us, on her duty."

From the shadows of her high-backed chair it was possible for Frankie to study her hostess. "I've felt now and again that you understand about your grandson and me, Miss Sarah. That we have been more than once-upon-a-time childhood sweethearts." Sarah sat still but made no acknowledgment of confidential communication. "I married James Davis because he wanted me to and I had to marry someone. I'd discovered that I was to have Benjamin's child."

"My dear Frankie!" There was compassion in Sarah's voice as well as distress. "If there is anything—"

"No, ma'am, nothing. Only, I wanted you to know, and I feel better for telling you."

Sarah remained quiet and began to rock her chair again. "I have perhaps been unjust but, if there is a way, shall try to make amends."

Frankie rocked her chair in rhythm with Sarah's, as if to confirm the new bond between them. "I remember a talk we had long ago, Miss Sarah, about Bessie Marsh. Benjamin had asked me to marry him and told me Bessie was pregnant with the child that turned out to be Leon. Do you recall how indignant I was, what extravagant demands I made? Well, I am paid out for it."

"I hope you do not think of it like that," Sarah said uncomfortably. It was one thing to feel sorry for the woman, but she could not quell her long distrust of her, and she did not want to enlarge the intimacy that had been foisted upon her.

"I despise myself."

"My dear, *please*."

Misinterpreting Sarah's toubled look as one of chagrin, Frankie went on. "There are mornings I wish I had died in the night."

"Do not say any more!" Sarah pleaded.

Frankie would not be stopped. "Who would care? I least of all. You cannot understand how detestable it is to accept the attentions of a man you do not love. Not love him? I hate him with all my heart when he touches me, and that is every hour of every day. Yet I must keep silent, be compliant, somehow endure—"

"Poor James!" Sarah exclaimed.

Frankie drew back as if she had been struck. "You pity him?"

"Poor lonely man!" She looked as if she would weep.

Controlling herself with effort, Frankie said, "May I ask why, madam?"

"So many reasons and none that I may tell you. If only Casey were here! I need him more and more—"

They were interrupted by Mabella. Her ears attuned to trouble, Sarah heard her before she arrived, excited to tears. "Miss Sarah, you got to come! Josephine has took the big butcher knife to Mercy—Miss Annabel's girl she brought? Hasn't cut her yet, but she's got her up on a kitchen stool and won't let her down till she prays forgiveness for pinching the icing off the angel cake!"

Tom Cooper was gentle, unlike his rackety sons, and having observed Frankie's sadness, spoke of it to his wife Elizabeth. Elizabeth thought about it and later spoke to Tom. Between them they conceived a plan to cheer their old acquaintance. Elizabeth had heard of the days he and the other farm boys of the neighborhood played collective swain to the pretty visitor from Savannah, Miss Frankie-Julia Dollard. Elizabeth reminded Tom of the evenings he and Hobart Kenning and Frederick Shields and John Baxter had serenaded Frankie and Jane on this very porch at Beulah Land. Might they not today re-create something of the kind to remind the sad woman of happier days? Tom would not sing, and the others were absent, but the Cooper sons, Jesse, Jacob, Marvin, Garvin, and Jeremiah, were enthusiastic songsters and loved any occasion of showing off. They were therefore easily persuaded to surprise Mrs. James Davis after the second eating of the day when, full of watermelon and cake and tea, the ladies lolled on the porches, the gentlemen at their feet, all waiting for the spirit to move them to get up and go home. That was the moment Tom chose to give the signal to his chorus.

Quick as hares they surrounded a startled Frankie and burst into the jolly bounce of one of her old favorites, "Glendy Burk." Alas, the response was not that intended. Frankie recognized the song and recalled the earlier occasions she had listened to it enraptured; but for whatever reason—the contrast of her circumstances then and now, the difference in her age now and then, the feeling that she had been severely snubbed that day by Sarah Troy, whose support she had thought finally to achieve—all perhaps combined to release in her heart an agony of grief that was not to be expressed except in high and hideous wails. The song ceased; the abashed chorus was led away by their mother to be reassured. Everyone at once offered excuses and explanations, no one listening to those of anyone else. The general and thorough commotion accomplished one result, the breakup of the gathering. Weary, Sarah did not try to stop them but let them go, only making certain they carried plates or baskets of the remains of the day's feast with them so that they would not have to prepare their own suppers. Their going, however, required some time, for there were horses to be harnessed to wagons and buggies and ten dozen last confidences and promises to be exchanged and lavish expressions of gratitude to be made their hostess.

Not until Frankie was being handed into her buggy by her husband did it occur to her to take Fanny with her, but suddenly she could not face even the ride alone with James. She called Fanny; Fanny came. "You must come home today. I cannot spare you any longer!"

The child protested that she was to remain another week or two. Sarah and Bruce and Benjamin added their pleas that she be allowed to stay. Her clothes were not ready. "She has plenty at home and the ones here may be sent after her," Frankie replied. There was no dissuading her from having the company of her daughter. So, after a little time was granted to gather the most urgently required personal familiars, Fanny climbed into the buggy, Frankie yanking her up and settling her firmly between herself and her husband. Away they drove, only now it was Fanny's crying that rent the air. Leon could not bear to be part of the scene but looked down upon it from a limb of their oldest magnolia where he knew he would not be joined because the climb had already proved too difficult for his cousins.

Sarah retired to her room. The Todds went to their own house. After checking the barns, Benjamin returned to the big house to find Leon alone on the front steps. He sat down beside him. "It was a full day, wasn't it?" Leon did not answer but stared off down the carriageway. Moving closer to him, Benjamin said, "Eat too much barbecue and got a bellyache?" Leon shook his head. "Just got nothing to say for yourself, that it?" Benjamin sighed easily and relaxed his elbows against the steps behind them.

Suddenly Leon burst out, "I don't ever want to leave Beulah Land!"

Benjamin put his arm around the boy and hugged him hard. Leon felt his fear and unhappiness dissolve as he let himself go slack against his father; and when Benjamin spoke, Leon understood that the words were for both of them. "This is home."

15

Mindful of Fanny's distress at going home, Sarah took Luck to town to see her when she and Bruce made the next ritual visit to the Oglethorpe house. As usual, grave questions were put to Bruce by her maternal antecedents, to which she gave dutiful answers that had been earlier provided her by Sarah. Bruce then was given a religious tract to admire while her elders conversed.

"It is the only place," as Sarah reported to Benjamin, "I find myself chattering. This is because I abhor silence with those I do not like. I surprise myself by telling—since there is nothing I want to *say* to them—about our crops and livestock, Josephine's progress in preserving fruit and vegetables, Jane's energy and skill in sewing, and the ailments of all the womenfolk on the place. Nancy would throw herself on the ground and roll with laughter if she heard me detail her gradual but now certain recovery. They once asked me the condition of 'the ailing Negress' after they'd paid their peculiar visit to her in the Glade, and I don't let them forget such Christian concern. I never speak of you. I never speak of any man lest it be thought unseemly. And when I have told them all these things, I discover that no time at all has elapsed since we entered the front door and were instructed to sit down. I always plant myself where I can see the mantel clock without craning or squinting. I never allow us to remain exactly as long as we did on our previous visit. You see why I chatter. I chatter now in the very recounting. Soon I shall be driven to reciting to them the manner in which we dry seeds for next year's sowing and the way we clear leaves from our wells. I only hope it wearies them as it does me. When we left after eighteen hours, actually thirty-seven minutes, I drove directly to old Mrs. Bascom's and bought enough candy to give an entire dame school the colic. Then back to spend an hour with Frankie while the girls ate the candy and played together. Frankie is still pale and appears distracted. I wonder if James would let us have her here for a few weeks along with Fanny? Beulah Land is good for everybody. I'll sound James out. While we were talking in her little parlor, Eugene Betchley came through the living room just next to leave some papers with James, who is at home with a cold in the head. Eugene bowed to us through the arched way as he left the house; and through the window I could see him pause in the yard to observe the children. He stared quite hard. As luck would have it, and I mean no pun, Luck's hoop went cock-a-loop and rolled into him. He caught it and looked as if he might break it, but then thrust it back at the child when she held out her hand to claim it. He obviously considered it *wrong* that she should be playing with them in the front yard like that. James does not look well, though I saw him for only a moment. I wish you would go to see him. I know how you feel, but go. With every cough—and his cigars make it worse—his ears go purple, almost black, as if with a sudden fever. Maybe we should have all of them here for a month and send them home well again. He usen't to smoke so, but he says it clears his head.

And Frankie confided to me—she is far too confiding for my taste—that he is often deep in claret. He was not ever a man for much drink, to my knowledge. — You see what a morning I've had? And you talk about the cotton yield!"

It was true, as she had long noted, that Eugene was keeping watch on Frankie. Busy and blameless as her days now were, awareness of his scrutiny was present in her mind during the hours she spent at the sawmill each day. She did not, as other women more vain with less cause might have, put it down to a susceptibility to her attractions. She knew what she looked like even tired, unhappy, and grossly pregnant; but it was not her beauty that kept his eyes on her. There was in his look something of speculation and waiting. What, she asked herself, was he waiting for? Had he not got what he wanted in the quarter share of ownership which, she reminded herself, had been denied her own husband while he lived? One man worked for a reward never given because he thought it would come without his asking, while his successor got it on demand as a condition of continuing to do the work he was already paid to do. Eugene Betchley won his way by threat, spoken or implied. Her first husband dead, her second blind, Eugene might watch her as boldly as he pleased, monitor her coming and going as he would, knowing she would not complain.

James's cold persisted, but it did not lessen his demands upon her. She protested. For his sake, she said, he must hoard his energies; but he would have her, and did so. When Benjamin tendered his grandmother's invitation for the James Davis family to stay at Beulah Land a month, James refused curtly for all of them.

"You are getting to be enormous," Annabel said to Frankie in August. "Surely it is far too soon. The babe will weigh twenty pounds at birth. Not due till December? By then we shall wonder whether the mother carries the baby or the baby the mother! James, I wish you could see what you have done, you cruel fellow!"

With five children grown and married, James yet remembered enough of their mother's pregnancies to become uneasy about his wife and to query her closely. She answered sullenly and, he considered, inadequately. When he pressed, she took proud offense, and then she wept near to hysteria, and then she turned silent.

On a hot night in September she sat by the open window of their bedroom praying that it might rain and cool the air, and with equal fervor beseeching heaven to keep James sleeping. Even as she did so, he woke to find himself in bed alone and called her name. When he began to grope about the bed, she said, "I am here."

"Why are you up?" She told him. "I don't mind the heat," he said. "Come back to bed."

"After while."

"Now."

"I am too hot."

"You must do as I say, Frankie." She made no reply and stayed where she was. Presently James said, "Are you thinking of him?"

"Who?"

"Whoever it is."

She sighed. "I think sometimes you are mad."

"The one who got to you before I did."

"I feel as if no one had ever touched me before you."

"That is how it must be from now on."

"You're suggesting the child is not your own?"

"You're so big so soon. I can feel you, and Annabel has spoken of it any number of times."

"She would accuse me of rutting with the devil if she thought it would turn you against me. You play into her hands, though you pretend to know her."

"Come here."

"Soon. Now go to sleep."

"I'm not sleepy."

"You need to sleep," she said. "You say yourself the heat does not keep you awake. Well, it does me. I must get cool, or I shall not close my eyes the rest of the night."

"Come to bed, Frankie. I want you."

"I am not well. Truly."

"Then you will not be any the worse for it, will you?" he said. "Lately you have complained much."

"I've had much to complain of. It is a difficult pregnancy. When it is over—"

"You complain overmuch."

"Only of your excesses."

"Do not make me come after you."

She left her chair and went to the bed, sitting down on the side of it. He took her by the wrist, but lightly, not as if he meant to hurt her. "Have you been unfaithful?"

"How could I be when we are never apart?"

"You were unfaithful to Bonard before me. I have thought so for some time. I'm no fool, though you may think so. It came to me after we married that you had contrived the thing because you had to. That's why I've never let you beyond my reach. I should have known it when you let me have you the first time; but I wanted you more than I was willing to doubt you. You don't love me, do you?"

"What does love signify?" she said tiredly. "You believe what others tell you or what you tell yourself. You have always been jealous; and jealousy such as yours requires little imagination to build an edifice of lies and false accusation. What is love to you but a license for fornication?"

"I warn you, girl, not to trifle with me. Take off the gown so that I may feel you properly." She continued sitting as she was. After waiting briefly for her to do as he'd said, he grabbed the gown at the neck and tore it down the back. It fell from her, and he raised himself, the more easily to pass his hands over her moist body. He then pushed her down so that she lay on her back, and stretching himself beside her, threw a leg across her thighs and moved to mount her.

"I don't know which of us has the bigger belly," she said. "You have grown fat on all the wine you drink."

"It gives me strength."

"That is what Bonard used to say, but it only made him disgusting."

He slid off her without achieving entry. "You must straddle me."

"No," she said.

"You have done so before. You say it's easier the way you are now."

"I shan't do it tonight."

"Yes, you will, my girl." He caught her again by both wrists. She tried to rise; he would not let her up.

"You are right to charge me," she said, struggling to twist away, spilling her held-in spite. "I have been unfaithful, but not to you, as you well know I could not have been. You watch me with everything but eyes, and at the mill Eugene watches me with his. Do you pay him to do it for you, as you must pay everyone for everything?"

"Are you telling me it's Gene you've been the whore with?"

"My unfaithfulness was never to you but to Bonard—if you call it that. Bonard had long ceased being husband to me when I found another."

"*Who?*"

"Your son Benjamin—now *he* is a man!"

His ears first, then his whole face went dark with a rush of blood and fever. "He is not my son! His mother was a whore like you! — Now climb astride, madam, and jog, or I'll make you sorry!"

"I will not—"

He rolled her over roughly and fell upon her, entering her from behind. When she cried out, he used a hand to close and hold her mouth. Heaving and thrusting brutally, he worked quickly to ejaculation, and when he slid off her sweating backside, panted himself to sleep. The sound of his snores increasing in volume and assuming a regular pattern at last freed her to move. She edged to the side of the bed; her feet touched the floor.

Pulling the rags of her discarded nightgown about her, she went to sit again at the window. It was no cooler; it would not rain. Eventually she fell a-doze sitting upright. Waking, she moved cautiously toward the bed. James was no longer snoring. She wondered if he was awake and would reach for her once more if she placed herself beside him. Finding a wrapper in the wardrobe, she left the room quickly and went into the hallway and to the room where Fanny was sleeping. Fanny did not stir when Frankie lay down beside her on top of the sheet that partially covered the child.

Exhaustion still held her oblivious when Fanny shook her awake. "Mama, it's nearly eight o'clock. Nobody got up, so Molly made Blair go in your room to see why. He says he can't wake Uncle James."

16

Although the faces they presented to Frankie were solemn enough, the townspeople responded to James Davis's death with more levity than they might have another's. The wink was common, accompanied by an earnest warning of the terrible risks to old dogs of behaving like pups. Wives took relish in nudging their husbands to mark a lesson in the event. If all were surprised, including those who claimed never to be, astonishment was reserved for Eugene Betchley. When the earth trembles twice under a man's feet, he must wonder if a fateful finger is not pointed at him. First, Bonard Saxon had died decades before due time, and now James Davis, who might have expected another twenty years of life—the two men to whom he owed such prominence as he had achieved. Eugene was given to think more furiously than ever. By natural rights, should not the sawmill now be his? It should be but was not, for there in her pew between son and daughter sat the twice-widowed woman who held his future, in billowing black that did not hide the new life she carried.

He knew who was responsible for that life. There was the man across the aisle with his granddam, son, and daughter in the pew that had been their family's as long as the church stood. The church itself was their creation, for they needed it to bear witness to the fortunes of Beulah Land. Eugene knew so much they did not think he knew. He had not yet decided how to use his knowledge, but the will to do so was behind the looks of speculation that had puzzled Frankie during her hours at the mill. He did not know how far he dared go, but there would be a way; of that he was certain. Otherwise, events had no meaning, and the examination of a single leaf showed form and order, not chaos, to be the laws of life.

Eugene let his eyes pick out two others from those present. Annabel Saxon and Priscilla Davis sat a few rows apart, the one flanked by husband and surviving son, the other shoulder to shoulder with her old scold of a mother. One hated Frankie Davis; the other hated Benjamin Davis—another thing he knew. Might they become his allies? But then he remembered one not present, his own wife. *She* was no ally, or one no longer. The chance of being caught poaching by Benjamin Davis had set him running to the farm of Bessie Marsh, which he saw on that morning for the first time as his opportunity to leave traps and seines behind him. *In the midst of life we are in the midst of death*—and truer words were never said, amen.

Waiting for the service to end, Eugene examined the backs of other heads before him. He had chosen to sit well to the rear, as suited his station. Why, he wondered, was Doreen Davis crying so? He'd not thought a dry old maid had so many tears to shed. She was only a sister of the dead man, yet she behaved like widow-mother-sister-daughter in one, while those who might more properly employ themselves in weeping sat like very statues of mourning. (Poor Doreen! She wept for lost love and innocence, for the days when she and James were children, before he began to need women, and she was the only one who loved and was good to him. Her heart cried, "James, James—turn time around and let us be boy and girl again! You have just come in from the field Papa gave you to plant as your own. Your hands are black with earth as you take the glass of tea I pour for you, and you laugh to thank me. — I was never happy till then; I have never been happy since. Lost, lost and gone!")

Ben Davis and his sister Jane were calm enough, Eugene judged, and back of them sat the dull daughters of the old man's second marriage, surrounded by their heavy husbands and pasty, restless children. It was well, Eugene mused, that a man never knew what his children would be, lest knowledge spoil his pleasure in the making of them. Finally it was over. The organ played; they rose together. He could not be the first to leave, though he itched to gallop out into the open air.

The hour James was discovered by his stepson dead, Frankie became the happiest woman in Highboro. She made no endeavor to disguise the truth from herself. Let her tears of relief be read by those around her as grief. When Annabel arrived to confirm the news that had been sent her, Frankie was better composed, but she almost laughed at her not bothering to condole. "Well, ma'am, what have you done this time?"

Ignoring the accusation in the grim greeting, Frankie answered, "It is true, sister. We have suffered a great loss and must comfort one another. I, you; you, me; for the kindest of brothers and the most loving husband."

"I know he's dead," said Annabel, "but what of?"

Frankie tried a sigh. "Dr. Platt says his poor heart gave way."

"That may be said of anyone who stops breathing. For such a diagnosis he will charge five dollars you can ill afford. You realize you will be poor again."

"No, ma'am, I shall not." How could she keep her voice low when she wanted to sing hosannas? Few people learn from experience. Frankie did. "James made a new will the day after we married and went to Savannah. He was much moved by my plight as a widow and determined that I should never be left so again. Neither of us saw reason to burden you with our confidence. There seemed so much time. Now, alas, none, which is why you'll forgive me for breaking the news so starkly. The son and daughter of his first marriage have provided for themselves, standing as they do to gain all of Beulah Land one day for their children. The daughters of the second marriage, Cora, Beatrice, and dear Rebecca, are themselves married and in the care of their worthy husbands. His sister Doreen requires nothing, having given herself to God and Miss Kilmer. All of us rejoice that his other sister, and mine by marriage, is the first lady of the town, being the wife of its banker. Everything James died possessed of is mine."

Annabel eyed her coldly. "It will be a hot day in December before I let you pocket a penny."

Frankie, who had anticipated the course of the interview, took a copy of the will from her reticule and handed it to Annabel, who knew exactly what to skip, and where to skim, and how to weigh each of the important words. The facts were hers in a minute. Noisily rolling the stiff legal paper into a tube, she twisted it and tossed it back to Frankie, who caught it triumphantly with one hand.

"We shall challenge it."

"I don't think so." Frankie smoothed out the will.

"It will be easy to prove your instability and unfitness. I'll claim a review of the estate for the sake of the children. Even you cannot deny that two sudden marriages indicate a predilection for shifting sands."

"If you try such a thing, I'll see you ridiculed before the whole town, and that's the truth. But I don't believe Mr. Saxon would allow you to be so foolish. He has the reputation of the bank to consider, however careless you might be of your own."

"My reputation is without stain, whereas you have more than once invited gossip, not least now."

"What can you mean?"

"I saw Bonard every day of his illness the month before he died. He cannot be the father of the child you'll bear."

"I don't say he was."

"You made great haste to marry again. I've asked myself why. It will be interesting to see when the child is born."

"Your wagging tongue cannot keep it from being legitimately that of James Davis."

Annabel waved a hand dismissingly. "The law may say so, but we may all be forgiven for wondering where your solitary buggy rides have taken you."

Frankie rose. "You are in my house, madam. I ask you to remember that now and in the future, should the future bring you back here to admire your grandchildren. Or is it your intention to put them on trial with their mother?"

Frankie saw her blink and noted the moment's hesitation. "You can't bribe me with the children."

Frankie moved confidently to the door. "Will you again handle the details of the funeral? You have much skill at it because you are older than I. It is something we all learn along the way, I daresay."

Eugene Betchley was another early caller when word of James's death circulated through town; but on that occasion exchanges were brief and formal, Frankie asking him to return to her after the funeral so that they might discuss the operation of the sawmill.

Fresh rolls were traditionally the one hot item of food in the cold supper enjoyed by the family of the deceased after a funeral. The yeasty smell of them from Molly's kitchen filled the house when Eugene arrived to receive his orders. Seated together in her private parlor, Frankie opened the interview by begging Eugene to assure the men that work at the mill would continue. She hoped they would do their best for her as they had done for her husband, and she thanked him for his own loyalty, adding that she expected things to go on much as they had done.

"Ah, ma'am, but that cannot be."

She had sat with eyes fixed on her hands in her lap in the widow's attitude decreed by decorum. She now looked directly at him for the first time, remembering their interview after Bonard's death. He had been nervous and awkward then. He was not so now. A new confidence replaced old uncertainty. He sat his chair solidly, legs firmly apart, hands easy on the arms of the chair. "How do you mean?"

"Mr. Davis is not here to guide us, making decisions and giving orders."

"It has long been clear to me, Mr. Betchley, that it is you who give most of the orders at the mill. As to larger decisions, I shall make them myself." She smiled slowly and flatteringly. It was such a smile as had put men at her service before.

But Eugene was not, apparently, schooled to respond as they had. "I am a quarter owner of the mill, Mrs. Davis, with years of experience of its men and machinery and markets."

"I am lucky to have so capable a partner. You have my perfect confidence."

He frowned. "I shall have to have more than that."

She looked troubled. "You are—bold."

"In business I find it best to be so."

"I can't think you are much different in personal affairs either." She smiled again and waited for him to blush or smile with her, but he did neither. She reminded herself that a man of his class would not understand the kind of innocent chaff that was part of a lady's social manner. She would have to teach him.

"There must be a new arrangement, Mrs. Davis."

"I believe you have thought about all this," she said as if bewildered.

"I have."

"What is it you propose?"

"A different sharing of the profits."

She appeared to be confused, saying slowly, "If you own a quarter of the mill, you are surely entitled to a quarter of the profits as before. I shan't hear of your having anything less because my circumstances are changed."

Eugene coughed and crossed his legs. "You're in no condition to attend the mill. To come with your husband was one thing, but you must come no more until after your child is born."

"I do not require lessons in deportment, Mr. Betchley."

"Leave everything to me. I'll take the responsibility of the mill and the marketing. No one else is able to do that, and don't think they are, not the bank, nor anyone, I tell you. So you see, we are not talking about things going on as they were, but as they will be."

Frankie took her time before answering, and he waited with no sign of impatience. Finally she smiled weakly. "I am, as you observe, to be presently without the capacity to direct the business my two husbands commanded and owned. It is true that much will depend upon you." Her face brightened as her voice gathered strength and decision. "I have not thought it through, as you have; but now that I do, I grant the justice of what you say, Mr. Betchley. I shall, for the time being, rely on you entirely, and we must come to an arrangement. I am, I declare, grateful to you for bringing the matter up without any regard for the niceties of feeling a time of mourning generally involves. I shall see that you are rewarded. Now, is that all?" She smiled upon him bravely.

"Well, no, ma'am. I have to know what the arrangement is to be."

"Good heavens!" she exclaimed good-naturedly. "You are in a hurry to settle things! Are you afraid I shall try to cheat you?"

"Best to know where we stand," he insisted.

"Well, let me think." She clapped her hands together playfully. "A manager's salary, that is the thing. In addition to your normal share of profits. That is perfectly fair, you'll agree?"

Eugene shook his head. "It's not the way, Mrs. Davis. As part owner, I don't fancy working for a salary."

"I am certain you will earn it," she allowed graciously.

"I'll earn a good deal more than that," he said bluntly.

She leaned forward in her chair. "What if I don't agree?"

"Then we can't go along as partners," he said carefully. "One of us must sell his share to the other. Are you prepared to buy back mine?"

"You take me by surprise," she said after a moment. "I suppose I might ask the bank to lend me enough to pay for your share, if that's what you want. Am I to understand, Mr. Betchley—?" She paused to study his face. "What will you do if I buy your share?"

"To begin: I'll ask more than you'll say it's worth. Then, if you pay it, I'll buy my own sawmill and put yours out of business, because I know the work, and you only imagine you do. I've put my back and mind into it, and I've learned it, Mrs. I can run a mill by myself. I've been doing it for a year, and longer too, for Bonard Saxon passed most of the work to me before he got sick and had to stay home."

"I shall talk with both Mr. Saxons at the bank, and when I've had their advice, I shall take my decision."

"Meantime?"

"Meantime, what?"

"How is the mill to run, or is it?"

"It will run the way it has run."

"No, ma'am. I don't leave here tonight until I know where my future lies."

"Mr. Betchley, I am being reasonable, and you must be. I own three quarters of the mill. Since I do, three quarters of the profits are reasonably mine. Very well. For the time I shall be unable to take active part in the operation, you will do the whole thing, reporting here to me. You say you don't want a salary. We are both familiar with the accounts. I am willing to let you have thirty-five per cent of the profits, keeping only sixty-five for my poor family."

"Your family is not poor, ma'am."

"Then we are agreed."

"I didn't say so."

"What *will* you have?"

"We must expand the business. I know the Highboro end and the Savannah end, and I know where and how I can get more business. Let's say this: If I keep the business the first year I run it only the same as it made the year before, I take forty per cent and you take sixty. For everything above last year's profit, we share fifty-fifty."

"I am not the helpless victim you may have fancied me, Mr. Betchley. I know you now for a conniving rascal, and I'll ask you to get out of my house instantly."

"Not with my tail between my legs. When you think it over, you'll come to terms." He got up from his chair. "One other thing. I know about your meetings in the woods near the old Marsh farm. My boy found a letter you dropped when you were there one day and a shirt stud I'd seen on Ben Davis. That put me curious, so I did some looking and asking without letting on how come. I found out about the winter place at the cotton gin. You don't want anybody else in on your secrets. I'll come again in the morning after I put the men to work. We mustn't miss a day if we're to show the kind of profits I think we can."

As he reached the door, she said, "You must have enjoyed the funeral, Mr. Betchley."

He looked shocked. "I thought it was real nice."

17

The following morning Sarah and Jane drove into Highboro to call on Frankie. "We must strike a new note," Sarah said, slapping the reins to encourage Buster into a brisker trot. "People crowd around a grave and call it sympathy, but they forget before the wreaths are brown. Like her or not, Frankie merits our attention."

They found her in a state of agitation, Eugene Betchley having just taken his leave with a signed agreement to his conditions for working the sawmill. As they offered comfort, accepting her fresh tears as continued mourning, Sarah renewed the invitation to Beulah Land. "Oh, ma'am," Frankie cried, "there is nothing I should like better!" It was settled that they would return for her and the children tomorrow, bringing Wally with a wagon for their trunks. When they had gone, Frankie told herself it was the very thing. Surrounded by those who must now wish her well, she would be safe. She would have time to think, and she would be away from Annabel, for Annabel was never eager to pose her dignity against Sarah's wit, and so her forays on the plantation house were infrequent.

Having only Molly to look after the house in town, Frankie left her there; and Sarah decided that she would need someone to attend her during her visit. On her regular daily walk to the Glade, she mentioned the fact to Nancy. "What with getting the last crops in, I've nothing at my disposal but girls and grannies, and neither will do. Something in between is required."

"Is she going to be here till she has it?"

"I don't know."

"Let me look after her."

"*You*, Nancy?"

"I'll be no danger to her," Nancy said ambiguously.

Taking one meaning, Sarah agreed. "You're as healthy as I am; but you aren't one of the maids, you're one of us. You live here."

"Let me."

Sarah considered the offer. "There'd be no need to do the common things, of course. The girls can do those well enough, but she'll want a woman near her who understands the problem of dressing, someone who knows more than just to scream and watch if she's taken suddenly."

Frankie was pleased, for she had been curious about Nancy. It was in her nature to try to charm and patronize her, but when Nancy only smiled at her efforts, she dropped her tricks, and the two got on well enough. If their feelings were less than affectionate, each found the other interesting and even, on occasion, amusing. It was the first time since her return to Beulah Land that Nancy had been regularly in and out of the big house. She still spent most of her day at the Glade, but she came down mornings and evenings to help Frankie with her clothes, and finding her grateful, began to look for other things to do to make the time an easier one for the pregnant woman.

"You're good to her, Nancy," Benjamin said during one of their hours alone at the Glade.

Nancy looked puzzled. "Why do I feel sorry for her?"

He pulled off his shirt and slung it over the back of a chair. "Because you've got me, I reckon."

"She's had you."

He took her hand and pulled her down beside him on the bed. "Not the way you have. — How come you're kinky down there?"

"How come you're not?"

Hands moved, his on her, hers on him. "I've missed my kinky-haired girl."

"Harvest time." Presently she lured him softly: "Give me, give me, give me."

He watched her face as he entered her, his eyes searching hers for the secrets they held.

When they were resting later, he said, "I see a gray hair."

"Getting old."

"That's not what you're supposed to say." Their heads were

close, and he blew his breath against her brow to make her frown. "You say, 'Get your big butt out of my bed and back to the fields—' "

She broke in to finish it for him. "—so's I can make up my bed. Made up this bed one time today, and now got to do it again!"

He smiled. "You remember the day I rode home ahead of Daniel and Floyd? We'd been off to get that Yankee—Sergeant Smede was his name—for what he did to you and Lotus and Lovey and Grandpa. Found you standing there on Aunt Nell's old bench waiting for me. You said, 'You have revenged my honor!' "

"So you had."

"That night was our first time."

"I just about had to make you do it," she gibed mildly, enjoying the familiar story as much as he did. "You were scared and eleven years old. Slow-maturing."

He cupped the side of her face with a hand. "If we'd found the others with Smede that hurt you, I'd have butchered every mother's whelp of them."

"You don't have to kill nobody for me."

Annabel did not come to Beulah Land because she had no new threat to make, her husband Blair having ordered her to mind her own affairs and leave those of her son's and brother's widow alone. He assured her obedience by telling her that if she stirred up the lawyers, he'd side with Frankie. Annabel had to content herself with blackening Frankie's name with her female acquaintances, but their response was disappointing. They couldn't believe anyone they knew capable of the sins Annabel said were Frankie's, though every one happened to be true in fact if not in the wicked intention Annabel ascribed to her. They'd have been more shocked to be told that she stinted butter and eggs to her cook.

Although Annabel stayed away, Eugene Betchley came every other day to report on the operation of the sawmill, as he'd promised he would. Frankie met him alone, Nancy stationed at the door both to act as chaperon and to see that they were not interrupted. The meetings were brief and businesslike, with Frankie listening closely to details and checking the ledgers he brought along. Eugene was getting the new orders he'd predicted he would, and from farther afield. She began to think she'd made no bad bargain, forgetting she'd had no choice in the matter.

For Eugene, coming to Beulah Land "by the front way," as he put it, was instructive. He watched to see how everything was done, how everything was kept; and one morning in the second week of his visits he paused where the carriageway turned to reveal the avenue of oaks with the big house at the end. "I want it," he said to himself, and smiled to be thinking such a thing. But he was reminded of another morning when he'd looked at Bessie's poor farm as a possible prize to be taken. "Yes," the inner voice told him, "but this is Beulah Land." The very name was enough to weaken the knees of every poor white in the county, with awe and envy. Well? He was used to feeling that he was a man chosen, and the future might open a way.

If he was one to dream, he also worked and figured and schemed. Since he'd lived in town at the boardinghouse he'd made it part of his business to attend St. Thomas's Church. Quietly, meekly, he became a familiar presence to the Annabels and Doreens and Priscillas. The big, crude young man began to appear, if not yet one of them, still a man who wanted to improve himself, one eager to learn their ways and abide by their rules.

On a Sunday morning in October he waited after the service at the foot of the church steps for Mrs. Oglethorpe and Priscilla to beg their advice on a delicate family matter. Priscilla looked alarmed; the word "delicate" was enough to send the blood to her head; but Mrs. Oglethorpe fixed him with a fearless eye and bade him explain. He wanted to bring his son Theodore to live in town so that he might attend school more conveniently and benefit from town associations. The lodging house where he himself found bed and board did not seem the right thing, for there were traveling men in and out, and the language, if they would forgive him for saying so, was not always such as to set the highest Christian example.

Priscilla ventured the opinion that his mother would miss him, at which Eugene put on a confusion of manner calculated to sharpen Mrs. Oglethorpe's curiosity. Did he, she asked with a penetrating stare, have *another* problem that had led to his decision to move his son to town?

Eugene hesitated, he swallowed, he shook his head, he took a big breath they might interpret as resignation. He admitted that he had become worried about the influence of Mrs. Betchley.

Aaah! Mother and daughter exchanged looks.

Having begun to tell them, he broke off with another shaking of the head, until he saw from the disappointment in Mrs. Oglethorpe's eyes that he might proceed a little further without fearing a reprimand. Glancing about as if to assure that he was not overheard—and indeed Annabel was watching the group with increasing interest—he mumbled phrases about past frailties, of his not having understood her thoroughly when he married her, of his having been hardly more than a boy and she an older woman with, he added haltingly, "a certain range of experience." He hinted at last that he feared for her very sanity.

Mrs. Oglethorpe would have verification. "In what way does she show herself daft?"

"Ma'am—" He hung his head. "She drinks." Mrs. Oglethorpe's eyes indicated that she was prepared to hear worse, and he hastened to supply it. "One time—I hate to tell this on her—I came home unexpected and found her eating supper at the kitchen table with the hired man."

"A nigger?" Priscilla asked breathlessly.

Eugene nodded.

"*With* her *at* the table?" Mrs. Oglethorpe wanted to make sure.

"Yes'm. I dumped him out of his chair and told him to get off to the field where he belonged."

"I should think so," Mrs. Oglethorpe agreed warmly.

"Mrs. Troy goes to see her, I believe." Priscilla sighed. "She always had easy ways with her coloreds, and Mrs. Betchley may have been influenced."

"My boy was upset, I may tell you," Eugene said.

"Poor child," Priscilla murmured.

Mrs. Oglethorpe squared her shoulders. "You've done well to come to us, Mr. Betchley, and I shall think over what you've told us and let you know what I advise. The boy must be got away from the mother; that much is clear."

Eugene was humble in his gratitude for their kindness in offering to help him with his problem. As soon as he'd excused himself, Annabel joined Priscilla and Mrs. Oglethorpe with such determination they were not long able to keep the confidence they had just received. Ready for a new project, Annabel said instantly, "You must take the boy in, Mrs. Oglethorpe."

"A *boy?*" Ann Oglethorpe shuddered as she pronounced the word. "In *my* house?"

"He won't eat you," Annabel promised her. "I am perfectly aware that those old railroad shares of yours stretch only so far and no further. The boy's board will provide you with a little extra incoming. Haven't you always said, both of you, that you've been deprived of the little girl? Well, take what the Lord sends; and I give you my word He has sent Eugene Betchley to you. If you don't take the Betchley boy, I'll hear no more from you of Christian duty. Think of it this way: you'll be doing the Lord's will and earning a profit for your goodness. And what better influence might a growing boy have than you, Miss Ann?"

Within the week Eugene Betchley had taken his son to the barbershop to rid him of his country look and settled him into a plainly furnished room at the Oglethorpe house, which appeared luxurious to both, compared to the old farmhouse. Every child likes to make a drama around himself, and Theodore needed only a hint from his father to supply substance to Ann Oglethorpe's dark imaginings of what his life on the farm had been. Since Ann and Priscilla did not expect any child to be good, and Theodore did not hope for any adult to be kind, they were not disappointed in one another.

18

Without reason, Sarah took alarm at the new development, sensing that more was involved than appeared to be. Annabel told her of it when they happened to meet at the bank. Delighted at Sarah's consternation, she boasted that it was her own idea. "So you see, Auntie Sarah, you are not the only one who can offer haven to Fate's unfortunates!"

"But why? Bessie will be alone out there—"

"Surely you see her often enough on your guardian visits to know she drinks?"

"Not a drop!"

Annabel sniffed. "You always believe what you like, naturally. Oh yes, it is all over town. Drinks. And she eats her meals with the nigger Gene Betchley hired to help run the farm. I don't know where it will end; it's a scandal, you see. But then scandal to the rest of us is something you've often had to take for granted. It's warped your judgment, as I've observed before."

Without stopping to argue, Sarah concluded her business at the bank and drove her buggy directly to the Marsh farm. She found Bessie listless and uncaring.

"Yes'm, well, Gene wanted to do it, and the boy wanted to go, so what could I do? With school started, he wasn't no help nor company to me, away all day. Maybe Mrs. Oglethorpe can make something out of him. She's welcome to try. He's got to where he don't mind me."

When Sarah mentioned the gossip about drinking, Bessie was amused. "No, ma'am, but maybe I should. Might keep me from getting that lonesome sometimes I could die." She spoke the words without self-pity, as a hard fact.

Sarah decided not to mention what had been said about her

and the hired man. She said as if asking a favor, "I wish you'd come see me when you feel like company."

Bessie laughed. "Lordy, Miss Sarah, you don't need me around with all your bunch of folks!"

"Any time you can come, know you'll be welcome. Plan to spend a whole day. Remember now, you hear?"

"Yes'm," Bessie said vaguely. "But I don't go no-where. Never have, never will. Just wait for everybody to come see me." She smirked ironically, but when Sarah made ready to leave a few minutes later, she became humble and eager. "I sure thank you for stopping by. Mama always said you was the best woman she knew."

Despondent as she felt on going, Sarah realized there was nothing more she could do, except continue her visits. Next time she came she'd bring Bessie a present, nothing to eat, nothing to wear, something pretty and bought especially for her.

As spring had been late coming, harvest was late finishing, and the opening of school was delayed. But now the children were settling down, beginning new friendships and rivalries to last the year or a lifetime, fixing on new teachers to love and to hate. Leon was given the responsibility of driving the wagon needed to transport the six and their books. He was easy but watchful with the reins, never trotting the mule or turning into the side roads Davy urged him to explore, as if they did not already know where every one would lead—usually nowhere, straggling to a halt in an opening in the woods. Bobby Lee sat beside Leon as suited his nearly equal status. Fanny and Bruce and Blair sat in short-legged cane chairs behind them, the girls with parasols opened, no matter the weather. Davy scrambled about, often leaving the wagon to dart into a field or wood branch and rejoin them with a stalk, stone, or feather no one considered a prize but him.

Unlike most of the children, who hurried to school but dawdled their way home, they were eager to get back to Beulah Land and its manifold life. The old mule, bored with waiting all day, often of his own accord broke into a trot as they bragged and joked and quarreled and sang.

On Thursday of the first week in November they returned to find a new living soul, bright red, sucking her mother's breast, and already provided with a name. When she was born, Nancy asked Frankie what to call her, and Frankie replied with no hesitation, "Edna May Davis. May for my grandmother and Edna for James's."

"She was my best friend!" Sarah told her happily, almost liking Frankie before wondering if there was calculation in the choice.

"Yes'm," Frankie said. "Benjamin told me so; I forget when."

Annabel arrived the next morning with a rattle and a ribboned cap she said Bonard had worn as a baby. "She's awfully red," she complained. "Red hair too, which is a handicap for a girl because it means freckles. It will be interesting to see who she favors as she grows."

Sarah said sharply, "Young children seldom look like anyone. People only say they do for want of anything more sensible to say."

"Nonsense, Auntie. Blood shows. The timing is so peculiar we all may be forgiven a little speculation."

Frankie regained her strength quickly, and after a week Nancy no longer came down from the Glade to attend her. Sarah did not ask why, but Benjamin did in one of their times alone.

"Because I don't want to love that baby," Nancy answered readily. "Because she's yours and I wish she was mine." Benjamin left her, knowing better than to touch her or say anything more.

It was as if Frankie willed herself to strength, having been helpless against pregnancy for so long. Suddenly she wanted to be in her own house again. She was tired of people in and out all day long, of the lack of any sort of privacy. Forgetting how gratefully she had come, she was impatient to go. She was unburdened, she wanted to reach ahead; and the thing she wanted to grasp was management of the sawmill. Eugene Betchley had seen his advantage and taken it. She vowed that she would now work to win back what was her own.

Fanny had hoped the baby would never come, because she wanted to stay at Beulah Land forever, or at least through Christmas; but she knew better than to question her mother's determination and had to be content with Sarah's invitation to come back whenever she could and to stay as long as she pleased. What Sarah could not feel for Frankie, she felt for her older daughter, and Fanny found in Sarah someone finally to admire without reserve.

Eugene continued to wait upon Frankie at Beulah Land; but when she returned to town, she also returned to the mill for the sessions that had been interrupted by widowhood and pregnancy. She went every day and usually remained the entire day, having her dinner sent to her. Molly grumbled at first, and the women of the town gossiped. A few said they admired her for trying to shoulder a man's work; a few said they pitied her. The majority condemned her, seeing her industry as a betrayal of their sex. Frankie ignored them. She no longer fed Edna from her own breast but hired a nurse to take care of her.

Fanny adopted the infant, allowing the nurse to do for her during the hours she was away at school but taking over her care the remainder of the time. Frankie made a joke of Fanny's devotion but seldom interfered, not caring about either girl. When Blair was out of school, he was most often with Annabel. As Fanny gradually took upon herself the management of the house, Molly more and more often asked her for opinions and decisions. Frankie encouraged Fanny's assumption of responsibility because it left her free. Luck came to see her every chance she got, always seeming to know when anyone at Elk Institute was going into town for a few hours. She teased Fanny, warning her not to become proud and bossy, and Fanny promised she wouldn't. Both were tired of dolls and playing house and found satisfaction in the real thing.

Eugene was too much involved in working the mill to show resentment of Frankie's regular attendance. Having won his terms, he was willing to use her when he could, but ready when she tired of routine to do without her. But as she persisted, he became accustomed to her and talked more easily about daily matters as they came up; and presently she knew, if he did not admit it, that he had begun to value and use her judgment. No fool, Eugene was aware that Frankie was none either. She had never in her maturity been more beautiful than she was now in her independence. Without the trouble of a husband—and having had two, she knew what trouble husbands may be—she owned a house and a profitable business. She bloomed with health and satisfaction. She was thirty-two and confident. He was twenty-five and ambitious; and he knew what he was going to do next.

Although they never talked of personal affairs, each was nervously alive to the other. One evening they strolled together along the creek, on the way back to the office after inspecting a load of pine that had been hauled to the mill; and Eugene found it natural to say with a nod toward the new buildings across the water, "If you hadn't given them that land, they couldn't have built and would've had to move, leaving more room on both banks for us. We're going to need it, and every drop of creek water too."

She found it natural to answer, "I didn't know then what I do now."

That was as close as they came to intimacy, but it was a kind of intimacy that enforced mutual understanding of their business. Frankie was too long accustomed to having her way with men not to consider the chances of bringing Eugene under her control, however careful she was in their daily dealings not to rely on anything but her eyes and understanding. If Eugene was crude, he was learning. One of the things he did now he used never to do was to smile. He smiled often and in a purely mechanical way. No one took it for good humor, but though it was not true coin, it smoothed his way. Unlike Frankie, he knew he must have the good opinion of the townspeople. His acceptance by Ann Oglethorpe and Annabel Saxon had been the beginning, and now he was ready for the next step of the ladder.

19

Petey was a man in his late fifties, neither dull nor bright. He'd work if watched, not quickly or well, but he would go through the motions of working. Picking cotton, he'd miss a few ripe bolls. Milking a cow, he'd never finish the job but leave a quarter of the yield in the bag. Chopping weeds, he'd miss enough to allow them to replenish themselves with the first rain. But when Eugene hired him two years ago to work on the farm, he'd been willing to accept the isolation of the place, and the wage he asked was almost as low as Eugene had in mind to pay. Critical of him when he came, Bessie had learned to tolerate him. As long as she didn't catch him resting from his work too often, she didn't berate him. Let him plow a little, draw the water, chop the wood, and never mind the hogs and chickens; she'd attend to them. Eugene expected more of him, and Bessie found herself in the position of defending the hired man, making his excuses. All Petey wanted was a peaceful life. There was, she told herself and her husband, no harm in him. And hadn't he gone and killed that big rattlesnake she saw down where the creek dried to a trickle every August? Why, if he hadn't done that, she'd have been afraid to walk there again. Or she might have been bit to death in her bed one night and nobody around to help her. The reminder that she had to live by herself was generally enough to silence Eugene.

Oh, she'd been wary of him at first. She despised Negroes and was afraid of them. But Petey went about the farm as if he didn't see her, unless she was standing right in front of him, and he always ate every scrap she put on his plate. In those days the boy Theodore was with her, and often, then sometimes—now never—Eugene; so how could she be afraid of the ugly black man who walked with a sort of twitch in his left leg she hadn't even noticed till he'd worked there half a year? It was worse in cold weather, and sometimes in the morning when she'd lit a fire in the cookstove and the kitchen was warming up, she let him stand a while after bringing in the milk. He slept in the barn and ate from a special plate by himself on the back doorsteps. The special thing about the plate was that it had a crack right across it and she never used it for anything but to feed him. He also had a special cup to drink out of and his own knife and spoon.

Bessie had never talked much to the man, nor asked about his folks, didn't even know if he had any, though she seemed to remember Eugene telling her he didn't. It was none of her business anyway. But now that she was alone with not another living soul to say boo to, no dog to kick, no cat to scat, she'd taken sometimes to talking at him. He said nothing, but he appeared to listen, and sometimes he nodded. Once or twice he'd laughed when she hit on a funny turn of words, or one he seemed to think funny. Lately, she'd found herself wondering what he liked best to eat, and on a Sunday, if she felt like it, she'd bake a little two-layer cake with plain icing. She told herself she was doing it in case Theodore came to see her, but he never did, and Eugene never said a word about bringing him. Of course, she could have gone to see him, she supposed. She knew Miss Sarah went to that house in town, taking Ben's other child to visit with her ma and grandma. But, well, she never got around to it, and the Lord's truth was she didn't think she wanted the trouble. It would be like begging; and wouldn't she look a fool if she happened to pick a day when nobody was home.

Now as the days shortened, it seemed to Bessie the nights were everlasting. Times she'd sit in her chair by the kitchen stove with it gone to ash and throwing no warmth, not bothering to build a fire in the one fireplace; or lie in her bed wondering what the hour was, not knowing because there was no clock. What did she need a clock for? She dreaded nights worst of all, for they'd get longer and colder before they got short and warm again and she could throw the quilts off and stretch herself, not have to scrunch up into a ball to warm her lone self.

She'd had no near neighbor since Preacher Paul and Miss Ona left. Little as they needed, they couldn't scratch even that from the country church, so they'd nailed the door shut and gone away. She'd walked over there one time to sit in the graveyard and found nobody. She wondered when Miss Sarah would come again. There was never any telling; she didn't keep to a regular day. One thing Bessie did was keep track of what day of the week it was.

Petey's leg twitch had come back bad with the cold weather. She hated to admit it but she had to say she dreaded his finishing his supper and going off to the barn. Not that he was that much company, but he was somebody there, and it gave her satisfaction to see the way he ate everything she put on his plate. One night was windy and rainy as well as cold, and she let him eat his victuals sitting on the woodbox by her stove. He looked grateful, and she told him he could go on doing it long as nobody else was there.

So what she'd do was cook supper and dish up her plate and eat it by herself at the table. Then she'd fix his plate and go to the door and call him from the barn. It got to where it seemed more awkward to her to have two sittings, so she began to fix his and hers at the same time and let him come in and sit on the woodbox while she sat at the table. She showed him he wasn't to take it as a familiarity by never addressing a word to him while they ate. He respected that, she thought. But then one time she said absently—she'd forgot what—just something about the cold weather or when he reckoned the Plymouth Rock rooster ought to be killed lest he get too old and tough to eat. Something like that, nothing at all personal.

It was the middle of December, a bitter black night when they sat together for the last time. She'd pondered aloud on whether she wanted to change the place she had her chicken house because it seemed like the wind was more and more from that direction and some days last summer she couldn't stand the smell. He'd answered nothing, as usual, nodding a time or two. They were just sitting, she at the table, he on his woodbox, each with a spoon at the mouth, when the door flew open and there, bless God, stood Gene coming at them with an ax in his hands. She knew, she'd always known after what he did to her ma; but she asked as if she didn't: "Gene, what are you going to do?"

20

"Have you heard, have you heard the terrible thing?"

"What? Tell me!"

"That poor man, oh that *poor* man! His own wife! What a thing for him to see!"

Not only the drifters about town and the idlers on the steps of the train depot, but the most respectable of women and estimable of men pitied the murderer and excoriated his victims.

"Caught them at it, him with his britches down and her with her dress up. Sheriff said long after he was dead his dick was hard as hickory."

"Smell of liquor ever'wheres."

"Bad enough with a white man, and she was never particular who. Ben Davis wasn't the only one to wash his feet in that spring. Matter of fact, though I hate to admit it"—sly wink and a wait for laughter—"but to do it with a *nigger*."

"Where are they, have you seen 'em?"

"Hauled them in town on his wagon, sheriff did. They say Gene split the nigger's skull in two and she don't look much better."

"Lost his mind when he saw them, I expect."

"No wonder—"

"What else? Tell all!"

"Well, when he seen what he'd done, poor man rode in town and found the sheriff and told him. Together they went back. Was just like he'd said: her and him on the floor side by side."

"Ought to drug 'em into the road and waited till the buzzards took and et 'em."

"Mighty right."

"What'll happen to Gene?"

"Sheriff ain't holding Gene."

"I should reckon not! Ought to put up a statue to him like we done for our soldiers."

"Old lady Troy and her Ben-boy come and got the woman. That rich darky Elk from over at the Institute come and took the buck. Shamed of his race, reckon; wants to get him under the ground so ever'body will forget."

"I for one ain't going to forget."

"Niggers all lying low, you notice. Not a one out of doors lessen they been sent on a job, and then they're hurrying right smart."

All manner of things were said, few of them close to truth, which none but Eugene could know for certain. Even at Beulah

Land the supposition of what had happened was admitted only between Benjamin and Sarah in the privacy of her office. Together they told Leon the facts, knowing he would hear them anyway, but stating their belief that his mother was innocent of wrongdoing. When Leon said, "He killed her like he did Granny Marsh," Sarah responded more temperately than she felt, "No one ever can know."

To Benjamin she confided, "I meant to take her something pretty, but I put it off because Leon was in school and I didn't want to go back. It was always easy to find something else that *had* to be done. The only thing I can give her now is a pretty coffin. — I hate pretty coffins!"

They bought her one though, together, and Jane and Nancy washed and dressed Bessie's butchered body and put her into it. The Reverend Horace Quarterman of St. Thomas's refused to conduct a funeral in his church, but Tom and Elizabeth brought over to Beulah Land the country parson who had married them, and he officiated at a short ceremony in the churchyard in Highboro. Sarah insisted that Bessie be buried in the part of the graveyard reserved for Beulah Land's dead, although everyone said it was a scandalous thing to do, if not blasphemous; and Annabel Saxon declared her intention of spitting on the grave every time she passed it. The sidewalks and front porches were empty at the hour the funeral party of three buggies and a wagon carrying the coffin made its way through the town to the graveyard. Besides the clergyman, who rode with Wally and the corpse, there were only the Todd family, the Cooper adults, Sarah, Benjamin, Bruce, and Leon. As they were about to begin, Fanny Saxon came running, out of breath, and joined them without a word. The preacher spoke simply and recited the Twenty-third Psalm. Together they sang "Beautiful Isle of Somewhere," Benjamin clutching Leon's hand, and that was all.

While the funeral was going on, Eugene Betchley and Frankie Saxon sat together in the office of the sawmill. She had expressed her shock and sympathy the day before when the news of what had occurred was told her. Since then the sheriff had passed word that Eugene Betchley was by no scales of justice to be faulted for what he'd done. It was the act of any honorable man. Since the woman was beyond redemption and the man beyond damnation, the matter was best concluded as it had been. Let it be a lesson to all, Negro *and* white.

Eugene had not hidden himself but arrived at the sawmill as was usual. No Negro now worked at the sawmill, and the white laborers lined up to shake him by the hand. Frankie watched the scene through the window, and when Eugene entered the office, she made a casual business about an order she'd found on the desk when she came that morning for a thousand feet of unscaled half-inch pine. From that they proceeded to discuss other orders. Only when he said he would go out to check the work did she venture a more personal remark to the effect that she trusted he would put the past out of his mind and think only of the future.

"I have already done so," he said.

She waited for him to leave or continue, and when he did neither, said, "I am glad."

He nodded. "Yes, and you are in it."

"I expect we shall continue to work as partners, with mutual interests as such."

"I think we had better be more than that."

"Do you?" she said, her voice sharp with surprise.

"Man and wife."

She stared at him.

"Yes, Miss Frankie."

"That is out of the question," she said coldly. "I suppose to be courteous I should thank you for the offer, but I am not flattered."

"That is a shame," he said slowly, "for it will be so."

"I say it will not be."

"Why else do you think I did it?"

Her offended look gave way to one of incredulity. "We'll never speak of it again. I promise you I shall never think of what you've said."

"Not next week, or next month. Even you must not have three husbands in one year. Let's say: May to marry."

"No."

"If I tell Mrs. Saxon what I know, she'll believe me and move against you, with me the sworn witness. Ben Davis won't deny it.

To do so would mean giving up any claim he might have on the baby he knows is his, and Beulah Land has always loved its bastards. Who understands that better than I? Mrs. Saxon will take the mill from you and she'll run you out of town. Then she'll sell me the mill at my price for helping her. Do you want to be poor again? I've seen your family in Savannah. You were the lily of the turnip patch, no better than I am. Marry me and you're safe forever, for we'll each hold a secret against the other."

Frankie was not a woman given to hysteria, although she had sometimes affected it when she saw it was to her advantage. But now she screamed furiously and with complete sincerity. The sound was, however, drowned in the singing of the saws outdoors as they cut through the wood that could keep her rich.

Arriving at home, Sarah sent Mabella to ask Nancy to come to her in the office. "Nancy," she said without preamble, "I want you to run the house from now on, for I'm no longer able to do it and no one else knows me and Beulah Land. It must be you."

Part Three

1895

1

For a long time there had been only one grave at Beulah Land, that of the slave Ezra, but now there were those of his wife Lovey, his son Floyd, Floyd's wife Lotus, and Selma, daughter of the earliest master of Beulah Land anyone alive could remember. Sarah had erected an iron fence around the graveyard to keep wandering animals away. There were flower borders, which Jane tended, one tree, and a stone bench nobody used. Visitors simply walked back and forth and in and out reading names and dates in a dutiful way; and those who loved the place enough to linger favored the friendliness of sitting on the gravestones. Sarah and Roman often sat on Lovey's.

"Do you think there really is a heaven?" Roman asked.

Sarah nodded and shrugged at the same time. "*Some*where for those we love. Those we hate go to hell, of course. There is certainly a heaven for these, and for Casey and Leon and my dear Edna."

"Proctor."

She touched his hand. "And Rachel."

"Poor Rachel!" he said. "Was she ever happy?"

"With James," Sarah answered after considering it, "and as a child. I remember her and Leon one time in particular, though it must have happened many. There used to be a pomegranate bush over there, and you and she had been taking a pod apart—"

"I remember."

"Leon swooped her up and threw her into the air. I can hear both of them squealing and laughing."

"Oh, the ache of love," he said quietly but with a hint of mockery. "Do you think Leon will call me son and love me in that place you say there is? — For I shall certainly be there!"

"Yes, certainly," she said to both question and statement.

Roman laughed. "Aunt Nell will eat sweet potato biscuits every day for breakfast."

"And a little squirrel gruel," Sarah said.

He gently mimicked Nell's voice. "I was ever partial to a gruel made from squirrel. — What about Lauretta?"

"So long since I've heard from her. I can't think she's dead, though. Someone would have written. I don't think Lauretta would leave without a curtain call."

"I can't think of her dying at all," Roman said.

"Well, she promised us she was going to *immediately*, when the good colonel soldiered off to paradise. June—six years ago? 1889."

"It wouldn't surprise me if somebody came and told us they'd seen her dancing the cancan in Paris."

"Roman, she's eighty-six."

"I expect by now she's pared fifteen years off that and takes care how she mentions things that happened long ago. Besides, they are said to admire old things in Paris."

"Then we must all pack our satchels and hasten there."

"What of Annabel? Heaven or hell?"

As if answering roll call, Annabel leaned over the fence to peer at them. "How can you sit there on that cold tombstone? Don't you know it's January?"

"We're warmly dressed," Sarah said.

Annabel surveyed the old woolen frock and red shawl worn by Sarah and sniffed. "Fashion is not your folly. You've never minded what you wear."

"I'm glad at least the bustle is gone. You all looked ridiculous."

"You're the one who looked a freak without one."

"Casey was content with my behind the way it is, and I saw no reason to alter it by putting a cart behind me like a pony."

"Don't be so country-coarse, Auntie. You wore hoopskirts; for I distinctly remember you in them."

"Everyone did."

"Except me," Roman said.

"Good morning, Roman. Why aren't you at school? Is it some holiday?"

"I've stopped teaching," he reminded her, "and come home to live."

She remembered with a cluck. "You see how distracted I am? Come along, Auntie Sarah, where I can talk to you, for I certainly will not sit out here and say what I have to." She walked briskly toward the house and into it, continuing to talk, taking for granted that she was followed. Past the drawing room she marched, as if she considered it too frivolous a setting for what was on her mind, and into Sarah's office. Roman whispered to Sarah that he would go, but she shook her head and pulled him along until he followed of his own accord. She never saw Annabel alone if she could help it.

"Oh, you've come too," Annabel said as Roman took a chair beside Sarah's. "It's all right, I suppose, for you were the first scandal at Beulah Land." Sarah and Roman burst out laughing. "I don't know why you're amused, I'm sure."

"Annabel," Sarah said, "being sixty-five does not allow you every rudeness."

Annabel rolled her eyes. "It should; there are few enough advantages. — Now I'm here, I don't know why I've come, except you're the oldest in the family, Auntie Sarah, and everyone comes to you, though I've never known you to say anything remotely Delphic."

"I don't give advice," Sarah said. "I listen, however reluctantly."

"It's about Blair Three. He's not going back to Charlottesville."

"I thought he was simply prolonging his Christmas visit."

"We've got to decide what he's going to do."

Sarah looked at her, puzzled. "What does he want to do?"

"Nothing," Annabel said.

"I see your difficulty." Sarah had learned not to ask questions of such as Annabel, knowing they made explanations more labyrinthian, trusting that she would pick up essential information as the speaker went along. "The bank perhaps?"

"No head for figures."

"Why doesn't Frankie make a place for him at the sawmill?"

Annabel wheezed with exasperation. "Can you see Blair at the sawmill?"

The three thought of the fashionable young man. "No," Sarah agreed. "Still, he wouldn't have to fell trees and order the men about. Mightn't he learn to think about orders and shipments? Something perhaps in the Savannah office."

"Gene won't hear of it. He will not have Blair in any of his business concerns and has ordered him to leave the house. Blair came to me, naturally. He dotes on me, as everyone knows. Even his mother has turned against him."

"Frankie loves the boy," Sarah protested.

"She may, but she's afraid of Gene and won't go against him. When I think of them owning that business, having stolen it from me! Surely a sister's claim is stronger than a trifling silly wife's—"

"You must tell us what happened."

Annabel fidgeted the drawstrong of her reticule. "Gene always hated the boy."

"Blair isn't fond of Eugene either."

"That's neither here nor there."

Sarah said, "Surely Blair is entitled to live in his mother's house until he has his own."

"Gene is furious."

"Why?"

"He's even threatened to kill him; he's an absolute, utter brute."

"I shan't argue that with you."

"There was a misunderstanding. Gene went into Theodore's room yesterday—I don't know what he was doing at home the middle of the afternoon; Blair says he never is. — I can't believe it; the man is demented. Blair denies it, but Theodore says Blair forced it on him."

"Theodore is a big fifteen to be forced to do anything."

"Exactly, but Gene will have it that *our* boy was holding *his* boy and kissing him! You see? He's insane. Males do not kiss other males unless they are father and son, or dying, or something like that." When Sarah and Roman exchanged a look, Annabel shifted her eyes to Roman. "I can see that you're just as astonished as I was. Men may have friendships sometimes like yours with that—what was his name—tutor who came to teach Adam and James and sort of adopted you. Advise me. Or at least say you agree with me. Shall I instruct Mr. Saxon to tell Gene we won't stand for it?"

"I don't think you had better do that," Sarah said cautiously.

Annabel subsided in her chair with an unhappy sigh. "Well, I've told you. Frankie won't even talk about it, only agrees that he must now live with me. I've always wanted him, and she wouldn't let me have him, and now she's willing to throw him away."

"Perhaps another school," Roman suggested.

Annabel shook her head. "They'd want to know why he left Virginia. You see, there was some misunderstanding—pure spite, of course. Blair belonged to a club with other sensitive young men who read Pater and Wilde and such, and the rowdies hated them and spread stories about them. They can be terribly silly at the University, you know."

They were quiet until Roman said, "Why not have him read for the law?"

The women looked at him and then at each other.

Sarah said tentatively, "Might Roscoe be able to help him? He read law."

"I'm sure he'd do what he could," Roman said. "The Institute is much in your debt, Miss Annabel, for your past patronage."

"That is so," she agreed, happy to be reminded of a debt anyone owed her. "Of course, Mr. Saxon and I don't lack for connections among the fraternity of the law—"

"Are you thinking of Philadelphia?" Sarah said to Roman, who nodded.

"No," Annabel said firmly. "It shall be here where he will have the support of those who love him. I will not have it look like he's being banished." She clapped her hands and rose. "You have hit on it, Roman. I was right to ask you to stay and listen, while you, Auntie Sarah, haven't been at all helpful." She nodded. "The law. I can see him in a courtroom with that fine figure and noble brow, telling the judge and jury in his thrilling voice exactly what to do. Oh yes, it is the very thing. A gentleman's profession, and who knows where it may lead? Why not one day governor of the state of Georgia—or higher? I shall go with him all the way, and his mother and Gene can go to the devil. Auntie Sarah, does it never occur to you to offer tea? Must I always beg? — The law! Respectable ever since Moses."

2

"Don't grieve, dear, any more."

Doreen Davis kissed Eloise Kilmer's wrinkled cheek, and Miss Kilmer wiped her eyes resolutely with a handkerchief already damp. "I cannot forget the cruel things Miss Annabel used to say. He ate the bachelor's buttons only because he loved them."

"It was a nice funeral," Leon said.

"He was fond of you," Miss Kilmer said. "I remember the first time you came to see us, he sat in your lap. I knew then you were a good boy. Toby was an infallible judge of character. The one time he saw Miss Annabel, she rocked her chair on his tail and he bit her ankle. She said I should have him destroyed because he was vicious! I'd sooner have had her destroyed. After that, whenever she came, he went to the attic."

"He must have been the oldest cat in Highboro," Benjamin offered in comfort.

"I believe he was," Doreen said helpfully. "Seventeen, and delighted us every day of his life. We may say that about few others."

"None," was Miss Kilmer's opinion. "I love them all, but Toby was the best I ever saw. Having made Toby, our dear Lord broke the mold."

Seeing that tears threatened again, Doreen rose hastily from her chair to offer the gentlemen more tea, which they declined, Benjamin saying they must go.

After protests and affirmations, Miss Kilmer rose to attend to her duty as hostess. "It was good of you to come. Toby would have been proud." She went to the box at the side of the fireplace and picked out a kitten from the drowsing litter of five, whose mother had already grown restless enough to leave them for an hour at a time. She looked at the all-black creature, who looked back at her with alert green eyes until she set him on Leon's knee. "He's yours if you will have him."

Leon offered a finger to the kitten, who grabbed the tip with soft forepaws and fought his palm with his hind feet. "Thank you, Miss Eloise; he's a beauty, and I need a cat." The kitten stopped his game and observed the young man's face with interest and calculation.

Benjamin said, "Thank you, ladies, for tea and, if I may say so in the circumstances, a most pleasant hour." He kissed his Aunt Doreen and her friend Miss Kilmer. Then his son, who was as tall and nearly as broad as he, kissed them too. The kitten mewed and held on to Leon's jacket with every claw.

"What will you call him?" Doreen said. "We've only called him Blackie for convenience, but it wasn't meant as his name."

Leon cupped a supporting hand under the kitten. "They say hell is black, but look at his eyes. I think I'll call him Hellfire."

Miss Kilmer was delighted, and they parted on the most friendly terms. Getting into Leon's gig at the front gate, they rode into the main section of town. Benjamin said, "I was thinking of that cold morning I found you and your ma in front of Sullivan's store and gave you a kitten. I'd been to the gin, and old Isaac, God rest his soul, made me take him. Whatever happened to him; do you remember?"

Leon told him, and after Benjamin brooded over it a little, he said, "Poor Bessie."

Leon looked down at the head of the kitten he had stuffed into his jacket front. "Nobody going to drown you, Hellfire." The animal ignored him, gazing about nonchalantly, as if being carried along the main street in an open gig was a common occurrence in his life.

"About time for the Up Train from Savannah," Benjamin said in an offhand way.

"Mm."

"Want to meet it? Just to be doing something?"

"Might as well, since we're here." Their eyes meeting, they laughed.

When they halted at the station, they found Roscoe Elk waiting in his wagon. All got down and went together past the station loungers who had come out of the warm freight office to watch for the train. On the platform Roscoe said, "If my girl hasn't brought half of Savannah home with her and put the other half on order, I'll be surprised."

"Maybe Nancy and Miss Fanny checked her," Benjamin said.

The three had gone to Savannah to buy clothes for Luck's wedding and were returning after a week's absence.

Though the three men paced impatiently exchanging routine comment and speculation, the train was on time; and when it stopped, Luck was the first to step down. Roscoe was ready to grab her and swing her around before letting her feet touch the platform. "Papa, Papa!" She hugged and patted him, breathing quickly with excitement. "Spent every penny you gave me and ran up debts everywhere they knew your name—didn't I, Fanny? —No, Papa, I'm only teasing you, but I bought me some mighty pretty things. Well, where is he? You mean to say he's not here when I've been gone a week? All he had to do was write every day and be here to meet me!"

He was there, but he had arrived early and decided to surprise her. When she had berated him until she had to stop for breath, he stepped out of the telegraph office and took her from Roscoe. At first she fought him with dumbfounded delight. "You scoundrel Abraham! Did you miss me a little or miss me a lot?"

The others, meantime, accomplished their reunions. Helping her with the smaller pieces of luggage, Benjamin managed a quiet welcome for Nancy, who loved him with a smile even as she spoke the most commonplace words for people to hear. Leon at first disguised some of his pleasure in seeing Fanny by showing her the kitten. The two heaped extravagant compliments and witty comments on the head of the puzzled Hellfire until they found themselves holding hands and talking directly to each other, the animal forgotten. Only when the engine started did they miss him and set up a panicky search, finding him as the train pulled away sitting patiently between a hatbox and a crate of oranges deposited from a freight car. Scolding and praising him, they regained a fair measure of social manner by the time Luck and Abraham subsided enough in their reconciliation to think of their friends.

"Come on, honey," Roscoe said to Luck. "I brought the wagon. Let's take just the things you want to show me first, or most, and let them bring the others."

"No, Papa! I must keep everything together. Fanny! — There you are. Isn't it good to be home again?"

Fanny agreed that it was. Luck saw that Leon was clutching one of her hands at his side and laughed. "You'll be next!" she declared.

"I brought my buggy," Abraham said. "I'll drive you home, and Roscoe can load *all* your things and haul them out for you."

"Oh, ho!" Roscoe exclaimed. "I'm to be no more than fetcher and carrier, am I? Damned if I'll do just as I'm told like that. Would you, Ben, if you was me?—Well, maybe.—All right. Go ahead. See that you don't stop and dawdle, because I want you to be there when I get home, girl, to give account of every nickel you spent of my money, you hear me?"

Luck drew Fanny aside for a whispered, giggled confidence, and then she and Abraham ran off together to his buggy, which he'd left across the tracks in front of Sullivan's store. Benjamin and Leon lent hands and backs to help Roscoe load his wagon with Luck's trunks, taking their directions from Fanny and Nancy to be especially careful with this one and to put that one next to the big wooden barrel, because the two items should be kept together. The thing that looked like a crated balloon was to be set on sacking, and Roscoe was to drive slowly so as not to jounce the contents. No, they might not know yet what was inside. It was for the new house Abraham had built, and they wouldn't understand until they saw it in place. Used to obeying the dictates of women about weddings, they did as they were told.

In spite of the cool day, they were sweating when all was loaded and ready. Hearing Leon's plea to Fanny to come to Beulah Land for a few days, Benjamin added his encouragement, saying that both Sarah and Bruce had missed her visits and were eager to see her. Clearly wanting to accept, Fanny said no but listened as they reasoned that her clothes were already packed and they had only to drive the gig to her mother's house and obtain her permission.

At that point Eugene Betchley appeared driving a wagon and told Fanny he'd come for her.

"We've other ideas, Mr. Betchley," Leon said, and explained the proposal that had been made and all but accepted.

Eugene looked earnestly at Fanny. "Your mama wants you at home."

"Is she not well?" Fanny asked.

"As well as she ever likes to say, but the house needs you," Eugene answered positively. "So does your sister."

"I've a present for her—"

"Where is your trunk?" She found it, and Eugene ordered one of the loungers to set it on his wagon.

"We'll go along after you and speak to Mrs. Betchley ourselves," Benjamin said.

"No call for that," Eugene replied flatly. "Get in the wagon, Fanny. It's my place to look after you."

Seeing that Leon was about to object, Fanny said to Benjamin, "Give my love to Bruce and Aunt Sarah and say I'll be out to see them very soon." Eugene helped her into the wagon and drove away without another word.

"I'll take Nancy," Roscoe said. "Plenty of room beside me, and it's on my way."

Leon handed up the last of the smaller articles to Nancy, who had set herself beside Roscoe. Neither had looked at the loungers, but they'd been aware of them. Watching them go, Benjamin said to Leon, "Might as well stop by the mill; Davy will be there." Leon nodded, and they got into the gig, leaving the station to the loungers.

"Hear it? Hear Gene?"

"I heard."

"He don't take sass from nobody, do he? Not the gal nor them Davises."

"Biggety niggers calling white folks by first names—"

"Je-rusalem!"

"Prissing around like the Queen of Sheba after going off to

Savannah to buy stuff for getting married. You reckon our Highboro lard ain't good enough for 'em?"

"I reckoned black apes nested in trees, didn't you?"

"Trying to out-white white."

"It's them Beulah Landers put them up to it. If I had my way, I'd run ever' nigger out of the county and kill them that didn't run fast enough to suit me."

"So'd Gene. He don't believe in spoiling niggers."

"It was old lady Troy started it all with that school out yonder, you know. Taught 'em to read and write and wipe their asses just like me and you."

"When'd you start wiping your ass, Raymond?"

They laughed. They spat, they repeated, they argued, they fumed; and when they had exhausted the variations on what they'd said a thousand times before, they went back into the freight office and sat around the stove in the middle of the room, hawking now and then and watching their spittle sizzle and disappear on the fat red belly of the stove.

3

Soon to be twenty-one, Leon was no longer thought of by the farm hands as a smart boy but as a knowledgeable man. He seemed to remember every bit of legend and lore that came his way concerning rain and moon, sun and soil and seed; and he had learned to temper hearsay with his own experience, to leave allowance for the unpredictable and the inexplainable. Animals were calm under his hands, and the men trusted him. While not indulgent, he was thoughtful of their welfare and quick to appreciate effort and care. Benjamin might be considered "big boss man," but it was Leon they worked with; and Benjamin, having responsibilities to the cotton mill and the gin and other properties, was happy to have such a son. For all there was to do, they were companions too. When not at work, and sometimes when they were, they were together, hence the plantation byword: "Find one and you've found the other."

At fifty Daniel Todd worked his own farm with the help of Bobby Lee, who had taken to the land as naturally as Leon. Daniel was given to saying with satisfaction approaching smugness that there were no holidays for farmers, adding in genial wonder, "Seems like there's twice as much to do as there used to be." Still, there was time for hunting, often at night; and it was this father and son who kept the plantation tables supplied with game: quail and wild turkey, rabbit, squirrel, even an occasional deer. Benjamin and Leon had no love of guns. Jane would grumble complacently that Dan and Bobby Lee were never happier than when they were out all night, returning at daybreak wet and noisy and smelling of feathers, fur, and blood. She was becoming more full-bodied, yet in spite of the eyeglasses she wore and the gray that showed in her hair, her face remained girlish. She reminded Sarah of her great-grandmother Edna. "Look at Dan," she would say to Sarah. "Eats a lot more than I do and lean as a fishing pole. Every bite I take goes here and here and, Lord help me, everywhere. Tell me why, Grandma?"

As for Davy, nothing bored him more than plowing and planting and waiting for things to grow. When he turned seventeen and finished the local school, he declined the suggestion that he continue his education at university and asked to work at the cotton mill. He liked the hum and clatter of the little factory, the buzz of talk, the comings and goings, the very dust and vibration in the air that made Leon on his occasional visits with Benjamin long for the rows of cotton and corn stretching to sky's end, the quiet fecundity of earth. Roscoe and Benjamin had made Abraham manager of the mill, for as they told each other, "If we hadn't, he'd have taken it away from us." It was natural enough for the young white man to learn from the Negro who was his senior by a dozen years and who had always been a friend.

Inclined as both were to mild foolishness, they tended conversely to act more soberly together than apart. They had their jokes, which the Negro factory workers enjoyed, but they worked hard and took work seriously. It was a small factory still, compared to the mills in Columbus and Augusta that employed thousands. They did not produce the variety of goods manufactured by their bigger brothers, who made everything from the finest muslins to the coarsest tenting. Abraham's factory made thread and only thread, and that of but four different sizes in black and white. They had tried dyes, but the sawmill across the creek shared the water supply and complained about it.

Eugene Betchley had expanded his holdings, now owning half a dozen small farms in addition to the one he had married Bessie for, a couple of thousand acres of backwoods timberland, and a few store properties in Highboro on the back street he rented to Negroes. He was not, therefore, inclined to bother his old enemies across the creek as long as their interests were not in conflict. But the men who worked for him despised the black workers and grudged them their decent wages. They even resented the state law that had passed in 1889 limiting the factory workday to eleven hours, boasting that they worked twelve and fourteen for their peas and corn bread and sow belly. There had been no violence, but the white men shouted taunts across the creek at the black men and women, while the latter, protected by the width of water, acted elaborate unconcern, or in the guise of comic asides to one another, displayed their scorn for the whites whose work was more menial than theirs.

The first thing Davy bought with money earned at the mill was a bicycle. Having decided he wanted to become a town man, he proceeded to use it instead of a horse to go back and forth to work, although the clay road between Beulah Land and Highboro was slippery in wet weather, and horse power would have been surer than rubber tires. He was sometimes forced to walk the bicycle the whole distance from home to factory, spoiling his boots and his disposition, for the sawmill workers laughed at him, including him with the Negroes he worked alongside.

One who observed him from across the creek and did not laugh was Frankie-Julia Dollard Saxon Davis Betchley. Determined to hold the major share of the sawmill, Frankie spent several hours there every day, confirming the suspicion of the town women that her earlier boldness in going to work was dictated less by necessity than a common, commercial streak she had brought with her from Savannah. Frankie had never paid much attention to them; nor did she now. She had given much to own what she did and had no notion of allowing Eugene to take it from her, although he ordinarily spoke of the mill as "mine," not "ours" or "my wife's." He made little mention of his wife to anyone. Having schooled himself to put on a patient and resigned public face about Bessie, he let it continue to serve for his second wife, which did him no disservice with the women of the town. ("Such a good man; never misses church, while she finds any excuse enough to stay home. No telling what goes on back of those closed curtains.")

But if Eugene, along with his show of piety, affected patience and resignation regarding his marriage, Frankie did not. The years had sharpened her temper and made her sour. Growing old with none to admire and love her was a bitter thing, she whose attributes had once made her belle of the county and might still have claimed some devotion and loyalty. It was a bitter thing for her to be married to Eugene, who taunted her with the reminder: "You will always be seven years older than I, and I've already been married to one old woman. She'd been used by Ben Davis too."

Memory was the worst bitterness, for she had only to look across the creek at the youth of Davy Todd to think of the time of her own youth when she might have married Benjamin Davis and had Beulah Land, but refused him because of his liaison with Bessie Marsh. The child of that connection was himself now in the very vigor of manhood and loved her daughter. Frankie had never loved Fanny, and it was a bitterness to think of her acquiring without effort or design the position Frankie had coveted. Her other daughter, Edna May, was a bitter reminder of the hours she had shared with the one man who had pleased her and who now and forever was denied her. Worse: he was not sorry to lose her, not resigned, but happy with a homely, pockmarked Negro woman older than he! Was there no comprehending a man?

The son she had spoiled and looked on with hope had, as she put it to herself, deserted her to live at Annabel's while reading law under the sponsorship of the retired county judge Claude Meldrim. Sometimes she thought of going away, freeing herself of the past to make a new life. But she was getting old, and those who have been poor and are a little rich do not easily abandon property. Feeding on bitterness, she walked lean and hungry, longing for a snake to cross her path that she might enjoy the release of killing it. No wonder when she heard laughter and looked over the creek she despaired, for there was no laughter on this side she could share.

"Abraham! Don't you think you're too old to marry a young girl like that?"

"A prince's daughter."

"Boss's daughter, you mean! Let you grow up in his house treating you like a brother—"

"'Open to me, my sister, my love, my dove, my undefiled—'"

"Don't know about 'undefiled' but she must be the blackest dove *I* ever did see!"

"Back to your looms and spindles, slaves—"

High, happy laughter flew across the little stretch of water that separated the sawmill from the cotton mill. The choppers and cutters of wood paused at their work to frown, and Frankie knew she would have one of her headaches that, at their worst, led her to close the curtains of her room and lie in the dark sometimes for two whole days with no one to comfort her.

4

Sarah had never used a maid to help her dress, nor did she now; but when they were making ready for special occasions, Bruce, who always dressed quickly, would come to Sarah's room and ask to sit and watch. It had begun when she was a young girl soon after Casey Troy died and continued now when she was sixteen. Luck's wedding day was a day of what they called typical March weather, with fast-moving clouds and squalls of rain, though it was late in the month and spring was well advanced.

When Bruce knocked and was invited to come in, Sarah was almost ready. "I have no patience with growing old. It's a matter of having one thing after another taken away until one day I'll wake up and find so little left, I'll say to the Lord, 'All right, take the rest, take *me* while You're about it.' Maybe that's the way it happens."

Bruce giggled, and Sarah looked at her warningly.

"Don't vex me, child; I'm doing my best." Bruce took a chair at the foot of the bed but close enough to the wardrobe and dressing table to follow Sarah's progress. Sarah had chosen a yellow silk dress that was nipped in sharply at the waist and left full in the sleeves. She tried to make the sleeves looked puffed, but being silk, they would not. With a twist she finished pinning her hair in a bun at the back of her neck in the fashion Mrs. Cleveland had made popular a few years earlier.

"I like watching you," Bruce said presently, as she said on every such occasion.

Standing, Sarah surveyed herself in the long mirror glass, tilting it, the better to catch the light. "I'm a bad example," she said critically, "for I don't care a fig how I look as long as I don't outrage public decency."

"You're original and independent, Grandma."

Sarah glanced at her suspiciously, then back at her reflected image. "Am I dressy enough to do Luck credit? She's particular about clothes, has been ever since she was a little girl. Always loved pink. So many colored people do, and why shouldn't they? They look good in it. I need something else." She pulled a drawer open. Its contents were a mess, and she tumbled them more before bringing forth a string of purple beads.

As she studied them, Bruce said, "No."

Without looking at her or questioning her judgment, Sarah dropped the beads back into the drawer and rummaged again.

Bruce said, "The opals Grandpa gave you."

Sarah found them, put them on, stood back from the glass, and looked pleased. "But I still look bare." She found a bunch of large red artificial cherries, but before she could hold them against the dress, Bruce said, "They look like something cut off a hat."

"They were. You remember it, a sort of green."

Bruce set her jaw and said nothing.

Sarah abandoned the cherries. "That will have to do. Maybe I'll carry a—what's blooming in the garden?"

"Nothing I'll let you wear." Bruce left her chair and kissed her. "You're pretty as you are, and you don't want to draw attention from the bride."

"*You* look nice," Sarah discovered.

"Will I marry someone too, Grandma?"

"If you marry at all, it will be someone, won't it?"

"You don't think—" She pulled her upper lip against her teeth.

Sarah touched the red scar lightly. "I won't say it isn't there, because it is; but it's part of you, and no one sees it as anything else."

"Papa and Leon are ready and waiting. We're using the six-seater so there'll be room to bring Fanny back, and the top is up in case it rains."

Fanny watched at a front window of her mother's house in Highboro, eager to be off. Annabel and Blair Three were to stop for her on their way to Elk Institute, they being the only other white townspeople who would attend the wedding. Edna May was at Fanny's side and once again begged her to save something from the wedding, if it was only a flower to press. She was eight and believed that every event should be commemorated because it occurred in her lifetime. When Fanny promised again, Edna May said, "I don't know why you can go and I can't."

Pausing at the living-room door on his way out of the house for his morning rounds, Eugene said, "You well know I won't allow it. It's a nigger wedding, and *his* to boot. Now get along to school."

"It's Saturday, Papa."

"There's no excuse to be idle." As Edna May ran past him, he remained in the doorway looking at the older girl at the window. "You're willful to go yourself. People think it wrong. If you were my daughter, I'd forbid it."

Fanny turned to look at him for the first time. "Yes, sir, you have said so."

"Yet you defy me. How you can even want to go—"

"Luck Elk is my friend."

"Her husband-to-be is my enemy, and people find it odd that you should go."

"It would be odder if I did not, since we have been friends all our lives."

"You're to come home immediately afterwards and not eat or drink anything with them, do you hear?"

"No, sir. I am staying at Beulah Land for a few days. I've explained it all to Mama, and she has agreed."

"You don't ask," he said provocatively, "you explain."

Ignoring his teasing tone which implied an intimacy she would not acknowledge, she glanced again out the window. "They are here for me. Grandmother is very stylish, and Blair a dapper dandy—"

"I forbade him to come here."

"Then I must meet them outside." She went quickly past him, taking up the carpetbag she had left in the hallway. Eugene looked about the empty room and then walked into it. It was quiet, and it held the girl's scent. His eyes went from the pendulum of the mantel clock to the portrait of his wife above it, and he frowned.

The grounds and houses of Elk Institute were a continuous purr and sometimes a roar of voices coming and going, of pleas and commands and, as the pupils of the school complained, of "doing and don't-ing." They were all to attend the wedding in the auditorium just as if it was a play. The starch in the dresses was enough to stiffen a circus tent and every drop of perfume on the premises had been used and used again. A drop spilled could sever a friendship.

At the Elk house Roxanne had been cooking for a week, and Claribell was firmly in control. A shy, retiring woman as long as Roscoe's housekeeper Geraldine had lived, she had, since Geraldine's death a year before, become mistress of her own house to the surprise of her husband and daughter, who had hitherto accepted her acceptance of the situation she had married into.

Today she was wearing peach-colored muslin, and the flow and flair of it was everywhere. Sarah greeted her warmly, but before she could word a compliment, Claribell was gone, so she made it to Roscoe, who laughed indulgently.

"You're very pleased with life these days," she said with a warning smile. "How is the bride?"

"Claribell talked her out of pink."

"Fanny told me about the dress she's to wear. Bruce was enchanted, but I'm afraid I got little from the description except that it's long and of an ivory shade."

"Just about everything else *is* pink," Roscoe said, "including the canopy over the altar she talked me into rigging. She said she wanted a frame around her and Abraham like a picture."

"I wish Casey were here to do pictures." She sighed, but not sadly. "Is she nervous?"

"Not a bit. She says why should she be, for she's planned the whole thing, including the songs and some new words she found in a book for the preacher. Whatever happens won't surprise me. She may come down the aisle leading a goat dyed pink."

Benjamin and Leon joined them. "Everything I smell, smells good," Leon said.

"Today you don't know whether it's victuals or people," Roscoe said, looking at his watch as Bruce approached.

Bruce said to Roscoe, "Fanny sent me to say you're to come. She's ready and it's almost time." Bruce beamed as she added triumphantly, "She's getting nervous!"

"Praise God," Roscoe said, and they laughed. He looked at his watch again in the bleak way of a man for whom time has run out.

Sarah leaned close and said, "Courage, my friend," which made him smile as he left them.

Sarah and Benjamin, Bruce and Leon made their way to the school building and to the door of the packed, buzzing auditorium. Many of the school's pupils stood on the sides and at the back to make room for other guests. Usually reluctant to enter the building, they had today needed no bell to command their attendance. They were encouraging and even politely chivvying latecomers to sit down and settle themselves. A young man acting as usher was trying to hurry Pauline and Nancy along the aisle. Pauline said, "I'm the groom's aunt, and this lady with me was his mammy. A swarm of bees couldn't make me move any faster."

With Roman, Pauline had shared the headship of the school since it had become Elk Institute, both stepping down only recently. Sarah caught herself thinking that Pauline was a very old woman and reminded herself that Pauline was but a year older than she. The usher who had led Nancy and Pauline to the front row on the right side of the auditorium returned and guided the party from Beulah Land to places beside Pauline and Nancy. Behind them sat Jane and Daniel and Bobby Lee, with Annabel and Blair Three. Blair was looking about indulgently and tapped Bruce on the shoulder when she seated herself in front of him. She turned, and he arched an eyebrow as if to say, "What amusing children they all are."

Seeing Sarah plunk in front of her, Annabel coughed disapprovingly. "A mistake surely," she said when Sarah looked around. "I am the school's sponsor."

Sarah nodded agreeably. "But we are the bridegroom's family. He is the youngest Kendrick, you know." Craning her neck frankly, she swept her eyes over the assembly. She did not know them all, but they knew her, and she guessed who they were. Everyone from the cotton mill who had worked there five years or more had been asked to come. Zadok and his family were there (Velma was pregnant again, and Rosalie kept her beside her) as well as the Beulah Land servants who had known Luck and Abraham longest and best. Old Otis, twin brother of Abraham's mother Lotus, sat with Wally, who liked better than anything else to ride or drive the horses too fast but who this morning looked as still as marble. Across the aisle sat Claribell, saving the place beside her for Roscoe. Beyond her were Roman and her old friend and mentor from the teaching staff, Mathilda Boland. Other teachers, male and female, young and old, surrounded them, giving the occasion an air of graduation day as much as a wedding.

On the stage above the altar was the battered school piano, newly polished and tuned, and a chorus of thirty schoolgirls. Led by the music teacher, a Miss Flutie Pierce, whose name delighted Sarah, they now sang "Abide with Me" and "Come Where My

Love Lies Dreaming," selected by the bride because she liked them. The preacher stood behind the pink-canopied altar frowning through rimless glasses at words on a piece of paper. Presently the singing finished, and the pianist struck the chords of the wedding march.

Fanny, the only attendant Luck would have, entered alone, carrying an armful of pink roses. Sarah turned her head, looking past Benjamin to see Leon's eyes shining with pleasure when he saw the girl. Abraham stepped out from the side with his chosen best man, Davy Todd. Sarah's heart caught when she saw them. "Floyd," she thought, "if you could see him, how handsome he is, how happy—" Benjamin was closer to her than anyone else living, but he could only imagine her thoughts and be a little surprised at her show of feeling.

Every head turned to see Luck come down the aisle. She was clutching Roscoe's arm as if she needed it. The proud, self-confident girl looked ready to weep or faint. At the altar, Roscoe responded to the preacher's ritual question and gave Luck over to Abraham. He then joined Claribell, and both of them sat rigidly attentive. As the preacher continued, the chorus of schoolgirls, cued by Miss Flutie, began a soft humming.

"Will you, Abraham, have this woman to be your wedded wife, to live together after God's ordinance, in the holy estate of matrimony, to love her, comfort her, honor and keep her, in sickness and in health, and forsaking all others, keep thee only unto her, so long as you both shall live?"

"I will," Abraham answered loudly.

"Will you, Luck, have this man to be your wedded husband, to live together after God's ordinance, in the holy estate of matrimony, to love, honor and keep him, in sickness and in health, and forsaking all others, keep thee only unto him, so long as you both shall live?"

"Yes, sir," she whispered, "I will."

Before the preacher could ask for it, Davy held up the ring, and in the second row Blair Three guffawed until he was silenced by a look from Bruce. The ceremony was soon concluded.

". . . By this act of joining hands you do take upon yourselves the relation of husband and wife, and solemnly promise and engage, in the presence of these witnesses, to love and honor, comfort and cherish each other as such, as long as you both shall live; therefore, in accordance with the laws of the State of Georgia, I do hereby pronounce you husband and wife."

For a second, such was its timing, Sarah wondered if the explosive sound was a part of Luck's program for the wedding, but the look of her frightened face as she twisted about told her that it was not. After the explosion there was silence. Brain lagged behind action, as Benjamin and Leon raced up the center aisle. Standing, as most of the others in the auditorium cowered in their seats, some beginning to scream, Sarah saw that the door leading into the auditorium was wide open. A white man unknown to her stood there laughing. Even as he drew back his hand to throw, Leon was upon him, and then Benjamin upon them both. But the man managed to fling the string of lighted firecrackers, and they exploded loudly one after the other, triggering a new burst of screams.

Davy and Roscoe were beside her when Sarah reached the front door, where the crowd, released from its first freezing fear, gathered thickly to watch the scene in the yard. Leon and Benjamin were fighting two white men in rough work clothes, the four of them rolling and pitching and pummeling, while a third man standing in an open wagon whipped the mule into a run. As the wagon rolled more rapidly, he dropped a lighted corn shuck into a barrel and rolled it over the side. It hit the ground smoking and exploding, and Davy jumped from the school porch onto the man's back and threw him off the other side of the wagon, falling upon him. Mule and wagon ran free as Leon and Benjamin and Davy fought the three strange men. The fireworks had by now all exploded or fizzled out.

Dazed by his leap and fall, Davy caught a fist on the side of his head. Ear bleeding and glassy-eyed, he sat alone on the ground until Bruce—where had she come from so quickly? Sarah wondered—knelt by him. The man Davy had attacked was helping one of his fellows to get free of Benjamin, and together they freed the third. All then ran after the wagon, the unattended mule slowing as they called to him, until they were able to hoist themselves up over the tailgate. As they looked back to see if they were pursued, their bodies heaved for air. Seeing they were in the clear, one of them whipped the mule into a fast trot while another yelled back: "Ass-kissing niggers! Nigger whores! Motherfucking-niggerloving-sonabitches!" With bold whoops of triumph they were gone.

Daniel and Bobby Lee were near Sarah, working their way through the crowd to reach Davy. "Where's Jane?" Sarah called.

"Taking care of Miss Annabel. She fainted."

"She has Blair to take care of her, doesn't she?"

"He fainted too." Daniel and Bobby Lee were gone, and Sarah inched her way back into the schoolhouse and auditorium. Presently, she found Roscoe holding Luck in his arms. It was Abraham who walked about trying to calm people, helped by the recovered Davy. Benjamin was tending a bleeding lip, and Leon asked across the intervening heads, "Have you seen Fanny? I'm looking for Fanny!"

Realizing that no one needed her, Sarah gave up struggling. Let everyone find each other, she decided. Abraham and Davy had become the center of the crowd, as any will who seem to supply information and calm in a time of panic. "It's all right now. — Nobody's hurt. — We know the men. — Sawmill workers. — That's right, we know them from seeing them across the creek. No, we don't know their names. Do any of you know their names? — Their idea of a joke."

With the explanation came indignation and condemnation, but eventually relief. The guests remembered the bride and bridegroom and the purpose of the day for which they had gathered together. By twos and threes and straggling lines they made their way from the schoolhouse to Roscoe's house beyond the japonicas he had planted long ago to make for himself a little screen of privacy. In time they were able to eat the food that Claribell and Roxanne urged upon them, and to drink the sweet, cool, pink wedding punch, to hug and laugh and, confidence returning, make their own jokes, feeble at first but growing in good humor. The event continued much as it had been planned; but there was not the same free and easy spirit there had been at the beginning of the day, not quite the same.

Sarah and Benjamin met briefly with Roscoe in his office, and while they were talking, Abraham entered without knocking. After working to calm others, he let his fury break with these he trusted. It was Roscoe who finally insisted that they not report the incident to the sheriff, reasoning that it would do no good. Even if the three men could be identified—and no one would swear to the name of a single man—they'd pass off their intrusion as a prank. There were always pranks before or after, and sometimes during, country weddings. There would be no charges and no arrests, only a stirring up of the bad feeling that already existed between those who worked at the sawmill on one side of the creek and those who worked at the cotton mill on the other.

It was late in the day the family party returned to Beulah Land, tired and thoughtful and glad to be home. Everyone went off to his room to find comfortable, common clothes, the women performing personal and household routine while the men went about the barns and cabins to witness end-of-day care of livestock and to speak about the wedding they had attended, which everyone who had not attended was eager to hear about.

The Todds kept to their house that evening, and Josephine, knowing the wedding feast, however rich, would have been mainly cold, prepared a plain hot meal of fried ham, rice and ham gravy, baked sweet potatoes, stewed tomatoes from a jar, spring greens boiled with hock, chowchow and beet relish, biscuits and thin corn bread, pitchers of fresh milk and buttermilk, and pound cake topped with custard into which Mabella had stirred peach preserves. At the supper table Sarah, observing the scratches and bruises Benjamin and Leon bore, suggested that they make a home day of tomorrow and not attend church, to which all thankfully agreed. Leon said after supper that he would go over and tell the Todds and asked Fanny if she would walk with him.

During the afternoon the weather had cleared and warmed, the wind stilled until no leaf moved, spring trying on summer manners. Leon and Fanny found the adult Coopers at the Todd house. Elizabeth had wanted to hear how fancy a wedding it had been. Having enjoyed only a simple one of her own, she was doubly fascinated by the show others made. Tom Cooper talked with Daniel and Leon about the larger acreage of tobacco he was setting and netting, wanting their assurance that he was not overextending himself.

The night was dark when Fanny and Leon took the shortest way back to the big house and they walked close as if afraid of night presences, Leon slipping his arm naturally about the girl's waist. At the little graveyard they surprised a figure in white leaning upon the headstone of one of the graves.

"Grandma!"

Sarah turned, statue made living. "Leon? Fanny, is that you too? I'm just going in to bed. I was already in my room when something told me the day wasn't over and I remembered I hadn't been here. Abraham married, you know, and no one had come to tell his mother and father and grandmother and grandfather."

"We'll walk you to the house," Fanny said.

"No, let me go alone; you stay. There is no place as peaceful as a graveyard at night."

5

Although the raid on the wedding party had not been Eugene's idea, he had not discouraged it when Stacy Winn proposed it to Perry Mitchell and Elmo Pitts, and his smiling had been taken as sanction. Certainly he was quick to see advantage in it. On Saturday night, following the common custom of walking about town to exchange news and views, he heard several versions of the event and by repeating what he'd heard, or said he'd heard, lent credence to the interpretation that it was a joke on the highfalutin Negroes, no meanness intended any more than there'd been other times in trying to spook the darkies about graveyards at midnight or laughing at their dancing at baptisms. He regretted that it had been taken in the wrong spirit, for it was further said, and he'd seen all the proof he needed, the jokers had been set upon by members of the wedding party, black and white, as if they'd been caught doing something they were ashamed of.

He had to admit that his own stepdaughter was there—but what could be done with young people these days who had little respect for authority and ignored the advice of their elders? Annabel Saxon did not join the Saturday-night walking and talking, and when queried at church the next morning stated that she had seen nothing of the disturbance, having fainted at the sound of the first explosion. By noon Sunday it was fixed to the general satisfaction that a vicious attack by Negroes upon innocent whites had been led by Benjamin Davis and his son.

"Is it true what we've heard?" Ann Oglethorpe asked gravely after the sermon.

With equal solemnity Eugene replied that he feared her son-in-law (with a bow of the head to Miss Priscilla) had been involved and that he knew no reason to doubt the facts as he'd heard them. They affirmed that it was a disgrace for white people to side with colored against their own kind, and that no good came of mixing and mingling, for it only led to debauchery and mongrelization of the white race.

Eugene Betchley had maintained and compounded the friendship begun when the Oglethorpe mother and daughter offered to take in his son Theodore. Theodore, under paternal threat, had behaved cautiously during the months he lived at the Oglethorpe house before joining his father at Frankie's after their marriage. Deception is easy enough when there is acquiescence on both sides.

"I don't believe I have seen Mrs. Betchley this morning?" Priscilla said in the cold bright tone she used in speaking of Frankie.

"A headache," Eugene announced with a sigh.

"Ah." Mrs. Oglethorpe sneered openly and invited Eugene and Theodore to take Sunday dinner with them. "I would include Edna May, but she will want to attend her mother."

Having sometimes taken a meal at Mrs. Oglethorpe's table, Eugene knew what he was in for, but self-interest dictated that he accept with a show of gratitude.

At Beulah Land it was a day of quiet enjoyment, a day none

would have remembered but for the visit that capped its routine events. After the usual large noon dinner, members of the family dispersed severally. Late afternoon found Nancy, after a conference with Josephine in the kitchen, pausing to pass time with Roman, who had been reading and dozing on the warm west porch. With much coming and going all day, they did not turn immediately upon hearing a buggy on the carriageway to discover who were its occupants. When they did, Nancy rose from her chair to usher the two visitors into the broad central hallway. She invited them to sit, but they were still standing when she went to fetch Sarah Troy and Benjamin Davis as she had been directed to do.

"Mrs. Oglethorpe and Mr. Betchley!" Sarah exclaimed.

"The *two*," Nancy emphasized.

"Put them in the office and say I'll be right along."

A few minutes later Sarah found Benjamin already there, the three sitting in silence as they waited for her to join them. "Good afternoon, Mrs. Oglethorpe. Afternoon, Mr. Betchley; and how is Miss Frankie?"

"Keeping to her room with a headache."

"I'm sorry. And Edna May?"

"Misses her sister."

"I wish you'd brought her with you to stay a few days."

"We've come on particulars, Mrs. Troy." Sarah sat behind her desk, not for its position of command but because she felt easy there. "We have come to hear an explanation of yesterday's event."

As host and hostess looked at them with surprise, Benjamin said, "I should think it is rather for you to explain, if explanation is necessary, since the men who interrupted the wedding were from the sawmill."

"Stacy Winn was hurt bad in the attack you made on him."

"I'd like to believe it, but I doubt it. Tell him next time he tries such a thing I'll crack his skull and have him thrown into jail."

The visitors looked at each other. Ann Oglethorpe commented, "You see: ever a violent man."

Sarah asked, "What is your concern in the affair, ma'am?"

"Dedication to justice. And however reluctantly I allow it to be so, I am connected with your family."

"A matter of mixed feelings for all of us." Sarah opened her hands in front of her on the desk top, telling herself she must not sit with them clenched.

"You do not deny that you attacked Stacy Winn?" Eugene said.

"I don't know the names of the three ruffians, but if he was one of them, my son and nephew and I routed them after they set off their explosions. Yes, certainly."

"The explosions you refer to were, so I have been informed, but innocent firecrackers. Were they on property of yours?"

Sarah said, "You must know, Mr. Betchley, the incident occurred at Elk Institute when we attended the wedding of Luck Elk to Abraham Kendrick."

Ann Oglethorpe said, "And what of the savages you unleashed against the poor men?"

"What can you mean?" Benjamin asked softly.

"The town knows." Eugene shook his head as if to dismiss any attempt at subterfuge. "Last night and this morning they've talked of nothing else. People are stirred up. It would not surprise me if something was to happen like happened over in Washington County last summer."

Sarah spoke sharply. "Do you mean the Negro they lynched for shaking his fist at a white man who tried to cheat him out of a bale of cotton?"

"They've got to be shown they can't go against us," Eugene said levelly.

"Or our women." Ann Oglethorpe looked directly at Sarah.

Seeing Benjamin rise in his chair, Sarah lifted a hand in a cautioning way. "I want you to understand this, both of you," she said, "and tell the people in town. No Negro touched those three jackasses yesterday. The fighting, such as it was, was between them and my grandson, joined by his son and one of his nephews. If, as you indicate, there has been such a thorough airing of the affair in town, surely Mrs. Blair Saxon and her grandson, who were at the wedding, will have already told you what we are telling you now."

Another look was exchanged by Eugene Betchley and Ann Oglethorpe. She said, "They were able to observe nothing, for they were unconscious, from shock and disgust I should imagine."

"So they were," Sarah remembered. "Very well: your own granddaughter, ma'am, and your stepdaughter, Mr. Betchley."

With a grimace Mrs. Oglethorpe replied, "They will say what *you* say, I've no doubt."

"There were hundreds of witnesses," Sarah said.

"Niggers." Eugene nodded his head. "Everybody knows their oath ain't worth a chew of tobacco."

Mrs. Oglethorpe said, "If your involvement was innocent and no Nigras were in it, why wasn't the fight reported to the sheriff? That it wasn't points to bad conscience. We talked with Sheriff Farrow before coming this afternoon. He knows exactly what everybody knows, no more, no less. *I* suggested that since none from Beulah Land attended church this morning, which is your usual habit although Sundays only, he had no opportunity to question you about it. I believe he is considering an arrest."

"On what charge?" Benjamin asked. "That of defending our friends against intruders? — And at what you, Mrs. Oglethorpe, must regard as a sacred moment, the exchange of vows between a man and woman in marriage."

"Don't *you* speak of sacred moments! I'm surprised the Lord doesn't strike you down as you utter the words."

"Let us all be calm," Eugene reasoned. "We have come on legitimate duty, that of asking for and listening to your explanation of what appears to be behavior that can have no defense."

Controlling himself, Benjamin said, "We have stated the facts. I do not offer them as explanation or defense."

"What you call facts don't satisfy me, and I don't think they will the town."

"Damn your satisfaction!"

"I told you he would be blasphemous," Ann Oglethorpe said with gratification. "Always a violent man."

"No need to remind me, ma'am. I was the subject of his attack on another occasion at the sawmill that now belongs to me."

"I thought it belonged to your wife," Sarah said.

"We are one."

Ann Oglethorpe frowned more deeply. "You persist then in siding with the Nigras?"

"They have always done so," Eugene said sadly. "Don't they own a big share of the cotton mill? Run by a nigger so that other niggers can make better wages than white men and brag about it. I've heard them myself."

Ann Oglethorpe said, "You, Mrs. Troy, will not deny that you were the instrument behind the starting of that school you call Elk Institute, where they teach Nigras to think themselves as good as white people. Before that you taught them here, when it was against state law too. You don't deny that, do you?"

"Why do you hate Negroes?" Sarah said.

"I hate only their low natures. If the darkies want to raise themselves, they are welcome to try, as long as they do it the way it's preached by their leader Booker T. Washington: to walk humbly and work hard in the station God has set them down in. I fail to understand how you of all people can love them after what they did to you. Common knowledge declares that Roscoe Elk's own uncle caught you in the woods and assaulted you when you were a much younger woman. That would have been enough to make any other white woman hate, fear, and despise Nigras the rest of her life."

"Well, I declare," Sarah said coolly, "what a memory you have. That was fifty years ago."

"It's not a thing I'd like to forget."

"No," Sarah said thoughtfully. "I suppose it isn't."

"It's not only my memory but the county's. The tragedy was shared by every white man and woman in the county."

"How generous of you all."

"You offend the Lord by making light of such things!"

"Many things, I'm sure, offend the Lord."

"For once you speak true." Mrs. Oglethorpe nodded with vigor. "That woman who brought us in here to wait—"

"My housekeeper?"

Mrs. Oglethorpe looked at Benjamin. "I remember her. She's the one you let live in your house in my daughter's place."

"She kept it better too," Benjamin said, "even though she was ill at the time. In any event, your daughter had deserted that house a good many years before."

"If she offered to come back now and be your wife, would you welcome her?"

"I cannot imagine her doing so," Benjamin said.

"She would do it to save your soul."

"I could not permit such a sacrifice."

Mrs. Oglethorpe's mouth stretched wide in triumph.

As if she had found a solution to a problem that disturbed her, Sarah brought both hands down flat on the desk top. "I am puzzled no longer. You are natural allies. You go to church and you want everyone to behave according to your ideas of right and wrong. Those who do not are to be damned. Well, we at Beluah Land have always followed our own ways, and if you don't like them, you are at liberty to peddle your opinions elsewhere, but not here. Yours, Mrs. Oglethorpe, are of no consequence. Everyone knows you for a meddling fool."

"The Lord has spoken to me!"

"If He told you to come here, I'll have to speak to *Him*."

"Blasphemy now from the granddam!"

"You, on the other hand, worry me, Mr. Betchley. There are so many things I don't understand about you. I remember you as a boy who would seine our creek and set traps in our woods. You used to leave creatures to die if they were no use to you. Next thing we knew you were entrenched at the Marsh farm. And old Mrs. Marsh died. She had been my friend, and so was her daughter my friend."

"We all know why you befriended her," Ann Oglethorpe said.

"Yes, mainly because of Benjamin's son, but I liked her too. And now she too is dead. I knew Bessie Marsh well. She would not have done what you accused her of, Mr. Betchley."

"That's a shocking thing to say, Mrs. Troy. The truth of my discovery has never been doubted."

"I've doubted it, though there was no way to challenge it."

Ann Oglethorpe said, "Don't countenance her, Mr. Betchley. All know you for a good and truthful man of God, as they knew Bessie for a frail vessel."

Sarah held her eyes on the man who had advanced to her desk.

"Don't make trouble, I beg you. I don't mean about yesterday's scuffle. You exaggerate the town's concern because it suits you to. Why, I don't know. But if you go further and try to harm us or our people, I will have no mercy on you."

"You beg and threaten at the same time."

"I want to be understood."

Benjamin knew that Sarah wanted him to remain silent, but he could not. "Get away from Beulah Land and never come back."

Ann Oglethorpe led the way.

When they had gone, Sarah and Benjamin sat for a time without speaking. At last Benjamin sighed with exasperation, then laughed shakily. "You heard them say I'm a violent man, Grandma. Let me kill them."

"Not today, boy. I know what we must do. I have so little regard for town opinion, or interest in it, I ignore it, and that makes bad feeling. Tomorrow morning I shall put on a pretty frock and drive my buggy alone into town, for only a woman may do what needs doing. First I'll have a talk with Sheriff Farrow, combining firmness with coquetry in a way that would make any man with his wits about him take a stick to me. But the sheriff is nothing if not stupid, or he wouldn't be our sheriff. It's one step maybe above the depot loungers, although the two callings have sometimes been combined. Then I shall put a bee in Annabel's bonnet. I've neglected her, and Annabel is like a child. Unless you give her something to do, she gets into mischief. Later in the week she and I together, perhaps with your aunt Doreen and Miss Kilmer, will pay calls. The name of Beulah Land will be fragrant again, I promise you."

Benjamin moved around the desk to stand beside her chair. "Grandma, I want you to know something. I never loved you as much as I love you today or had better reason."

6

Finding it easy to climb the trailing quilt Leon had kicked off in the night, Hellfire picked his way alongside the body until his attention was caught by sudden movement under the sheet. Something bulged where nothing had been. He sat to study it and put out a paw to investigate. Leon woke smiling from his dream, and when he saw Hellfire, his erection began to subside. He drew his knees up slowly under the sheet, which further alarmed the kitten. When its gaze was fixed unwaveringly, Leon slipped an arm from under the sheet and swatted the creature lightly. Hellfire scampered off the bed and away, pausing at the door to see if he was pursued.

Leon got out of bed and stretched, going to the window to look out as every farmer will on rising. He opened both shutters full, feeling the warm sun and air on his hands. Mabella was crossing the yard, her back to him, on her way to the well, and as he looked beyond her and the barns into the fields, he remembered that it was April 8, 1895, and his twenty-first birthday. By gum and by God, he thought with a thrill of anticipation. Turning, he took the slop jar from the bottom of the commode and peed, but heard his name called before he finished. Cutting off his water and clapping the lid on the jar, he returned to the window to see Bobby Lee and Davy.

"Going to swim?"

"Wait for me," Leon said. They did not yet go every morning as they would in summer, but it was warm enough today, and the water would feel fresh and cold. They would holler when they jumped into it but then brag that it wasn't so bad after all.

Davy winked at his brother. A minute later Leon joined them, still barefoot, wearing loose cotton trousers, shirt half on and unbuttoned. They were just beyond the stand of sunflowers that screened the privies when Bobby Lee turned on his cousin. Leon tried to run, but they caught him and held him, Davy whacking him across the buttocks with a stick he had appeared to pick up idly on the way. Laughing and shouting the count, they accomplished the ritual, whereupon Leon broke free and the cousins chased him across a field and into the woods and along the old path to the particular creek bank from which the men of Beulah Land had swum for more than a hundred years.

They might hardly have known each other, so few were their exchanges as they splashed and paddled and stroked up and down, across and back. Often on their morning and evening swims they played and shouted; today they were quiet until they were dressing and Davy said, "There's going to be champagne at dinner tonight and brandy in the punch for the ball."

"Well, surely," Bobby Lee said tolerantly.

"Don't say it as if it happens every day. I never had champagne and neither have you, and I can't remember a real *ball* at Beulah Land before and I'm eighteen."

"Nearly," Leon corrected him. "They used to have them in the old days, Grandma says. She met Grandpa Casey for the first time when he came to a ball at Beulah Land."

Combing his hair, Davy said to Leon, "I reckon you think you're something getting to be twenty-one."

"Never mind, little man," Leon answered. "We'll let you be twenty-one in a few years, won't we, Bobby Lee?"

Bobby Lee put on a doubtful expression. "If we do, it'll take the whole meaning out of it."

The ball had been Annabel's idea. Annabel took vast pleasure in large parties if they were at someone else's expense; and when Sarah enlisted her help to improve town feeling toward Beulah Land, the idea of a ball to mark Leon's coming of age seemed an inspiration. Sarah's fence mending was seen to be serious, and because it offered more than it asked, it was successful. What the townspeople really wanted was to be noticed by the family at Beulah Land—flattered by them, consulted by them, consoled by them. The best way to the hearts of inferiors was to ask a favor of them that was easy to grant. Sarah sometimes forgot it because she didn't like to believe people so simple. Eugene Betchley and Ann Oglethorpe contended no more, merely picking at old sores and harboring old scores, but no one paid them much attention. What is pride to the advantages of a ball? Eugene had not, in truth, expected to win anything in this challenge over the Negro wedding but had looked upon it as an exercise and a test.

Leon was last to arrive at the breakfast table that had for a month been set up on the east porch to get the early sun; another month and they would avoid it and breakfast on the west porch. Sarah and Bruce and Benjamin had begun, Mabella having already brought a platter of fried eggs, another of fried beefsteaks, bowls of grits and gravy, biscuits, a pitcher of milk and a pot of coffee. As they served themselves and each other, he sat down at his place and lifted his plate, which was turned down on the tablecloth, to discover beneath it three small packages. Smiling but making no comment, he opened the one with the prettiest wrapping, knowing it would be a gift from Bruce. Inside were mother-of-pearl cuff buttons she had commissioned Fanny to choose for her in Savannah when she went there with Luck and Nancy. He admired them and kissed her and opened the next. It was a plain, gold, old-looking wedding ring. He looked at Sarah questioningly.

She said, "For your wife when you marry. It was my ring when I married your great-grandfather Leon. Every time the Yankees came during the war I hid it in my mouth, ready to swallow if they touched me. I didn't wear it after the war, and Casey gave me another."

Blushing with pleasure, he left his chair to hug and thank her. The third present was a gold watch and chain. He opened it carefully and read aloud the wording that was delicately engraved on the inner lid: "Leon Marsh Davis of Beulah Land from his loving father." The watch was wound and keeping time, but its sound could not be heard even when he held it to his ear. His fingers trembled as he examined it, as if he feared it might melt in his hands. It was the most beautiful thing he'd ever had, and when he looked up and across the table at Benjamin, his eyes held tears. Bruce took his plate and served him a large beefsteak and three fried eggs, the tops dark with pepper the way he liked them. Sarah added a biscuit to the plate, and Mabella poured coffee into his cup. They began to eat and talk and laugh, until presently their attention was caught by Davy's waving goodbye as he sounded the bell from his bicycle and pedaled away to work at the cotton mill.

It was a busy day for everyone at Beulah Land. The men went about the work of the barns and the fields, glad to be out of the way of the women, whose concentration on food and flowers and furniture arrangement was total and terrible. The aroma of cooking mingled with the smell of beeswax and new dresses and the fragrance of blossom. The wide central hallway that stretched from front to back would contain most of the dancers as well as the musicians; but since the weather was warm and there would be many guests, windows and doors were to remain open, that the dancers might use the porches too. Oil lamps had been cleaned and refilled, but candles also were set about to provide further light and cheer.

Sarah told Jane: "I will not bustle about, I'm too old. Let them come to me now." And so they did for answers Jane and Nancy and Bruce could not give, because no one at Beulah Land other than Sarah had ever prepared for such a large entertainment. There would be eighty or more who would dance and that many again too young or too old to indulge in the refined savagery who would lurk and smirk, gossip and tease and yawn among the potted ferns. The branches of blossoms from the orchard they now set so carefully would shed petals as the rooms warmed with humanity until some became no more than bare limbs sketching air.

Noon dinner was a hurried affair on the side porch where they had taken breakfast, but Mabella made it the occasion to present Leon with the chocolate pie she had baked, a part of birthday ritual since his first one at the plantation. He paid her with surprise and pleasure that never seemed less than then and remembered to stop in the kitchen to hug her and Josephine after the meal. He and Benjamin rocked and nodded on the porch until Otis rang the tower bell that signaled all hands to return to the fields for afternoon work. Sarah retired to her room to rest, Jane to her house, Nancy to the house in the Glade, and Josephine to her cabin, leaving Mabella to superintend the extra workers in the kitchen. But the pause was for less than an hour, as there was so much yet to do and see done, baths to be taken, hair brushed and curled and coiled and pinned.

Late afternoon found Benjamin and Daniel, Leon and Bobby Lee and Davy scrubbing themselves in the creek before going indoors to put on their party clothes. As dusk came on and the lamps were lighted, the whole of Beulah Land began to assume a quickening air of expectation. Sarah and Bruce found Benjamin and Leon in the big living room, and Sarah said with satisfaction as Benjamin handed glasses of wine, "We four."

They had taken their first sips when they were joined by the Todds. Bruce giggled at Davy's embroidered shirtfront, and he told her she was ignorant. Shortly after, Annabel's party arrived in her carriage. She looked very fine in black brocaded silk, and she carried a new ostrich fan. She was attended by Blairs One and Three (number Two would come later with his wife Prudence in their own carriage) and brought with her Frankie and Fanny and Edna May. During the half-hour transit from Highboro, Annabel had, after telling Edna May that she was getting fat and Frankie that she was so thin as to look positively gaunt and Fanny that her left sleeve was surely shorter than her right, contented herself with speaking only to Blair Three. Frankie and the most senior Blair Saxon exchanged civilities; and Fanny assured Edna May there would be many little things she might choose from to remember the evening and preserve in her "memory" book. Forgetting her grandmother's criticism (at eight she was too young to mind substance), Edna May set her face toward Beulah Land with the happy anticipation of the historian approaching Nineveh and Tyre.

Sarah had intended early supper as a simple one for those who lived at Beulah Land, but Annabel would have it otherwise and prevailed. "I despise arriving with everyone else; it's common and tacky. You must feed us early and late, Auntie Sarah; and it won't hurt you either with your army of retainers to fetch and carry. You have so many, you have so much."

To the which Sarah replied, "Whatever we have we've worked for."

"It helps to have a little 'live' dough as starter if you want to make bread though, doesn't it?"

So down they sat fourteen together to enjoy Josephine's feast of whole roast pig and asparagus and salads. When that and all the other dishes were no more and sherbets had been passed, Josephine herself bore the birthday cake in lighted triumph to the dining room to flattering exclamations and applause led by Leon. As Davy predicted, there was champagne, and Leon was wished long life and good fortune so many times that Mabella, who considered him her own boy, was overcome by emotion and had to be led away to be comforted and petted, to the derision of Josephine and the amusement of the guests.

The sensations of individual attendants of a gathering are never the same, however single the purpose of their assembling, and while some of those tonight were sincere in their regard, others were envious and bitter. Looking at Frankie with pity as she drank more than she ate, Benjamin marveled that he had once wept to lose her and expanded courtesy to courtliness until Frankie suspected him of trying to revive their old love affair. But then when she saw how often his gaze returned to Edna May, she told herself that Benjamin Davis cared for no woman, only his children by them, and that she was glad to have married Eugene Betchley. Eugene was right about those at Beulah Land: they thought they ruled the world. Their very instinct to generosity was arrogance. Having so decided, she narrowed her eyes as she listened to the laughter of her elder daughter and observed the familiar, almost familial affection in which she was held by Sarah Troy, the Davises, and the Todds.

The youngest Blair Saxon admired the room. It was not, of course, fashionable; still, there was a richness and a kind of *decision* about it that carried its own authority, none of the hesitant assertion that often betrays the new rich when their vulgarity does not. He weighed the silver in his hand and turned the crystal goblet of champagne appreciatively. There might be something worth considering in his grandmother's suggestion that he ally himself to the girl at Beulah Land.

Sarah presently led the ladies away to the living room to drink their coffee while the gentlemen smoked and talked farming and politics. Of the one topic they knew, among them, everything; of the other little or nothing; yet they spoke cautiously about the first and conclusively on the second. Blair Three longed to be with Annabel and yawned against the cigar smoke. His eyes slipped from one face to the next. All were florid from weather or overindulgence at dinner, but he could admit that his three young male cousins were handsome, if only in a rude country way. There was, however, something almost sensitive in the nose and chin modeling of the elder Todd boy, something melancholy in his eyes, and Blair wondered what lay behind his thoughtful detachment. Bobby Lee's thoughts were indeed at that moment detached from the company; he was speculating on the sex of the calf due to be born soon to a cow named Daisy he had taken special care of all winter.

Roman had wanted to be part of the evening and knew that discretion forbade his appearing as a guest, so he appointed himself factotum: which permitted him to wander freely about, but not to sit. As much as Sarah dared, she would never have Negroes as guests with townspeople who were not part of the family. It was all right for the annual barbecue on the Fourth of July. That was a family affair and outdoors. She knew that Roscoe and Claribell, Abraham and Luck understood the rules and wouldn't have enjoyed the party anyway; but if Claribell and Luck had doted upon balls, they could not have been asked. And so tonight Roman, who was Sarah's oldest friend and the only man alive who called her Sarah without a "Miss" before it, limped about fussily instructing the orchestra.

He spoke now to the violinist who led the musicians, and they began to play. The sound drew the gentlemen from the dining room and the ladies from their coffee cups into the wide hallway just as the guests from town and county began to appear. They came in anything with wheels—buggies, carriages, wagons. There were even a few bicycles. Wally and his stableboys would have a busy night of it. Sarah and Leon on one side of the door, Benjamin and Bruce on the other welcomed their guests, with Nancy behind them to direct the disposal of their wraps.

Everyone knew everyone else, but eyes tonight were ready to make fresh appraisals. China silk was argued against Japanese, the cut of a dress admired or pitied, this complexion praised, that figure deplored, manners declared to be refined or disgusting. Almost every female carried a folding fan of paper or silk; all were adept at using them. Only Annabel boasted an ostrich fan, and when her old girlhood friend Ann-Elizabeth Dupree complained that it was far too long and got in everyone's way, Annabel replied loftily, "The length of feather depends on the size of the bird, you know." If there was much that was comical and superficial in the yearning after alien sophistication, still it was only for an evening, and there was an exhilaration in the event enjoyed by everyone.

When she was ready for the dancing to begin, Sarah whispered to Roman and he spoke to the lead violinist. Finishing the tune they were engaged upon, the musicians paused long enough for the party to grow quiet with expectation. The leader held his violin at an alert tilt and the orchestra began the first waltz. Leon went to Sarah and bowed; she gave him her hand, and he led her to the floor. When they had danced a few bars, they were joined by Benjamin and Bruce, then Jane and Daniel. They were followed by Bobby Lee and his great-aunt Doreen, and there were whispers of speculation as Davy bowed before Fanny Saxon and led her into the dance. With tossing head and a flutter of ostrich plumes Annabel achieved the floor with the obedient Blair Three. Laughing heartily enough to draw a pained glance from that young man, Elizabeth and Tom Cooper followed them. The ball had begun and from that moment sustained itself.

Leon knew his duty and found himself happy doing it. After Sarah he danced with his aunt Jane and his great-aunts Annabel and Doreen. Next there was Miss Joyce Kilmer, and when he bowed over the thin hand of ancient Miss Emmy Goldthwaite, she shooed him with her fan. "You are going through us old ladies like reciting the multiplication tables!" she accused him. "Go and dance with someone young—"

Leon laughed. "I love old ladies!"

"Then you will surely go to heaven and I shall dance with you there, for we shall all be young and fair."

To rest the musicians there were pauses and promenades through the open rooms and porches. Annabel found a moment to say to Sarah, "I'm so glad little Bruce is finding partners. Not that I thought she wouldn't, for she is, of course, the young lady of Beulah Land; but you must watch out her head isn't turned by someone sly who wants more than her hand in marriage!" Sarah looked at her sharply and then as the music began searched until she discovered Bruce.

"Her new partner is Blair Three. That would seem safe enough," Sarah said.

"What a handsome young man he is," Annabel said complacently. "I declare he is quite the favorite, so good and thoughtful too. He is getting well up in the law, you know. Judge Meldrim tells me he is amazing."

"Annabel," Sarah said warningly, for there was a time neither had forgotten when Annabel had tried to arrange a marriage between her son Bonard and Jane.

"How suspicious you are. Only remember: youth is fleeting and unheeding and will have its way."

Just before midnight supper Bruce found herself with Davy. "You danced three times with Blair Three," he told her as he might have pointed out the number of melons on a vine.

"He waltzes better than you," she said.

"If that's all you care about, you might as well do every turn with old Midas Mott over there. He used to *teach* dancing."

Bruce giggled. "I don't think he's moved from his chair since they settled him in it. He must be a hundred."

Sweeping her about in a bold swing that lifted her off the floor and caused Mr. Mott to shake his head in disgust, Davy said, "The other girls all like my new shirt."

"Elvira Kennedy would like anything as long as there was a pair of britches below it. She stands too close to her partners."

"I haven't heard any of them complain."

"I don't know one girl her age that doesn't purely despise her for the way she acts with boys."

"She never wants a partner, does she?" He smiled at her smugly, and she stuck out her tongue at him.

Having satisfied his own ideas of duty by dancing with Annabel, with Sarah, and with his mother, Blair Three had proceeded to dance with whomever he pleased to ask or, as happened more frequently, not to dance at all, but to loiter and wander, ignoring females needing partners. At the punch bowl he asked Bobby Lee what he thought of *The Picture of Dorian Gray* by

Oscar Wilde. Blushing, Bobby Lee answered that he hadn't read it and he'd thank Blair not to mention that rascal's name where ladies were present. Setting down his empty cup, he moved away, and Blair laughed to suggest that they had enjoyed a joke together.

"An interesting book, though not universally admired."

Blair turned; the speaker was Roman. "Have you read it, Uncle?" he asked jocularly. "Oh—you're the one they call Roman Kendrick." He nodded his own confirmation. "Taught in Philadelphia and all that before coming home after the war. Used to—" He stopped, remembering other things he'd heard about the old Negro man, and as he did so, saw awareness and warning in his eyes. With a shrug he moved away.

After supper, instead of joining the dancing that then resumed, Leon and Fanny left the house together, and as soon as they entered the shadows of the yard, began to run, stopping abruptly when they came to the little graveyard that had become their favorite place of tryst. Inside the iron fence, the young man fastened the gate as if doing so separated them from the world, pulled the girl to him and kissed her. After a moment Fanny pulled gently free, saying, "I wish, oh how I wish!"

"Give me a real birthday present, Fanny, better than all the others. Tell me and let me tell them when we're getting married."

"I can't."

"Why?"

"I've told you: Mama, Edna May. I won't leave them with him."

"Your mama knows how to take care of herself, I'd say."

"You won't understand."

"Well, she married him; you didn't."

"They don't sleep together any more, but they quarrel. The things they *both* say make me so afraid. He's bad, Leon."

"I know he is, but that doesn't mean you have to spend your life watching so he doesn't harm Miss Frankie and Edna May; now does it?"

"Yes."

"What if it goes on ten years?"

"By then Edna May will be grown."

Leon groaned. "And we'd be old! *Fanny!* How can you think of it? Everybody wants you here; you belong here. But that isn't it, that doesn't begin to say it. *I* want you, Fanny. I lie awake thinking about you, *us* together. I could cry some of those times.— How can I think about farming with you on my mind every minute!"

"Well, I'm sorry if I interfere with the cotton, I'm sure!"

"You're just stubborn," he said.

"You're bossy. You can't order me around the way you would a field hand—"

"You know I don't do that," he said sternly.

"I'm sorry," she said softly. She found his hand and held it against her until he put his arms around her again. He was reaching with his lips to kiss her when she said, "Let's go back in."

"Oh, my God," he said, "do you have to be such a *girl?*"

"You'd like it better if I was a chicken?"

He tried not to laugh and laughed. "If I'm not to have you, at least let us stay here a little longer."

They sat on the cool tombstone of Selma Kendrick and held hands until the sound of music ceased and then began again. Then without a word they rose, still holding hands, and returned to the house.

7

"Good night, good night, *good* night!" Frankie caroled facetiously after Annabel's carriage as it rattled away, leaving her and her daughters at their front gate. Frankie stumbled twice on the brick walkway but recovered herself without help from Fanny or Edna May. In the dim light of the oil lamp Molly had left burning in the entrance hall Frankie looked her normal self, no worse than pale and tired, and when Fanny asked if she might help her undress, refused curtly and said the girls must go directly to bed. The three climbed the stairs with Frankie, lamp in hand, leading the way. She merely nodded when her daughters told her good night—they never kissed—and entered the room they shared. The house was large enough for them all to have separate rooms, and Fanny was of an age to want her own, but she knew Edna May was nervous alone and sometimes woke at night, scared.

Fanny found matches and lighted their own lamp, turning it high for cheer so that it smoked the glass chimney briefly before she adjusted the flame. They smiled at each other, glad to be by themselves. Looking at the little mantel clock Leon had given Fanny her last birthday, Edna May marveled, "It's a quarter to three! I've never been up so late, indeed only to just after midnight before, to say I'd welcomed the new year."

Undressing, Fanny teased her sister. "How you begged the first time you were allowed to, saying, 'What if I die in the night and never see the new year?' "

Edna May smiled to think she could ever have been such a child. "There wasn't as much to bring away as you said there'd be, but look. This bud will press well; it isn't too thick, is it? And here's a ribbon bow, two colors—"

"Get ready for bed."

They shook out their dresses and hung them carefully in the wardrobe they also shared, then began brushing their hair; but Edna May yawned and her strokes became languid, stopping altogether. Fanny finished tying her own hair and, taking Edna May's brush, started brushing briskly, which brought the younger girl awake again.

"Do you like dancing with Leon?" Edna May asked.

"Of course."

"More than with anyone else?"

"Much more."

"He's very handsome, isn't he?"

"Yes."

"Do you think him the handsomest boy in the world?"

"I don't know all the boys in the world, do I?"

"Well, of the ones you do know."

"Mama and Grandma both think our brother better-looking."

"Brothers don't count. What about Roger Shields?"

"Well," Fanny said, "he's nice-looking too."

"I can't tell Marvin and Garvin Cooper apart, so I don't know if I danced with both of them or one of them twice. The young-uns were dancing out on the porch, you know. Sometimes. Only the boys don't really like to, and you have to dare them to get them to do it. Marvin and Garvin are always playing jokes at school because they look alike. One of them took a whipping due the other last year, so they tell."

"That will do." Fanny laid down the brush and found a ribbon.

"Do you think Nigras can be pretty if they're girls and good-looking if they're boys?"

Fanny laughed. "Yes. I think Luck is pretty."

"That's because she's your friend. I mean ordinary Nigras. I think they can only be good-looking to each other. The way some cats like some cats and don't like others, so it must be how they look."

"You're silly."

"I bet I'm right."

Fanny, done tying her sister's hair, pushed her toward her bed. "Say your prayers so I can blow out the lamp."

Edna May knelt beside her bed and bent her head over folded hands. "Now I lay me down to sleep, I pray Thee, Lord, my soul to keep. If I should die before I wake, I pray Thee, Lord, my soul to take. God bless Mama. God bless Fanny. God bless Leon on his birthday, and you might as well bless Marvin and Garvin Cooper." She hopped into bed as she said, "Amen," and pulled the sheet over her. "I don't ask Him to bless Papa and Theodore any more. Is that wicked?" Without answering, Fanny blew out the lamp and got into her own bed. "I don't know why you don't kneel any more and say your prayers out loud."

"I've told you: I like to say mine in bed to myself."

"Do you have secrets you don't want me to hear?"

"Maybe. Go to sleep."

"I'll bet they're about Leon. Well, *I* have secrets too, and I'm going to tell them to myself right now while you're telling yours to yourself." When her sister made no reply, Edna May said rapidly, "All right, I'm asleep! Good night, dear Fanny!"

"Good night, Edna May."

Down the hall a door opened and Frankie's words—Fanny guessed she had gone into her husband's room—were like a mockery of the words the sisters had spoken. "Good night! Good night! Wake up, Eugene, and say good night!"

When he answered, Eugene's voice sounded harsh and sticky with sleep. "Shut your mouth and get to bed, old woman."

"*Old?* You wouldn't say so if you'd seen me dancing with this one and that one—"

"I don't give a shit who you dance with."

Frankie laughed triumphantly. "Got the sore head like a sick rooster, have you? Because *you* couldn't go to the party. *You* couldn't go because you weren't asked, and *you* weren't asked because they don't like you because you're common!"

"Get out!"

"Common! — Oh, they're genteel and aristocratic out there. Everybody loves everybody and speaks so nicely. Nobody wanted to leave—that's why we're so late. You never heard so many good-nights. Kept saying 'Good night' and not going, 'Good night,' but standing in the door or on the porch or from their buggies, hoping they'd be made to stay a little longer. Nobody wanted to leave ever."

"Get your drunk face out of mine."

Her laughter was pitched high and spiteful. "You're not good enough for Beulah Land! You're only good enough for Bible-toting old buzzards like Priscilla Davis and her ma, and you're good enough for them only when you wear your Sunday God-face!"

"Go to bed, bitch."

"Call *me* that, you murdering devil!"

There was the sound of a slap Fanny had known was coming and had waited for. She began to slip out of bed, but hesitated when Eugene's voice came again, low and controlled. "I told you. Now, go." Doors opened and closed, and there was silence.

As she eased herself back down, hoping that her sister had not heard, a whisper said, "Can I get in with you, Fanny?"

"Yes."

Edna May eased herself under Fanny's sheet and lay trembling. "He makes me call him Papa, but I'm glad he's not. He's not, is he?"

"No." Fanny patted her arm. "Sh. Sh."

The younger girl's trembling gradually ceased, and soon she breathed evenly in sleep, but Fanny lay long awake.

8

The telegrapher at Highboro's train depot was still in his twenties, and as he received the message from Savannah for Sarah Troy of Beulah Land, it provided him with no meaningful intelligence; but when he showed it to Gideon Trim, who had been stationmaster since, as people never tired of saying, Hector was a pup, the old man exclaimed, "Rotten bananas!"—an expletive he had long used to indicate that urgent action was of the essence. The message was: *Expect Mrs. Ward Varnedoe afternoon train.* Mr. Trim himself delivered it within the hour.

Sarah had not seen her sister since Lauretta married the Union commander Colonel Ward Varnedoe after the war and went to live in Maryland. They corresponded irregularly; that is, Sarah wrote promptly when she received a letter from Lauretta, and Lauretta wrote when the spirit moved her. They had mentioned visiting each other but never done so. The message struck Sarah as peculiar on two scores: its formal wording and the fact that Lauretta had never before announced that she was coming to Beulah Land but simply arrived, more often than not in dramatic, not to say melodramatic circumstances more suitable to her career upon the stage than her life off it. Distracted, Sarah ate little of her noon dinner and was on the front porch ready to go to Highboro long before Leon brought the buggy around, followed by Wally with a wagon for Lauretta's trunks. It was May and hot, and Leon would not trot the mule, there being no need to do so, though he was aware of Sarah's impatience. As it was, they were half an hour early. Leon urged her to spend the waiting time in the comparative coolness of the drugstore across the tracks from the station, but she would not, pacing back and forth before the station loungers, all of whom knew from the telegrapher why she was there.

"Thirty years, Leon! Will I know her? She's eighty-six, my sister! Impossible. Day before yesterday we were girls in Savannah, living with Aunt Pea on Broughton Street. Lauretta in love with that Shakespeare actor—Savage was his name, Douglas Savage, yes—at the playhouse on Chippewa Square. Lord, how quickly it goes. Do I look all right? You'd say so anyway, but Bruce would tell me. I hope I've warned you sufficiently what to expect. She hasn't a sane or sensible bone in her body—or used not to have. Perhaps life with the Colonel has sobered her, though I doubt it. He was a good man, though a Yankee. Everyone said she was the pretty sister and I the plain, and so she always took what she wanted, and I was left with what she didn't want. Oh, how I used to mind all that! And what does it matter, a lifetime ago? Yes, I must *steel* myself to seeing a very *old* woman. She is two years older than I, you know, and I must not show it if I am shocked by her appearance. I'm glad I didn't bring Jane and Bruce, just you. It would have looked smug. I have so many and she has no one, now the Colonel is dead and gone. No child, no grandchild—hence, naturally, no great-grandson as I have." She patted his chest. "Call her Grandma; it will make her feel welcome. No, don't; call her Miss Lauretta and flirt with her a little. That will make her feel more welcome. I don't know that she likes men, but she likes them to like her. Oh, saints and sinners, give me strength, for here it comes!—"

Yet even as the train slowed and stopped with its usual discharge of steam and creaks and clanks, Sarah had a sense of anticlimax, as if she did not really expect Lauretta to be aboard. The feeling was reinforced when no passenger came down the steps that had been set ready. But then as they waited, Sarah clenching Leon's arm, the doors of the baggage car slid open and a coffin was lowered respectfully to the baggagemen on the platform.

Sarah did not breathe as she moved forward, with Leon's hand now gripping her elbow to support her. Even the loungers stirred, some of them rising from the wooden crates they sat on. Was this then to be poor Lauretta's last "curtain call"? There was a large label on the coffin, and as her eyes registered the words, *Mrs. Ward Varnedoe in care of Beulah Land*, Sarah fainted. Because there was no bench, Leon eased her down where she was. Presently she came to and saw his anxious face above hers. She must be, she *was* lying flat on the splintery floor of the station platform alongside the coffin—sister by sister. She moaned with the thought. Then behind Leon's face, another pair of eyes gazed at her curiously. "Can it be you, Sarah? Why are you lying there like some creature in the slums of Baltimore overcome by drink? Get up and kiss me, for I surely cannot bend down there to you."

Sarah recovered abruptly, using Leon's arm to rise, then turning upon Lauretta. "How dare you!"

Lauretta blinked. "You never greeted me like that before. Aren't you glad to see me?"

"I thought you were *in there!*"

"Why should I be? They do say Sarah Bernhardt sleeps in hers, but I simply carry mine with me because at my age I never know when I'll need it. Who is this young man?"

"Leon Davis, my great-grandson."

"Mine too then. We share, although you've always had odd ideas about that sort of thing, haven't you? Howdydo, Leon; you may call me Aunt Lauretta. And this—" She waved her hand toward the black-as-coal woman who was officiously supervising the unloading of trunks from the baggage car. "This is Pearl, my own rarest Pearl who takes care of me, arranges my life, who was, in fact, the one to insist that we come and sent you the telegram. Surely you got it?" She laughed. "How could you have thought I was in there? Leon, is she getting queer? Pearl! Tell him gently with the hatbox—there are butterflies inside!" To Sarah she explained, "Gauze on black straw; you'll see; very pretty."

Every roll of the buggy wheels through town and along the road to Beulah Land brought a gush of remembrance or a question to account for a change. Arms open, she embraced every sight, mourned loss and alteration, wept happily to see it all again, as she said, "Like a sleeping princess in a fairy tale who wakes after thirty years to survey my old kingdom!" At Beulah Land there was further marveling, and her embraces were more tangibly completed. Daniel was her own dearest favorite, having guided her "home to Beulah Land" when the Yankees burned Atlanta and forced them to flee. Roman was thanked again as well as embraced, for *he* had saved her in 1861 (she would never forget that hour) from an angry audience in Philadelphia who accused her of being a Confederate spy. And there were Jane and Benjamin, Bruce and Bobby Lee and Davy to discover and be begged to love her. The house servants were agog, and Mabella thrilled to the soles of her feet, although Josephine, who remembered Lauretta, managed a more measured response.

The day went swiftly. Lauretta was settled into her room. Pearl attended to the unpacking and pressing of dresses before they were stored in the wardrobe, which, it became obvious, would be inadequate. "I'm so glad you have put me at the front so that I may know who is coming and going. I'd have been bored to suicide looking over the fields at the back. I have never been agriculturally inclined, if you remember." She asked a thousand questions without pausing for any to be answered. She laced her talk with references to her life in Maryland and visits to Washington and New York, where the Colonel had business and government interests. She mentioned sumptuous feasts that made ordinary fare as flavorless as gruel. "How I dote upon terrapin, though I shudder when I think of the poor things having to be put into the pot *alive!*" It sounded a rich and glamorous life; and if Lauretta never boasted of social eminence, still there was an assumption of being highly regarded by the world she and the Colonel had moved in. She remarked familiarly that a certain rich recluse whose name everyone knew was "as rare a sight as the wife of the Chinese ambassador." She laughed over the Colonel's insistence on her wearing the jewels he had given her, speaking with partiality of a pair of diamond earrings presented to her on their very last wedding anniversary before his death. "As beautiful as they were costly—and every time I shook my head I shook five thousand dollars."

The spell she cast over the inhabitants of Beulah Land (all, that is, except Sarah and Josephine and Nancy) continued during the days that followed her arrival. What with their hanging on her stories and the usual traffic and responsibilities of life on the plantation, Sarah had no chance of a private conversation for nearly a week. Nancy had received permission to store the coffin, covered carefully with old quilts and then burlap, in one of the barn lofts. "Before he died, the Colonel chose two that were identical, one for him, one for me. He thought of everything—almost."

Sarah asked if she wanted to store her jewels in the office safe, not that she suspected any of the house servants of being light-fingered but because Lauretta had been so fulsome in her references to their cost. "No," Lauretta said. She had not brought anything really valuable with her, only trifles; this bracelet—she held out her wrist to show it—only rhinestones. No, Sarah might keep her safe for her own jewels and money, of which Lauretta trusted there was an abundance.

"We manage tolerably."

"Tolerably! Beulah Land breathes prosperity."

"There is enough, but everyone has his job to do."

Lauretta laughed. "You mustn't expect me to pick cotton."

"Oh, that won't be until August." She said it without thinking.

"Well, I've come for a long visit. I hope I'm welcome."

"You know you are."

"You don't mind Pearl? She's so good to me, but she *is* a little bossy."

"Nancy and Josephine will keep her in her place. They take no nonsense. Do you have someone reliable looking after your house in your absence?"

Lauretta's hesitation was brief. "Oh, I've got rid of it. Being alone, you see, everything reminded me of my beloved. It was too much in all ways."

"Then where will you live?"

"I doubt that I shall go back." Lauretta laughed again. "They call themselves Southerners, but you would not think them so. They can be very sharp in their dealings and cool in their affections. They are not like us."

"When it comes to business, it's as well to be a little sharp perhaps."

"I have no head for it." Lauretta sighed. "I am an idealist. You've said as much yourself."

"Have I?" Sarah said with surprise. Lauretta was fussing contentedly with the contents of a glass slipper on her dresser top. It was full of buttons of many sizes. "I hope, Lauretta, that Colonel Varnedoe provided well for your future."

"No one could have done better than he, I suppose."

"Do you mean that now," Sarah said carefully, "you find yourself—a little at sea? Surely he'd have used a reliable firm of lawyers."

"Why yes, I believe he did, but who am I to judge? They have not managed well."

Lauretta's fussing with the slipper became pettish. "I cannot find them! I am certain I have two little buttons covered in gold silk, and I want them in the worst way for a—" Her voice trailed off.

"You'd better sit down and tell me."

Lauretta sighed and plumped herself into the chair beside Sarah's. She smiled hopefully. "You were always quick to see things. I wish I were like you in some ways. I haven't a penny."

"How can that be?"

"I don't know!"

"When the Colonel died, didn't the lawyers explain everything?"

Lauretta shrugged. "I never understand lawyers; do you?"

"Well enough," Sarah said grimly.

"There seemed no need to worry, but as time went by, the dividends were not what I thought they would be, and I spent—you would perhaps say too much—after dear Ward died. I was lonely. They had accepted me as long as he was alive, and I never knew they resented me all the time. After he was buried, they began, one by one, to neglect and then desert me. I was not invited everywhere as I had been. I thought at first it was respect for my grief, but even the callers became fewer and gradually stopped altogether."

"Had you made no true friends?" Sarah asked.

"I've never made friends with women, you know." Her eyes hardened with fright and awareness. "And I'm too old to make friends of men. Besides, the wives don't like it. And men have always—except Ward—taken advantage of me, although they've never betrayed me."

"One or two perhaps," Sarah said drily.

"I don't hold grudges."

"No," Sarah admitted, "you don't. I sometimes think it's because you have a short memory."

"Don't you think that's best?"

"It isn't a matter of choice, I suspect."

"Why are husbands taken first," Lauretta said, "leaving us alone and defenseless?"

"If the Lord had come right up to you, Lauretta, and said, 'All right, I'm going to take one of you; which shall it be?' what would you have said?"

" 'Be merciful, Lord, and take us both!' "

Sarah shook her head. "If the Lord said, 'One; which?' Take care how you answer, for they say He can see into every heart."

"You are provoking, Sarah."

"Tell me the rest of it."

Lauretta settled back again. "I saw a chance, or what looked like one, to make a great deal of money. If all had gone well, I should never have had to worry. I might have snapped my fingers at those lawyers and at those detestable Maryland biddies who had dropped me like a stone. Oh, how I should have liked that. I was tempted, and temptation has ever been my downfall. You must understand. This man—"

"Ah."

"Don't say 'ah' in that irritating way. You make me feel silly."

"You are silly."

"He was not what you think: no gold toothpick, cigars, and flattery. *I* had to approach him. When I asked if it might be possible for a poor widow to invest a little in the new silver mines he had made mention of—"

"Not silver mining!" Sarah shook her head. "I thought no one could be swindled with those again—"

"I tell you, the whole proposition was sensible."

"The lawyers, didn't they advise you?"

"Lawyers are always overcautious. Mr. Worthington said—"

"Worthington? Perfection!"

"I wish you would not try to be funny—"

"Go on," Sarah said contritely.

"There's nothing to tell. I put up a modest amount, but of course I had to turn stocks into cash to do so."

"Then you added more."

Lauretta nodded. "Finally, all. I fear a little more than all.—Sarah, I owe them seven thousand dollars, they say. Everything is gone. The Colonel should not have left things so that I was allowed to speculate."

"No," Sarah said, "but he loved you, and it would have looked like not trusting you to tie everything up."

"I wish he had!"

"You'd have abused him the rest of your life."

"I didn't want to bother you, Sarah, but Pearl made me see there was nothing else we might do. I even considered the stage again, but—"

"Pearl is right."

"I'm *so* glad you think so." Lauretta brightened. "You say I've done right by coming?"

"Of course."

"Wherever I've been, I've always known that you were here to catch me if I fell. You and Beulah Land, a haven." Lauretta rose from her chair and went to look out the window. Presently she said in a strained voice, "There is Jane, dressed as if she's going to town. I wonder if she'd have time to look for suitable buttons—" When she broke off, Sarah knew she was crying, though her back was to the room. "It's so awful to be old and poor."

Sarah rose stiffly and went to her. "None of us can avoid getting old. As for 'poor,' you've come home, and you've no need to think yourself poor."

"I haven't paid Pearl for a year."

"She will be paid," Sarah promised.

"I wish—I hate knowing they laugh at me up there and say to each other, 'I told you so.'"

"I'll have Benjamin write to the lawyers."

"If you will only tell me when we may settle accounts, I'll write to them myself."

"Let Benjamin do it. They'll do things properly if they see they're dealing with a man."

"Perhaps you're right. I'd hoped we needn't tell anyone else about it."

"Benjamin is master of Beulah Land. Nothing happens here without his knowledge."

"I thought you owned it all. One should never give away to children; if you do, they'll treat you like a child."

"Good of you to advise me."

Lauretta laughed uncertainly and blew her nose. "I feel better. They say confession is good for the soul."

"Let's go ask Jane about buttons."

9

Frankie entered the sawmill office to find Eugene behind the desk staring with concentration at nothing. "What are you doing?"

She had surprised him, and like a woods animal, he hated being surprised. "What does it look like?" He raised the revolver he held on his lap and aimed it at her head.

She hesitated only a moment. "Go ahead. That would make your score three—that I know. I don't count the darky you found with your wife, or say you found."

"You make bad jokes." He blew his breath into the barrel tip, spun the bullet chamber with a flourish, and laid the revolver on its side in a desk drawer.

"Like the time I walked in to find you fooling with yourself. You jumped like a little boy caught." She laughed shortly and took two ledgers from the shelf behind the desk.

"Better than fooling with your old bones."

"I bless the day I decided on separate rooms," she said.

"I get what I want."

She sat down at a side table and opened both ledgers flat, her back to him. "I don't mind your nigger sluts."

"It's only one until her tricks grow familiar—the way yours did. Then I have a new one. That's a thing about this county: always a crop of poontang coming ripe, no matter the season or whether it rains or shines. They all like to feel a peter between their legs, or wherever I put it. I do it all whichaways, from the front, from the back, between the tits—you sing it, Mrs., I'll dance to it." She turned pages in a ledger, checking the arrival date of an order for cypress boarding against its delivery date. She might have forgotten him, but it suited him that morning not to let her do so. "For all your I-don't-care, I reckon you miss it sometimes. I know I do it good; women can't help let me know. Some squall like dying calves."

"Contrary to your country-boy thinking, women don't enjoy that kind of talk."

His face assumed a laughter grimace, but he didn't make a sound. He allowed her to turn a few more pages in the ledger before he said, "I wonder what Priscilla Davis would be like."

"Why don't you ask her husband?" She closed both ledgers but continued to sit with her back to him, studying a wall calendar. "Are you thinking of wooing her to take my place? It occurs to me, not for the first time, that you make a habit of following after Ben Davis."

"Miss Priscilla is naught to me but a funnel for town opinion. She's got nothing to tempt me."

Frankie faced her chair toward him, crossing her legs and swinging a foot in a way she knew irritated him. "No money, no property to speak of, and a vile old crow of a mother." She nodded. "Besides, she has a husband. You might get away with killing me, although someone would be bound to remark on the coincidence in your luck; but Ben wouldn't be as obliging as his father was."

He smiled at her. "Which did you like better, father or son?"

"If it's comparisons you want, you come a poor third."

"Not everybody has your experience. My own preference is for virgins."

"I'm surprised you know any."

"I do though. Got my eye on one in particular, a sweet and pretty heifer right down the hall from where I sleep."

She rose and came slowly toward him, her head trembling on her neck as she sought to control herself. "Don't you dare think of her."

He winked. "Protective mother or jealous wife? Or only scared it'd drop her price when you're ready to sell her to Beulah Land? Something in that. Davis men don't always marry to get their stuff, as you know."

She returned to the side table and began to leaf through a letter file. "What is the gun for?"

"I'm getting some convict help."

"We talked about it and decided not to. The town would be against it, to say nothing of our own men. I'm not sure they'd work with convicts; are you?"

"They're coming tomorrow, a dozen with a guard. We feed them slops twice a day and give a few dollars to the state. More money for us. That ought to appeal to you."

"Can we risk it?"

"I stand good with people, better than you. If I tell them I have to hire such because the mill's hard up, they'll accept it."

"What kind of men will they be?"

"Niggers mainly, a white or two—but they'd only put the worst in with niggers."

"Our men won't stand for it."

"They'll have to. I'm sending the big gang from here today up to my high thousand acres to cut pine and set turpentine troughs. They'll be there a week before they start hauling down; and when they get back, they'll find the convict gang. I'll play it poor-mouth, say I had to have help in a hurry with them gone and special orders. If they don't like it, they can quit and I'll get me another gang of convicts."

"You're asking for trouble," she said.

He nodded. "Got my reasons."

"What are they?"

"Tell you sometime," he said with another wink. Rising from his chair, he stretched and farted.

"They won't like it across the creek."

"I sure hope not." He opened a drawer and took out the revolver. "Guard carries a shotgun, but I figure won't hurt to have our own protection. You know how to use it?" She shook her head. He motioned her with the revolver. "Come on, I'll show you."

The sound of regularly spaced shots drew Davy and Abraham from the factory a few minutes later. Abraham had been in the office, Davy making rounds of the factory floor. They met at the front door and looked at each other questioningly. Sometimes they heard a shot from a hunter in the woods around them, but nothing like the sounds now. Stepping out, they saw across the creek Eugene Betchley standing close behind his wife, guiding her arm and holding it steady. Then they spied a puff of smoke an instant before hearing the report. They continued to watch until she had emptied the pistol. As he reloaded, Eugene glimpsed them out of the corner of his eye; he was expecting them to show themselves. When they did nothing but stare, he waved a hand, and after a moment both young men waved back, first Davy, then Abraham.

Over the years, what had originally been the cotton mill and a few acres around it had become a settlement of cabins in which many, though far from all, of the millhands lived with their families. Such a thing had not been intended, but when one cabin was allowed, another followed and another until now there were two dozen, all small and crowded together because there was not enough land for them to spread out. The men and women who lived in these complained as soon as they saw the convicts, because of their children and old people. The day after, all the Negroes who worked at the mill were voicing objections to Davy and Abraham.

No, they had not been bothered directly, but black men working in chains (all but two were Negro, as Eugene had predicted) made them feel low in their minds and was bad for the young ones to see. There was no way to forget them, for even when they were inside they could hear above the racket of their own work the rhythmic dirges the convicts made up to keep time as they sawed and toted.

That evening when the convict gang left on the wagon, Davy crossed the creek to talk to Eugene Betchley. Eugene apologized and explained. His best men were off cutting and would be gone a week. When they came back, he probably wouldn't need the convicts. He hadn't thought about its making any difference to them at the cotton mill. Any time they had a complaint, Davy should come and say so and they would oblige, if they could, only this time they couldn't—no hard feelings. Davy reported to Abraham, and they decided they would have to wait for the week to pass, appealing to their now-sullen work force to be patient.

On the factory side of the creek outrage gave way inevitably to curiosity. At first the smaller children stood and stared, although they had been warned to keep back from the bank, not even to *look* across. One of the bolder, friendlier black men in chains called over. He enjoyed the indulgence of the guard because he worked hard and was always cheerful, thereby serving as both model and pacifier to the other convicts. Most of the children ran, but two stayed to answer, and the others crept back when they saw lightning didn't strike. Next day there were brief exchanges between two or three of the black convicts and some of the adult cotton-mill workers. It was discovered that the convicts were only men, after all, black men like them and wanting to be friendly, *not* like the white sawmill workers now absent. Among the more eager were unattached females who were always curious about men forced to live without women and ready to show sympathy if only by a smile, a quick jest, a flirt of skirt. Abraham was troubled by the development but bided his time.

Word of the convict gang at the sawmill had passed around Highboro as major news the first day they came to work, but utterance of disapproval dwindled to muttering by the second and third days because the convicts did not have to make wagon passage through Highboro to go between the sawmill and the jail at the county seat seven miles to the west. The townspeople were not directly involved, as they began to tell each other. Both sawmill and cotton mill were on the edge of the town anyway, not in it. The workers at the latter were all Negroes except for Davy Todd, who had chosen to work with them. The sawmill crew was made up normally of the town's rougher element who didn't matter much because they had tried every other way to make a living and failed at it before going to the lumber camp.

The white work gang returned on Saturday, which was payday. Although the convicts received no pay, Frankie passed out plugs of chewing tobacco and small sacks of sugar, a thing they much craved. Eugene, who had already made his payment to the county jail office for the gang's work, slipped five dollars to the guard. As if to seal the success of the venture, Priscilla Davis and Ann Oglethorpe were present to read aloud passages from the Bible and to distribute printed tracts to the convicts, none of whom, black or white, could read them. Their good work had not been solicited by Eugene Betchley; it was their own idea. But they would not have been inspired to do it had not Eugene established himself as a God-fearing man. In the present instance, they argued to their fellow citizens, he was doing positive good in employing heathenous villains outside prison walls where they might benefit from the sight and example of Christian folk.

Eugene had not planned it so, but he was gratified, and he learned from it an essential factor in successful roguery: get right with those who monitor the morals of a community and the rest is easy. The white gang of regulars might be angry, but they hardly knew with whom. And so, as they had long done, as Eugene had conditioned them to do, they looked across the creek.

10

Of the trio who had carried out the firecracker raid on Luck and Abraham's wedding, the youngest was Perry Mitchell. Since the morning he appeared asking for work, he had become something of a favorite with Eugene, because he reminded Eugene of himself when young. Eighteen, the red-haired, freckled farm boy had run away from what he called "a mean daddy" to try town life.

Eugene took him in, and since he was the youngest at the camp, the men made a pet of him, as men often will the runt of a litter. He was ignorant and saw them as experienced, responding to their rowdy manners with eager amiability; but on the evening one of them playfully tried to take his tin plate of supper from him at the mess shack, Perry knocked him down and jumped on top of him. He had to be pulled off by Eugene himself. The scuffle earned him respect. "He's no troublemaker," they now said, "but if you step on his tail, he's quick as a rattlesnake. See him?" To reward him and to confirm his manhood, they took him to a whore they all frequented and paid for his turn with her, standing around the couple to comment ribaldly on the progress of their exertions.

On Monday evening after the Saturday return of the white crew to the sawmill, Eugene discovered Perry by himself, day's work done and waiting for suppertime, sitting on the creek bank and staring across at the Negro workers drifting out of the cotton factory to go home. They exchanged no greeting, having seen each other a dozen times during the day, but Eugene's pausing seemed an invitation to talk, and the boy had something on his mind.

"Mr. Betchley, when I come begging work here, I thought them over there was as close as I'd have to work alongside niggers."

Eugene looked surprised and took a tin of cigarettes from his pocket. Putting a cigarette between his lips, he then offered Perry one, a rare and flattering gesture that disarmed the boy. Sharing a match, Eugene appeared to consider the remark. It was the first open criticism any of the regular crew had made on his hiring the convict gang, their initial displeasure having confined itself to oaths made to each other.

"You got it wrong," Eugene said, and sat down beside Perry. "Nobody telling you to work with niggers, is there? They do their job, you do yours—separate. I'd never mix and mingle my crews."

Perry stared down between his raised knees as if trying to appreciate Eugene's reasoning. "Yes, sir," he allowed finally, "but they nigh enough to stink."

"Keep on the windy side of them."

The boy nodded as if the suggestion was intended seriously.

"Nothing to worry you. You-all are my regulars and I treat you good. The convicts work for no pay; pay goes to the state—to you and me, you might say, because we're the state. When I'm through with them, I'll be getting rid of them."

"Yes, sir," Perry said, and took a long puff from his cigarette, carefully tapping ash into the creek afterwards.

Eugene smiled his quick, deliberate smile. "Get your mind on something else. — Like that over yonder. Know who she is?"

Perry shifted his eyes to see a young Negro woman, smartly turned out, driving a trap into the factory grounds across the creek. "That nigger manager's wife, I reckon."

"Ought to recognize her—it was you tried to liven up her wedding!" Eugene slapped the boy's knee. "When I was your age, only black thing on my mind was black pussy. How'd you like to lay on that one and let her rock you off to dreamland?" Unwillingly, Perry smiled too. "Better than that old woman with washboard tits they took you to, wouldn't you say?"

Luck halted the trap and jumped down, leaving the horse to mind himself. A group of three men and two women were leaving the main building. She did not know their names but was certain they would know hers. "Where's my good-looking husband? Any of you seen him, or has he already gone home to the wife he thinks is waiting?"

As they laughed together, Abraham and Davy emerged from the building, Davy wheeling his bicycle, which he kept indoors out of the weather. "What are you doing here?" Abraham demanded of Luck.

Instead of answering him, Luck continued her joke to the group of five. "Don't sound to me like he's as glad to see me as I'd hoped!" With appreciative whoops of laughter they went on their way.

"Why don't you answer *me?*" Abraham said peevishly.

"Come to take you home."

One of the leaving women turned and cried, "Tell him!" to show she had heard.

"Can't you get it through your head you're a married woman?"

"Well, I sure had better be!" Luck declared. "How you, Davy?"

Davy beamed at her. "Fat and sassy as a puppy dog teething. You're looking fine!"

"You too."

"Well, good night to you both." Davy mounted his bicycle.

"Want to hang on the side of my trap? We go straight by Beulah Land, you know."

Davy looked offended. "*I'll* be home before you're good started—make your horse look lame and blind and like every other wheel spoke is broke!"

"Don't let it rain on you—"

Davy looked up anxiously. "Do you think it will?"

"Never know about June evenings," Luck teased. "They can bring surprises." She laughed hugely.

Davy began to pump the pedals, and the bicycle shot down the road as straight as a flying bird.

When he was gone, Luck faced Abraham with her fists on her hips and a confident smile. "You mad with me, hubby?"

Abraham returned from retrieving the reins Luck had let fall to the ground when she halted the trap. "No," he said severely, his tone contradicting denial, "but you are *thoughtless*, you are *spoiled*, you act like you can say *any*thing to any*body* any *time*."

"Me?"

"Don't you know better than make fun of me with people that take my orders?"

"I wasn't," Luck protested.

"Making light; you sure were."

"*I* see." She giggled. "They won't respect you because they'll think I henpeck you. Now, is that it?"

"They know good and well your papa owns most of the mill."

"Then they ought to feel sorry for me having to buy a husband."

"I don't think anybody'll feel sorry for you, the way you behave." His voice was not yet good-humored. "I've told you, honey: better you don't come around here, or take me home. Especially now they got convicts working over there."

"They're gone," Luck said. "I passed their wagon on the road. They spoke up real nice to me, a lot nicer than you."

"You see?" he said, exasperated. "What am I supposed to do with my horse?"

"Leave him for California." California was the name of the man who swept out and locked up when everyone else had gone from the mill for the day.

"What'll he eat?"

"Cotton thread. Give him his choice, black or white."

"See how fooling you are?"

"Sure wish I had something to tell you to make your disposition sweet again. Let me see. — Oh, yes, there was a thing, if I could only remember what. You put it right out of my mind."

"You made a new pink dress. You baked a cake and made pink icing to go on top."

"No, I remember. I'm making us a new pink and black baby."

"What'd you say?"

She went to the trap and pulled herself up into it as if with great effort. As he joined her, she threw the reins into his lap. "You drive, Papa boy. I got to take care of myself and think over names to call him."

"Did you say what you said?" he insisted.

"I sure did."

"Son of a gun." He sounded out of breath.

"Maybe daughter of a gun; won't know for a while."

He put arms about her and hugged her. "You sure you're not doing a Luck-joke? If you are, I'll put you over my knee and spank you right here and now."

She held her head back to stare at him with satisfaction and interest. "Let's go home," she said finally. He picked up the reins, and as they trotted away, she leaned against him, sliding her arm about his waist.

It was dusk. On the other side of the creek Perry Mitchell was alone. He had watched them without being aware of Eugene's departure. The cigarette had gone out and he felt a little lightheaded. Occasionally he chewed tobacco, but he seldom smoked. In the near distance one of the sawmill crew raised his voice.

"Black-eyed peas *again* and the sow belly is fatter than ever!"

"You want fried chicken, you have to cross the creek and work at the cotton mill!" The cook followed his answer with a high laugh.

"Where's the youngun?" the first voice asked, and another called, "Perry, come running! Where be ye, lonesome fucker?"

11

Old adversaries will sometimes relish their jousts as much as old friends their reunions. Annabel Saxon and Lauretta Varnedoe had, or fancied they had, adequate reason to dislike one another, but their not meeting for several weeks after Lauretta's return was accident. Annabel paid few visits to the country, and Lauretta's excursions into Highboro had not involved her in stops at the old Saxon mansion. It was not until late June that they came face to face.

It was the afternoon of a fine, hot summer day. The air was alive with the ripeness of corn and melons in the fields. The eye was hypnotized by the endless rows of cotton, its tight bolls ready to burst, as they would in another week. The ear was charmed by the wind in the trees and the occasional buzz of all but satiated bees as they stumbled in and out of flowers like tipplers leaving a wineshop. The sweet-briny aroma from the kitchen quarters tickled nose and made tongue water, for Josephine was putting up cucumbers in quart and half-gallon jars for winter consumption.

The four entertaining themselves on the shady side porch had gathered with no plan after rest followed noon dinner. Casual comment became reminiscence, and a reference to dancing sent Bruce to her room to fetch her guitar. She was playing it; Lauretta was clapping her hands; and Roman and Sarah were doing a sort of polka that took them from one end of the porch to the other, when Annabel arrived in her buggy. They continued while she handed over horse and buggy to Clarence, the stableboy who had come running, his ears catching the sound of strange wheels. Mounting the steps, Annabel glowered at the scene before her, and as Sarah and Roman swept past without so much as a nod to acknowledge her presence, she cried, "Unseemly!" and plunked herself into a rocking chair with one cracked rocker. It broke under her weight, and she listed like a sinking ship. Guitar, dancing, clapping stopped, laughter taking their place. Recollecting themselves, Sarah went to help Annabel to a sturdier chair beside Lauretta's; Bruce offered to bring iced tea; and Roman announced solemnly that he must finish a poem he had begun that morning. Fixing Lauretta with challenging eyes, Annabel said, "Well, ma'am, I'd heard you were back again."

"Happily back," Lauretta agreed, "with my dear sister who is pleased to call her great plantation my home too."

"Indeed." Annabel laughed rudely. "I thought we'd seen the last of you when you married the enemy colonel and went North to live among them."

"During the years of my exile," Lauretta confided, "the faces of old friends here would sometimes rise in memory to sadden me, but yours was not among them."

"I am glad you were spared the melancholy."

"I should never have recognized you, ma'am. You have altered beyond anything. Once so pretty, everyone said. And then what they called a handsome woman. But now—what tragedies we may live to see reflected in our own mirrors!"

"I am astonished that age has left you vision enough to see the tragedies in yours."

"It has, dear madam; otherwise, how might I know what you have come to? Sarah dear, you might have warned me—"

"You haven't been to church since your descent upon us, or I'd have observed you. Are you very infirm?"

"At my time one has little need of spiritual guidance. It is too late to ask the vital questions and too early to expect final answers."

Shifting her chair so that she sat between them, Sarah said, "I declare, you are better together than a play. What brings you, Annabel?"

Annabel frowned and stirred the air with the palmetto fan she had found on the wide arm of her rocker. "What is Josephine cooking at such an hour? It smells horrendous."

"Cucumber pickles."

"Delia puts alum in mine. See that you give me a couple of jars when you have done turning them to the light to admire them!"

Annabel laughed at her own wit, although neither of her companions did, and Bruce returned with a tray on which were glasses, a pitcher of iced tea, and a plate of sliced pound cake. She served her elders and excused herself, saying there was sewing she must attend to. Annabel and Sarah and Lauretta sipped their tea and nibbled their cake, and Annabel, who had watched the girl while she was present, observed, "The hot weather draws out the redness of her scar. Without it she would be almost pretty."

"She is pretty as she is," Sarah declared firmly.

Annabel continued. "A pity it isn't the fashion for ladies to wear mustaches."

Through cake crumbs, a few of which took to the air, Lauretta said, "I knew a woman once whose beard was as heavy as Lincoln's."

"All of us have not the advantage of your theatrical background."

"Nothing to do with my years on the boards," Lauretta replied. "She was the widow of a senator and had a fortune in copper. The only disadvantage, she used to say, was that people couldn't see her pearls for the beard."

"You don't mean to say she appeared in public with it?"

"What was she to do? She enjoyed society and disliked shaving. She solved it by parting the beard and wearing it in two plaits. You could see the pearls perfectly well then."

When Annabel stared at her wordless, Sarah said, "I think Lauretta is teasing us."

"What odd fancies possess the elderly," Annabel said. Her tone was deceptively casual as she went on, "By the way, I understand from my husband that Benjamin recently transferred a sizable sum of money to a law firm in Maryland." Facing Lauretta, she said, "That was your last roosting place, I believe, ma'am?"

"Yes, I—Benjamin was settling a business affair for me. A temporary arrangement—"

Sarah said, "Blair had no right to tell you that."

"My dear Auntie Sarah," Annabel said placidly, "you well know there is little of importance at the bank I don't hear of one way or another."

"I shall speak to him."

"It wipes you out of ready money, doesn't it?"

"Certainly not," Sarah said, "as you would know if your spying had been really thorough."

"Don't be offended, Auntie. I understand how rich you are in land and crops, and I'm not forgetting certain shares and bonds, but it would be madness to touch those. I hope you won't have to."

"How is Blair Three progressing with his law studies?" Sarah asked, and Annabel launched enthusiastically into a preening of herself and her grandson. Lauretta nibbled her cake again, but in a troubled way. Sarah exerted herself to nod and smile. When the subjects of Blair Three's brilliance and promise had been explored more thoroughly than her listeners cared about, Annabel asked, "What are you going to do about her?"

Alert to defend the fortress again, Sarah said, "Who?"

"Bruce, of course."

"How do you mean?"

"She's sixteen. Has she any prospects or offers?"

"I hope not," Sarah said.

"You don't know. That means there haven't been any, for girls are always ready to boast of them. Well, she isn't likely to be really pursued, even with Beulah Land behind her. Things are so peculiarly arranged among you all, it's hard to know who owns what and holds the power."

"It isn't a question that much concerns us," Sarah said, "and there's *no* reason it should concern you. Our only rule is that two of us must sign a document that binds us all."

"Now you're huffing at me again when all I've done is express concern over the child's prospects. Benjamin *is* your grandson; I think we are all agreed about that." She smiled complacently, but Sarah and Lauretta exchanged a look. "Bruce *is* his daughter; no question there. But Leon is his son, not legitimate but legitimized. Where does that leave Bruce and her expectations? Any suitor will want to know."

"When she decides to marry, she will choose someone who won't be looking at her chances of an inheritance. She isn't likely to be the target of fortune hunters, and if she were, is too sensible to be deceived."

Lauretta, who was fond of matchmaking and had remained cautiously quiet for longer than she enjoyed, said, "It's my belief she'll choose someone close to home."

Ready to welcome even an unexpected ally, Annabel began to smile with gratification, then asked, "Who do you mean, ma'am?"

"Both of Jane's boys pay her particular attention."

"They're close cousins, so that won't do," Annabel said. "Her looks would not be entirely against her as the wife of a politician or statesman. Indeed, it is better that a woman in such a position not be too pretty; it loses votes for the man. My Blair is a cousin too, but less close."

Lauretta had been pondering. "Davy and Bobby Lee aren't all that close."

Annabel laughed indulgently. "Of course they are; you're forgetting. My great-grandfather Benjamin Davis had two sons, Bonard and Bruce. You ran away to California with Uncle Bonard and let him die there, so you should remember him; and later you set your cap for my father Bruce, and you ought to remember *him*."

"He wasn't interested in me," Lauretta said. "It was Sarah he wanted to marry."

"No such thing!"

"Tell her," Lauretta urged Sarah.

Sarah shrugged as if in apology. "I didn't take it seriously. It was after Leon died and before Casey came back."

"Well, *I* never knew!" Annabel exclaimed.

"Now you do," Lauretta said demurely. "Would you like us to go on explaining relationships?"

"Thanks to you, Uncle Bonard had no children—"

"Nothing to do with me," Lauretta said. "I could have had children. In fact, did."

"None you can admit to, I'll vow."

"Rachel was mine, wasn't she, Sarah?"

"You bore her, but she was *mine*," Sarah said judiciously. "After all, Leon was her father."

Annabel closed her mouth, then opened it again to say, "There must have been scandal—"

"Not much," Sarah said. "Of course I was vexed for a while."

"I should think so!" Annabel turned belligerently upon Lauretta. "To continue: my mother had four of us. Doreen doesn't count because she didn't marry. Adam died young before he could. James married—Rachel."

"My daughter," Lauretta said.

"And mine," Sarah repeated.

"Well, you're sisters, so let's say it doesn't matter to the *bloodline*. Then Rachel and James had two children, Benjamin and Jane."

Sarah choked on the cake she had begun to nibble again. When she could speak, she said gleefully, "*You're* forgetting. Benjamin's father wasn't James, but Adam. So Jane and Benjamin are only half brother and sister like Bruce and Leon."

"But their fathers were brothers!" Annabel declared desperately. "That makes Bobby Lee and Davy and Bruce and Leon—oh, God in heaven!" She left her chair and began to shout through the open doorway for someone to send her buggy around.

Lauretta and Sarah were silent until Sarah said, "Don't forget my Fourth of July party—it's a family reunion, you know." The sisters dissolved in laughter as Annabel withdrew from the porch with what dignity she could assume to wait for her horse and buggy on the brick walk.

When she had gone, they leaned their heads back in the rocking chairs and rested a little while. Sarah said, "Annabel always tires me out."

Lauretta asked, "Is it true about the money, Sarah? Have you enough? I'm so miserable about it—"

"It's nothing for you to worry about," Sarah assured her. "Annabel just likes to talk. No good my speaking to Blair One. She could twist secrets out of Torquemada."

12

For the first time anyone could remember it rained on the Fourth of July, not steadily but hard enough and often enough to keep the family party at Beulah Land under shelter. The house was large, with many rooms, and the porches were broad and long. The women and girls commanded the comforts of these; the men and boys had the excuse of dawdling in the barns, which they preferred anyway. Old Otis had, as usual, superintended the barbecuing even though he was ailing, but the two younger men who helped him this year had to rig a canvas roof over the smoldering pits when the rain began at dawn and looked likely to continue.

As the guests arrived, Lauretta was made much of, to Annabel's vast annoyance, for many of the young ones of the large family had never seen her at all, only heard hushed references to the adventures of the old lady who now sat in the midst of them so mild and twinkling. Annabel, counterattacking, bludgeoned everyone with details of her new Turkish Corner—actually a small room off her large living room. She and Blair Three had made two train journeys to Savannah already, first to ransack shops and pore over catalogues, second to inspect the furnishings ordered from New York when they finally arrived. Blair had, she boasted, done it all. It was, in fact, his idea, and with old Judge Meldrim in Atlanta for the summer (his married daughter), he was free of his law studies to give the Turkish Corner his entire attention. The project had filled many happy hours for them both. Tiring of the recital of glories they might all be privileged to admire in the fullness of time, Lauretta declared after two vehement yawns that Turkish Corner had been "the thing" among her acquaintances in the East "a few years ago" but that she and they were now "quite bored by them," and even the best of them had reminded her of nothing so much as "the parlor rooms of a nookie house."

Annabel broke the thrilled silence that followed this remark by stating that the elderly should not presume on the indulgence of their juniors to the point of arrogant coarseness and that perhaps the younger members of the company should be removed from Miss Lauretta's influence for their own good. As for her—if Miss Lauretta meant what she thought she meant—she did not believe there was anyone present, male or female, who had the frame of reference to appreciate the comparison—save, evidently, Miss Lauretta herself. Sarah stood ready to douse any further fire, but that was as far as it went, Blair Three comforting Annabel with the whisper, "The old crone is really too grotesque for society." There was, however, no more talk that day of Annabel's Turkish Corner, and Lauretta did not suffer for want of an audience for her further anecdotes.

Luck and Abraham and Roscoe attended the family celebration, Luck abloom with pride of pregnancy and begging everyone to tell her how big she was getting. They smiled and obliged her, although her figure was as yet no fuller than were those of her contemporaries who had nothing in the way of her expectations. Luck and Fanny and Bruce spent much of the day in Bruce's room weaving small plans and big dreams in the way of women absorbed by samples and scraps of clothing materials and drawings illustrating the magazines they followed. The wetness of the windowpanes only reminded them of their snug isolation from the world.

Roscoe and Abraham passed most of their day in one or another of the barns, not much attending the cattle they were pretending to inspect, or the hogs at whom they aimed occasional dry cobs, but reviewing the affairs of the cotton gin and the cotton factory, in particular the way the factory was affected, indeed threatened, by the sawmill.

The conflict between the two was surely, they decided, coming to a head. Never friendly, relations had deteriorated to the trigger point of danger. Because of their color, the convict laborers had been provisionally accepted by the factory workers, who knew that shackles prevented contact more intimate than a few suggestive remarks. They felt sorry for them and were inclined to disregard if not condone verbal approaches to their females. The new situation had, however, altered an old one. Whereas before there had been few words between the white sawmill workers and the cotton-mill hands, the whites were beginning to copy and enlarge upon sallies made by the convicts they despised. In brief: white men were shouting crude invitations across the creek to any tolerably comely female who came in view. Soon or late, and sooner than later, Roscoe feared, there would be a fight, possibly a killing.

They talked of ways to avoid confrontation. Davy and Abraham had already spoken to Eugene without effect. He smiled his frozen smile at Davy and said that human nature was beyond him, and what could anyone do? Abraham, he merely stared at until Abraham went away. Roscoe would not approach the lumber camp. Benjamin was reluctant to do so, having ordered Eugene away from Beulah Land at the time of his intrusion with Mrs. Oglethorpe. The dilemma was resolved in a way Benjamin only later guessed had not been happenstance.

Frankie, with little aptitude for what she considered the inconsequential concerns of her own sex, was not popular with them and tended to drift at such a gathering. Benjamin encountered her during a rainless half hour sitting on the surround-bench of one of the old oak trees, alone. "Isn't it damp for you?"

"No matter," she said quietly.

He sat down beside her. He had been a little surprised at her joining them today, for although she was often invited, it was understood that when she came it would be without her husband. In recent years she seldom went anywhere in the social way. Most of her acquaintances were resigned to her neglect of them. Of those at Beulah Land only Leon and Bruce continued to call at Frankie's house in town. It appeared to Benjamin that Frankie had deliberately cut herself off and that she showed the effects of a too constant reliance upon her own company. She was like a rope pulled tight: he marveled that she held, even as he waited for her to snap. To try to dissolve her gravity he said, "You choose not to loosen your stays and rest with the other ladies."

"I use stays no more, and nothing is more boring than to lie down in a communal bedroom with snoring women."

He laughed to encourage her. "I have never done so."

She did not laugh with him, but she seemed to relax, he thought. "Besides, I require little rest."

"You work too hard."

"I like to know what is happening."

The opportunity was too clear to ignore. He began to explain the fears they felt of trouble between the sawmill crews and the factory people. She listened carefully, nodding but making no comment until he had finished, whereupon she said, "I was against hiring convicts, but it has worked well enough, I've had to admit. There is no friction between them and our whites; they ignore each other. I'm surprised at the white men annoying your women. They do not do so in front of me."

He assured her that it happened often, that even Luck had been challenged when she came and went to the factory to see Abraham.

Suddenly her face softened and she put a hand on his. "Poor Ben—you who so easily should understand the appeal of the dark ladies! — I've shocked you." She patted his hand briskly and withdrew hers to her lap. "There is always bad feeling between your factory and our sawmill. If it weren't this thing, it would be another. The only solution, I expect, is for you to go somewhere else, or for us to. I believe Eugene was wise and farseeing that time: I should not have sold you the land you needed to expand. Then you'd have moved and we'd all be easier in our skins. By now, moving for either of us would involve a good deal of money. I've thought about it, I'm ready to admit." She paused a long time, and when she spoke again, it was as if reluctantly. "I think I know a solution, but Eugene is against it and would need a great deal of persuading."

"Tell me."

She outlined a plan by which the cotton factory would buy the land presently occupied by the sawmill. The sawmill would move to a new location on the other side of town, down the railroad tracks. A short sidetrack might be laid from the main tracks to the new location so that the shipping of lumber would be simplified.

The plan interested Benjamin and he said so. He would consult his partners if she would talk further with Eugene. Did she know, he wondered, who owned the land she had in mind as a new location for the sawmill?

"You do," she said.

When the exact acreage was made clear, he acknowledged that it was his. He and Sarah had acquired it after one of their richer harvests and left it untenanted because it was rocky and nearly bare, unfit for farming and unpromising for grazing livestock. They'd not bought it but taken it in a swap for a farm they owned in a remote part of the county, thinking one day to sell it in lots if the town grew that way.

"I see no obstacle. I'll certainly talk to Leon and Grandma about it."

"Leon?"

"We make no decisions without him now."

Saying she would present the advantages of the move to her husband again, she rose. "We mustn't be seen sitting together for so long. The others will begin to stir and wonder, perhaps be jealous."

Together they walked toward the house. "It's beginning to sprinkle again," he said.

"Is Nancy jealous?"

He forced a laugh as if she had meant a joke. "When are you going to allow Fanny to marry Leon?"

"*I* do not forbid her. — So you think I grudge her winning so easily what I was denied."

"No one denied you anything. You chose Bonard and left me with a sore heart."

"Has Leon been complaining to you?"

"We talk. He hopes; but it seems Fanny won't come to the point."

"It's nothing to do with me, you see."

"She would agree if you encouraged her."

"I've no stomach for matchmaking."

"The match is made. Only the timing is in question. Fanny won't set it because she is reluctant to leave you and her sister. — Why don't you *all* come?" he suggested exuberantly, cheered as he was by the possibility of settling the problem of the factory and the sawmill.

"Eugene too? I can't see Miss Sarah welcoming us, to say nothing of your faithful Nancy—even if she is not jealous. Is it because you give her no cause?"

"Frankie, don't," he said.

"I am a shocking woman. Doesn't everyone say so?"

When she went home at the end of the day, she was able to report to Eugene that his plan was working out as he had foreseen. They went upstairs together, and at her door he said, "You've done well. Do you want me to come to bed with you?"

"My reward?" She shook her head.

He smiled. "I could pretend you are Fanny."

Leaving him in the hall, she entered her room and slid the bolt.

13

The porch was a comfortable sitting height from the ground, and Leon's feet touched earth while the rest of him was supported by the porch. He lay flat on his back, face covered by a wide-brimmed straw hat, ragged at the edges from a summer's use in the fields and sweated to softness. He might have been dead, so still was he except for the slight rise and fall of his chest. It was the end of day, the end of August, almost the end of summer, and he was aching tired. He'd picked two hundred and sixteen pounds of cotton that day, a good amount for any man; the record day's pick was two hundred and forty-four pounds. He didn't usually pick, but it was the peak of the harvest and every hand was useful. After weighing the yields and entering a sum against each picker's name in the record book he carried in his hip pocket, he had come to the porch to wait for his father, instead of accompanying Daniel and Bobby Lee to the creek to wash and cool off. Benjamin had taken a buggy into town after noon dinner, according to Nancy, who always knew where he was, and he had directly joined his grandmother in the office on returning a quarter hour ago.

A few feet from Leon, Hellfire was washing himself. He was now grown but in Mabella's phrase "had yet to fill out." Up went a hind leg like a salute. The sudden bolt-upright rigidity always made Leon laugh, and as if remembering this, the cat paused, flicked his ears, and gazed at the young man disapprovingly. He did not like to see him asleep and usually woke him when he discovered him so. Slowly he lowered his leg without washing it and shook his head. Walking deliberately over, he began to sniff delicately at Leon's curled fingers. As he woke from the shallow sleep of fatigue, Leon thought it must be night until he recognized the straw hat's sweaty smell, a little like that of boiled peanuts.

"That tiger's about to eat you up."

He removed the hat and raised himself on an arm to see Sarah and Benjamin looking down at him from the office doorway.

"Scat." Hellfire hightailed it off the porch and around the house.

"Come on in here with us." Benjamin held the door open and Leon followed, sprawling in the chair he usually took when they were there together. "Eugene has finally said he'll talk about selling."

Leon studied his father's face briefly. "It took him a while to make up his mind."

Sarah shook her head as if to rid it of gnats that plagued them so in August. "I never liked Frankie's acting the go-between."

"You've just never liked or trusted Frankie," Benjamin told her.

"No more do I now," Sarah admitted, "so I'm glad Eugene has come into the open. Not that they won't have their heads together."

"They're married," Benjamin reminded her, "as well as running the sawmill business together."

She thought about it. "There's something I don't understand."

"Well," Benjamin said to Leon, "he's ready to talk, and he wants to do his talking with you."

"Me?" Leon was astonished, for although he was part of their business discussions as well as the day-to-day operation of the plantation, he had never been singled out for such responsibility.

Sarah said to Benjamin, "Frankie's told him the way we do things. I can see why he wants Leon to come to him. He's afraid of me and he can't abide you. He also hates colored people—I don't know why, but white trash like him always do—and he won't consider selling his old site to Roscoe and Abraham. Won't deal with them at all, so it's up to us."

Leon said slowly, "Him and me aren't friends either."

"No, but he imagines he's superior to you," Benjamin said.

Sarah said, "You're to go see him tomorrow morning. That's the message your papa brought home from Miss Frankie."

Leon sat thinking about it as Benjamin said, "You listen to what he says and we'll talk about it when you come home. You won't have to settle anything on the spot; he knows that. On the other hand, you can surely tell him as much as we can."

"Yes, sir." Leon looked from his father to Sarah. "Yes, ma'am."

"Let's go to the creek," Benjamin said.

"Wish I could go with you," Sarah said.

"Well, you can't," Benjamin told her, and the three smiled for the first time.

The next morning Leon saddled a horse and rode to the sawmill. He had never been there, only observed it from the other side of the creek. He'd seen Eugene irregularly but often during the years he was growing up, could indeed remember to the month his age when he was able to say to himself, "Now I'm as big as he is." With the memory of the time the man had beaten the young boy almost to death, they were wary of each other, and when they met briefly at church or on Leon's visits to Fanny, tensely watchful.

At a little distance he saw Theodore Betchley talking to three men who were trimming a cypress log. One of the men stopped and motioned, and Theodore looked up. Leon removed his hat and waved it, but the boy made no return gesture, only said something to the men, whereupon one of them laughed and spat and, detaching himself from the little group, came to meet Leon. "If you're looking for the office," Perry Mitchell said, "why, it's yonder." He pointed. Perry worked shirtless in the heat, freckled back and shoulders running with dirty sweat and smudged with his own hand marks where he'd slapped mosquitoes and rubbed their bites.

Through the open doorway Eugene saw Leon approaching, but they proceeded formally. Leon knocked; Eugene called, "Come in," without getting up from his chair at the flat table he used as a desk. He was alone.

Entering, Leon said, "Miss Frankie told Papa you'd be expecting me."

Eugene pretended to suddenly recollect. "Yes, so she did. Take a chair if you want to."

Leon sat down facing the man at the table and keeping his hat on his lap. "You've talked over an idea she put to Papa about moving the sawmill to another place."

Eugene smiled; the smile set, then disappeared as quickly as it had come. "She thinks we ought to accommodate you, but I can't see doing it unless you make it a whole lot to my advantage. Let me hear how you tell it."

Leon and Benjamin and Sarah had discussed the plan often during the last few weeks, and it was easy for Leon to review it simply and clearly. Eugene studied his hands folded on the table, opening them, flexing fingers lightly, scratching resin off a thumbnail, frowning, appearing to consider, his expression now doubtful, now bored and amused, not at Leon's recital but as if he remembered something that had nothing to do with the topic under discussion, so that Leon sometimes had the feeling he might not be listening. But then the hands folded themselves again; the older man nodded and sighed and shrugged.

When Leon stopped talking and waited a full minute, determined to say no more until the other responded, Eugene cleared his throat importantly. "I can see some advantage to me about the shipping, since most of my lumber goes to Savannah for the office there to reroute. But let me tell you again: I can't waste my time moving unless you-all at Beulah Land are prepared to make it worthwhile. Way I see it, I've had this land many years, since not so long after your ma died. Everybody knows where to find me; a blind mule could bring a load of pine without nobody leading him. Then too, I hate the notion of giving up my place here to niggers' use, and that's how it's going to look unless I got something mighty big to show. You want them to take this over and us to go. Well now, Mrs. Betchley is on your side, I reckon you know." He laughed indulgently. "Have to admit it. She's more on your side than mine in this matter. Makes me feel plum lonesome. But while Mrs. Betchley is on your side, she's also got a quick eye for the passing of money, as maybe you've noticed. Just how much you figure your pa and old Mrs. Troy are willing to turn loose?"

"You'd better tell me what you have in mind about that," Leon countered.

"Then you'll say yes or no?" Eugene smiled at him mockingly.

"No, Mr. Betchley. I'll go tell them, and we'll talk it over, and I'll come back."

"Oh." Eugene looked sly. "I thought me and you was going to do this negotiating ourselves, you such a grown man and all. But *I* see, you're just the—" He opened his hands and turned them palms up. "No offense meant, naturally."

Leon's face burned enough to show beneath its weathering. "We generally agree on what to do."

"That's good." Eugene affected reassurance. "That's just fine." He looked around the rough office like a man who hates to think of leaving a place he's used to. "Lot of trouble for me, and it'd have to wait a month till I get out some hurry-up orders. Let me put it square to you. The sawmill gets that piece of land up the railroad tracks, so we're out of everybody's way and your niggers can expand their business or just use my old property—all this here—for a watermelon patch if they want to, though I don't reckon they'll be doing that. Anyway, you, they, whoever—takes my place over and I take that land of your papa's; but an even swap's not to my advantage, way I figure it. I got to have me something more. Let's say: I get yours, you get mine, and you-all give me five thousand dollars to sweeten the sadness of leaving."

Leon had cautioned himself not to react openly; even so, he sat blinking in surprise for a few moments. "You mean that, Mr. Betchley?"

"Sure do." Eugene's voice was firm. "Unless you want to offer me more?"

"That's a lot more than anybody could say it's worth, Mr. Betchley."

"Well, 'anybody' ain't doing the bargaining—Mr. Davis."

Leon turned his hat on his lap. "You're asking two hundred and fifty dollars an acre for a worked-out creek bank."

"No, you're the ones doing the asking; I'm doing the answering. I'm talking cash money, not a promise to pay. Unless you want to put up a piece of Beulah Land against the price. That might make a further talking point."

"Beulah Land is not for sale, Mr. Betchley."

"There, you see? I know how you feel, though you wasn't exactly born to it. People get attached to a place a stranger mightn't see as all that valuable, get their own ideas as to what it's worth. You go talk to the boss man and the boss lady, then come back and see me if you want to. I don't much care either way."

Leon nodded grimly and rose from his chair. "Good day to you, Mr. Betchley."

Eugene put on his smile. "I'll expect you when I see you, Mr. Davis."

The sight of a Davis, or anyone from Beulah Land, at the sawmill had been unknown for so many years the men paused at their work to watch as Leon walked his horse out the way he had come. There was no sign of Theodore, but Perry Mitchell stopped work and leaned lightly on his saw, eyes on the horse and rider.

Sarah and Benjamin were waiting in the office at Beulah Land, and Leon quickly told them Eugene Betchley's terms.

"The whole parcel isn't worth five hundred," Benjamin said.

"He knows how much we want it," Sarah said. "Frankie will have told him that, if he needed telling. What must we do?"

"Tell him to keep his land," Leon suggested.

Sarah sighed unhappily. "If only Lauretta's debt hadn't come the same year. That's twelve thousand dollars cash, and cotton bringing the lowest price I can remember."

"You're not even considering it, are you, Grandma?"

"We've gone this far. If we can do so much for Lauretta, we must do it for Abraham."

"Aunt Lauretta's us," Benjamin said. "It's a question of family pride."

"Abraham is family too," Sarah said. "Floyd was his father, and we owe Floyd's son anything we can give him."

"If he understood it, he wouldn't let you do it," Leon said.

"Then we mustn't let him know."

"It means tight living for a long time and watching every penny."

"We've done that before. It also means being rid of Eugene Betchley. How dare that scoundrel even *talk* of taking a part of Beulah Land!"

Benjamin said, "Grandma, I don't think we can do it. After Aunt Lauretta's debt, we're short. We've got a lot of cotton nobody wants to pay even what it cost us to grow it."

"We'll find a way. We've been worse off than now."

"Not since the war," Benjamin said.

"Without Floyd we'd not have survived that."

They sat quietly until Leon said, "All we've talked about is Abraham. I know how you feel about him and Uncle Floyd, Grandma. We all know, and we all feel that way. But if we do this thing, I don't think it should be just for Abraham."

"What are you suggesting?" Sarah asked.

"That Davy should own a part."

"Davy's just a—"

"Davy's a man," Leon said, "and he's our family too. Bobby Lee will come into his papa's lot one day, so Davy has to be thought about."

His father and his great-grandmother looked at each other with surprise before they smiled.

14

The heat of early September was no letup on that of August; but as the days passed, there was a gradual relaxing of harvest fever. Except for a scattering, the cotton was picked and ginned, with many bales still stored at the gin because no one was eager to buy, and the warehouse was full. Nights became a little cooler, and the younger folk turned their minds to the country frolicking there would be when the sugarcane was cut in quantity and its juice boiled into syrup.

Annabel Saxon held a series of social evenings to show off the completed Turkish Corner, managing frugally by serving sugarcane juice and thin dry cakes, the recipe for which, she claimed, had come to her "almost directly" from Byzantium. When inviting those at Beulah Land, she employed exaggerated winks and a voice to trumpet the dead awake on Resurrection Day: "*Of course, those who have seen so many Turkish Corners, however inferior, and care to see no more may not feel any compulsion to attend!*" In the event, Lauretta begged Sarah to say she was too engrossed in rereading Deuteronomy to set foot out of the house. She spent the evening playing cards with Roman, cheating and losing.

Annabel's final entertainment honored those acquaintances nearest Blair Three's age. In spite of the enjoyment of his grandmother's company during the summer months, Blair had been lonely for his own kind. Despairing of discovering a patrician soul among the plebeians of Highboro, he had written desperate letters to former college friends, receiving few replies, for all their shared allegiance to the spirit of Pater and Wilde. Warmed by Annabel's confidence that any suit of his would be met by a grateful response, look where he might, he had determined to ask Bruce

Davis to become his wife. He was not inspired by passion but had decided with his grandmother's encouragement to settle himself in anticipation of rising into the majestic realms of the law. He did not look to an early marriage but saw a long engagement to his young cousin at Beulah Land as a step toward independence and consequence.

He and Annabel had thought of this final party as the occasion of his making his proposal. The guests duly arrived. Hands respectfully behind backs, they inspected the wonderful room. The low seating, the prevalence of velvet and abundance of cushions, the brass trays and ornamental tapestries were much admired, as was the dying palmetto wrenched from its swamp home and transplanted to an urn to pose as palm. The long blade displayed on one wall discreetly in shadow, Annabel called a scimitar, although it was no more curved than any common sword and the initials of the Confederate States of America might be seen on its hilt by any who leaned and squinted. However, the whole effect was declared a marvel, the young party subsequently repairing to the dining room to find there a supply of thin cakes and cane juice.

They were fifteen altogether, mainly family connections, for Blair Three was not popular with his local contemporaries. There were, however, a sprinkle of those not kin interspersed with the familiar presences of Bruce and Leon Davis, the Todd brothers, Fanny Saxon and Edna May Davis, and the daughters of Prudence and Blair Two Saxon, whose names were Clementine and Amaryllis. They were not so few then as to make a mean gathering nor so many as to become careless and destructive. They fidgeted more than they might have done elsewhere and tended to laugh at anything that could be thought even remotely amusing. They looked furtively at clocks and wondered when they might take their leave and who would dare be first to break free. Neither Annabel nor Blair Three possessed the happy gift of making a guest feel welcome. With his mission in mind, Blair was less talkative than usual and stayed close to Bruce, which made her nervous and Davy Todd suspicious. When the host, flatly and without finesse, invited Bruce to return to the Turkish Corner for reasons that would become clear to her, Davy slipped after them.

The sliding doors between living room and Turkish Corner had been removed and standing screens substituted, the panels of which showed infidels gushing with blood as they toppled off minarets at the moment of capture by Christian knights accompanied by languid greyhounds. Davy kept a distance while Blair directed Bruce to compose herself on a nest of cushions for the most important occasion of her life. When he set the screens as a wall between them and the world, Davy crept closer and, concealed by the screens, heard all.

"Is it some kind of new game?" Bruce asked, surprise veering to concern.

"No," said Blair Three. "I am about to offer you the most precious gift a man may offer a woman." Bruce stared at him. "My name."

"Thank you," Bruce said, "but I have a perfectly good one myself. All things considered, including the fact that 'Bruce' generally indicates a man or boy, I like it because Papa insisted on giving it to me. You've probably never known a girl before who likes her name, have you? Most of them say they hate theirs so that whoever hears will tell them how pretty it is, like birdsong, or bees in clover, or faraway bells—"

"You don't understand," Blair interrupted her. "The thing I am about to propose is one we both shall remember forever. I have made up my mind to marriage. That is, I do not plan or desire to be married soon, but Grandmother and I have talked it over and decided the time has come to settle the future. You will agree and be flattered by the confidence when I tell you I am certain to rise from the law into politics, eventually perhaps to be—"

"But you've only begun to read the law with Judge Meldrim. Must you plan so far in advance?"

"I daresay most young men would not; the wiser do. I do not profess a great love for you, the sort the poets rhyme, the stuff of troubadours. Nor, possibly, do you entertain such a regard, as yet, for me. Nevertheless, an alliance between us would emphatically be to your advantage. You are, after all, a girl. That is to say, unlike your half brother Leon, you are not going to inherit very much, although it is no bad thing to have what Beulah Land stands for behind you. — Then too, there is your disfiguration, no trifle if you were to count solely upon charm of appearance to win a place in life. But Grandmother and I, Grandmother particularly, see some virtue even in that flaw, for plain ladies, so she tells me, are assumed to be above reproach and that will be advantageous in the wife of a governor, or even—who is to say not?—a senator or cabinet minister, even if the presidency is too much to hope for a Southerner nowadays."

"Stop, Blair."

"How you blush! That is a sign of virtue too, we think. You are obviously overcome by what I have suggested."

"I am flabbergasted."

"I understand. Let me tell you that *I* should not have thought of you at all if Grandmother had not—"

Blair was again stopped in mid-thought, not this time by words, nor by the action of one hand, or even two, but by four. In front of him, Bruce picked up a brass tray as she rose and brought it down smartly upon Blair's head as she attained elevation. Behind him, Davy abandoned subterfuge and tipped over the screens. Hands grasped both shoulders to spin Blair around, and not tenderly either.

"Saracen!" Davy called him, and smacked him on the jaw.

Not given to endure alone and suffer in silence, Blair screamed, and the trio was almost instantly joined by the entire company from the dining room, led by Annabel with a grandmother's anxiety for the cry of her innocent.

Consternation was followed by contradictory half explanations from Bruce and Davy and Blair, but the essentials of the situation which had brought them all together so quickly were comprehended. Blair was comforted and led away by Annabel while the others stole guiltily but delightedly back into the dining room, where they had abandoned their Byzantine cakes and half-drunk sugarcane juice. In a little while Annabel returned, but Blair Three did not. The hostess told the guests coldly that her grandson was unwell and that the party was over. Meekly, they spoke their thanks and regrets and left the house.

Bruce, who might have claimed some justification for mild hysteria, was furiously calm. Davy was puzzled and garrulous, but some deeper instinct kept him at Bruce's side, and when Leon, who had driven her to the party in his buggy, said he would take her home, Davy announced curtly that Leon might attend Fanny and Edna May if he so pleased and that *he* would see that Bruce returned home safely and with no more ado. Leon pointed out that he had only his bicycle, whereupon Bruce declared that she had ridden many times on the handlebars and that she should like nothing better than to do so at this moment.

To the further astonishment of the little party sidling about indecisively on the boardwalk in front of the Saxon mansion, she proceeded to do just that, sitting the bars as graciously as another might have sat the tamest mare, while, chest high with pride and importance, Davy spun the wheels through town toward the road to Beulah Land. Bruce wore a hat which their propulsion forced her to hold with one hand, but they pedaled along prettily enough, to the amusement of the many they passed, who told each other what several generations of the town had told one another, that there was no accounting for the behavior of anyone who lived at Beulah Land.

When they had left Highboro behind, Davy, who had not spoken a word since the beginning of the ride, said simply, "The cur." Bruce nodded; that much could he tell from the bobbing of her hat. And suddenly, hat ribbons in his face, it was as though his whole life became clear to Davy, for he then discovered and proclaimed, "You are going to marry me and nobody else. Put that in your pipe and smoke it."

Bruce turned to give him a wrathful look.

"Did you hear what I said?" Davy asked.

"You're a silly little boy," she answered.

"I'm eighteen, and Uncle Ben and Grandmama have promised me all their share of the cotton mill when I'm twenty-one if I turn out well. So I'm not a boy, I'm a man, you see." He continued with exhilaration: "What a good thing it happened so! I've always dreaded the idea of growing up and having to think about some girl to marry—and then do the courting, you know, not knowing if she'd say no and it would all have gone for nothing. Ugh! What a waste of time it would be! So I'm glad it's all settled, I sure am. I'd have just plain hated to go through all that with some stranger, but you're just Bruce, just old Bruce that used to smell of milk—"

"What do I smell of now, I'd like to know?"

"Nothing, thank the Lord, absolutely nothing!"

"Well, let me tell *you* something, you factory hand: I wouldn't marry you *or* anybody else if I was promised ambrosia every meal the rest of my life! Put that in *your* pipe and smoke it!"

"You'll see," he said cheerfully. "You'll marry me when I'm twenty-one and you're—what'll you be?—nineteen."

"Great businessman you are!"

"Don't you worry," he said, and actually began to chuckle, making much the sound of barnyard fowls when they have discovered pickings that please them. "Imagine—married to old Bruce!" He couldn't get over the wonder of it and laughed all the way home.

15

It was not until the third week of October that papers were signed and payment made—"cash money" as had been demanded; but that done, the sawmill began to move immediately to its new quarters. The sidetrack was laid to the main railway line, and the chain gang was employed for most of the clearing and burning, while the main body of the white work force, under Eugene's supervision, set up the new yard and began operations there. Eugene had promised that, once things were right, the convicts would be dismissed, and he'd put Perry Mitchell in charge of a smaller crew of whites to complete the abandonment of the old campsite.

Eugene had watched Perry over the summer and autumn months and knew the boy still had Luck Kendrick on his mind. She did not come every day, and sometimes nearly a week passed without her visiting the cotton factory, but Perry always noted her comings and goings. Eugene teased him a little, but did not discourage him. "You won't be seeing her when we get finally moved; reckon you'll miss her?" Another time he said, "Maybe you ought to catch her on the road one day. She's never known anything but nigger dick and she'd drop her drawers in a second if you asked her, I bet. They all want it white."

Twice after that, Perry, seeing her arrive across the creek and knowing she never stayed long, left his men with the excuse of having to go into the woods and shit. Instead, he went up the creek on the sawmill side, wading across at the shallows, and hid in the bushes beside the narrow woods road to watch her leave. The second time he did so, she paused at the bend as if she guessed his presence and stared into the woods. His heart pounding, he touched himself to encourage a hardening and might have called out, but she suddenly slapped the mare's rump with reins and was gone.

Eugene was in his glory. He boasted of his triumph over Beulah Land, wanting everyone to know, and he was the hero of the town idlers. "Got the best of old lady Troy and her pet coons, he did! Why, Gene hates niggers same as me and you, pure despises 'em—" Theodore too took on some of his father's glory and was made much of by the loungers as he took his strutting, crowing way to the depot twice a day to watch the trains come and go. He had been put to no regular work, although he'd done occasional jobs at the sawmill during the long summer break from school.

If Eugene was gratified by events, Frankie was less so. She had insisted that the sale money be deposited in a new bank account neither she nor Eugene could draw upon without the other's countersignature; but at the time the final papers were drawn, she was confined to her room for three days with one of her worst headaches. When she emerged still weak and trembly, she discovered that Eugene had put the new site in his own name and that she owned nothing. They quarreled, she with bitterness, he with pretended surprise that she could object to having the business bear her husband's name. She wavered and gave way only when he threatened to cancel the agreement. Eugene had already signed, and so had each of the triumvirate of Beulah Land. She added her name reluctantly to the documents, and the sale was accomplished.

With the harvest all but over, Leon brought a work crew from the plantation to build a bridge across the creek where the cotton factory faced the old sawmill site. It was during his work there he became aware of Perry Mitchell's interest in Luck. It appeared plain to him, although no one else seemed to notice it. Perhaps being in love with Fanny made him more sensitive to the other young man's obsession with the Negro girl. At first he thought Perry stared at her with the resentment poor whites felt for any Negro who had risen above a menial station; but though Perry frowned, his intensity was not one of hatred. That too was plain; there was a burning constancy, almost dedication in the steady gaze.

Eugene knew that Perry was drawing out the cleanup of the old site and let him do it. For the last few days Perry had gone alone on one of the mules. Eugene was about to stop him altogether, but when the boy begged, gave in, saying, "Only till the end of the week. You want any of that stuff, move fast, you hear?" With a wink and a laugh he let him go.

Perry watched desperately for any chance. It came at the very last, on Saturday about eleven-thirty in the morning. He had given up hope, knowing his work was over and that he could make no further excuse to return to the site. He saw too that Leon Davis had become aware of his deliberate lingering. Mounting the mule, he rode up the creek bank and crossed the shallows into the woods road. With the diversion he'd be only a little late getting to the new yard to line up for his week's pay with the other men. Slumped on the tired mule, he heard suddenly the clatter of approaching wheels on the rough-rutted roadway, a turning of which brought him face to face with Luck Kendrick. It was like a dream. He slid off the mule's back and grabbed the harness of the mare Luck drove. She was as startled as he and did nothing at first as he led her trap off the roadway into the underbrush. It happened suddenly and quickly, and by the time Luck realized, still without understanding, what had happened, she jumped out of the trap. Perry grabbed her by the arm, and she began to strike him about the head any way, anywhere she was able, speechless with agitation.

"I been waiting to get you," Perry told her. "Now I got you, I'm going to fuck you, girl. You let me, for I'll do it anyhow—"

No one before had laid a hand on Luck she didn't permit or invite. She had been treated with deference and affection by her black family and white acquaintances, and although she knew the racial divisions as well as did every Southern Negro, she had not believed them bone-deep until this moment when the strange, strong white boy let her know he was determined to have her and that he expected her to acquiesce. Breathing as hard as he, she began to shout for Abraham; but Abraham was not there.

Leon was. He had left his men at the new bridge to put away their tools in the factory, because they would be returning on Monday morning to continue the job; and he was riding his own horse back to Beulah Land to join his father and Daniel and Bobby Lee for a wash in the creek before noon dinner, as was their Saturday custom. Davy and Abraham were still in the office working over the week's figures. Leon knew from a remark made earlier that Abraham was expecting Luck to come for him today in her trap. That was why he became uneasy when he saw Perry ride away and heard him cross the creek. Following only a few minutes later, he found Perry's mule returning riderless to the old sawmill site. Going faster and directed by Luck's cries, he soon found and separated the pair. For a long moment the three stood apart from each other, Luck almost retching in her need for air and her relief at rescue. Leon was first to find voice. He said to Luck, "Go to Abraham—tell him whatever you will, but *don't let him come!* I'll take care of this man—" Nodding, still gasping for breath, Luck led her mare and trap back to the roadway and disappeared.

As he paused to see her get clear, Leon was surprised by Perry, who jumped on him from the back and brought him to the ground. They rolled and fought, each trying to overpower the other, and because he was the bigger and stronger, Leon soon prevailed. He beat Perry only enough to be certain his resistance was over, but when they both drew themselves to upright positions, Leon wiping blood from the side of his head where his ear was bleeding, Perry said, "You ain't taking me!"

Leon grabbed him again and shoved him roughly ahead to the

roadway. The mule was long gone, but Leon had his horse. He ordered Perry to mount and, taking the bridle, he began to walk them out of the woods to the main road.

Perry no longer resisted. "Where you leading me?"

"To your boss."

"Through town?"

"Only way."

"Everybody'll see!"

"Don't you care about that!"

Directly through town they went, with people staring from the sidewalks at the odd sight of Leon Davis leading his horse, which they recognized and on which sat Perry Mitchell, whom some identified as one of the sawmill hands, both young men looking grim and as if they had been in a fight. Turning up alongside the railroad tracks, they were soon at the new millsite. From the office steps where he had finished paying the crews, Eugene saw them coming and waited. The three went into the office without words having passed, and Eugene closed the door after them.

Leon told him what had happened, and Perry made no objection or comment of any kind. At the end Leon said, "He's your man, Mr. Betchley, and I reckon you had better be responsible for him. I don't want any more trouble, for we both know how ugly it could get. If you promise to have him out of town by tomorrow morning and promise he'll never show himself here again, I'll try to calm our people. I may have to tie Abraham Kendrick to a tree, but if I don't stop him, he'll come after your man, and somebody will be killed. If it's this one, then Abraham will be killed too, with no regard to reason and right. Will you agree to that?"

Eugene looked at Perry, who stood to one side of the office, then back at Leon and nodded. "I'll see he goes. Now you go." Leon found his horse at the door and rode away through the crowd of wondering men.

Eugene closed the door.

The boy said, "I don't know what happened, Mr. Betchley."

"All hell, it looks like."

"What must I do?"

"You'll have to go, like he says."

"Where? I got nowhere, I got nothing. I can't go back to no farm, even if they'd have me. — You said she'd let me do it, Mr. Betchley, but she wouldn't. — I'd like to kill that Leon Davis. I almost had her. How come he got into it—you reckon he's been fucking her? Lend me your pistol so I can go kill him now!"

"Do that and you're in real trouble. They wouldn't wait to try you; they'd hang you today. Think of something else."

Perry shook his head hopelessly. "Can't ask nobody for help but you, Mr. Betchley."

"Let me study on it." Eugene took a tin of cigarettes from his pocket, put one between his lips, and after a pause handed one to Perry without offering him the tin. They smoked for five minutes without speaking, Eugene appearing to cogitate, Perry giving him anxious looks as he waited. Dropping the end of his cigarette to the floor of the office, Eugene crushed it out. "I've thought of something, but I don't know if you're man enough to be trusted."

"Try me, please, sir," Perry said humbly.

"If you ever breathe a word, God help you."

"No, sir!"

Eugene shrugged. "I'm going to give you fifty dollars and a mule. When I let you go, you're going to vanish like you been wiped off the face of the earth. You'll ride what's left of tonight and ride every night, hiding days. Get to Savannah by directions I'll give you and get the first boat headed anywhere. I can help you there with a note to my lumber office in Savannah." Perry began to cry, and Eugene looked at him with satisfaction. "Before I let you go tonight, I got a few things for you to do."

"Anything you say, sir."

"You mean it about wanting to get even with Leon Davis and all them nigger lovers?"

16

Omitting most of the details and choosing her words with greater care than she was used to doing, Luck still thought it necessary to give her husband a clear account of what had happened. She was calm enough, but neither she nor Davy was able to reason Abraham out of his rage. Far from being grateful to Leon, he resented his being the rescuer and blamed him for not killing the attacker on the spot. Davy finally made him see the sense of taking Luck to Beulah Land while he, Davy, went to fetch Roscoe Elk. They would wait together for Leon to return and tell them how he had disposed of the man.

Sarah insisted on putting Luck to bed. Luck insisted on getting right up again, just as Fanny Saxon arrived, having heard incomprehensible reports of Leon's walking his horse through town carrying a captive rider, both men bloody from fighting. She had come to discover what had happened, but was able at least to tell them that the rumors made no mention of Luck Kendrick.

Luck and Bruce welcomed Fanny and after the first emotional explanations the three young women adjourned to Bruce's room, where they were to go over Luck's misadventure a hundred times while Leon and Benjamin, Abraham and Roscoe, Davy and Sarah talked together in the office. Roscoe was first to congratulate Leon on his handling of "the incident," as he chose to call it, hoping thus to diminish it. He argued that all of them must understand the probable consequences of doing what they felt like doing; for if they responded violently, there would be killing on both sides, and no end to the affair.

They agreed that no good could come of informing the sheriff. He'd only hem and haw, ask impertinent questions and draw wrong conclusions from whatever answers he received. The longer they talked, the plainer it became that Leon had acted well. If the man went away, and if they let him go, Luck's name would not be in every gossip's mouth. She had been attacked, but she had not been raped. If the man was accused of rape, he would accuse Luck of enticement, and Eugene Betchley would find it easy to get his men to swear to it. Davy reminded them of the calling back and forth between female factory workers and sawmill crews. There could be silence, if no justice and no forgetting; for even as they went over the affair, present in everyone's mind was the fact that Sarah Troy had been raped fifty years ago by a black man: Roscoe Elk's uncle.

They must wait and see if Eugene Betchley kept his word. Sarah said he would because he was self-seeking above all else, and no credit would come to him from a complete airing of the episode. When there are accusations from two sides, both are believed. She would seek him out at church tomorrow and ask what he had done. Meantime, since they were all here and had talked away the afternoon, offending Josephine by ignoring her calls to dinner, wouldn't they stay for supper? They did, and Fanny was persuaded to spend the night. The stableboy Clarence was sent to town with a note for her mother.

Roscoe and Abraham and Luck set off for home at nine o'clock, after something like a party atmosphere had enfolded them for a few hours. It was one of the graces of Beulah Land that even in bad times they could find comfort there. Everyone was gay, not callously so but as an assertion of themselves and their consideration for each other, as people will sometimes exert themselves to be cheerful after a funeral.

The Todds were next to leave; and after a last yawning review of the day, Sarah retired, and Benjamin took the path to the house in the Glade to spend the night with Nancy. He wanted Nancy, and he needed to be quiet with her. When Leon went to his room, he passed Bruce's door and heard her and Fanny talking in the soft tones of self-comfort women use when brushing their hair and making preparations for bed. Closing his own door, he set down his lamp to discover Hellfire asleep on the pillow of the turned-down bed. He picked him up and deposited him on the floor. "Off! God knows where you've been; you smell like—you got a polecat for a sweetheart?" Hellfire ignored him, scratching his ear thoroughly before shaking himself and walking under the bed. One by one the lamps and candles of Beulah Land went out, and the world was dark.

Clarence slept in the horse barn, and with his ear trained for arrivals and departures, it was he who first heard and ran to meet the messenger two hours after midnight. At the word "fire" he turned to look toward town and saw reflections of burning in the sky. Running, he caught the rope of the bell used to send them to the fields to work and bring them home for food and rest. "Fire" was the terrible word for the terrible thing all country folk most dreaded, for there was no weapon against it but God's will. They might fight it, but even as they passed and threw the inadequate buckets of water, flames spread, to die only when there was nothing left to destroy. Any fire was awful; a fire at night brought everyone from his bed, for there was an element of the supernatural about it: flame against blackness suggesting hell to the susceptible, and with always the question of how it had come about. "Struck by lightning" was the most common explanation, but there was often the suspicion of a vengeful hand. Fire killed livestock and sometimes people, destroyed hay and cotton, grain and dry goods. It was called an act of God but feared as an act of the devil. It was the great leveler of men, more evenhanded than democracy and disease, for it accomplished its ends more swiftly.

For those at Beulah Land it held particular horror, for Sherman's army had used it against them and the neighboring Davis plantation. Before that, the first Roscoe Elk had tried to confound Beulah Land by firing its warehouses in town. And so now, when the field bell rang in the black early morning, they left their beds hastily to hear the word "fire" echo from one house to another. Benjamin came running from the Glade to find Leon already in the horse barn with Clarence and Wally saddling horses. As they rode around the house and away, they passed Davy on his bicycle, and behind them heard the clatter of buggy wheels on the hard road, for Jane had insisted on going with Daniel. Bobby Lee caught up with them on a horse he had simply bridled and not bothered to saddle.

On the road to town they were joined at every crossing by other farmers, all drawn in the direction of the light in the sky. They came first to what had been the old Campgrounds and more recently the site of the cotton factory and the sawmill. The cabins that had mushroomed around the factory buildings were all burned or burning, having caught fire from the factory, which still blazed like the jaws of hell. People ran or stood amazed, some holding each other in thankfulness at being spared, some carrying meaningless things they had grabbed on their way out of burning rooms, a chair, a chamber pot, a picture from the wall. People came and went; although some lingered, others turned away, for there was nothing they were able to do. Even as they wavered, there was a fresh alarm.

"Look!" someone cried, pointing to a distant light. At first it was said to be only a trick of reflection, but as Benjamin and Leon rode to see, word came to meet them that the cotton gin was afire, and that would mean the warehouses adjoining it too.

Waking, Doreen Davis had seen the walls of her room glimmering with shadow-light. For a few moments she thought only how pretty it was against the flowered wallpaper, and then she left her bed and stumbled across the hall to throw open the door of her friend's room. "Where is Pharaoh?" she cried. "The Yankees have come for him, and I must hide him from them!"

It was the old familiar nightmare, thought Eloise, of the killing of her horse, but she hurried from bed nevertheless to soothe her companion. "No, my love, it's all right—only a dream. There are no Yankees."

Doreen drew her to the window. "Look there! — Where are the cats? They will be so afraid—"

Edna May Davis was wakened by the high-pitched laughter of her stepbrother Theodore; and when she remembered that Fanny was not in the bed beside hers, she screamed and ran out into the hallway to Frankie's room. Finding it empty, she raced through the house and onto the porch calling, "Mama, Mama, Mama—" There she found Theodore holding the banisters with both hands and still laughing as he looked off toward the fire. Beside him, Frankie said, "Be quiet! Has everyone gone mad?"

How they came there, they never remembered, but they arrived separately and met in the old graveyard. They had seen the cotton factory burn and known there was nothing to be done about it. Too late to worry about the already leveled cabins, they left Roscoe and Abraham to quiet the people as best they could, and Davy shaking his fists and cursing. Leaving together to investigate the other fire, they discovered that it was theirs too. It was a holocaust. Because of the tightly baled cotton, it would smolder for days, and there was no way to put it out.

Wandering back through the town, they heard talk of their ruin: "Who could have?" "Judgment of God!"—until they were sick of every fearful voice. And so they continued walking, walking here and there and finally to the old graveyard, as if they sought counsel of their forebears. Leon found Benjamin with his arms about the marble angel hovering over the grave of Rachel, the mother who had not loved him and whom he had not loved.

"Pa?"

Benjamin turned and saw him. Opening their arms, they embraced, weeping.

17

Benjamin found himself inordinately regretting the loss of Isaac's wooden leg, the way people faced with catastrophe will hold on to one inconsequential thing as if it represents all past order. On the death of Isaac, Benjamin had kept his peg leg under a great bell jar in his office at the cotton gin. No one considered it a morbid relic but rather a tribute to the man who had spent most of his life taking care of the gin.

The same questions were asked a thousand times over. Who? How? Why?

Both factory and gin had a watchman, but no one man may bar another bent on evil. It was inconceivable that any who worked in either had started the fires. Then wouldn't someone in a cabin near the factory have waked in time to give the alarm? Wouldn't a dog have barked at a stranger? They remembered the bridge Leon and his men had almost completed. A man might have crossed it and been directly before the factory without going through the cabin area. As for the gin, no matter what a watchman swears, he may steal sleep, or step into the outdoors to relieve boredom or to empty his bladder.

If that was how it occurred, then who and why?

Before the night was over, Leon and Benjamin had gone from their reunion at the graveyard to Eugene Betchley, and he'd told them he had dismissed the man Perry Mitchell as requested and sent him on his way with the warning never to return. He could have had nothing to do with the fires—and no, Eugene did not know where he had gone; he was a poor worker and would have been dismissed anyhow in another week or two. They might not believe him, but they could not send parties in every direction to find and question the man.

Morning light left no doubt that the fires had completely destroyed factory and gin. There was insurance, but only for the buildings and some of the machinery, and they were the least of the loss.

When Sarah came into the kitchen after the long night, she discovered Mabella crying with ostentatious modesty as she sidled about her duties, but Josephine was dry of eye. "Miss Sarah," she said, "I dreamed about Napoleon last night. Do you reckon it means something?"

Startled, Sarah took a moment to remember that Napoleon had been married to Josephine many years ago, but she was glad of the distraction. "He must have left Beulah Land with that girl—when would it have been?" Josephine waited for her to study on it. "Two years after the war." Both nodded.

"I don't dream about him often, just sometimes. He couldn't resist a sassy butt, could he, ma'am?"

"No, he couldn't, Josephine."

"You reckon he'll ever come back to me?"

"He'll be over sixty if he's alive," Sarah said doubtfully.

"Somebody'd surely have killed him before now." Josephine

sighed. "That leaves me only the Lord. Is it so, Miss Sarah, what they all say about us going to be poor?"

"I'm afraid so. Is that coffee ready?"

Josephine took the pot from the stove and poured out cups for her mistress and herself. Her kitchen was her kitchen. "Well'm, I ain't forgot how to cook lye hominy. You can fill a lot of hollow bellies thataway with a handful or two of shelled corn. We been poor before."

"Well, *I* never been poor before!" Mabella wailed.

Sarah patted Josephine's arm. "Josephine, you are a comfort. Mabella, if you don't stop that sniveling and blow your nose, I'm going to feed you to the hogs."

It was important for them to go to church that day, and they did so in good style: the Todds in the four-seat rockaway, and Sarah, Benjamin, Bruce, Fanny, Leon, and Lauretta in the six-seat barouche. Sarah understood that if they did not present themselves, half the town would come to visit, some to express genuine sympathy and others to gloat, for however correct their words on the occasion, their eyes would give away their satisfaction at seeing the mighty fallen. All the family members mingled freely; they talked freely; they hid nothing, thereby disappointing a few, disarming others.

Annabel said to Leon, "I suppose you will now be in a great hurry to marry my granddaughter, seeing how poorly you'll all be situated. Well, I don't know that it mightn't be wise to postpone thinking about it. Fanny may look like a rich heiress to you, but the money is only *behind* her, on my side and her stepfather's, if you understand me. How well *he* has done for himself—"

Overhearing, Sarah moved to join them. "Annabel, some of my happiest daydreams have been of doing you bodily harm."

"Auntie Sarah, you are shocking!"

"So you always say when I allow myself to speak the truth."

"I'm only telling your great-grandson that he mustn't expect anything particular in the way of financial consideration if he marries into what must now seem to him great affluence. And how are *you* bearing up to adversity?"

"Tolerably."

Annabel sighed with exasperation. "You make me tired, always so inhumanly accepting. Once, only *once* I'd like to see you curse your fate and vow vengeance."

"Don't be silly, Annabel; you're only trying to sound interesting."

Annabel continued, "I'm glad that 'silly' notion of mine about Blair and Bruce came to nothing. He's well out of it, and she mustn't expect another such offer. My guess is she's cut out to be an old maid like sister Doreen. – I've news for you. Judge Meldrim has found a place for our dear boy in an excellent law firm in Atlanta! He goes in a week to continue his reading and studying. I shall miss him, but what does my sacrifice signify?"

"I wish him well," Sarah said.

Annabel was looking at her narrowly. "You'll have to convert all those bonds and securities."

Sarah took Leon's arm and led him away. Ann Oglethorpe and Priscilla Davis nodded from a distance but attempted no more intimate approach. They did not look unhappy, and they did not lower their voices as they speculated with Eugene Betchley on the mysterious ways of the Lord.

Of those expressing their concern for her, none spoke more truly than Elizabeth Cooper. "Miss Sarah, if there's anything we can do, ask. You've been good to us, good friends and good neighbors. Anything we've got except our rascally boys is yours for the asking."

Smiling, Sarah thanked her. "It's the boys I wanted."

Lauretta, who did not often attend church services, had today insisted on coming, not liking to miss a dramatic occasion. Sarah heard her saying to Eunice Hightower, "I may be compelled to return to the stage to earn my bread. I daresay there are some who have not forgotten my name—"

At last they were free to go home for Sunday dinner, which the Todds enjoyed with them, Josephine not finding it yet necessary to put them on lye hominy for sustenance. Mabella had defiantly made three chocolate pies.

Their problems were real enough, however.

The cotton gin would have to be rebuilt before next summer. This year's cotton was lost because they had stored it to wait for the price to rise. They had also engaged to store part of the ginned and baled harvest of other farms, and that must now be paid for. The factory too would have to be replaced. Meanwhile, there were those to pay who worked at Beulah Land and those to support who would not be working at the cotton factory. Roscoe came immediately to offer any help he could. They decided to use the workers to clear the destruction and to begin rebuilding. Sarah and Benjamin converted bonds and securities to working currency to meet immediate obligations, and Roscoe arranged further credit for them at two banks in Savannah.

Every day they figured and talked; every night they figured and talked again, Sarah, Benjamin, and Leon in Sarah's old office. The father and son would sip one glassful each while Sarah consumed two or three of the peach brandy Otis made for her every year. Benjamin was always first to go to bed after yawning and offering no comment for half an hour before doing so. They were all three bone-tired, going to bed so and waking little refreshed. Soon after Benjamin left them, Sarah sent Leon off, saying she wanted to sit alone awhile. "You oughtn't to be here anyway. Tomorrow night, go into town and court Fanny."

"Can't, Grandma."

"Why?"

"No courting to do. She's willing and I'm not."

"Don't you know the best thing a man has to offer a woman is the chance to help him?"

"Grandma, you're forgetting something. I was born poor. My name is Leon *Marsh* Davis. I won't ask my wife to be poor with me when she's put me off before now."

"If you're thinking about Annabel Saxon and what she said—"

"It's what everybody would say, Grandma."

"What matter? At Beulah Land we don't care what people say about us."

He kissed her cheek. "Good night, Grandma."

"Come back here!"

But he did not.

18

Eugene Betchley was triumphant. Everything had happened according to plan and better than he'd foreseen, because he was able to use the advantage of the unexpected. The sawmill in its new position was operating at full production. Shipping was more efficiently done than had been possible from the old Campgrounds, and new orders were coming in every day from the Savannah office. He was even afforded the bonus of selling lumber to Roscoe Elk and Benjamin Davis, which they needed to rebuild the factory and cotton gin and warehouses. He had money in three banks in Highboro and Savannah, and that was power. He was negotiating the purchase of another thousand acres of woodland, and that was power. Having asserted himself over Frankie, he could be certain that everything in the future was in his name alone, not theirs together; and that was power.

"There's no stopping me," he said to her.

"You won't get Beulah Land, which is what you want."

"Wait and see."

"You're trash and always will be; you can't change yourself."

"Watch what you say," he warned her.

"I say what I please, and don't *you* forget I can bring you down any time I want to with what I know."

"Nobody'd believe you. They think you're crazy, way you drink, way you lock yourself in your room days at a time, way you paint your ugly face and powder your old neck and think you look sixteen. Even Molly believes you're crazy. *You* be the one to watch out, for I can have you locked up in the lunatic asylum."

She laughed, deliberately exaggerating her scorn and confidence until she sounded a little crazy even to her own ears. He left her, and she subsided, frightened.

One morning after the train arrived, Sarah and Leon waited in the post office for the mail to be sorted. Eugene was only one of the dozen or so who waited with them, but he came over, removed his hat, and bowed. "Morning, ma'am. You're a rare sight except for church these days; and we never seem to have a chance to do more than speak when we meet there. Of course I could come out to see you, but I know not everybody's welcome at Beulah Land."

The post office had gone quiet.

Feeling required to say something, Sarah managed only, "As you say, Mr. Betchley."

"Well, ma'am, no hard feelings—on my side, that is; and I want you to know how much I appreciate doing business with you all for the building you're engaged in."

"There is but one sawmill in Highboro."

"And it used to be yours."

"We sold it after the war to James Davis, as you know. It was he who first gave you a job of work there. Am I not right?"

"Yes, ma'am, so he did, and I've been ever grateful, for it set me on my way. As my fortunes improved, those of Beulah Land have waned."

"Wax-and-wane is one of the rhythms of life, Mr. Betchley, like breathing in and out."

"I hear you-all are having to take help from niggers? I sure hope it's not so, but you know how people will talk about things."

"We're in business with Roscoe Elk and Abraham Kendrick," Leon said.

Eugene looked at Leon as if he were just discovering his presence. "That's the way to look at it, as long as you can. His own granddaddy used to work at Beulah Land, one of the slaves, you might say."

"If you did, you'd be wrong," Sarah corrected him. "Roscoe Elk was a free man before he came to us."

"Still, it does seem queer, having to take help from his grandboy."

Sarah said, "Maybe the moral is that if you're 'nigger lovers,' as I once heard you describe us, they love you back. Good day to you, Mr. Betchley. The grill is opening and your mail is waiting."

"Yes, ma'am," he said, parodying contrition. "Good day to *you.*"

Elaborations and embroideries of the scene were repeated all over Highboro within the hour, and there were few who did not take Eugene Betchley's side in the matter, seeing Sarah Troy as arrogant and over-proud. As for the town idlers, he was more than ever their hero. "Gene stands up to 'em," they bragged.

One afternoon Eugene discovered Frankie in the office. She did not come to it as often as she had the old one. She was at the heavy oak desk he'd recently bought himself, so absorbed in opening drawers and rummaging through them that he was able to observe her for several minutes before she knew he was there.

"Can I help you find something?" he asked politely when she glanced up.

She answered with fair composure, "Why do you lock one drawer?"

"Secrets," he said, and winked.

"I know your secrets, and the business is ours together."

"It don't say so on the papers, you know. What are you looking for?"

"The gun. Now the convict crew is gone, I want to take it home."

"You don't need a gun."

"I might."

He smiled. "Who'd you use it against? Not that *I'm* afraid, you understand. You're the one to bolt your door at night, not me. I just don't consider you stable enough to have a gun lying around. You might hurt yourself, and everybody would blame me."

"I get scared when you're out at night. I've heard there are prowlers, and everybody knows you're gone a lot of the time."

"I've things to do."

"You can't get enough of your nigger, can you?"

"I get enough," he said quietly, "and I won't let you have the gun."

"We're only females and a young boy, alone and niggers roaming free."

"Practice screaming, in case you need to."

Like a number of men in Highboro considered otherwise respectable, Eugene kept a Negro mistress. It was a custom discreetly ignored, although many were aware of it. The woman Eugene was currently keeping was named Myrtle. She lived alone not far from the sawmill, and Eugene saw her almost every night for an hour or two. His sexual appetite, always strong, had increased with his recent successes as if it were part of new energy he found himself generating. Myrtle was a plump, bold woman twenty years old, and she boasted of her position to her friends, who were always keenly aware of the changing status of whites in the town. The way she put it was: "White ladies like us-all to do their washing and ironing and clean their houses; reckon it's just another step to let us do their fucking." It made them laugh. Eugene found her more satisfying than any woman he'd ever had. As his station had changed, Eugene had learned to observe the common rules of cleanliness, but he was not a fastidious man, and he never bothered to wash himself after bedding with Myrtle. If he saw Frankie on his return at night, she invariably wrinkled her nose and told him, "You've got nigger stink on you."

"Never mind, I won't be getting it on you."

On the evening after finding Frankie at his desk he came home at midnight as Leon was leaving Fanny at the door after a town dance they had attended. Eugene waited for her in the hall, and when she entered, commented jokingly, "Didn't look to me like a very romantic good night between you."

He had planted himself directly before her, and she made as if to go around him. "Good night, Mr. Betchley."

He took her hand, which she immediately withdrew. "You never trouble yourself to talk to me. I'm tired of being treated like that, you hear me? You live under my roof, and it's time you learn some manners."

"I'm sorry you think I lack them," she said. "I must go to bed."

"I haven't heard any more about you getting married. Have the recent setbacks to Beulah Land stopped your plans?"

"We've set no day to marry or you'd know it from Mama."

He followed closely behind her up the stairs, drawling, "You tell your mama everything, do you?"

"We must be quiet. Mama and Edna May and Theodore are surely asleep."

Before she could enter her room, he took her hand again, and this time she could not pull away. "Kiss me good night like a good daughter."

"No, sir, we are not on those terms."

"I'm a mighty loving man." He clasped her firmly against him. "God, what a pretty thing you are. If you're getting no loving from that boy from Beulah Land, you ought to be willing to let me show you some—"

"Let me go!"

"A little fight feels good to me. Now, come on, kiss me like I said. I won't tell your mama; won't nobody ever know but me and you. Your mama's too old to want to do it; don't you feel sorry for me just a little bit?"

When Frankie opened her door, Fanny managed to wrench free. Slipping quickly into the room she shared with Edna May, she bolted the door and leaned against it. She waited and was surprised that there was no sound of voices. A moment later she became aware of the regular breathing of Edna May and was thankful that she had not waked. She listened a little longer but heard nothing from the hallway. As quietly as she could, she began to undress in the dark.

Eugene and Frankie had stared at each other when they were alone, his lips forming the words "old cunt." But when she made no move toward him, he went down the hall to his own room, entering and closing the door behind him. Frankie closed and bolted hers, but she did not go to bed. She had been sitting by the lamp table with a novel by Mrs. E. D. E. N. Southworth, which she'd found Edna May mooning over recently. She returned to the book but her mind would not follow it, and after a while she closed it and poured whiskey into a glass.

When the clock struck three downstairs, she was awake. The sound made her feel the stillness of the house and her own aloneness more than ever. She had drunk two glasses of whiskey but was as sober as the day she was born. Leaving her chair, she realized that she was cold and took a winter wrapper from the wardrobe. Possessed suddenly of a wish to examine something she passed fifty times a day without looking at it, she went downstairs.

The heavy curtains had not been closed, and moonlight played through the thin inner curtains of the living room, making it almost as bright as day. She had not brought a lamp, nor did she need one to see the portrait Casey Troy had painted of her sixteen years ago. She saw that she had indeed been a great beauty and remembered what Annabel Saxon said the first day Casey came to the house to make drawings. "We must catch the bloom before it fades." Frankie had been aware of her beauty all her life and had used it to advance herself, but she'd never had the overweening vanity of most belles. Nevertheless, it had shocked her to have Eugene ridicule her as being old and ugly. She told herself that she was neither, but without beauty, without youth, what was she and who could love her?

Turning from the portrait, she went into the hallway. It was not bright enough for her purpose, so she lighted a lamp and held it to the mirror glass into which she habitually glanced to check her appearance before leaving the house. Now she studied her face, and her heart turned cold. Annabel Saxon had been right to say her thinness made her appear haggard. It was a mistake to worry about her figure; the face and neck mattered more. She blew out the lamp and stood where she was, tears coming, as if she had to be alone in the dark to cry.

Without design, she went into the living room, noticing this and that, remembering what each item had cost and how pleased she had been to acquire it, finding worth and reassurance in belongings she had not discovered in herself or anyone else. As her hands passed over the surface of things, she came upon Fanny's sewing basket. On top and used as a weight was a pair of scissors. Taking them up, she looked at them as if she understood for the first time what scissors were for. They were not a large pair, but they were very sharp.

She went upstairs carefully, although she was not drunk and there was no reason for her to creep. Everyone would be asleep. Outside Eugene's door she listened to the sound of his snoring. Opening the door, she went in and to the bedside. He was sleeping heavily and had thrown the top bedclothes off himself. She could see him quite clearly, the rise and fall of his hairy chest in the partly unbuttoned nightshirt. She rested her fingers lightly on his penis and after a moment felt it respond. As it became warm and began to lift of itself, she was seized by the greatest rage she had ever known and plunged the sewing scissors into his groin again and again as he woke kicking and screaming.

19

"Mercy! Hurts just to think about, don't it? And him a gent'mum set so much store by his peter." It had taken Myrtle a little while to grasp what had happened, but then she accepted it readily enough. A practical woman, she passed word to her friends that if they heard of anything, she might be willing to do a little washing and ironing until something better turned up.

The town idlers put it with awed simplicity: "She took his manhood away."

There was no suppressing the affair. Eugene had been dispatched by train to the Savannah hospital, accompanied by Dr. Platt, who stepped out of near-retirement to make the journey, and, to the general surprise, by Priscilla Davis. Priscilla and her mother felt that Eugene should be accompanied by "someone close," and since no family member volunteered, Priscilla did so. As Ann Oglethorpe explained, "In the circumstances, we consider no chaperon necessary."

Before leaving, Eugene and Dr. Platt signed an order committing Frankie to the state asylum for the insane, and there was no voice to oppose them. Most of the townspeople had considered her mentally disordered for years, and if the violent act was not final proof, Frankie furnished it by vociferously accusing her husband of having murdered both his first wife and that wife's mother. A few might have wondered about Bessie's death, but Bessie herself had sworn that old Mrs. Marsh died by an accident she was witness to. Only those at Beulah Land believed Frankie, and they understood there was nothing to be gained by doing so openly. Frankie must be put away, for if she were not, she would stand trial for attempted murder.

Sarah, however, would not have her go to the state asylum. With Benjamin she approached Annabel. "You must postpone this present project of yours and help us find a place for Frankie, a private one suitable for ladies."

Annabel retorted, "I shall do no such thing."

"You must," Sarah said.

"Please, Aunt Annabel," Benjamin begged her.

"Why should I?"

"You ask such a thing when she was first your daughter and later your sister? You are doubly responsible. Furthermore, Eugene has let it be known that he won't pay to have her privately kept. *We* can't afford it, so you must pay for her."

Benjamin said, "Think how the town will praise you, Aunt Annabel."

Sarah rephrased it. "Think how the town will condemn you if you refuse. You boast constantly of doing your duty. Now *do* it."

After long hesitation, Annabel muttered a grudging "Very well," but she looked at Benjamin as she said it. "Perhaps I'll think about it."

"Blair Three should come home and see to his mother," Sarah said.

"I won't allow that." And on this point Annabel did not give way. "He mustn't be associated with her again in the public mind; it would shadow his future."

Within a week Annabel found the right place less than twenty miles from Highboro. It was near the town of Sandersville and called itself "a private home for difficult cases." It was in effect an asylum for gentlewomen. Its governess had to be persuaded that Frankie was no longer violent, but Annabel was a practiced persuader and Frankie was docile. Since the night of the attack she had been given morphine, and it was no wonder the governess found her "tractable and genteel."

"Thank goodness," Annabel said, "that is arranged. So much

has depended upon me. However, 'rank imposes obligation,' as I am the first to admit. Now I can return to my *important* project."

Later, Benjamin asked Sarah what that was.

"Surely you've heard. A skeleton was found over in—I think it was Emanuel County. In the woods in a shallow grave, hardly a grave at all. Nobody knows who it is. There are no identifying marks and no clothes. It might be the Missing Link for all anyone could prove, but Annabel has got it into her head that it was one of our soldiers who fell before Sherman's advance and was buried hurriedly by retreating comrades."

"Where was he found?" Benjamin asked quietly.

Sarah wasn't certain. He went to Annabel, and what she told him sent Benjamin and Daniel away on a day's journey of investigation. When they returned, Benjamin asked his grandmother, "Just what does Aunt Annabel propose doing?"

"Why, adding it to the Confederate Memorial. A sort of urn at the foot of the statue she had us erect, with the skeleton in the urn and a nice inscription along the lines of 'unnamed but not unremembered'—something like that."

"She mustn't do it."

"Oh, it's harmless enough, and it keeps her busy."

"Grandma, I know whose skeleton it is."

She stared at him. "You amaze me."

"Sergeant Smede." She continued to stare at him. "Yes, ma'am. Dan and I went to the place they found him, and we remember it well. We buried him there after we followed and killed him."

Sarah said slowly, "The man who killed your grandfather and Annabel's father. Who raped Nancy and Lotus, killed dear Lovey, and dug up Uncle Ezra's grave looking for silver. The man who looted Oaks and Beulah Land."

Benjamin nodded. "That's whose bones Aunt Annabel proposes to honor."

"Well." Sarah sat thinking until she came to a decision. "We must let her do it. What does it matter? May God forgive him, for I never shall. May God forgive us all."

"You don't mean it, Grandma. You can't."

"Yes. We'll have it to hold over Annabel as long as she lives, for if she ever gets out of line, she's done for. If there's one thing Annabel fears more than eternal damnation, it is ridicule. Were the truth known, she'd be the laughingstock of the county."

"You're a wicked old woman," he said, and kissed her cheek.

"Have you heard what your wife is doing?" Benjamin shook his head. "They say she's all but moved into Eugene Betchley's house and taken over. Molly insisted on going with Frankie to Sandersville, so Priscilla has brought in her own cook to take care of Eugene and Theodore, thereby assuring the same low standards prevailing at her mother's house. To call it Spartan would slander the Greeks."

Fanny and Edna May were staying with Annabel, who disliked girls and complained of the arrangement. One evening at Beulah Land after a long whispered conference with Bruce and Luck and Nancy, Fanny took Leon aside.

"I will no longer be an old maid dependent on relations. I must have my own place. You are to marry me now, Leon Davis, or never."

Nonplussed, Leon talked to Sarah and Benjamin. Sarah said, "If you let that girl go, I shall disown you. I want her for Beulah Land. I can't live forever, although I think I can."

"Let's call it settled," Benjamin said.

Annabel was vastly relieved when Benjamin told her that both Fanny and Edna May were to move to Beulah Land after the Christmas wedding. "So good of you, Ben, to think of keeping sisters together." He blushed, and Annabel thought it from modesty.

At long, long last Benjamin Davis was to have all his children under his own roof.

20

Leon and Fanny were married at the church in Highboro two days before Christmas, and of those who loved them only Luck was not there, having the night before given birth to a son, whom she and Abraham named Roscoe.

"A Roscoe Kendrick!" Sarah said to Roman. "Think of it, after everything that's happened between the different Roscoes and Kendricks! You see, my dear? All things are reconciled in the end."

After the wedding Sarah took an armful of holly that had decorated the church into the graveyard, where she and Jane put a sprig on each family grave. "The first warm day in January we'll come and work," Sarah said. "Much wants doing."

Fanny and Leon would take no wedding trip, although Benjamin offered them one. Instead, Leon drove his own buggy from the church back to Beulah Land. As they turned from the main road into the private one that would carry them through the orchard and along the avenue of oak and cedar to the main house, Leon stopped the horse. "The first thing I remember," he said, "is stopping here one morning. Mama and I were taking our wagon to town to sell eggs and chickens. It was cold, and she pointed through the trees and said, 'That's where you belong.' Welcome to Beulah Land, my love." He lifted her hand and kissed the ring Sarah had worn when she married Leon Kendrick.

Sarah and Beulah Land were to thrive together for many years to come, her reign over it exceeding that of Victoria's over England, as Annabel Saxon once pointed out dyspeptically. But one day Fanny took Sarah's place, and by that time, she was ready. It had come about so gradually no one felt any change. Benjamin stayed more and more in his house in the Glade, where he and Nancy were husband and wife in all but name.

Frankie never recovered the mind she had lost, although she was said to be not unhappy in the home that cared for afflicted ladies of means. Of the family, only Fanny and Leon went to see her, for she wanted no one else and became agitated in the presence of any others from the past. She learned to play the piano, and they allowed her to care for a patch of garden and call it hers. When Fanny told her that they'd taken her portrait to Beulah Land, where it was hung in the entrance hall for everyone to admire, Frankie smiled as if she understood. Yet when Fanny was ready to leave, Frankie clutched her hand and asked anxiously, "Where will you go?"

"Why, back to Beulah Land, Mama."

Frankie smiled again but a little vaguely, as if she could not recollect the name, she for whom it once had been the sum of all she coveted of consequence in the world. "Beulah Land. It sounds like heaven. Is it far?"

Thou shalt no more be termed Forsaken; neither shall thy land any more be termed Desolate: but thou shalt be called Hephzi-bah, and thy land Beulah: for the Lord delighteth in thee, and thy land shall be married.

Isaiah 62:4